THE KING ARTHUR TRILOGY: BOOK TWO

Warrior of
the West

Also by M. K. Hume

The Merlin Prophecy: *Battle of Kings*
The Merlin Prophecy: *Death of an Empire*
The Merlin Prophecy: *Hunting with Gods*
The King Arthur Trilogy: *Dragon's Child*

THE KING ARTHUR TRILOGY: BOOK TWO

Warrior of the West

M. K. HUME

ATRIA PAPERBACK

New York • London • Toronto • Sydney • New Delhi

ATRIA PAPERBACK

A Division of Simon & Schuster, Inc.
1230 Avenue of the Americas
New York, NY 10020

First Atria Paperback edition January 2014

ATRIA PAPERBACK and colophon are trademarks of Simon & Schuster, Inc.

For information about special discounts for bulk purchases, please contact Simon & Schuster Special Sales at 1-866-506-1949 or business@simonandschuster.com.

The Simon & Schuster Speakers Bureau can bring authors to your live event. For more information or to book an event, contact the Simon & Schuster Speakers Bureau at 1-866-248-3049 or visit our website at www.simonspeakers.com.

Designed by Dana Sloan

Manufactured in the United States of America

10 9 8 7 6 5 4 3 2 1

Library of Congress Cataloging-in-Publication Data

Hume, M. K.
    The King Arthur Trilogy : Warrior of the West / by M. K. Hume. — First Atria Books trade paperback edition.
        pages   cm.
    ". . . second book of the King Arthur trilogy . . ."—ECIP galley.
    "Originally published in Great Britain in 2009 by Headline Review"—T.p. verso.
    1. Arthur, King—Fiction.   2. Guenevere, Queen (Legendary character)—
Fiction.   3. Marital conflict—Fiction.   4. Political stability—Great Britain—
Fiction.   5. Decision making—Moral and ethical aspects—Fiction.   6. Great
Britain—History—Anglo-Saxon period, 449–1066—Fiction.   7. Folklore—
Great Britain—Fiction.   I. Title.   II. Title: Warrior of the West.
    PR9619.4.H855K58   2014
    823'.92—dc23   2013018966

ISBN 978-1-4767-1520-9
ISBN 978-1-4767-1521-6 (ebook)

Warrior of the West is dedicated to my parents,
Ronald Henry Smith (1920–1980) and
Edna Katrina Ellis Smith (1920–2004).
These two extraordinary people raised three
children to believe that the only limitations
that exist in this world are those that we
build for ourselves, stone by stone.

Myrddion's Map of
Pre-Arthurian Roman Britain

Trimontium

Bremenium

Onnum

Hadrian's Wall

Magnis

Bravoniacum

Lavatrae

Verterae

Eburacum

Bremetennacum

OCEANUS HIBERNICUS

Mamucium

Lindum

Mona

Deva

Aquae

Causennae

Ratae

Durobrivae

Viroconium

Venonae

Salinae

Camulodunum

Moridunum

Venta
Silurum

Isca

Glevum

Corinium

SABRINA AEST

Abone

Londinium

Aquae Sulis

Calleva Atrebatum

Lindinis

Venta Belgarum

Cadbury

Glastonbury

Sorviodunum

Noviomagus

Tintagel

Isca

Anderida

Dumnoniorum

Durnovaria

Vectis

PROLOGUE

Horses whickered nervously, and the skittering of their hooves on the flinty scree was the only sound of discord in the still morning. Within the nearby wood, the rooks, ravens, and crows waited silently with their blue-black plumage almost lost in the shadows of the old trees. Only the bright eyes of the birds glinted with signs of life, and they were malicious and hungry.

Weaponless and wary, the six envoys waited impatiently, even though their armed guards ringed them, ill at ease, a little way from the nobles. Twenty in number, the guards rolled their eyes expressively, and were inclined to jump at every shadow. Here, where Saxon hands held the reins of governance, a Celt was unwise to ride incautiously through woods where every tree could hide a Saxon with a battle-axe.

"I don't like this place," one warrior hissed at his neighbor. "It's too damn quiet for my liking."

His companion tried to peer into the impenetrable woods, but the darkness was absolute.

The envoys of Artor had chosen a large patch of open ground where they could wait for the planned parley. Above their heads, the white flag of truce snapped and curled in the wind. Their escort waited five spear shafts from their masters, looking outward at the dense trees that surrounded this bare, grey knoll.

As the proposed meeting place was deep within enemy territory, their guards were fully armed but had been ordered by King Artor to keep their weapons sheathed unless the envoys were under direct attack. Only their loyalty and impassioned devotion to the High King kept these veterans calm in the face of brooding menace and the threat of impending attack.

The Celtic emissaries had come to this parley at the express wish of the High King in a last attempt to reason with the newest war chief of the western Saxons. For well over fifty years, these barbarian tribesmen had been a thorn in the Celtic heel.

Artor had sickened of death over twelve years of brutal battles. He had smashed the eastern Saxons again and again, but his enemy was implacable, and every summer brought new, leaf-shaped ships across Litus Saxonicus or the huge, grey seas of Oceanus Germanicus. Although Artor struggled with a growing dread that his wars achieved only minor gains, battle by battle the High King began to stop the Saxon advance. But he sought a better solution than brute force, and he had sent six of his most loyal noblemen to Saxon country to broker a truce.

Now, his envoys and their warrior escort doubted the good faith of the barbarians.

"It's a cold morning," Gaheris murmured quietly, more to calm his nerves and to break the eerie silence than to begin a conversation. "Spring seems so far away."

"I wouldn't have thought you'd notice," Cerdic ap Cerdyn muttered sarcastically. "You Otadini like the cold in the north. The eastern Saxons must enjoy it well enough too . . . since they're so cozy with your father."

Cerdic ap Cerdyn was a blunt man, thick in neck, chest, and thighs, and possessing red hair and a temper to match. Artor trusted him completely as a young son of the King of the Silures, for Cerdic had followed the High King from the first desperate forays out of Cadbury Tor at a time when the Celts had struggled to stop the Saxon advance. Focused and rigid in his thinking, Cerdic would follow Artor's orders to the letter, but he lacked his master's quick empathy and cold reasoning.

The insults that Cerdic chose were sufficiently offensive to warrant a challenge to armed combat. Gaheris bit his lip until he tasted the salt of blood. He was the younger brother of Prince Gawayne, Artor's most ardent champion, and shared a familial tendency to sudden, searing explosions of temper. But Gaheris acknowledged that the Silures warrior spoke the truth, albeit with unforgivable lack of courtesy. King Lot, Gaheris's father, was an ally of the western Saxons of Caer Fyrddin.

Gaheris breathed the frigid air deeply into his lungs to avoid the temptation to snarl an offensive retort. What would be the gain?

Gaheris was Queen Morgause's youngest legitimate son and, undoubtedly, the most beloved. Sunny-tempered, with tawny hair, pale green eyes, and a rich, golden tan deepened from months in the saddle, Gaheris had a face and a form that drew the swift interest of women and the easy camaraderie of men. But, for all his maturity, Gaheris was young—not yet nineteen—and ardent to prove that he was loyal to the High King rather than to the treasonous dictates of family.

"You're very quiet, Gaheris," Cerdic taunted. "Why did you come, unless you intend to betray us to your friends? Or perhaps you're afraid."

Cerdic even refused to use Gaheris's rightful title, but the young prince knew the surly noble only spoke aloud what other warriors were thinking. Unlike his brother Gawayne, Gaheris had an agile brain that was nearly the match of the High King's, and he refused to take offense at Cerdic's slurs.

"I travel along my own road, Cerdic, and my path follows that of Gawayne and the High King," Gaheris said patiently. "My father may be my liege and my tribal lord, but he has decided on an alliance of his own choosing. Like you, I wait here in the open and will parley with these Saxon animals—for I obey the orders of the High King and I follow the loyalties of my brother, Prince Gawayne."

"Give the lad a rest, Cerdic," one of the other warriors interjected. "Gawayne has been killing those fools who ally themselves with King Lot up and down the mountains for years. Fair is as fair does!"

The warrior who spoke was a bastard Roman, born in the lands to the north of Aquae Sulis in settlements that were close to the Saxon hive in the old Roman forts, so Cerdic bit off an acerbic retort. But the other envoys lowered their eyes so that Gaheris would not see the distrust that lurked in the lines of their faces.

A horse shied violently, and the startled men tugged on their reins to prevent their own horses from following suit.

"Can't you control that sodding animal, Ulf?" Cerdic snapped, his nerves taut with the strain of waiting.

"Someone, or something, approaches," Ulf warned, his eyes darting from side to side in alarm. "My mare always knows."

The captain of the escort rolled his brown eyes as Ulf's horse shied again, sending pebbles rolling and clattering.

"Keep the beast quiet then, so we can hear for ourselves."

An eerie silence descended.

A hawk circled high above the ridgeline, its wings spread wide as it hovered on the wind. Even the crows in the ancient oak trees were silent and waiting. The whole world seemed to be still, except for the gelid air that the men heaved into their straining lungs.

Through the strange blood of his mother, Gaheris felt the weight of his approaching death come upon him like dark, implacable wings. He was not afraid, precisely, but his senses were heightened as if his body knew that it would soon cease to breathe and think.

Then, as if they had sprung from the aching, icy earth, the Saxons, dozens of warriors, armed and eager for combat, appeared before them on the open ground. These men were the children and grandchildren of the warriors led by Vortimer and Hengist, shaggy barbarians who had been brutally decimated into near extinction by the forces of Uther Pendragon and his fearsome son. They had been born on British soil in one of the few bastions of the west that the Saxons had been able to hold, and their hatred for all things Celt knew no limits.

Greasy, oiled hair was bound with silver and bronze wire, and clothing that was once brightly dyed was now dun with dirt and hard use. Although their bodies were comely and heavily muscled, their furs and leathers made them look like hulking creatures born out of nightmares. The Roman crossed himself, and several warriors of the guard clutched stone amulets and muttered prayers. In response, Ulf began to draw his sword out of its sheath, and the hiss of sharp, well-oiled metal was shocking and loud, but Cerdic raised one hand to still the warrior's instinctive response. He lifted the flag of truce so that it could be clearly seen by the Saxons.

Wheeling, Cerdic waved the banner again, shouting in Celt, Saxon, and Latin that this meeting was to broker a truce, but the Saxons were oblivious to everything this flag meant. They loathed the very air that Celts breathed. Cerdic carried the words of Artor, but the message was as arid to Saxons as dry leaves in the northern wind. Approaching in a loping, mile-devouring run, the Saxons surrounded the Celts in a ring of steel, and, even for warriors on horseback, there would be no easy way out of this circle of death.

One huge man, well over six feet four inches in height, moved casually to face Cerdic's horse and, with blinding speed, buried his axe in the brain of the animal. As he expertly twisted the blade free, and the horse collapsed at his feet, the Saxon snatched up the white banner, spat on it, and then trampled it into the bloody earth.

Cerdic struggled to rise, but one leg was trapped beneath the body of his stallion. The men-at-arms wheeled their horses and tried to free their weapons, but the Saxons thrust spears at the undefended chests of Artor's emissaries. Cursing, Cerdic's warriors dropped their hands, for they were outnumbered, ten to one.

The Saxon leader was fair-complexioned, as were most of his race, but his hair was greased to the color of old honey and his nails were black with grime. Gaheris registered all these small details as if he was caught in a nightmare, but he was preternaturally calm.

The Saxon pointed to Ulf and two other warriors in the guard at random. With a jerk of his head, the brute indicated that the rest of the troop should move to his right and dismount. Gaheris was surprised. The Celts stood with their horses' reins held loosely in their hands, but the Saxons had presented no threat to the animals so far. He had not expected the Saxons to appreciate horses for their usefulness. For all their wild and brutal appearance, perhaps these hulking warriors would still allow Artor's emissaries to go free.

"I am Glamdring Ironfist, the Thane of Caer Fyrddin. I reject your pitiful flag of truce, as I reject all those horse lords who fought against Katigern Oakheart."

Gaheris stared at the white flag of truce, ripped haphazardly across its length and muddy from the Saxon's feet, and he was reminded that no mercy had been shown to Cerdic's horse, now only so much meat that would be smoked for food during the next winter.

Then the leader of the Saxons grinned widely—and made the universally understood action of throat cutting.

The Celtic warriors on the right were slain before they could defend themselves, and death came slowly to them as their bodies were hacked and stabbed to prolong their suffering. The men bled to death in front of the envoys, while begging for help with mute, bewildered eyes.

The terrified horses were led away from the bodies and then slaughtered, but at least the beasts merited clean, killing blows. Several Saxons immediately applied themselves to the task of carving horseflesh into slabs of bloody meat for easy transport.

These Saxons are truly barbarians, Gaheris thought with an odd, calm detachment as he assessed the carnage. They will never learn.

He shook his head in confusion at the knowledge that his father, King Lot, had allied himself with the savage Saxon invaders rather than pursue his original dream of achieving power within the Celtic tribes. Gaheris knew that wild things could never be trusted, and he could conclude only that his father had been a fool—and a fool he would always remain.

Glamdring cleaned his axe of blood and brain matter on a fold of his woolen cloak. The blade was well oiled and very sharp.

He pointed a huge finger at Gaheris.

"You! You are the son of King Lot, a man who is a friend to the Saxon peoples. You have my permission to ride away to join your father. The fate of these others will convey my message to your High King."

Glamdring's last words were so scornful that they cut through Gaheris's passive calm and released him from its thrall. He forced himself to breathe normally, and once again he felt like a man.

"I don't wish to die, Glamdring Ironfist, but I have sworn an oath—a blood oath—that I will serve no king but Artor, he to whom the gods have given the sword and crown of Uther Pendragon. Even if I wished to save my life, I cannot do so. Nay! I will not do so!"

He looked directly into the cynical, smoldering eyes of Glamdring.

"Do as you choose, Glamdring," he said to the Saxon. "My death will bring you no advantage, but it might bring you much harm—for I am defenseless."

Glamdring Ironfist returned the open gaze of the boy, who was barely beyond his first blooding.

"Well spoken, lad. You have my permission to die like a man as you wish—but I will kill you last for your impertinence."

Then Glamdring's axe flashed and Cerdic's head rolled over the scree to rest beside a small rock. The Saxon ignored the fountain of blood that pulsed from Cerdic's throat and soaked him from the knees down. The fetid reek of voided bowels and hot urine almost choked Gaheris, but he found he could not look away from the grisly sight.

He willed his face to be still and to remain devoid of fear.

"This man carried the standard, so at least he had the balls to be singled out as leader. We are not unduly cruel to those enemies who show courage." Glamdring leered knowingly. "Now, who among you wants to be next to die?"

The Saxon leader obviously intended to make the Celtic warriors suffer as they awaited their fate.

Suddenly, the Roman envoy moved. Against all the rules of the truce, and less trusting than his companions, he had secreted a knife in his boot. With a sudden lunge, he managed to put out the eye of a burly Saxon who had failed to take the slight man seriously.

7

The Roman died quickly from a devastating sword thrust that split him from groin to breastbone. As the man died in the hot stink of his own entrails, Gaheris wished he could remember the warrior's name.

Three other envoys were hacked to pieces, slowly and deliberately, so that the Saxons could choose when to grant the welcome boon of death. Only Ulf, two other Celtic warriors, and Gaheris now remained standing on the bloody earth.

The air was still, as if the whole, slate-grey earth held its breath. Gaheris stared intently at Ulf, who was trying hard to stand nonchalantly and display the fearless arrogance of a Celtic cavalry officer. Bloodstained, and with his fingers trembling and one knee twitching despite his best efforts, Ulf embodied what was most noble in a Celt, and Gaheris was oddly comforted. This was not reckless, brainless courage. Ulf represented the ordinary man who was faced with an extraordinary situation, and he had mastered his terror when most men would have wept or voided their bladders.

Now that his fate was sealed, Gaheris saw the Celt and Saxon races so clearly that he was surprised he hadn't realized the purpose of Artor's long wars years earlier.

"Whatever you do to these men will change nothing, Glamdring. Surely even a barbarian can give credence to the words of a man who is about to die. I can smell your death upon you, and it will be worse for you than for these brave men, for you don't know Lord Artor. You judge him by the standards set by my father, King Lot, and by Artor's father, Uther Pendragon. Artor is not an ordinary man, and he will exact the worst punishment upon you that he can devise . . . and my lord is a master of imagination. You will wish that you had listened to my warnings when you hear your children scream and burn."

Glamdring's face reddened slightly beneath his grimy skin, but Gaheris relentlessly goaded the Saxon, hoping for a quick and painless ending. He stared at the sky, where the hawk still circled, oblivious to the human raptors below him. Gaheris turned his frank green eyes towards his executioner.

"I have the same gift of Sight as my aunt, Morgan, so I can read your death clearly in your eyes. Artor would have had the sense to keep the horses alive, and he would have fought fire with fire. Artor wouldn't stoop to kill the defenseless and sully his honor by slaying unarmed envoys. Even Lot will be sickened when he hears of your cowardly murders."

"Lot is a fat fool," Glamdring blustered. "And your Morgan is a whore." In his rage, the Saxon's fingers gripped his axe so tightly that his knuckles were ridges of white bone.

Gaheris smiled with a young man's bravado, and the contempt of a prince.

"Those insults are the only truths that you have spoken on this blood-soaked day. You are a condemned man, Glamdring, because, like most Saxons, you'll never learn."

Glamdring gave a great cry of rage, swung his axe above his head, and struck Gaheris on the shoulder, cutting deeply into his breast.

Even as the prince fell, choking on a sudden rush of blood into his mouth, Gaheris managed the ghost of a chuckle.

"Never learn . . . never . . . change."

Then Glamdring struck off the boy's head with a vicious blow to the neck.

The shale and gravel were thick with congealing blood. At sword point, Ulf and the other two survivors were forced to collect the six heads of their masters, place them reverently in their leather provision sacks, and then string them round their necks. At any moment, the warriors expected to be hacked to pieces, and their nerves were stretched to screaming point.

Glamdring looked scornfully at the three shaken Celts who were bowed over by their hellish burdens. Then he delivered his message to Artor.

Ulf was forced to repeat the message three times until each phrase was perfect. Sickened, the cavalryman knew that he was doomed to live.

"Now, run away, little dogs, and tell your master that Ironfist is waiting. Tell him also that the bodies of his men will have no burial.

Their souls will wander in the void forever, as will all Celts who dare to set foot on Saxon soil."

And, to his shame, Ulf fled, closely pursued by his companions. Their despair knew no bounds because, by random chance, they lived when better men had died. They hadn't struck a single blow to save their masters from death, so honor demanded that they should also perish. But stronger than terror or shame was their oath to the High King. Artor must receive Glamdring's message if the Saxons were to be punished for their crimes against the helpless. Ulf must bear witness to what he had seen and heard, although desperation coiled in his belly so that he vomited until his throat was raw.

Although his cloak and tunic stiffened with blood and serum, and the two leather bags thudded wetly against his sides, still he ran until he could no longer move without weeping.

Eventually, the three survivors found their way to a Celtic settlement and begged horses to speed their journey. They did not stop to eat, or to clean their bodies of the blood that had seeped from the heads of Artor's ambassadors, until they finally reached Cadbury Tor and their long and ghastly task was completed.

Chapter 1

BLOOD GUILT

Then all the councillors, together with that proud tyrant Vortigern, the British king, were so blinded, that, as a protection to their country, they sealed its doom by inviting in among them (like wolves into the sheepfold), the fierce and impious Saxons, a race hateful both to God and men, to repel the invasions of the northern nations.

—GILDAS

Artor stood on the summit of the imposing earthworks of Cadbury Tor and stared down at his domain. Below him, like the peeled skin of an apple, the ramparts and cobbled roadways leading to the flagged fortress curled around the tor. Regular redoubts guarded heavy log gates that could be closed and barred to seal any enemy between its walls of wood and stone. If any fortress could be considered impregnable, then Cadbury was one such, for in its long history it had never fallen.

As he stared down at what he had rebuilt, Artor recalled his first, crucial campaign against the western Saxons twelve years earlier.

Older Celts still remembered, and resented, the foolishness of

Cadbury and Environs

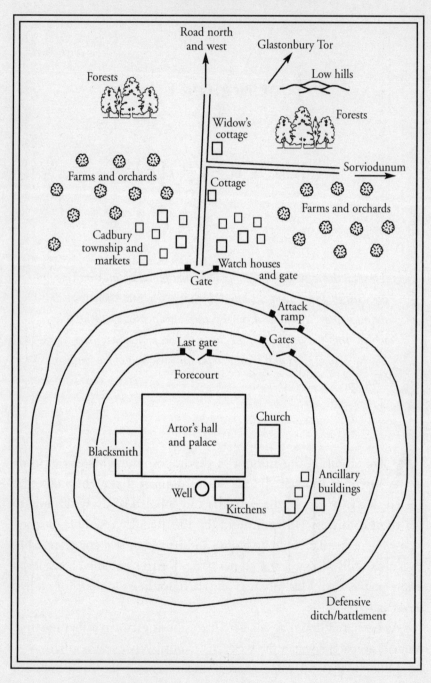

Road north and west

Glastonbury Tor

Low hills

Forests

Forests

Widow's cottage

Sorviodunum

Cottage

Farms and orchards

Farms and orchards

Cadbury township and markets

Watch houses and gate

Gate

Attack ramp

Last gate

Gates

Forecourt

Artor's hall and palace

Church

Blacksmith

Ancillary buildings

Well

Kitchens

Defensive ditch/battlement

Glastonbury and Environs

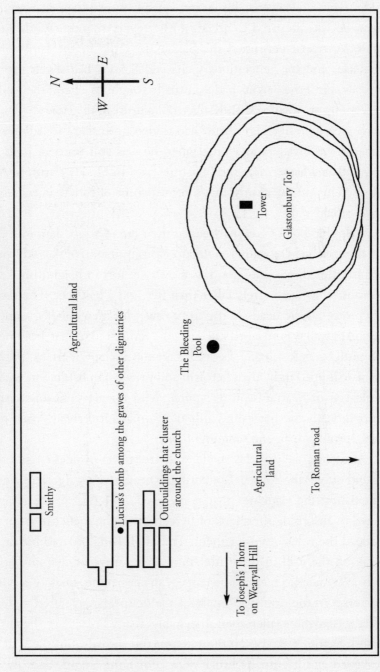

King Vortigern, who had been so lost to reason that when the strong, golden legs of Rowena, his Saxon queen, were wrapped round his waist, he was prepared to accede to her every request. While in her thrall, Vortigern permitted the Saxons to settle in the lands of the Demetae, and for generations Celts and Saxons had dwelt together uneasily, until the Saxons had eventually sought to extend their power by forming an alliance with Katigern Oakheart in the east.

But early in his reign, Artor had ridden north out of Cadbury and defeated the invaders at a time when he was still untried, both as a king and as a leader. For the first time, and in bloody attrition, Artor had used his cavalry against that most fearsome of barbarian tactics, the Saxon shield wall.

A double line of Saxons wedged their circular wooden, bull hide, and bronze shields together in unconscious imitation of the old Roman tortoise. But the Saxons stood well over six feet in height, unlike the Romans, who were rarely taller than five and a half feet. The second row protected the heads of the front row with their shields, and once the shield wall was engaged, the warriors refused to retreat, holding the line until every last man was dead. Like the ancient Spartans, the Saxons worshipped individual heroism and prowess in battle, but without the leaven of Spartan iron discipline. Wild for glory, Saxon warriors courted death and heroism, while the Romans had always been pragmatic, professional, and sanguine fighters.

Artor had viewed the shield wall from a convenient rise in the ground above the forked Roman road near Magnis. He had sighed, anticipating the slaughter that it presaged. The Saxons were accustomed to absorbing the shock of fiercely attacking men, but Artor had changed the rules of engagement. The High King ordered his cavalry to pound the wall in wave after thundering wave of charging horseflesh. No man, no matter how large, can absorb the shock of a galloping horse. As the cavalry disengaged, Celtic spears were used to deadly effect to slaughter fallen men. Inevitably, many horses perished as the berserk Saxons risked everything to gut the animals, but the wall was weakened and eventually broke. The remaining Saxons fled into the inhospitable mountains. Through inexperience, Artor had mercifully permitted them to escape.

"You'll have to crush them sooner or later," Targo, his old sword master, had grunted as he cut the throat of a horse whose leg dangled at an unnatural, painful angle.

"True," Artor replied philosophically, and stepped to one side to avoid the jet of arterial blood as the horse kicked convulsively, and then died. "But I must soon face a larger Saxon force in the east, and I don't have the men to deal with enemies on two fronts. These curs will keep till a later time."

"You'll not succeed with cavalry so easily again," Targo warned softly. "Still, I suppose there's many ways to trap a rabbit, as my old sergeant used to say. They'll continue to breed until they become a problem once again."

"Give over, Targo!" Artor snapped, his eyes momentarily cold. Then he laughed ruefully. "I still lack the stomach for carnage."

"You'll learn," Targo replied without a trace of humor or rancor in his cracked old voice.

Half starved and ill equipped, the Saxons had squabbled and skirmished on the rocky hills of Dyfed like parasites until an emerging new leader had bludgeoned them into a fragile unity, linked only by their old hatred for all things Celt—and for King Artor. Intolerant and obdurate, these warriors were born and bred as Saxons, not as Britons, regardless of their mixed bloodlines. They swore that they would never again retreat from their enemy.

After that first successful campaign, the war with the Saxons and the traitorous Celtic kings had raged for twelve long years. Now, all the Celtic tribes south of the great Roman Wall were united against a shared barbarian threat. Now, at Cadbury, Artor waited.

"So many dead warriors, and all good men," Artor sighed. "Why was so much violence necessary? Reason and compromise could have saved hundreds—nay, thousands of lives. But compromise is another word for cowardice in the Saxon vocabulary."

"Talking to yourself again, Artor?" Targo muttered, leaning upon

15

a heavy staff. "When an ancient like me can sneak up on you, then you're dead."

"Why do our conversations always hark back to my mortality?" Artor smiled as he spoke. "How goes your day, Targo?"

"Slowly, slowly. As it does for you, my lord. You still await news of your proposed truce from our envoys?"

"The waiting tries my patience, Targo."

"Your attempts at peacemaking won't work, my boy. You'll receive your ambassadors back in little pieces, and the Saxons will believe that you're growing soft and are too frightened to engage them in battle. I told you in times gone by that they'd breed to cause you trouble."

Artor sighed with resignation. "Yes."

The single word fell like a stone into a deep and very empty well.

Targo peered up into the younger man's set face. Artor was no longer a beautiful young man, and the light of excitement and pleasure had left his eyes. Something harder, more bitter, and wounded had taken its place and Targo regretted the loss of the boy whom he had loved so well.

"I imagine that it's difficult to send good men to certain death. I wouldn't fancy it, so I always served in the ranks. No responsibility— no guilt."

"I will not permit the latest of these Saxon thanes to endanger the west, and I'll no longer ignore King Lot's treason when he gives aid to the enemy. He'll see sense and draw back behind the Roman Wall, or I'll slaughter every warrior and camp follower that praises the Saxon might."

"Even King Lot?"

"Especially King Lot."

Artor's words were bitter, and as rigid as a bar of iron. Yet Targo cherished this mature, hard, and stern Artor as well as he had loved the boy, Artorex, for he gave his all to protect and guide his people.

To the north, beyond the apple and pear orchards, and the hamlets of conical huts with their thatched roofs, Artor saw the glitter of sunlight on horsemen. A small troop of cavalry was riding in haste towards Cadbury Tor, the light glinting off bronze and iron discs sewn on leather cuirasses. With the cold reason of his brain, Artor knew the answer to his silent plea already, although his heart prayed that his instincts were wrong.

Flanked by his body servants, Gruffydd, Odin, and Targo, Artor watched and waited for the riders. The way leading up to Cadbury Tor took some time to negotiate, for it was an uphill journey through rich fields, orchards, and pastures of fat-tailed sheep and contented cows. Civilization had sprung up under the protection of the fortress as peace and security promised a chance for a better way of life. In the shadow of the tor, village groups prospered, and life here was sweet-scented and deceptively peaceful. But soon the spring thaw would arrive, and, with it, the months of killing weather as the Saxons moved out of their winter quarters.

"This ordered way of life will last only as long as I continue to win," Artor stated cynically. "Those same warriors who now swear eternal devotion to my sword will kill me when my back is turned if, like Caesar, my luck doesn't hold."

Odin, his Jute bodyguard and one of the last of the Scum of Anderida, knelt on the flagstones, held his arms wide, and looked up at his lord.

"You are wrong, my king. Any of your warriors would die for you if you desired it. They'll obey you without question, whether your orders are just or not. You are our master, but you are also the High King, and are above us and better than us. We obey out of love, my lord, so please don't reject what we feel, even though your heart may be heavy." Odin spoke with a thick, guttural accent but twelve years of close contact with his king had remedied his language deficiencies. In fact, Odin now spoke with all the grace of his master, with simple and profound truth.

"I've still got one last battle in me," Targo offered, "and the Saxon advance in the east is almost at a standstill. You aren't responsible for their evils."

"No. I'm not." Artor's response permitted no further discussion.

He placed one hand gently against Odin's face, and the huge Jute rose to his feet, his eyes moist with unshed tears of devotion.

Targo patted his master's shoulder, before moving carefully down the cobbled courtyard towards the great gateway. If he could intercept the horsemen on arrival, he could discover the Saxons' work for himself. The report to Artor could then be softened to spare his master some of the consequences that were bound to result from this ill-advised mission. Thus, these two very different men struggled to shield their master from pain.

The small troop of cavalry drew closer and became visible as no more than a trio of warriors. Finally, as the first gates opened before the riders, Artor accepted that there would be no truce, for he could see the leather bags hanging limply across the front of each of the horse blankets. Men stepped aside as the three horsemen rode slowly through the narrow, earthen corridors to the second gate, and then the third. At each stage, warriors clutched amulets or crosses as the leather bags slapped odorously against the horses' sides, and women turned away, their faces pale and nauseated by the putrid smell.

"Hail, warrior! What name shall I give when I bring you before the High King?" Targo asked as the riders negotiated the final gate and dismounted from their lathered horses.

One warrior stepped forward. His leathers were filthy with dried blood and mud, and his face was grey with exhaustion.

"I am Ulf, from Caerlion, and I ride with Bryn ap Cydwyn and Justus of Aquae Sulis. We bear tidings from the Saxon war chief, Glamdring Ironfist." Ulf held his head high, although twin spots of color stained the thin skin of his cheeks. He was alive, and he knew full well that any honorable man would now be dead.

"We were ambushed in the hills northwest of Nidum while under a flag of truce. Without any warning, the Saxons slaughtered the emissaries and our brothers in the guard," he explained dully. "We alone were left alive to bear witness to the brutality of the leader of the Saxons. He gave us these 'gifts' for the High King, and the filthy bastard forced us to swear that we would bring them to Cadbury Tor with his message for King Artor." Ulf grimaced, and his ashen face flushed with shame. "Lord Targo—for so I believe you to be—please beg the king to forgive the tongues that bring such arrogant words to insult him."

The warriors were half fainting with exhaustion, yet still seemed determined to fulfill their obligations to the dead, so Targo gave them a grudging nod of respect.

"Artor is a just ruler; you have nothing to fear from the High King as long as your hearts are truly loyal."

Artor emerged from his dark reflections and strode towards the cluster of men at the gate. The horsemen abased themselves. With their foreheads pressed against the flagstones, the three warriors trembled guiltily, for they believed that the king would order their executions.

"Rise, good sirs," Artor commanded the warriors. "It is I who should be kneeling before you, for I should be paying homage to those poor men and their servants who went so bravely to their deaths for the chance of forging a just peace. And to you courageous men who have ridden hard to bring home the remains of our heroes—for I can guess what your burdens contain."

"Aye, my lord," Ulf replied, as unacknowledged tears spilled over his lashes and ran unchecked down his cheeks. Yet neither Artor nor Targo considered that Ulf wept out of weakness, but for the dead, for the failure of his oaths, and for his consuming guilt.

"We lacked the heart to see friendly faces left in such ugly cir-cumstances," Ulf continued, "so we stayed alive when honorable men would have preferred death to this dishonor. We chose to return the heads to you so that their kin should have some part of them. We couldn't save the lives of our masters or our brothers, so it is fitting that we should be ordered to carry the heads back to their loved ones. Their bodies were left for the scavengers, and I now regret that we couldn't lift our swords in their defense."

A small group of women, some clutching children, had approached the gates. Targo knew at a glance that they were the kin of Artor's emissaries, and he tried to spare them from the ugliness of what had happened to their loved ones.

"Women, this is no place for you." Targo spoke gently. "We will send word to you when we know the fate of your young men."

But Artor turned to the women, beckoned them forward and then, to their consternation, knelt on the cobblestones before them.

"I may be king, but I beg your forgiveness, daughters of this good land. I knew the risks taken by your menfolk when they agreed to obey my orders. Mine is the blame for sending them into danger. You may hate me if you wish, but I confess that I would still order six more men to parley with the Saxons if there was any chance of bringing peace to the west. I regret that your sons or your husbands were victims of the viciousness of politics."

One grey-haired matron stepped forward and stared down impassively at the king's stern, controlled face. Her simple peplum and cloak hinted at her Roman ancestry, but the garnets in her ears, red as dried blood, shouted her quality. Then, with a wry twisting of her lips, she pulled him to his feet.

"Two of my sons have died at the hands of the outlanders for you, my king. The head of another lies in a bag on one of your horses—or so I guess. I've one more son who is near old enough to bear a sword, and, if God chooses to take him from me to serve you, then I will make no complaint. You must drive the Saxons, and all who are allied with them, into the dirt."

Artor nodded his appreciation of the old woman's savage patriotism, and stripped a golden arm ring, carved with his personal dragon motif, from his wrist.

"The Saxon women are fierce creatures, Mother, but they are no match for matrons such as you. Although gold is no recompense for your losses, I beg that you take this bauble as a gift from a grateful king. And more gold shall be given to the mothers and widows of these brave men who died at my behest. I am ashamed that I can only offer you coin for your loyalty."

"My grandson will hold it sacred to his house, my lord. But for now, I ask that you give me leave to take my son's remains and see to his honorable burial."

Artor inclined his head in permission, and the elderly woman approached the grisly bags, checking each dead face until she found the one she sought. Then, regardless of the odor and the vile ooze of corruption that enveloped it, she clasped the bag to her heavy breasts and uttered a single, high-pitched cry of grief. Then she pattered away down the roadway.

One by one, the heads were claimed and loud were the cries of grief and rage that circled the tor like the screams of hunting birds.

Finally, only one unclaimed head remained.

"Gaheris, my nephew." Artor sighed. "They didn't even spare the son of King Lot."

Targo stared disbelievingly at his king. "What sodding stupidity! How could the Saxon oafs have been so foolish as to kill the beloved son of King Lot, their most loyal ally? Gaheris followed Gawayne into your service, and, at the time, King Lot almost swallowed his beard in rage, but even Lot won't tolerate such a fate for his son."

"My lord," Ulf interrupted, blood suffusing his face at his impertinence. "Prince Gaheris was the very last to die, and he defied the Saxons to the end. He was offered his life if he would resile from his oath to you and return to the halls of his father, but the boy refused. He perished bravely, and died cursing the Saxons as he fell. He said he saw the fate of the Saxon thane. He warned Glamdring that you would exact justice on all Saxons in the name of the dead envoys and their escort."

"He was a good lad." Targo offered Gaheris the highest praise he knew. "He was far too good to die without a sword, or the opportunity to defend himself."

"Tell me every detail of the Saxon treachery," Artor ordered. "Leave out no detail of your experience. I know the telling will cause you pain, but I must understand the depth of Saxon perfidy."

Ulf bowed his head and began to speak in little more than a whisper. So vivid and heartfelt was his report that, as his voice began to gain in strength and passion, the listeners could visualize the deaths of the envoys and experience the quiet courage of Gaheris.

21

Artor cradled the bag containing the young man's head for several moments, and then opened the drawstring and kissed the purpled lips that were still curved in the rictus of death. A trick of the late afternoon sunlight played about Gaheris's dead features and captured a trace of Artor's daughter, Licia, in them. Artor shuddered that Licia could die so easily, just like her cousin, whose head spoke so eloquently of the family ties between them.

"Mine is the blood guilt, Gaheris," the High King murmured. "And it shall be paid in full."

The cold part in Artor's brain whispered that the Saxons had gone too far this time, for even Lot and Morgause could not ignore the murder of their unarmed child, regardless of his allegiances. He turned to his sword-bearer. "Find a box of aromatic wood, Gruffydd, the finest that can be purchased. Wash and wrap the head of my nephew in fine, perfumed linen, and then send it to King Lot and Queen Morgause. They, too, should have an opportunity to mourn what is left of their child."

Gruffydd came forward. He had aged in the past twelve years and grey sprinkled his hair and his close-cropped beard, but his eyes were still as warm and as sharp as they had ever been. Now they rested on his king with open concern.

"If you approve, my lord, I'll carry the head of Gaheris to King Lot in person," he volunteered. "Should I bear a message of sympathy from you to the boy's father?"

"We wait upon the message from Glamdring Ironfist, but you can recount Ulf's description of the death of their son," Artor ordered. "They are entitled to know that he could have lived if he had been prepared to break his oath."

Gruffydd nodded. Privately, the sword-bearer thought that Artor should use the slaughter of Gaheris to advantage himself over King Lot, but the High King was a man to love because he scorned to cheat or lie.

Gruffydd bowed low, although his back twinged with the bone ache that attacked his joints and made long journeys so painful. Yet, out of love for his king, he would brave the journey and the rage of the grieving parents. Artor had raised his status in the world, and Gruffydd always paid his dues.

When Gruffydd heaved the leather bag and its grisly contents over his shoulder and turned to leave, the High King called Ulf to his side.

"Wait a moment, Gruffydd," Artor instructed. He turned to face Ulf. "You may now tell me the exact message sent by the Saxon barbarian."

Ulf gulped in near panic. "Please don't judge me by the words I bear, my king. We wouldn't have survived if we hadn't been needed to return to your fortress with the remains of your emissaries."

Artor stifled his impatience. He was fully aware that couriers were often executed when their masters were angered by the content of a message.

"You will be safe, Ulf, regardless of what the Saxons have instructed you to say to me. The words come from Glamdring, not from you."

Ulf heaved a deep sigh, looked skyward as a memory aid, and began to recite his message in a stilted voice.

"To Artor, who is an impostor and a dog. In the name of the dead Vortigern, Vortimer, and Hengist, I, Glamdring Ironfist, demand that you cease all hostilities against the holdings of the dead king, Katigern Oakheart. I command you to relinquish your crown to King Lot, who is the rightful heir of Uther Pendragon. If you comply, you will be permitted to live. If you meet us in battle, you will surely die."

Ulf stepped back quickly, well out of reach of Artor's sword blade, but his caution was unnecessary. The High King's eyes glinted with what looked almost like amusement.

"Gruffydd, you may give King Lot my condolences and inform him of the substance of Glamdring Ironfist's message, that his son was murdered so that the father could take my place. You will also remind the king that those who trust to the honor of the Saxons are fools. And they are worse than fools, for they are traitors to the Celtic cause. You will say to King Lot that, if he should give aid or comfort to any person involved in Ironfist's war against me, then his own crown will be considered forfeit by the Celtic kings. And I will not forget the slight when I arrive at his gates."

"He'll not like such a message," Gruffydd replied dryly, although his mouth smiled within his grizzled beard.

"You may inform him that all of our lands will not be wide enough to save him from my wrath if my messenger is harmed in any fashion." Artor grinned. "Just in case he determines that he doesn't like you, my friend."

"I take your kind addition gratefully, my lord," Gruffydd responded. "I'm fond of my head just where it is."

"And if King Lot rails against my decision to place his son in danger, or complains that the offer of a truce was weak and foolish, you may remind the king and my sister that they have constantly pressed me to cease the bloodbath of racial hatred."

"I will be happy to remind them of their old loyalties."

"But you should also tell my sister that I weep with her for her lost son. Gaheris was a better man than I am, and would have grown to be a leader of other men because of his purity of spirit and clarity of mind. Good Celts everywhere share in her loss, for all the kingdoms are the poorer without his grace."

"I will say all that is necessary, my king. Of this you may have no doubt."

"I don't, Gruffydd. Take an escort suited to my consequence. You will do all honor to King Lot and Queen Morgause, regardless of past insults and allegiances, for they are the parents of Gaheris, one of the heroes of . . ." Artor paused, and looked to Ulf for an answer.

"We met the Saxons at Y Gaer, my lord."

"One of the heroes of Y Gaer. I will not permit that name to be forgotten, nor will I forget the appalling cowardice of Glamdring Ironfist. He will suffer for every drop of innocent blood that he shed so unnecessarily at that accursed place."

The High King was a man who paid more than lip service to the notion of protection for the innocent, Gruffydd knew. He thought of

24

his foster daughter, Nimue, and how Artor had ensured that the infant would grow and blossom.

Artor transferred his gaze to Odin. "Find shelter, ale, and clean pallets for these good men. Honor them, for theirs has been a terrible burden."

Odin departed at a run.

Turning back to Gruffydd and Targo, Artor issued his orders.

"Gruffydd, you have my leave to proceed with your task, with my gratitude. Targo, call the captains to attend me for a council of war. Ironfist had best be like his name, for I plan to lock his hands in a vice and squeeze him dry. Then I will rid the earth of this Saxon. We've reasoned with him for long enough."

"It will be a pleasure, Artor, a great pleasure. We have sat on our arses for three years." Targo grinned evilly.

A WAR COUNCIL was held four days later, long after the remains of the dead were burned with aromatic woods and their souls had been sent to the heroes. The hall atop Cadbury Tor was filled with warriors and chieftains, the greatest of whom sat on sturdy benches and drank from Phoenician glass as the day surrendered to evening.

Many of their number had ridden far, for they had come from the far-flung outposts of Ratae, Venonae, Viroconium, Aquae Sulis, and Venta Silurum. Their horses had been ridden to the point of death, and men had driven themselves, without sleep or pause for food, in order to answer the call of the High King. A sophisticated network of communications made meetings such as this one possible, but only the loyalty and obedience of the captains could bring them to Artor's court at Cadbury so expeditiously.

Artor's hall lacked the heavy ornamentation or the pretensions seen in Uther Pendragon's formal rooms in Venta Belgarum. In true Celtic style, the hall was longer than it was wide, and no anteroom forced visitors or petitioners to cool their heels until the High King

chose to admit them. Simple, beautifully polished benches were provided close to the doors so that weary men might rest their tired legs.

The ceiling was very high and was shaped to draw smoke from
the fire pits into a circular hole in the roof that possessed its own
cover to prevent inclement weather from entering the building, yet
permit the fire smoke to escape. The wooden walls were softened
by great lengths of woven fabric, an amazing luxury that provided
splashes of woad blue, jewel-bright crimson, and cheerful yellow. The
flagged floor was unremarkable, except for the figure of a dragon that
celebrated the might of Artor's totem, the red Dracos. Made of glass
tesserae, it was rumored to be the work of Myrddion Merlinus. This
Roman dragon, whose origin was virtually forgotten, stood proudly
rampant directly before a low dais on which a single, use-polished
curule chair rested.

For this meeting, King Artor rejected the raised dais in favor of a
long table with benches for seating. The High King sat at one end and
his chief adviser, Myrddion Merlinus, was seated at the other; all the
men present were equal, and were free to speak and openly express
their opinions. Goblets of wine in rare Roman glass and large platters
of sweetmeats, fruit, nuts, and even cold meats provided food and
drink that would tempt even the most epicurean of tastes, although
Artor and his adviser chose nothing but clear, cold water. Wall sconces
provided a pleasing light and the wood in the fire pit had been soaked
in a subtle, aromatic oil to sweeten the air.

As the council began, Ulf was instructed to relive the tale of the
death of the truce bearers and their escort. His face was suffused with
blood, but he recited the brutal story with increased confidence.

"I was forced to watch these treacherous murders without the arms
to strike a single blow. I will not rest until I have either killed ten Saxons for each of my companions, or I am dead. So do I swear!"

Ulf's formal words caused a ripple of unease and anger throughout
the packed hall. Peace is a strange and addictive state, and Artor had
provided three years of relative quiet. The land was in the process of
rebuilding after years of neglect, and only fools would choose to cast

away the comforts of soft beds, willing wives, and full bellies for the discomfort and uncertainties of battle.

Now that three summers of relative peace had passed, fields that had been left fallow and had been choked with weeds and nettles were now cleared and plowed. Homesteads, villages, and fortresses that had been neglected were now blessed with the luxury of time to make repairs, neaten fences, rethatch roofing, and repack stones into walls from which they had fallen.

But, while some warriors present seemed unwilling to take offense, other men rumbled their rage and frustration at the insults hurled at them by the Saxons, a white-faced Gawayne foremost among them. The prince took great pride in the bravery displayed by his younger brother, and he was also experiencing a measure of guilt at the premature ending of the young man's short and glorious life. By Gawayne's code, the truce breakers had no honor, for they had slaughtered Artor's emissaries out of hand, like oxen.

Twelve years of warfare had transformed Prince Gawayne from a lanky, enthusiastic boy into a mature, engaging, and handsome man. Of middling height, Gawayne was powerfully built and possessed a horseman's natural grace. His blond-red hair, a scattering of freckles across his cheeks, and his pale eyes gave him a boyish appearance that was accentuated by his frank and open gaze. Many men underestimated Gawayne because he spoke freely without first censoring his tongue, and his ready smiles deceived them into overlooking both his remarkably acute instincts and his loyalty to his uncle.

Gawayne was ruled by his libido, which was probably his greatest flaw. Women were instinctively drawn to him and the prince loved the fair sex, whether they were old or young, married or unmarried. No woman had any cause to complain of his attentions to her, but many husbands did.

But the prince was now angry, so his good humor had fled. Someone would pay for the spilled blood of Gaheris, for Gawayne had pressed his younger brother to prove his allegiance to King Artor. At the time, Gawayne was being mischievous and was tweaking the nose of his rigid father. Guilt, as well as rage, now flayed the prince, and Gawayne was determined that the western Saxons would be obliterated.

Myrddion gazed impassively at the assembled group and gauged the mood of those kings who had arrived at Cadbury, and the emissaries of those who could not attend in person. Slowly, he rose to his feet and took Ulf's place in a spot where he could face all the warriors and kings within the hall.

Vortigern and his yellow-haired Rowena were long dead, but not forgotten, so it was incumbent on Myrddion to recount the memories of his childhood to the assembly. Only Artor knew the full details of the tale that Myrddion told. Only Artor knew how shamelessly Myrddion tampered with the truth to manipulate these superstitious, cautious men.

"I was born a devil's spawn at Moridunum, and raised near a small town that the Romans called Segontium. Most of you know the story of my birth, even if I have often wondered if my mother concocted a tale so fearsome and strange that no one dared to expose me on a hillside for the wolves to devour. Suffice to say that my mother swore that she was raped by a demon in the privacy of her room, so I grew up with the taint of evil as my birthright." He smiled across the table at the assembled nobles. "But I need not prattle on about tales you already know."

The warriors nodded, for all men knew that Myrddion Merlinus was the son of a demon who mated with a virginal Cymru princess.

Now that Myrddion needed their compliance, he was playing ruthlessly upon their prejudices.

"Instead, I will recount to you the tale of how Vortigern's tower at Dinas Emrys tumbled down again and again while it was being constructed, and how his sorcerers convinced the king that only the blood of a devil's child could cement the foundation stones together." Myrddion paused for effect.

Although they might have argued that Myrddion's story had no bearing on the current problem, his audience listened, gape-mouthed.

The smallest child in the land knew that Myrddion had spirited himself out of Dinas Emrys through the use of sorcery.

"I did not intend to be sacrificed in order to mortar the stones of a Saxon fortress."

The members of his audience nodded wisely, and Artor grinned appreciatively from behind his hand. Even Targo stared at Myrddion with an odd mixture of reverence and recognition, and Artor marveled anew at how the strongest and shrewdest of men prized the glamour of magic in a world that was bloody and prosaic.

"Any fool could see that the foundation stones were wet with underground water that had soaked upward through the soil. I was barely eleven years of age, but I had two good eyes and I told the sorcerers and their unholy master, Vortigern, to dig into the foundations at a certain spot where they would find a pool of water."

Myrddion's listeners were captivated. Their eyes shone in the flare of the torches at the thought of a boy issuing orders to a High King, especially a lord who was so lost to reason that he had welcomed the Saxons into the lands of the Celts. They remembered that the first Saxons to settle in Dyfed had come at Vortigern's invitation.

"Vortigern accepted your advice, I take it," Targo stated flatly. "Or else you'd not be here."

"Aye, Targo. They dug through the foundations and they found the pool, exactly as I had predicted."

Myrddion's eyes clouded and Artor could swear that those same eyes rolled back into his head. The warriors' breathing hissed between their teeth, and the air seemed colder and thicker.

"Within the pool, two dragons coiled and struggled. I could see them quite clearly, although other, wiser men present swore that they could not. One dragon was as white as hoar frost and its breath was gelid with cold. Its claws were curved blades of ice and its tail lashed the pool into a storm of sleet and snow."

The audience leaned forward, mesmerized by Myrddion's fair and compelling voice.

"The other dragon was red, and the plates of mail that covered its body were hot and steaming. Fire poured from its nostrils, and its claws made the pond water boil at a single touch."

He paused, dramatically.

"The dragons leapt at each other and fire met ice. The struggle was terrible as the breath of the white dragon turned the flames of the red dragon to steam. But where the red dragon clutched with its great claws, and where its plated tail wrapped round the body of its enemy, the white dragon shrank and melted. Terrible was the struggle, but at last the red dragon was triumphant and only whitened, glacial bones lay at the bottom of the pond to testify that the ice dragon had ever existed. Then the red dragon of the Celts spread its wings over the land, rose, and hovered on the breast of the wind. The white dragon of the Saxons was defeated, and Vortigern was doomed to lose his crown and die."

The warriors sighed, but one princeling wasn't satisfied. He broke the rapt silence.

"Did Vortigern see this battle? Did the sorcerers not try to aid the white dragon?"

"They couldn't see the battle, they only witnessed the roiling and bubbling of the water. I fell into a faint, and many of those who were there swore that I prophesied—but I can't speak for the accuracy of their recollections. One thing is certain. I've carried the weight of this prophecy for forty years, and I know it is true. The red dragon of the tribes will destroy the white dragon of the Saxons, and we'll strike Glamdring Ironfist like fire on ice. I cannot promise that we will always defeat the dragon of the north, but we will be triumphant while the Red Dragon of Artor rides high. We will strive until we turn this troubled land into a haven of peace. This I do swear, as long as Celtic hearts remain faithful and as long as the High King dares to stand against murder and brutality. We will prevail and we will defeat the western Saxons of Dyfed, King Vortigern's poisoned legacy to the Celtic people."

All eyes swiveled towards Artor, who stood stiffly, his hands on the hilt of his sword and his head bowed as if in prayer. Slowly, so slowly, he raised his eyes, and even those doughty warriors, his allies, quailed before his angry, flaming face. His eyes were not veiled as was his usual custom, and the nobles swore later that they saw fire burning deep in their grey depths, as if the dragons of ice and flame still struggled within them.

As, perhaps, they did.

"This High King will not brook the murder of his ambassadors under a flag of truce. Artor will not be content until every Saxon west of the great mountain chain is dead, or else herded back into the sea whence they came. Choose, men of the west, for now is the time for the testing of our hearts and of our courage. Until now, the Saxons have come to us, battering at our defenses and seeking our weaknesses, but we have always managed to drive them back."

Loud were the cries of assent in the hall.

"Now we must risk all that we hold dear to our hearts. We must do battle with a man who is thane of a country so barren and ruled so cruelly that his forces have withstood all the efforts of Llanwith pen Brynn, and Llanwith's father before him. The Celts of the Demetae tribe of Dyfed in Cymru are so battered into submission by the descendants of Vortigern's guard that they wait sullenly for relief. And, fellow Britons, do not think that Glamdring Ironfist and his debased and bestial Saxons are no threat to us. They are at our backs, and a child can kill a warrior if he strikes hard, unnoticed, behind a man twice its size. This particular Saxon hive must be destroyed."

The room became silent, and Artor could feel doubt in many of the downcast eyes and the covert glances that slid back and forth between the assembled kings.

"Ulf, what did Gaheris say to Glamdring Ironfist when he faced certain death?"

Ulf faced Artor squarely. "He told him that the Saxons never learn—and they never change. Then Ironfist struck off his head."

Artor turned again to his audience. "Is this not true? Did the noble young prince perceive the Saxon weaknesses clearly? Aye! They do not learn, and they do not change their barbaric practices. They destroy Roman-built garrisons to build their own wooden palisades. They

31

smash stone towers into rubble. They kill horses and use them only for food. And they don't change!"

Each word was spoken with measured, bell-clear emphasis, so that each man in the great hall was forced to consider the weight of the message delivered by Gaheris.

Eventually, murmurs of assent became more audible. The spoken words weren't loud in Artor's keen ears, but a level of agreement was growing inexorably within the assembly.

Caius, Artor's foster brother and steward of Artor's household on Cadbury Tor, rose smoothly as the council wavered uneasily in the face of the High King's determination. A snap of his slender fingers summoned servants, who refilled wine cups and removed used platters. His clever, black eyes gauged his brother's determination.

We go to war! Good! Caius thought excitedly, although no trace of his eager anticipation reached his controlled face. Caius was tired of peace and weary of counting hams and the weapons in Artor's armory, or overseeing the collection of the High King's taxes. Men such as Caius are only ever comfortable and at peace in the midst of war, when the violence they crave is readily on offer.

"All races are born with the same measure of courage," Artor insisted. "And courage is a resource that can be used or wasted. Never forget that the Saxons are just as brave as we are."

The audience stirred nervously.

"Many of the western Saxons have been born in these isles, as were our forefathers. Ironfist is as much a Briton as my foster brother, Caius, who stands here with you. And Caius, for all his Roman bloodline, is still a proud and noble Briton."

Snickers of amusement ran through the gathering. For, while Caius enjoyed considerable respect as Artor's steward, his pride and arrogance won him few friends, and most of the kings present were aware that the relationship between Artor and Caius was strained.

Respect among fighting men is a strange and hard-won reward. Caius had proved his courage again and again, just as he had proven his prowess as a fighting man and as a leader. But few men really liked

32

him, for there was something about Caius that was mildly repulsive. His mouth was a little too full and too red; his eyes glittered a little too brightly; and his manner was just a fraction too obsequious to be pleasing. Prince Gawayne had been heard to say that men such as Caius were either at your knees or at your throat, and most of Artor's captains would have agreed with this view if pressed for an opinion.

Two hot coins of color appeared on Caius's cheekbones. He was well aware of how his peers thought of him. He realized that he wasn't trusted, even though he had served the High King with conspicuous gallantry for twelve years.

Caius willed the color to fade from his face. He hated these smug Celtic lordlings with their crude and simplistic view of the world.

As if he could read his foster brother's mind, Artor smiled encouragingly.

"No, Ironfist and his warriors are no different from our Celtic ancestors," he continued. "They are no different, except for their refusal to learn from their mistakes. As their fathers lived and built, so do the Saxons of today. As their grandfathers fought and died, so do the Saxons of today. But, in time, the Saxons will be forced to accept new ideas from other races, just as we Celts were forced to accept changes in our outlooks and in our lives. We took Roman knowledge, and we used it to our advantage. And now we maintain their roads and we recognize the strength of their fortresses. And we've learned to use the horse to maintain our military might. At this moment—this rare, fleeting moment—we still have an edge over our enemies. May the gods help us if we cast our advantage aside out of timidity and ineptitude."

Targo flushed with pride, for Artor had used the voice of authority to force his message upon the great ones. All the wiser heads in council now nodded in agreement.

"When Ironfist falls, the Saxons in the east will be forced to halt their advance. They will settle in the east, and they will bury their roots in our soil. They will marry Celtic women and their lives will change until the day eventually comes when all the races who inhabit these lands may be prepared to call themselves brothers. But that day has not yet come. Nor will it happen in our time." Artor gazed into the attentive faces of his nobles. "Do we let Glamdring's aggression remain unchallenged? Do we hide in our fortresses until Ironfist and King Lot surge out of the wilderness to lay waste to our fields and rape our women? Are we in our dotage that we must accept their uncouth insults?"

"No! No! No!" roared the war council.

You fools! Caius thought contemptuously. Artor can manipulate you at will.

"Even if all of you should vote for peace, it is my intention to ride against Ironfist, even if I must go alone. Make your choices, and make them quickly, for I leave within the week, even though death may take me."

Then Artor strode from the hall, and the assembled nobles and warriors bowed before him. The High King's eyes veered neither to right nor left, but were focused on the north.

And the eyes of the shark were pitiless.

Caius wiped his suddenly sweaty hands dry on the sides of his tunic before striding out boldly behind his foster brother. His red lips were curved into a gentle smile of satisfaction.

Slowly, stalwart men followed, both nobles and vassals, and the word raced through Cadbury and the villages like Greek fire.

"We go to war."

Chapter II

THE LOST CHILD

One day, the old Roman road would be called Fosse Way, a pedestrian and comforting name for something made for bloodletting. Built to facilitate the movement of men at war, the road stretched out ahead of Artor's cavalry, straight and wide, over the gorse-covered slopes leading towards Aquae Sulis. Winter still clutched at the land, although the snow had gone, promising that the spring thaw was coming and the winds would soon blow warmer. A few shivering and naked aspens raised skeletal branches over the bare earth, while domestic animals turned their backs to the wind and grazed in places where the grasses of last autumn waved brown, withered fronds on the lee side of slow-rolling hills.

In disciplined ranks, the cavalry had ridden out of Cadbury Tor towards the north, and then camped at the highest point of the Roman road where the signal fires were lit. As the warriors hobbled their horses and erected simple hide tents, the lights of small fires were visible over the land like fireflies clustered around a larger, glowing blaze. The silvery sound of tinkling bells sounded through the twilight as the horses wandered to find what sweet grass might be found under the trees. Throughout the night, drawn by the signal fire, riders joined the main force in small groups.

Two days later, when Artor led his army out of bivouac astride the ancient Coal, his favorite horse, he did so with grim deliberation. Except for the dragon symbol on his shield and breastplate, he dressed carefully in the deepest sable. Peasants stared hard at the king and his similarly clad warriors as the army passed, and searched each face for a funereal sadness. They sought in vain. Rather than mourning, the army's somber clothing was the dress of inevitable death, so that under their dyed cowls and helmets, the warrior's faces appeared to be leprous and skeletal in their whiteness. Even the afternoon sun was bone pale, as if it sensed that only the blood of many men would renew its vitality before the warmer months were done.

The baggage train was small for a force of several hundred men, excluding the horse handlers, who moved a herd of spare mounts in the wake of the dark-robed cavalry. Later, a growing contingent of foot soldiers and archers from Ratae and Venonae swelled the force that pushed ever northwards, without making any attempt to disguise its movements.

"I want Ironfist to be warned that I am coming for him," Artor told his captains. "And if human blood runs through his veins, he will begin to sweat under all his bravado. We will let him wait, with his nerves stretched taut, until we make camp on his soil. He made our emissaries suffer, so we will do the same to him. Imagination plays tricks on the bravest man, and when I am on his soil, Ironfist will know that I intend to exact my revenge. When we enter the Saxon lands, we will paint our faces in the old Pictish ways. Each man will wear the mark of a skull under his visor when we eventually meet up with Ironfist and his warriors. I want him to understand, irrevocably, that he is facing an army of the dead."

Some of Artor's captains were nonplussed by his plan that they should wear blue woad and white clay on their faces. "Does Artor admit to the possibility of failure before we strike even a single blow?" some of the warriors whispered over their flickering campfires.

But Myrddion walked from fireside to fireside, explaining that their Saxon opponents were deeply superstitious men. They should suffer before they faced just retribution for their crimes.

"Your king wants our warriors to mimic the wights of those men that Ironfist murdered," he said. "And he hopes that the Saxons will believe that those defenseless victims have returned and are multiplied a hundredfold. It is better that Ironfist is afraid, not us, for we are the death bringers, and the harvesters of fear."

Whenever he spoke, Myrddion gave heart to the most superstitious of men, so that the veterans came to think of the disguise as a great joke and a fitting tribute to the dead ambassadors.

When the growing army reached the outskirts of old Aquae Sulis, the population met them with exuberant joy. Broad, open fields on the banks of the river offered water and feed for the mounts and the baggage animals. Artor and his captains rode onward, through ever-broadening streets, until they reached the original Roman walls that encircled the administrative heart of the city. There, the chief magistrate and the city councillors awaited them.

The High King was greeted with due pomp and ceremony, for neither Artor nor the city dignitaries would countenance any lack in common courtesy. In fact, the chief magistrate, who had been woken from an afternoon nap by news of the king's arrival, appreciated the honor that Artor offered by paying his respects to the city fathers before he made camp. Such small details, Artor knew, were crucial elements that firmly cemented his alliances with his subjects.

"I welcome you, my lord," the magistrate, Drusus, intoned solemnly. "The city is yours to do with as you choose." His obeisance was low, but not subservient.

"As always, it is a pleasure to rest at Aquae Sulis, for it reminds me of the joys of my youth," Artor responded as he warmly embraced the Romano-Celt. "My brother, Caius, will beg your assistance in the provisioning of my combined forces."

"Of course, Your Majesty." Drusus smiled, knowing that Artor's war chests were always deep and that the king would never quibble over details of payment. "I will order our scribes to hold themselves ready to receive instructions from Lord Caius."

"My commissary will be hard at work long before dark," Caius said courteously with a low bow. "My thanks to the citizens of Aquae Sulis for the assistance that is always given to Lord Artor's servants so willingly."

The magistrate flushed at Caius's fair words, and Artor smiled with a certain element of sardonic humor that Caius was finally learning the value of flattery. His foster brother's smiles were far more effective than his tantrums, and he was a superb steward.

After all the courtesies had been completed, Artor and his captains rode back through the darkening, cobbled streets to rejoin their troops. Women bowed low over their baskets, while small children and young boys ran parallel with the horsemen, whooping and shouting excitedly like savages, but the welcome wasn't as warm as in the Celtic towns. The king understood. The people of Aquae Sulis were Roman in their thinking and, although Artor had been raised in the ancient traditions, his amber hair and his great height marked him forever as a sympathetic stranger. And so he cherished the bowed heads of the citizens, for such respect held more worth for him than the wild homage of the more volatile tribes. Artor knew that Roman Britain would never fail him.

Aquae Sulis, queen of cities, Artor thought, as he dismounted and looked back in the direction from which he had come.

Situated on a branch of the old Roman road, Aquae Sulis seemed awash with a multitude of contrasting pastel colors in the light of the afternoon sun. In its soft, fertile lowlands, the city glowed with old stonework, jetting water fountains, and painted walls that brought rainbows to tangible life. The delicate mosaic floors that were intertwined with dolphins, sea creatures, and brilliant tessellated fish seduced those Celts who had never seen the wonders of a Roman city, or experienced the delights of a Roman bath. The complicated rituals of hygiene, which many Celts had adopted in the time of their Roman conquerors, came as a sybaritic delight to the novices.

The Celtic warriors weren't excessively clean by habit. Britain was a cold country for the most part, and lacked the hot, sometimes steamy weather and disease-breeding humors of Rome. But the Roman invaders had prized personal hygiene, so public bathing was now enjoyed by all the citizens of the city. With oils to remove deeply ingrained grime, hot water to open the pores of the skin, and cold water to close them, men and women could turn cleanliness into a luxurious experience. Wherever the Romans traveled in the world, they brought the notion of public bathing with them, along with the heated floors that were a by-product of the calidarium, so Roman towns such as Aquae Sulis, with its plentiful mineral springs, became thriving centers of sophistication.

The pleasures of Aquae Sulis were possible only because Artor determined to rest his men for twenty-four hours, ostensibly to replenish their rations. In reality, Artor wished to pay a short social visit to Ector, his foster-father, at the Villa Poppinidii, where his life had once been so simple and peaceful. Besides, the very fiber of his being demanded that he should gaze once more upon the lovely face of Licia, his beautiful daughter, who was being raised by Ector. The child was ignorant of her noble connections, for Artor had made the hard choice to relinquish his daughter for her protection. Frith's great-grandson, Gareth, was her sworn bodyguard, and only those trusted intimates who had known the king's first wife knew Artor's deepest and most closely guarded secret.

Artor had only to close his eyes and the faces of ancient, beloved Frith and his beautiful Gallia were there with him, faint and translucent with the passage of the years. Frith had fulfilled her oath to her dearly loved master, the boy Artorex, and died protecting his heavily pregnant wife. Regrets! Rage at his long dead father, Uther Pendragon, who had demanded their deaths, surfaced out of Artor's repressed memories, with the same heat that he had felt before that old monster was dead.

So, once the captains had been briefed on the behavior expected of their warriors during their sojourn in Aquae Sulis, Artor rode out of the camp in company with Caius and Targo. The High King left his staff in no doubt that any infringements of discipline by his warriors were to be punished without mercy. Artor always insisted that friendly cities, towns, and villages should be treated with respect. His warriors knew better than to indulge in the soldiers' pastimes of rape, robbery, or violent drunkenness. The High King was a realist; he knew young men would always seek out prostitutes and drink if left to their own devices, but any public disturbance was punished brutally and expeditiously. Artor always paid for any damages with red gold, so the cities of the west greeted his arrival with pleasure.

A man is not always a hero in his home community, or so the Christian Bible warned Artor. Aquae Sulis was outwardly pleased that one of her sons had risen high in the world, and the young men of the city were eager to serve in his armies, but all the citizens who had known the youthful Artorex were either dead, ancient, or already serving the High King at Cadbury. Those who might speak knowledgeably of his youth, such as Ector, Julanna, or the house servants at Villa Poppinidii, would never betray the boy and the man that they still loved.

The evening breeze was mild when the long and meandering road leading to the Villa Poppinidii loomed out of the dusk, leaving Artor feeling strangely displaced in time. On a number of occasions, many years before, he had watched with anticipation as the three travelers who had changed his life so unexpectedly had ridden up this same rutted track on their irregular visits.

Myrddion Merlinus, Llanwith pen Bryn, and Luka—Uther's chief courtier and two nobles—had arrived unheralded at the Villa Poppinidii when Artor was a twelve-year-old boy. The High King sighed. The three men had changed his life, honed him to become a weapon against the barbarians, and then they had torn him away from everything he had known and loved. Had he ever really mattered as a person of flesh, blood, and spirit? Or was his birth, his physical strength, and his potential as a High King all that the three travelers desired?

On reflection, Artor decided that the three travelers had known what they were doing to him, and were willing to pay any price. He was tangible proof that hope still lived in the Celtic breast, and that the west need not burn behind the Saxon marauders.

Now, he was visiting the villa on his own mission of hope.

As the party reached the villa gates, they spied a tall young girl with amber hair as she ran towards the villa doors to alert the house of the arrival of visitors.

That must be Licia, Artorex thought to himself in amazement at the many inches of growth that had taken place since he had last seen her.

Ector came shuffling to the door of the villa, followed by the house servants, who bowed so low that their heads all but touched the ground. Ector attempted to kneel, an effort that caused his swollen knee joints to creak painfully. His old blue eyes were filmed with cataracts and fresh tears as he recognized Caius, his son, in the company of the king.

Dismounting, Artor clasped the old man to his breast.

"You need not bow to me, Father. Nor should you ever be on your knees. I do not expect you to carry out such empty gestures."

"They're not empty to me," Ector replied simply, with his head held high. "I am a Celt, and you are my king."

A hot, red flush began at Artor's throat until it reached his cheekbones. Unwittingly, he had offended the proud old man, and he was deeply ashamed of his shallow courtesy. Kings learn to flatter without thinking, a habit that Artor had adopted all too easily.

"By the gods, Artor, you're blushing," exclaimed Ector. "Who'd have thought that you could still color up like a callow youth?"

Immediately, Artor felt sixteen again, ignorant and awkward.

As usual, Targo leavened the embarrassment of the moment by simply clapping Ector on the back, quite forgetting that he had once been a servant of the house.

"The lad will never feel like a king at the Villa Poppinidii, Sir Ector. You knew him when he was a great lump of a lad, all elbows and knees, with his head in the clouds and wearing a dirty tunic."

"Licia takes after him then, for she is of similar appearance, although she is a sweet little thing." Ector sighed gustily. "And Caius. My son. I am so proud that you ride with the High King, my boy—and that you are his steward. Come, let me embrace you."

Caius enfolded his father in his muscular arms. His coarsening face was almost content as he basked in his father's unqualified approval.

Caius was the last of the three visitors to be embraced, and the last to be recognized. Only Targo saw the faint glitter of resentment in his eyes. He didn't blame Caius for his jealousy, for it must be difficult to be second best in his father's eyes to a person he had actively despised during his youth. Until his death, a shadow would lie between Ector and his only son, the shade of Lady Livinia, whom Caius slew in his rage and frustration.

So long ago! Targo had listened to the villagers when the young master rode with the dead Severinus and his friends. The downcast eyes of the simple, peasant farmers were murderous. Child killers! Pederasts! The accusations had turned the air to acid, had the aristocrats, on their fine horses, cared to notice the ordinary men who watched them with hatred and disgust.

In one dreadful night, Caius had tried to kick his pregnant wife to death, and had lifted a blade against her, only to kill his mother in error. Targo had been present when Artor and the three travelers had threatened Caius with unspeakable pain unless he explained his actions.

He had.

Old Targo had lived too long to mince words or to seek pleasing, meaningless platitudes. The Villa Severinii had given up the bodies of seven small boys, tortured and murdered by an evil ring of pederasts. Caius had sworn he was a victim, driven to madness by blackmail and terror, but Targo had doubted the boy, because he knew that Caius had often shown cruelty towards his servants and his horses.

But Targo also knew that Caius had shown his mettle in battle a hundred times over the years, and the veteran was prepared to quash the worm of doubt that wriggled uncomfortably into his thoughts.

"You are as hale as ever, Father." Caius smiled at his sire. "You never seem to age like the rest of us." He placed a protective and possessive hand over his father's age-spotted old paw.

With the affection that had grown during the many years that Artor had lived and worked under his roof, Ector examined every considerable inch of his king. Eleven battles, and twelve years, had managed to sit lightly on Artor's thirty-seven years. His hair was as curly and as golden-amber as ever, his form was still strong and beautiful, and only the white weather lines at the corners of his eyes spoke of his many years in the saddle. Artor was almost too beautiful to be a man, and was therefore doubly beloved by Ector, for the semblance of youth was a reminder of old times and lost loves.

By comparison, Caius had thickened. He was superbly fit, because he prized the skills of battle and regularly exercised his skills at Cadbury, but his physique had gradually become overlaid by a layer of fat. His face was coarser and the pores of his skin had widened, especially at the end of his aristocratic nose. His complexion was ruddy, not with health but from extremes of temper, and Ector felt a twinge of worry for the well-being of his son. But Caius's smile, his white teeth, and his clear eyes were encouraging, and Ector failed to notice a telltale flatness that marred his son's expression when he saw his wife, Julanna, standing in the doorway. She quickly melted away into the shadows of the villa.

Overjoyed by the visit, Ector dashed away the traitorous welling of his emotions with the back of his hand.

"Come in! Come in! Old friends and kinsmen! The Villa Poppinidii cannot match the royal palaces you now frequent, but we still offer good meals and soft beds. Julanna will be organizing your comforts even as we speak."

As Artor stepped over the threshold, he imagined he could see old Frith, smiling at him from the shadows before the kitchen entrance. And here came Gallia, the insubstantiality of her form belied by the brilliance of her eyes. And Livinia Major looked up from her loom with her customary elegance and grace.

All these fine people were long gone now. All were lost for the remainder of time.

A shudder of regret ran through his body as he surveyed the familiar surroundings with the bittersweet memories of his youth.

Ector noticed, and gripped Artor's sword-calloused hand.

"I often see them too, Artor," he whispered. "They comfort me as I wait to join them at the last. I am not afraid of death, for their love still embraces us."

Then, suddenly, Artor could smell flowers and sweet perfumes, and his imagination conjured up those invisible hands that had stroked and comforted him. His eyes filled with unshed tears, which he brushed away while the others were occupied with Julanna's welcome.

Little Livinia Minor, now nearly fourteen, stood directly behind her mother. She was struck dumb with awe, and her dark eyes were wide with fascination as she stared at the tall, powerful visitors.

Artor grinned at her. He winked, and the girl giggled.

He embraced Julanna and congratulated her on the beauty of her daughter. Julanna herself was softly rounded and petal-faced. She was still a beautiful woman, and the frightened girl of yesteryear had grown into an assured Roman matron.

"You are well, wife?" Caius asked.

"Yes, my husband, and little Elynn flourishes."

Julanna's second daughter, Gallia Minor, sucked her thumb and hid behind her nurse's skirts. Caius embraced her, and the child endured his caress with a rigid indifference. The nurse carried Elynn, who had been named for Ector's mother, to meet her father.

The two-year-old wriggled and smiled in the nurse's arms, and Caius patted the child on her fine, baby-soft head.

Ever the perfect wife, Julanna's face was fixed on her husband with a pleasing and compliant smile. Artor wondered if it was only his imagination that her large, deer-soft eyes were wary and careful.

"Greetings, Papa," Livinia Minor murmured hesitantly, and planted a nervous, damp kiss on her father's cheek. The girl was like a skittish fawn, for she hardly knew her father; Caius's duties kept him far from home for over ten months of the year. She flinched as he hugged her.

Familiar and strange servants showed Artor and Targo to the best rooms, while Caius stowed his traveling kit in his own apartments. Already, the aromatic smells of the evening meal wafted through the atrium, and Artor remembered those occasions when he had served the three travelers with his own young hands. Time swept him back to the days when he was an ignorant young boy, and a greater part of him regretted his rise to supreme power and the demands of his duties.

Artor, Caius, and Targo dressed and met for a small feast that was timed to coincide with the long dusk. Targo would have excused himself as not fit to eat with "his betters," but Ector overrode all arguments presented by the mercenary. As the family reclined to eat, it was almost as if Livinia Major still lived and was present with the company. Livinia Minor was permitted to stay awake later than usual in honor of the occasion, so she could savor the fine smoked ham, eggs stuffed with honey, freshwater crayfish, and sheep's stomach filled with jellied eels and plover's eggs. Artor would have preferred a simple repast, but he understood that the villa was offering its best to entertain the High King.

But of Licia, there was no sign.

Julanna seemed to read Artor's mind.

"Licia's maidservant is attempting to clean the scamp. She is always in the fields or in the forest, so she hardly owns a robe that isn't torn or stained. Gareth will bring her to us presently."

"How goes Gareth?" Artor asked.

"He has become my steward," Ector answered jovially. "And I cannot imagine how the villa would run without him. The scrawny stable boy has grown into a formidable young man."

Ector had barely finished speaking when Gareth entered the room with a freshly scrubbed, coiffed, and uncomfortable girl at his heels.

Artor nodded to Gareth, a mark of respect that the servant deserved for his many years of guardianship. As a boy and as the great-grandson of Frith, whom Artor had loved as a mother, Gareth had killed to protect Licia during an attack on the Villa Poppinidii by Uther Pendragon's guard. Artor could still picture Gareth then. The lad's striking white-blond hair had already been long, and his golden skin and northern-blue eyes had marked him as an outlander by blood. For all his barbarian ancestry, Gareth and his grandame, Frith, had given many lifetimes of service and loyalty to the High King.

Licia had certainly grown. The dark hair of babyhood had lightened to the color of amber honey, enlivened by a pair of eyes that were an odd shade of brown. At certain angles, especially by the torchlight in the dining room, the flecks in her eyes seemed almost green. With a wry grin, Artor noticed that the child had scabs on both knees and the long scratches that always seemed to result when adventurous children came into contact with briars and low branches.

"Licia." Ector held out his hand to her. "This gentleman is King Artor, who grew up inside this very house. He is the High King of all the Britons, so make your bow, child."

Licia bowed prettily, glancing up into Artor's face through smudged, sooty eyelashes that gave her eyes and smile a special loveliness.

"Sire," she said, "did you *really* grow up at the Villa Poppinidii?"

Artor knelt so that their eyes were level. "Yes, I did, Licia. I used to play in the forest too. And Frith, Gareth's grandmother, would scold me because I always came home dirty with my hair all tangled."

The child grinned engagingly. "Gareth says he'll beat me black and blue if I go into the forest—but he won't. He loves me, you see."

"Then you are a very lucky girl, little lady. To be loved is the best feeling in the whole, wide world."

"Doesn't anyone love you, sire?" the child asked seriously.

"Some do . . . but there are many more people who would like me to vanish in a puff of smoke." Artor blew out his cheeks with an audible pop, and Licia giggled.

Then her compelling eyes became serious once more. Artor felt their force as they examined him dispassionately.

"I'll try to love you, if you like," Licia said carefully. "But I can't promise, because I don't know you very well."

"Thank you, Licia. I'd be very honored if you could like me."

Licia giggled again. "Oh, I can do that. I like nearly everybody."

Artor smiled, but he felt the hollow pain of the loss of his wife stab through the space under his ribs. Although Gallia had been dead for over twelve years, she often entered his thoughts. He could recall the smell of her, the silken quality of her skin, and the erotic softness of her touch, but he couldn't remember her face. Even now, as he looked gently into the eyes of their daughter, he couldn't picture Gallia's features and he mourned the betrayal of time.

"Enough, Licia," Ector said gently, recognizing the sheen of moisture in his foster son's eyes. "It's time now for you to go with Livinia and eat your supper. Then it's off to bed for both of you." He patted the heads of both girls with affection.

Livinia looked dismayed, but Licia hugged Ector impulsively.

"I'll go if you say so, Grandfather," Livinia said softly. "But I'm not the least bit tired,"

"Do I win a hug, my little ones?" Artor asked.

Livinia did not hesitate, and clasped her arms round the shoulders of the kneeling Artor.

Licia considered the matter more carefully and then, quite visibly, decided in Artor's favor. She approached him and lifted his curling hair away from his brow with the same deft touch that her mother had used so long ago. Then she kissed him on each eye.

"These kisses will help you to sleep well, my lord," she explained neatly. She studied him for a moment. "Your hair curls just like mine. Gareth says that my curls are just like the tendrils on the wisteria vine where Mama lies. Did you know her, sire? Did she have hair like ours?"

"No . . . Your mother's hair was thick and glossy, and was far shinier than even the mane of my horse. Your mother's hair was very beautiful, but it was not as curled as yours."

"Then I must have inherited this mop from my father." Licia smiled at him. "Did you know him, sire?"

Artor laughed softly, but only to disguise his reluctance to answer the question.

Targo had turned away on his dining couch, and Ector's eyes were misty.

"Yes. For, to me, he was like a twin brother. You should always think of him as being brave and strong, and he loved you, and your mother, very dearly. But he is no longer with us, for the life he lived with your mother ended a long, long time ago. He had no will to live without her by his side."

Licia sighed happily. "How lovely." She smiled up at him. "No one will ever quite tell me, you see. Don't you hate it when people don't quite tell a lie but they don't quite tell the whole truth either?"

"Yes, Licia, friends often act just as you say, but it would be wise of you to remember that people can often appear to be cruel when in fact they intend a kindness towards you. You should be proud of your parents. They were devoted to each other, and their memory remains with me."

"Thank you, sire. I hope you sleep well."

Then Licia tripped away with the awkward, stumbling gait of a child who was still growing into the length of her very long legs. Artor drank in every careless movement, every swing of her cascade of curls, and the sweet sway of her burgeoning body.

The men present felt his pain, but, trapped in their masculine inability to express the depth of their sympathy, they said nothing. Julanna reached across the table to grip Artor's hand with her own, which he wordlessly kissed.

He shook his head to clear his dismal thoughts, and rose to his feet.

"You have wrought miracles, Father Ector," Artor congratulated his host. "And you, too, friend Gareth. Licia is delightful and free of care. She has been raised to be herself, and I am encouraged for her future." He turned to Julanna. "And you, Julanna, should be especially proud that the girl has such pretty manners and is so natural in her dealings with adults. Gallia would be so grateful to you."

Tears formed in Julanna's eyes. "I wish Gallia was here with us. I miss her still."

Ector fiddled with his white beard and changed the topic, for he could see the old horrors were welling in Artor's eyes. It was time to divert the conversation in a new direction.

"What is your destination, Artor?" he asked. "I can't believe your presence at the Villa Poppinidii is motivated by a friendly family visit. Targo will always accompany you, I know, but why does Caius ride with you? What is amiss?"

"We go to war with the western Saxons, Father," Caius cut in self-importantly. "Our emissaries to the Saxons in the mountains to the north were murdered under a flag of truce, so we must march to answer the Saxon challenge."

Ector's eyebrows rose. To Caius's chagrin, he addressed his questions to his foster son.

"That rat's nest has been entrenched since the time of Vortigern. Uther permitted them to breed because the mountains and the loyal tribes kept them enclosed. I thought you'd dealt with them at Magnis, so why do they show their heads now?"

"Katigern Oakheart and his eastern Saxons, Angles, and Jutes were beaten soundly ten times, but they never surrendered. Although Oakheart died in the second ruinous battle, the Saxon settlements in the south and the east regrouped to live and to fight another day. Scores of his erstwhile warriors have chosen to strengthen the old fortresses used by Vortigern and his kin, so they must now be eliminated. They will be difficult to dislodge, for they have set their eyes on the softer lands beyond their own borders. I am no Uther Pendragon who would be happy to leave sleeping dogs lie. As they were born in our lands, I offered them an honorable peace, but they rejected my overtures in the bloodiest way possible."

"Then they are fools," Ector replied stoutly. In the old man's prejudiced regard, no Saxon invaders could stand against the might of his foster son.

"No, Father Ector, I wish the Saxons were fools, but they aren't. To deal with this particular enemy, we will need to draw on all our resources and courage. The only truly foolish thing they have done so far was to slay our emissaries in such a brutal and cowardly fashion. And the execution of Prince Gaheris gained them no advantage, for their treachery serves only to strengthen my resolve."

Ector's mouth dropped open in amazement, for even in quiet, peaceful Aquae Sulis, the sons of King Lot were well known by name.

"Why would the Saxons kill the son of their closest ally?" he asked Artor. "Where is the honor in such arrant stupidity?"

Targo snorted his agreement, but Artor was more pragmatic.

"Gaheris chose his own fate, for he refused to break the oath that he had sworn to me, even when the Saxons offered to spare his life. Their leader had no choice but to treat Gaheris like the other warriors. But I would have found some way short of murder, had I been in his boots." He paused. "At least King Lot will now be forced to think for himself. Morgause and Morgan have influenced his decisions for decades, but their motives are based on their hatred for Uther Pendragon and, by birth, myself. Their spite can have no place in how King Lot decides to respond to the killing of his son."

The discussion moved on to family matters, and Ector informed the king of the latest news of his fields, his orchards, and their yields, and the various benefits of different agricultural methods. Artor took considerable pleasure in talking of such simple, homely matters, and he luxuriated in the warmth and comfort of the rural life.

When he finally made his way to the most luxurious sleeping room, Artor recalled those times as a young boy when he had stolen oil to read in the scriptorium, and he wondered again what had happened to the hopeful and curious Artorex of that long-ago time. Then he slept.

• • •

ARTOR BROKE HIS fast with fresh bread, new honey, and a handful of nuts, and in the clarity of the early-morning sunlight he strode briskly across the fields to the ruins of his old home. He had lacked the heart to visit Gallia's memorial for many lonely years, but now, as he prepared for a new series of battles, he was drawn once more to that quiet and secluded place.

The stones used in the construction of the walls had weathered during twelve winters, and the ravages of the fire that had destroyed the house had been disguised by wisteria, ivy, and a network of flowering vines that twined around the singed rafters to provide a living roof over the building. The roots of a young hazel tree had broken the flagstones in the courtyard close to a pond that had been created by Gareth's careful hands. An ancient carved stone rested in the shallow water, its flanks glistening with dew in the early blush of the sunshine. Artor knew that daisies and poppies had seeded in cracks all around the ruins. In the summer, the daisies would look like a carpet of white snow dotted with the blood reds and vivid yellows of the poppies.

Clever hands had placed a number of pale river stones, worn smooth by the weight of an untold number of spring thaws, in a rough but graceful circle. The rocks supported rich soil in which a rose tree grew in a profusion of early spring buds. Smaller buttercups and wild flowers nestled between the roots, and, when the flowers bloomed, they would fill the air with a riot of color and scent. Artor smiled at the sight of wild rosemary, thyme, sage, and mandrake root growing freely among the flowers, for the garden mingled Gallia's sweet presence with the soul of Frith, the healer and wise woman. Old Frith had raised him as much as had Livinia Major, his foster mother, and these two women, between them, had shaped his character and turned him into the man he had become.

A salt-glazed ceramic urn, banded with red gold and sealed with beeswax, stood in a rough-built stone niche. The urn contained the ashes of two of the only three women whom Artor had ever loved wholly and selflessly.

"Have my labors pleased you, my lord?"

Gareth had walked, cat-footed, behind the king and was waiting patiently for Artor's attention. The steward was now a fully grown man, near to thirty, with long white-blond hair secured at the nape of his neck. Like most of the men of the Villa Poppinidii, his cheeks and chin were bare of beard, and the clean lines of bone under sunburned skin reminded Artor of Frith, his grandmother. In this man, her spirit and blood ran true.

Grey eyes met blue.

"Aye, you have made beauty out of pain. Gallia and Frith are very strong in the bones of this memorial; I can feel their touch."

Gareth's eyes dropped. His hands twisted with his tunic, with fingers that were roughened with work but undeniably clever and artistic.

"I ask a boon, lord, a promise for my faithfulness. I have stayed within the safety and security of the villa for most of my youth, to keep Lady Licia free from harm."

"Aye." Artor sighed. "You have earned the right to ask anything of me."

"When Licia is eventually married, I ask that I be permitted to ride with you as one of your warriors. I have trained diligently with our weapons master so as to be ready to serve you. This has always been my dream, my lord, as you know."

Artor smiled. He remembered Gareth as a boy, impatient to become a warrior and ride away to war.

"I confess that I have never considered those sacrifices that I asked of you in the past. I should have known better than to chain you to the Villa Poppinidii for life." As always, Artor made his decision swiftly. "Yes, I will release you from your oath once Licia is safe in another man's household. At that time, your life will become your own and I will gladly invite you to join my staff."

Gareth smiled Frith's sweet, knowing smile in gratitude for Artor's offer. He bowed his head, and left his king alone with his memories.

In the trees, a lark sang clearly and cleanly, and small finches dived among the flowers in their never-ending quest for nectar.

Despite himself, Artor felt his heart lighten. It would be difficult for any person to remain melancholy and consumed by self-pity in this enchanted garden.

"I pray that I will see your grave once again, my Gallia, for where I go, there will be no flowers or birds, except for the crows of death."

Artor remembered the texture of the dead, purpled lips of Gaheris, and thoughts of revenge immediately stirred in his hardening eyes. Whether or not his anger was fueled by guilt at the murder of another innocent was irrelevant. Artor was consumed by the need to have wanton bloodletting expunged from his kingdom. But bloodshed and death followed him, and left its stink of carrion in his wake. He couldn't help but be the hunter that Targo, in collusion with the three travelers, had wrought. Wracked by the weight of kingship and stifled by the heavy cloak of rule, Artor had learned that he must look to the final goal, and not consider the fine details leading to the achievement of his ends.

Was the slaughter of his emissaries and their guards one of those fine details? Had he depended upon Glamdring's brutishness to achieve his ends? Had he recognized that those deaths were the only means to fight a legitimate war against Glamdring? And had he wanted to strike at King Lot and Queen Morgause, to revenge their treachery by using the fair and decent Gaheris as a weapon?

Artor's brow furrowed. He had truly hoped for peace, but the responsibility of kingship was not so simple. For years he had known that this war would come.

Sickened and confused, Artor mounted his horse and tried to smile at Ector, Julanna, and the children without the shadows of cares that were massing behind his face.

He knew it was almost as easy to stop the inflowing tide as it was to still the desire to inflict pain in the human character. The crows knew.

They waited in the Old Forest for Artor's departure. And, perhaps, they chose to follow him, for every scavenger knows when the raptor takes to the wing.

When the three visitors rode away, they were watched by black, knowing eyes. The woods were alive with blue-black shadows . . . and a memory of stirring feathers.

Chapter III

INTO THE WEST

A week later, the army of the Britons finally reached Venta Silurum and prepared for the coming campaign.

Venta Silurum was an insignificant settlement, ancient even before the Roman invasion, and was named Castell Goronw in the old tongue. The envoys from Artor's court had perished in the hills to the north of the old fortifications, so there was a grim appropriateness in the High King's choice of bivouac. Situated overlooking the threadbare lowlands of the coast, the town had proved to be an easy site to fortify and hold, and the granite bones of the Roman walls still served the Silures well.

Gruffydd gazed upon the place of his birth, where he had taken a plump wife after many painful years in Saxon slavery, and felt a fierce surge of pride in his heritage.

For years Gruffydd had been Myrddion Merlinus's best spy in the east, where his knowledge of the Saxon tongue had made him an invaluable tool. He was present when Artor recovered the crown and sword of Uther Pendragon at Glastonbury, and it was there that the High King had appointed him to the position of sword-bearer. During the last twelve years, Gruffydd had been privy to secrets so fearsome that his toes still curled to think of them. When he had returned to Venta Silurum in the past, he had always come alone, and was viewed by the citizens as an ex-slave. Now, in the full livery of one of the High King's most trusted servants, the whole city could see his status in the hierarchy of the west as he bore the enormous blade, Caliburn, on a jeweled sheath on his back.

As the army rode through the streets of the town to a plateau of land that would serve to rest the troops, Gruffydd watched his master's face with concern.

The High King rubbed his gritty, sleep-starved eyes. Aquae Sulis seemed a lifetime behind them, although only seven days had passed. The physical demands of a campaign were far from new to Artor, as he had fought eleven major battles in the past twelve years. But the strain of devising strategies that would diminish the vast cost to his realm in human tragedy drained his mental resources. The aftermath of battle came with guilt so crushing that he had often believed he would die of it after his first wars against Oakheart so many years before.

His second battle, at Magnis, was a huge success because of his use of the horse. But Targo had been correct. That strategy had never again possessed the element of surprise, but Artor had studied the campaigns of Caesar in Gaul and was determined to integrate the use of bowmen, cavalry, and infantry to ensure that the three parts of his army worked as a united whole.

At Pontes in the south, where the Tamesis River branched in four directions and the small town was hemmed in by water, Artor used the soggy landscape and the spring flood rains to encircle the Saxons and wait for them to foul their drinking water. When sickness struck at the besieged Saxons, Artor used his bowmen to confine the enemy within the killing fields. Then his infantry and a range of war machines, built in situ, pounded the Saxon force into bloody flinders. The remnants of the Saxon force retreated back to Londinium, having learned the deadly accuracy of catapults. When Artor saw what the stones of the catapult did to human flesh, his gorge rose, but he had schooled his face to reveal nothing.

Targo constantly reminded his king that every battle was part of a learning process that wise leaders used if they desired to save lives.

Artor learned his lessons well, in campaign after campaign, and he was flexible in his thinking, but he was no longer sure if it achieved anything, apart from the loss of friends, the destruction of the lives of simple men, and the ruination of the land.

By rote, Artor saw to the comfort of his troops. Camp was set and his large, leather tent was raised. With a joke and mild teasing, the High King released Gruffydd from his duties to spend time with his wife and adult children, and retired to his spartan quarters where he was assailed by the thoughts that had grown increasingly despairing over the years.

"How can we become one united Celtic people when our first loyalties lie with our own tribes?" Artor had once asked the tribal kings. "We must become one unified nation, a force of Britons, regardless of our tribal or racial origins."

He had been so naïve. He had never really belonged to a tribe, for the Villa Poppinidii and Aquae Sulis had been his only roots, and they were Roman. He snorted when he remembered the eager, hopeful self that had believed it was possible to overcome the hatreds of generations in a few, short years. He had succeeded, superficially, as mixed cavalry troops and squadrons of bowmen testified, but the tribes weren't reconciled towards brotherhood, as King Lot's treaty with the Saxons had proved. The High King had been deluding himself when he took pride in the force that ultimately marched against Katigern Oakheart at Eburacum all those years before. Effective rulers couldn't afford the luxury of pride.

The High King could still taste the blood on his lips from that long forgotten battle. It was his first, brutal realization of human frailty, especially his own, and marked the death of ideals that shook his soul to its foundations.

Eburacum had been a relatively easy conflict compared with the task that was now ahead of him. Situated at another crossroads, and surrounded by swamp, rivers, flat undulating beds of reeds and rushes, and totally unsuited for a pitched battle, the old Roman fortress had fallen to the eastern Saxons some twenty years earlier. Eburacum became a deadly base for parties of Saxons who cut communications along the roads to the north every summer. When Katigern invited the Saxons, Angles, Jutes, and Picts to join him in an alliance at this unpromising site, Artor could no longer avoid the inevitable conflict. Eburacum must be taken and Katigern Oakheart must be smashed, for he had now proved his capacity to broker alliances that could destroy the frail Celtic defenses. Artor had marched north with a heavy heart, feeling ill equipped to fight such an important and pivotal campaign.

The battle had been fought on level ground, and the Saxons had outnumbered Artor's Celts by two to one. Katigern Oakheart had taught the High King a painful lesson about the Saxons, and himself, although Artor had taken the offensive from the beginning for only through attack could any advantage be gained over fierce and motivated barbarians. The field was hopeless for charging men, so Artor's infantry was ineffective even before he began. Similarly, his catapults and siege machines were useless in the reeds, marsh, and soggy fields. But Artor still had one edge because the Saxons used the shield wall, their one certain battle technique, on this fatally flawed occasion.

In their old, outdated way, the Saxons encircled the battle chief and fought ferociously in hand-to-hand combat, but they could not prevail over Artor's cavalry and archers. His bowmen cut down the shield wall with a rain of arrows, scarcely aimed but driving inexorably into the heart of the packed walls of Saxon flesh. Again and again, the deadly iron rain fell down on the press of men, until shields must be raised over their heads to protect the warriors from above, thereby exposing their torsos to even more volleys of arrows.

Then, Artor ordered his cavalry to target the weakest points in the wall of shields and charge through flesh, bone, and iron. As the interwoven shields crumpled under the force of tons of horseflesh, Artor whipped Coal hard into the press, searching for Katigern Oakheart. He could still remember the judder of the blow through arm and shoulder bones as Caliburn cleaved through Oakheart's armored head.

Even with their leader down, the barbarians had refused to surrender, and the High King's cavalry had been forced to kill every Saxon left standing.

Artor tasted bile as he recalled the stench of the battlefield. The Celts had moved between heaped bodies of the dead and the dying on earth so rich in spilled blood that it was the color of old rust, and Artor had winced each time a wounded Saxon was given the coup de grâce, for these men would neither be taken prisoner nor beg for mercy. The evening had been filled with the sounds of wounded men and dying horses. Artor had walked on the battlefield with Myrddion, who had blanched as his booted feet skidded on a slurry of blood and entrails.

"How can you look on such carnage without sickening?" Myrddion had asked his king on that bloody plain. "I can remember a time when you were as squeamish as I am."

Artor glanced over at Myrddion Merlinus's solemn face. "Within the hour, you will join your healers, stripped to the waist and dressed in a leather apron, with your hands deep in the bodies of wounded warriors. You heal what I harm, so how can you feel squeamish on the field? You saw the trade of death many times beyond counting before I was born, and you chose this road for the journey of my life."

Surrounded by the bloody detritus of war, Myrddion had been forced to acknowledge the accuracy of Artor's jibe with a curt nod of his head. "Aye, I have seen men die like dumb beasts, row on row, and I've labored uselessly to drive death away from too many suffering souls. But still, the sight of a battlefield turns my stomach. I wish it did yours, Artor, truly I do."

Then Artor had laughed, and the sound was so harsh and cynical that his chief counselor and healer had flinched away from that ugly mirth. When Myrddion looked into his protégé's face for explanation, those cold, grey eyes were more flinty than usual, and Myrddion realized that Artor was very angry with him.

"What use would a softhearted High King be, Myrddion? Am I not what you and your friends created? Does my ability to think clearly when I am surrounded by the consequences of my actions offend your sensibilities? Don't I please you as Artor more than that sensitive boy, Artorex, once did? No, I can see you admit that I am what you made, for better or for worse."

"You're angry with me, and, given the circumstances, I can understand how I seem ungrateful," Myrddion whispered. His eyes were downturned, so Artor couldn't read them.

"Aye!"

The High King's voice had been bitter, although Artor tried not to blame his old friend for the direction his life had taken. Unfortunately, that coldest part of his brain told Artor that Llanwith, Luka, and Myrddion had chosen to shape him, as a youth, into a weapon, regardless of the terrible personal cost. They would do the same again, regretfully and with guilt, but nothing mattered more than the land, least of all a High King.

"Because I must be harsh, my friend," Artor had replied, spreading his arms wide to encompass the muddy field and the wall of corpses. "I can finally understand why Uther came to hold life so cheaply, and why the suffering of others meant nothing to him. But every man who died here lies heavily on my soul, and I pray to all the gods that I do not forget what it is to remain human."

They died because of the rigidity of a warrior code that wouldn't permit them to live and fight another day, Artor brooded to himself later in the safety of his tent walls. And because we adopted the notion of massed cavalry from the Romans, for which the Saxons have no tactical answer. They didn't learn from Magnis or Pontes, so they lost once again. It was a slaughter.

Now, sitting quietly at Venta Silurum many years later, he stared down at the flawless pearl ring upon his right thumb. It stared back up at him like a blinded eye rimmed with a crust of dried blood. How long can I keep fighting, he asked himself, when everything I have learned seems useless?

In the darkening of the day, Artor felt weary and lost. The pearl of his thumb ring, which had formed a knob on the top of Uther's box of horrors, was a tangible reminder to care for the people who bled for him. Then Artor would avoid the poison in his bloodline, inherited from his birth father. Each day that the pearl remained clean of spilled blood was a fortuitous day, or so thought the boy, Artorex, who still lived somewhere in Artor's soul.

"You're sitting in the dark, Artor. What ails you?"

The High King jerked upright and his quick eyes recognized the familiar form slipping through the leather flap in the tent.

"Targo! You startled me. I've been sitting over Myrddion's maps for hours, and I was thinking about the battle at Eburacum . . . and how it all began . . ."

Targo crossed to the camp desk where his master sat on a rough stool. He found the jar with its store of oil and a simple wick, and struck his flint with the economy of action that comes with years of practice. Once the tender fiber began to smoke, he blew on the tiny flame until it burst into vigorous, active life.

Artor's leather tent was exactly the same as those used by his warriors, except that it was much larger and was carried in the baggage train because of its tall posts. Through an open flap, Artor could see the dying sunset, so that now only the remaining banks of cloud were edged with bloodred. The simple camp furniture, light tin plates, and goblets chosen for ease of transport, rather than beauty, and Artor's chests of maps were laid neatly on the sod floor. Odin had filled one jug with clean water and another with red wine; Targo filled a goblet of the latter almost to the rim, found a comfortable bench, and drank delicately.

Then, when he had wiped his mouth on his sleeve, he turned his attention to his master.

"You've been brooding, boy—and counting your losses, instead of your successes. Do that too often and you're—"

"Dead," Artor cut in. "I know, Targo, I know."

He selected one of the maps in the chest, unrolled it, and thrust it towards Targo. The old mercenary turned it in several directions, squinted at it with eyes set in deep wrinkles, and then shrugged.

"Where are we?" he asked. His eyes were too weak to follow the details of the terrain.

"We are here," Artor pointed with one long finger. "And there is the water. Outside the tent you can see the Sabrina Aest."

"Hmm."

While Targo struggled to interpret the rough map, Artor mentally ticked off his preparations for the coming war. He had contrived to strip the fortresses of the central mountain chain of all but small, token forces of cavalry and archers. His flanks were protected by the range of mountains to the rear of Venta Silurum, and the tribal chieftains of the Silures could be depended upon to protect any retreat.

The mountains themselves were steep, rain-swept, and coldly arid, and any edge Artor could devise would be needed if his cavalry were to be effective. But where his army was going, force of arms would never be enough to take the fierce heights that the Romans had named Moridunum, with its suggestion of death. The sound of the word rolled from his tongue as he said it aloud, much like the hollow drumming of thunder.

"What?" Targo raised his shaggy grey head.

"Moridunum, where we are going, old man. Or Caer Fyrddin, if you prefer its name in the old tongue. It's at the very heart of Ironfist's country." Artor pointed to a rough location on the map, and Targo grunted irritably.

"The Romans knew their business, didn't they, Artor? Look. He who holds the high ground rules the coast."

Artor nodded in agreement.

Myrddion had spoken of the fortresses strung along the coast like stone beads linked by cobbled roads. The Romans had known that the Sabrina Aest gave access to the greener, more fertile fields of the southwest. The old garrisons controlled the heights from Gelligaer to Glevum, but Moridunum controlled the heights of the far west of Britain.

The Demetae had once held the long finger of bleak mountains that reached out into the rolling grey seas of the west. But generations of Saxon incursions had cut these Celts off from their brethren, and now the Saxon influence had further weakened the traditional culture and sense of self of the Demetae tribe until they had become an embittered people who were withering in the new, perilous winds of the west. Artor had smashed the children of Hengist far into the north beyond Deva, but the flea-bitten, sullen settlements in Demetae country had been ignored.

For now, the Saxon influence was strong, and they had become arrogant after years of domination.

With relative ease, Artor's warriors had moved to positions where they were within range of Ironfist's strong right arm. Now was the time to eliminate the usurper and all his works.

"We must teach Ironfist that he is the thane of a dung heap, not a nation," Targo growled.

Myrddion, Luka, and Llanwith, Artor's inner circle and the three men who had shaped his life, entered the High King's tent bearing wine jugs, wooden cups, and handfuls of nuts, dried meat, and apples. With them came the pleasant scent of newly cut grass, fire smoke, and sword oil, and the High King felt his spirits rise.

Since Artor was no longer alone, Odin shrugged his way into the tent and stood, ever watchful, in one corner. He looked like a very large and excessively hairy troll. Time had barely touched the Jute, except to dull the redness of his beard.

"Shite, lad," Targo hawked, and dropped the map on the table. "This terrain's even bleaker than Deva, and the gods know that the north is a freezing pimple on the arse of the world. I suppose it rains on each and every day."

On cue, a light drizzle swept in from the sea, gradually becoming heavier until the leather roof began to sag under the weight of water collecting faster than it could drain away.

"Stop complaining, Targo, and have some more wine," Luka offered, pouring the old legionnaire another cup, and passing him a rough pottery bowl of dried apples.

Twelve years had turned Luka and Llanwith into aging men, and countless days in the saddle had cured their skins to the texture and color of seasoned oak, but Luka, in particular, still retained the grace of a hound, whether on foot or astride a mount. Both men wore kingly beards liberally streaked with grey, and lifetimes spent in battle gave their torsos thick roped strength, although Llanwith carried too much weight on his belly to be nimble. The heirs of both men guarded their tribes at home, but younger sons served as captains in Artor's cavalry.

Only Myrddion defied time. His hair was now mostly silver, except for the odd, disconcerting streak of black, still with the bluish hue of a raven's wing. His face remained taut and smooth except for deep frown lines between his dark eyes, which still possessed all of their luster and brilliance. He did not look young, yet he did not appear old. Rather, to the Celts of Artor's Britain, Myrddion was simply Myrddion. He was a force of nature in his own right.

"Have you any thoughts yet?" Artor asked Targo who was relishing an apple with the last of his yellowed fangs.

"I know that this coast is shite ground for horses."

"Would you prefer to walk then, my friend?" Artor grinned with a flash of his own still-youthful, white teeth.

"As if I could. My days of forced marches in the sodding rain with a full pack are long gone, thanks be to Mithras."

"Do you have any other suggestions, Targo?" Myrddion asked the old soldier silkily, not entirely to defer to his experience or to flatter him. "You must have fought in the mountains often enough."

"Your sodding map speaks out the problem, clear as clear, or at least what I could see of it," Targo retorted, his wrinkles deepening around his sharp, raisin eyes as he squinted in the half-light. "It's the damned high ground. The Saxons will always try to command the high ground, Artor. Caesar may have beaten that heathen Vercingetorix when he sulked in his fortress on the high ground in Gaul, but Caesar always had the devil's own luck. And he had soldiers from the legions who were trained to obey him without question. And, if you'll pardon me, my lords, Celt warriors aren't a patch on the soldiers of the legions when it comes to discipline." Having said his piece, and ruffled the feathers of every man present except for Artor and Odin, who were impossible to insult, Targo gulped a mouthful of wine and grinned evilly.

"Granted, friend Targo, but horses are capable of charging uphill."

Luka may have been provoking Targo deliberately, but his affection for the Roman shone from his narrow, bearded face.

"Would you like me to list the number of ways a good strategist can repel cavalry from above?" Targo looked around the assembled faces. "The very first weapon I would consider is the use of rocks and stones." The old man gestured bluntly, and the listeners could picture a tumbling avalanche of scree engulfing men and horses on the hillsides. "Even children can throw stones—and, all told, horses are surprisingly fragile creatures."

Targo's eyes did not smile although he spoke as if in jest.

"If I was in the Saxon positions, I'd dig deep pits full of nice, sharp stakes to impale you as you charge up the hill. Then I'd regroup on another steep grade, and do it all over again. Your losses would be horrific."

Artor nodded grimly. "It's just as well that you aren't Glamdring Ironfist," he said, acknowledging Targo's wisdom. In the practical aspects of warfare, Targo was a master without peer.

Artor came to a sudden decision.

"Odin!" he called.

His huge bodyguard stepped forward into the circle of light and bowed his head.

"Find Ulf—and try not to scare him silly."

Odin was almost at the leather door flap when Artor spoke again.

"While you're at it, order someone to pluck Gruffydd from his wife's bed. He knows these particular Saxons well, and if anyone can provide us with some insight, then Gruffydd is our man."

Odin nodded and slid out of the tent on silent feet.

The men resumed their hunched examination of the maps. The oil fire smoked in its pottery jar, and the flame flickered so that even Artor's handsome face was turned into a grotesque mask in the half-light.

The inner council was still no further into their deliberations when Odin returned, impassively ushering Ulf into the tent. The Celt immediately fell to his knees in the presence of his king.

"Up, Ulf, I can't talk to a warrior when he's on his knees."

Ulf rose to his feet.

"You're the only person available to me who has seen this Ironfist and lived," Artor said. "Describe him for me, Ulf, for I must understand the man if I am to defeat him."

In those short weeks since the massacre of Artor's emissaries, Ulf had tried to banish all thoughts of Ironfist from his conscious memory. The Celt felt physical pain at the possibility of returning to face the Saxon chieftain and having to revisit that slate-grey expanse of open ground, soaked with the blood of men and horses.

But Ulf tried.

"Ironfist is big, near to your size, and he's arrogant and ruthless. He had us surrounded before we knew it, so he commands with confidence. And he plans ahead. The Saxons must have been hiding in the woods long before we arrived."

Ulf's voice trailed away, but, conscious of six pairs of eyes fixed upon his face, he hurriedly lurched back into speech.

"The man lives by some semblance of honor, my lord, for he offered Gaheris his life in deference to King Lot. But when the prince refused, the Saxon didn't seem surprised. He seemed . . . well . . . pleased that Gaheris had defied him. He forced us to watch the murder of our friends until every one was dead. Gaheris was obliged to watch the other emissaries as they perished."

Ulf lapsed into silence.

"Take your time, Ulf," Artor said gently, for the warrior's face was paper white, and his lips and cheeks seemed bloodless.

The silence continued until Artor spoke again.

"Odin, step forward. Does Ironfist look similar to Odin? Come, lad. I have urgent need of your eyes."

To his credit, Ulf raised his head and examined the giant Jutlander carefully. He moistened his lips, hawked, and once again began to speak.

"No, Ironfist looks nothing like Odin," Ulf responded more steadily. "For one thing, Odin is taller and cleaner."

"Is there anything else you can recall, my friend?" Luka urged.

"I've scarcely heard Odin speak, although he is always in your shadow, my lord," Ulf said thoughtfully. "Ironfist seemed to be boasting and bragging while he was carrying out his treachery. And Odin seems so much more . . . substantial . . . so much larger, though I swear there's only inches between them in size." Ulf paused, unable to clarify his thoughts any further. "I beg your pardon, my lord, but I lack the words to explain my meaning."

Artor studied Ulf dispassionately. The king knew that Ulf was not a clever man, but he had discerned a serious flaw in Ironfist's nature.

"Perhaps our friend Ironfist is a man of straw, a shallow boaster who doesn't think overmuch of the consequences of his actions," Artor mused. "I know I'd never have killed Gaheris, even if my own life depended on it."

Ulf remained silent.

"Did Gaheris die slowly?" Artor asked. "You said the emissaries were hacked to pieces by Ironfist's men."

"No, my king. Lord Gaheris, Cerdic, and Cessus all died very quickly on the orders of Ironfist, or by his own hand."

"Why?"

Ulf looked blankly at his king and Artor stifled a flutter of impatience at the slowness of the Celt's thought processes.

"Why did these three men merit a merciful death?" Artor tried again.

Ulf examined his feet, and his voice was a thin croak when he answered.

"Cerdic was dispatched first. He was beheaded. His death was swift because Ironfist respected his courage in leading the emissaries. He refused to be cowed and he continued to hold the flag of truce to the end."

Artor nodded his encouragement.

"Cessus was the warrior who had hidden a knife in his boot. He stabbed the nearest Saxon through the eye."

"Ave, Cessus!" Targo murmured, in approval of the warrior's prudence in preparing for all eventualities.

"And Lord Gaheris continued to goad Ironfist. He said repeatedly that the Saxons would not win because they wouldn't change their ways. He ridiculed Ironfist, and it was almost as if he welcomed death as a consequence of his actions. He swore that you would take vengeance, and predicted Ironfist's death."

"Thank you, good Ulf." Artor smiled. "You may return to your comrades now."

Still puzzled, and visibly upset, Ulf left the tent.

"Ironfist cannot control his temper," Artor stated quietly, as Ulf was swallowed by the night and Gruffydd entered the tent. "It's likely that he can be goaded into taking precipitate action."

Targo nodded, amused, as he watched the wheels turning within Artor's mind. "Now, that would be an edge . . . if we could play on it. We could maneuver him into a foolish mistake before he realizes that we have tricked him." Targo snickered wickedly.

"Ironfist reaches very high when he claims the crown of Vortigern, who was, when all is said and done, a Celt," Myrddion added. "Ironfist's pride will work against him if we exert pressure on him. Perhaps we can lure him out of his fortress and cut his forces up piecemeal."

Gruffydd stirred. He grinned at his king with the familiarity of a man who knows his master's mind, for Gruffydd had stood at the king's right hand for twelve years, bearing the sword of kingship.

"You need my services in Ironfist's fortress, my lord," he said. "And I was just getting comfortable, too. Nothing beats a good stew cooked by a warm wife." He spoke seriously, although his brown eyes danced with humor.

"Tell me all that you've learned of the western Saxons during your travels," Artor said without the usual courtesies.

Gruffydd's eyes immediately shadowed. "The Saxons of the east are an interesting people, as are the Jutlanders. I respect their tenacity as they carve out a life far from their own frozen homelands. But don't ask me to speak well of the bastard Saxons of the southern mountains. They butchered my parents, and they made me a slave. I will bear their brand on my chest for the rest of my days." Gruffydd bared one freck-led and heavily muscled shoulder and there, upon his right breast, was the outline of a spearhead that had burned deeply into the skin. The wounded flesh was white and puckered at the edges.

Myrddion winced visibly. The men in the tent were silent. Gruffydd drew a single, rather ragged breath, and answered as his king commanded.

"The western Saxons have held parts of Cymru for a long, long time, certainly longer than I have lived. Vortigern welcomed them to these shores, and they have proved to be as stubborn as grass ticks, and near as impossible to dislodge."

"Are they true Saxons, like Katigern Oakheart?" Luka asked. "Now there was a man to respect."

"No!" Gruffydd snorted his scorn. "The bloodlines of Hengist's brood were purer than the breeding of these barbarians. These Saxons have taken Celt women and interbred for several generations. In all that time, they have laid waste to everything that the tribes praised as good, burning the Sacred Groves to cook their meat, destroying the Roman forts that offered protection. They steal what they cannot grow, and kill what they cannot use."

"Charming." Myrddion expressed his contempt with a slight curl of his well-shaped lips.

"Yet the very intermarriages that should have tied them to the land and made us stepbrothers elevated their pride in their ancestry to such arrogant proportions that they reject every concept that is not Saxon in origin. They are backward and ignorant, my lord. Prince Gaheris was accurate when he said that they will never learn. They don't choose to change."

With a wry grimace, Gruffydd stroked his slave cicatrice through his woolen tunic. With the cadences of the natural storyteller in his voice, nuances that made even horrors into songs, Gruffydd continued to describe the western Saxons.

"I was treated far worse than any dog. On many evenings, as a joke,

I would be forced to fight the dogs for scraps of food from my master's table, and I was barely nine years old. I learned how to hate as I cowered in the filthy straw at their feet, and at their whipping blocks. I have the scars, my lords, to remind me that life is precious and should be lived with joy."

Gruffydd glanced at Artor, and those strange sharklike eyes bored into him. Artor wasn't easily seduced by soporific imagery and phrases. He was searching for an edge.

"They sing the ancient songs in their drafty halls, with only a hole in the roof to release the smoke, so grease covers every surface. All the nobility has been bred out of them, but not the hunger for blood, women, and glory. Their ravenous desire for personal honor drives them to take stupid risks, while they consider all other peoples in the land barely human.

"But only a fool would underestimate the western Saxons. Despite their appetite for violence and their casual wallowing in filth, they are consummate warriors. They hold to the old ways, the old gods, and the habits of another time and another land, no matter how senseless they might appear to our eyes. They will embrace a suicidal charge against their enemy for the sake of personal glory, and in the gory business of hand-to-hand combat, their skills are exceptional."

"So we will be facing eight or nine hundred warriors who fight as a rabble, and not with a single fighting mind?" Artor asked, his eyes very sharp in his weathered face. "I wonder, if personal honor is so important to Ironfist and his ilk, would they act rashly if they saw a chance to strike us in one single, killing blow?"

"I have no knowledge of this Ironfist, Lord Artor, but the Saxons of the west simply turn on each other when they have no other enemies to fight. Any slight is paid for in blood." Gruffydd shrugged expressively. "Although they half starve in the long winters, they scorn agriculture and live for battle. After all, those warriors who were fools or inept are already long dead. Katigern Oakheart would applaud Ironfist's fighting skills, yet deplore the primitive remnants of the past that the man represents."

The silence fell heavily, and only the sound of the rain tapping on taut leather broke the eerie stillness.

"My thanks, Gruffydd. You may go back to your warm bed and warmer wife with my good wishes. We should enjoy this brief period of rest, for we must be gone from Venta Silurum within seven days."

Gruffydd bowed and disappeared into the night, whistling between his teeth.

"How lovely. A race of killers that are full of piss and shite," Targo stated. He had a disconcerting habit of stabbing to the very heart of any problem. "Stupid men are just as difficult to defeat as clever ones, especially when they outnumber us and are prepared to fight to the last man. If necessary, they may even be able to starve us into failure. And Ironfist appears more intelligent, or at least better counseled, than the usual outlander."

Discussion and planning for the operation then moved on to matters such as arms, food for the baggage train, fodder for the horses, and the order of march to Caer Fyrddin. Artor was confident that Caius could winkle a snail out of its shell, so provisioning the army was safe in his capable hands. Meanwhile, Myrddion's spies were busy, watching the roads and blending into the Saxon villages. Llanwith was the supreme commander of the cavalry, second only to Artor.

And Targo? Well, Targo was in charge of sound common sense.

"To bed, Artor," Targo advised with a wink. "There's no sense in worrying yourself all night, trying to outguess a fool. You'll find the edge—you always do."

Once alone, Artor slept fitfully in his sleeping furs, and, as predicted by Targo, his mind chased strategies round and round in a never-ending spiral. When he eventually dropped into the deep well of nothingness that he welcomed, he was attacked by strange visions of swords and crowns hanging in space, or spining wildly until they became disembodied heads that smiled and spoke gibberish at him. But far worse for the shrunken inner self that was truly Artor was the shade of Gallia, striding out of the darkness, carrying a naked infant who stretched out its immature arms towards him. Artor's shivering, inner self saw the dragon tattoo on the infant's ankle and, as his gaze lifted, he recognized that the child was a boy.

He awoke in a lather of sweat, with a pounding heart and ragged breathing.

Chapter IV

MORGAUSE

In the heavy darkness that precedes the dawn, Artor decided that any attempt to return to sleep would be fruitless. His rest had been disturbed and his flesh felt hot and swollen within his skin. Around him, his leather tent felt like a dark carapace and he was a sweating, helpless moth, struggling to be born.

Just before first light, he rose, dressed, and prepared his horse for an inspection of the bivouac. Behind him, Venta Silurum lay quiet and lightless, except for the occasional servant about his master's business. Sentries bowed as he passed their positions, before resuming their solitary watches. The warriors were alarmed that the High King was abroad alone, but Artor paid them no mind.

Initially, Artor simply wished to breathe clean, empty air, free from the distractions of rule, but as he rode aimlessly, he heard gulls calling from the coast, and, in his fancy, it was his name that was carried on the light, early-morning sea breeze.

A meandering path in the green carpet of grass led the High King across the fertile strip of earth that formed the transition between mountains and sea. Cowbells tinkled as unseen cattle grazed on the higher slopes, adding to the eerie translucence of the earth and the sea in the early-morning light. A beach of smooth, water-bleached pebbles

Myrddion's Chart of Pre-Arthurian Cymru

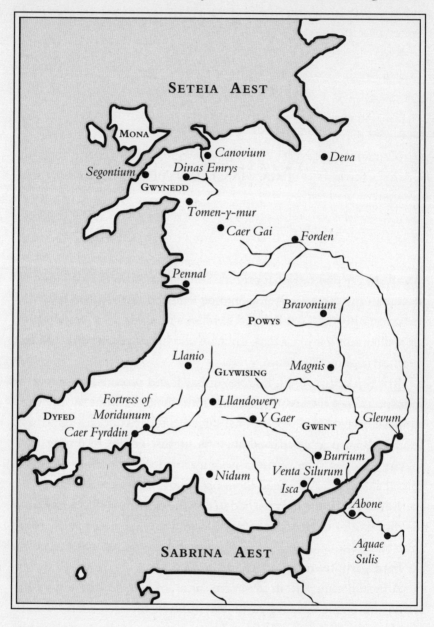

SETEIA AEST

MONA

Canovium • Deva

Segontium • Dinas Emrys

GWYNEDD

Tomen-y-mur

• Caer Gai • Forden

Pennal

Bravonium

POWYS

Llanio

GLYWISING Magnis •

Fortress of • Lllandowery

DYFED Moridunum

Caer Fyrddin • Y Gaer GWENT Glevum •

• Burrium

• Nidum Venta Silurum

Isca

Abone •

SABRINA AEST Aquae
Sulis

and pale sand marked the very edge of the land where grey wavelets, scalloped with lacy rimes of white foam, delicately tasted the beach and then crunched the gravel in their teeth.

Artor dismounted, and Coal wandered off to seek out sweet grass.

Sea, sky, and wheeling gulls were painted in shades of grey that were set against a strip of viridian so green that it hurt the eyes. Behind the grass slopes, the land rose gradually until it was punctuated by more grey rock, now smoky and dark. And above these uplands were the mountains, basalt grey and black, beetling, towering, and spinning in Artor's lowland eyes until his whole vision was filled with rising fortresses of grey stone.

The sea looked cold, and Artor's warm breath steamed in the early light, so why he should choose to strip off his clothing until he was naked was a mystery, even to him. Targo had taught the boy Artor to swim decades earlier, and now the adult enjoyed the feel of smooth pebbles under the soles of his naked feet and the scent of salt and sea-weed borne to him on the light wind. His skin rose in a rash of cold, and the curls of his bright hair seemed to tighten. The cry of seabirds reminded him of the small noises that Gallia had made in the night as he explored the fields of her body. Half erect with memory, Artor plunged into the icy sea.

You need a wife, you fool, his inner voice told him as the water struck him a hard, frigid blow, and then his pores, his capillaries, and even his hair roots were flooded with a warm rush of heat as he began to swim. For a suspended, thoughtless time, he pitted his muscles against the thrust of the sea. Then, pleasantly weary from his exertions, the High King of the Britons lay on the bosom of the sea and stared at the warming sky.

Finally, chilled and hungry, he walked out of the waves, throwing his darkened mane of hair back from his eyes with a swift toss of his head.

"Ah, lad. But you're a dead man."

Targo sat negligently on a good roan stallion above him, one knee hooked casually across the neck of the beast. His white hair was a nimbus of light as Artor looked up at him, into the low morning sun. He shaded his salt-stung eyes with his hand. For one brief moment, Targo looked like a man of black slate, his eyes and the old planes of his face flinty in the prevailing light.

"Targo?"

Artor's tunic slapped hard against his bare chest. He scarcely had time to clutch the rough woolen garment before his leather leggings were thrown at him as well.

"You'd best hide your nakedness, boy. It's not likely to impress me, but it might add a little something to Queen Morgause's day."

Artor gaped wordlessly, while Targo used a long spear to lift another garment from the sand and throw it at his bemused friend and master. Targo was dourly angry.

"Morgause? What are you babbling about, Targo? What would Queen Morgause be doing here? It takes a week of hard riding to reach Venta Silurum from King Lot's kingdom."

"Shite, boy, don't ask me! Who cares what I think? But King Lot, his wife, and a sizable troop of cavalry and spearmen are almost at your bivouac. Pinhead saw them coming and rode like the wind to warn us of their approach. He seemed to think that another small army on our heels might make us nervous."

"Pelles?"

"Yes, I've just said so! Damnation, boy! I'll never get used to calling that old whoreson by the name of Pelles. To me, he's always been Pinhead, and he'll be that forever, regardless of his finery. He's the very last of the Scum of Anderida still alive—besides us, that is. I'd never have believed that one-eyed thief would last half as long as he's managed to do."

"Pelles is a survivor from the top of his head to the tips of his toes. But don't change the subject, Targo."

"Get dressed . . . master." Targo's response was laden with irony and hurt.

Wordlessly, Artor obeyed his old friend and dressed swiftly and with economy.

Targo's voice was sullen and his usual dry wit was wholly absent. Phlegmatically, the king quashed the questions that leapt to his lips and continued with his dressing. He could feel the vibrations of Targo's disapproval tremble between them, but Artor pushed his personal concerns aside. As Targo was so fond of saying, "First things first."

Sand and small pebbles crunched under his shod feet as he hurried up the green, shelving slope. He whistled, and Coal came instantly, ever vigilant and obedient to his master's wishes. The horse skittered playfully as his master caught the reins. Before Artor leapt onto the back of his horse, he scooped up a handful of stones and thrust them into the leather pouch that always hung from his belt.

Targo watched this performance with mounting irritation. His king was wasting time with misplaced sentiment.

Artor leapt agilely into the saddle and engaged Targo's mulish eyes.

"Now, begin your news," Artor ordered.

Targo drew an audible, exasperated breath.

"Pinhead has ridden hard from Deva in the north down the old Roman road. The old reprobate turns up in camp on a half-dead horse and almost too tired to ride any farther, even if he wanted to. He reports that King Lot is heading in this direction with armed horsemen at his back."

"And my sister is with him?"

Targo grunted irritably. "Yes, she is."

"When will they arrive?"

Targo shrugged, and turned his craggy face away from his king. "Mithras knows." The old Roman paused for a few seconds before continuing, anger roughening his already gruff voice.

"In passing, I must tell you that Odin is very cross with you. He very nearly spoke out loud and swore this morning when he awoke to find you missing from the camp. He takes his duties as your guardian very seriously, and, if you wander off again when he's at rest, I'm certain he'll start sleeping with only one eye closed—if he sleeps at all."

Artor frowned with a mixture of irritation and something akin to shame. "I'll speak to Odin about my bad habits, but for now, we'll ride back to the bivouac."

Targo swung his horse and urged it into a canter with such unnecessary force that the beast whinnied in protest and pain.

"Targo?" Artor shouted after the retreating back of his most loyal servant. "Are you angry with me on Odin's account?"

Targo didn't deign to reply, but sat even more stiffly on the back of his roan. His every movement screamed disapproval.

Artor kneed Coal in the ribs and set off in pursuit.

"Spit it out, Targo! You're angry about something."

Targo pulled his mount to a bone-jarring halt and swung towards his master.

"By all the gods of Hades, Artor! Pinhead came posthaste to warn us of an important matter, and you were nowhere to be found. You gave the watch the slip as well . . ." Targo's voice drifted into sullen silence.

"I wanted some time to think. It's near impossible in camp because I'm hardly ever alone." Artor knew his own voice was petulant, but he was feeling a surge of resentment towards the two men who loved him best. Surely he was entitled to some time free of human company.

"I seem to remember another servant of a High King whose feelings were ignored. But I'll say no more on it." The old soldier stared fiercely at his king for a long heartbeat. Then, abruptly, he wheeled his nervous horse and rode away at a reckless gallop.

"Who? What?" Artor shouted after his old friend. "What are you talking about?"

Targo refused to turn back.

Artor sat motionless on Coal's back as he chewed over Targo's words.

He plundered his memory in a search for servants who had been abused by their master. Was it Frith? Cletus? No and no. Targo himself? Gruffydd? Botha?

"Ah, Botha!" Artor whispered softly, remembering a tall, proud man long past his middle years who had served Uther Pendragon as the captain of the High King's guard. Botha had loved Uther in his golden youth, and had remained true to his vows of loyalty, although his heart had been broken in the process.

Yes, Targo had been speaking of Botha.

Then, like a bolt of lightning from a storm cloud, Artor realized Targo's meaning. He kneed Coal into a swift gallop, and caught Targo within moments.

"I'm truly sorry, old friend." He spoke earnestly at Targo's stiff back. "All I can say in apology is that I understand your meaning."

Targo slowed his horse and then halted. His bony shoulders heaved, but he refused to turn his close-cropped head.

"I'll apologize to Odin as well, my oldest teacher," Artor added. "I acted without thought, and I regret my lack of consideration for you. All I can say in my defense is that I sometimes forget that my responsibilities lie with others as well as myself."

Targo muttered something under his breath and avoided eye contact with his king.

Artor pushed Coal forward and captured the gaze of his friend. He commanded Targo to speak his thoughts.

"Where would we be if you weren't here to lead us, Artor?" Targo's arms were spread wide. "What would we do if one of the Saxons cut your throat while you were lazing about in the shallows? Do you believe that either Myrddion or King Lot could lead the Celts in war or in peace? Do you suppose that Llanwith or Luka could replace you? If you should die, we all fail in our quest. Who can unite the tribes but you? Would the Roman settlements follow Gawayne? No. Without you, the Saxons win. Without you, the cities of the west will burn and the churches will be razed to the ground. Blood will defile holy Glastonbury, and the peaceful Villa Poppinidii will be smashed into rubble. Venta Belgarum will become a cluster of mud and thatch huts and the Roman fortifications will be destroyed. Is that what you want?"

The beauty had fled from Artor's morning, and he began to feel like a mongrel dog.

He could readily conjure up the greying, leonine head of Botha as he had first seen the man in the hall of the High King so many years before. Botha had been straight and noble in the beauty of his honor, until Uther's orders had turned him into a murderer. Botha had obeyed his king, but his honor had been irretrievably lost. A king has a responsibility towards those who serve under him.

Artor urged Coal closer to the roan's side and awkwardly threw one arm round Targo's shoulders and embraced him. Coal sidled nervously, and both men laughed awkwardly as their mounts drove them apart.

Targo's stiffened mouth slowly relaxed into a grin.

"Just so you understand, boy."

Artor could once again enjoy the beautiful dawn.

ARTOR DRESSED WITH scrupulous care for his noble visitors. Out of respect for the dead Gaheris, Artor donned his sable tunic, cloak, and armor, enlivened only by his golden ornaments and the red dragon rampant on his cloak pin. Scorning the crown as unnecessary with kinfolk, he plaited his brow locks and bound the curling ends with golden wire. Then he thrust his pearl ring on his right thumb and a plain gold ring, faintly imprinted with the form of a clenched fist, on his left thumb. The gold ring had been a gift from Lucius, Bishop of Glastonbury, many years before.

Earlier that morning, Artor had left Odin speechless by kissing his bearded cheeks and begging his pardon. The huge bodyguard had abased himself before his lord and master.

He treats me like a god, Artor thought sadly. It's a heavy burden to carry.

Now, with his emotions in check and surrounded by his captains, including the irrepressible Pelles in all his finery, Artor awaited the arrival of King Lot and Queen Morgause.

He did not have long to wait.

Lot and Morgause halted their cavalcade beyond the Celtic bivouac, and sedately approached Artor's camp on horseback. An honor guard of Celtic warriors clashed their weapons on their shields in the old Roman greeting. Alone, and with only a token guard of two men, the King and Queen of the Otadini drew rein before their High King.

Morgause was dressed in her usual opulence of furs and fabrics, but now every item of clothing that she wore had been dyed to the deepest black. As he gazed up at her marble face, Artor saw the resemblance to her mother, Ygerne, and her sister Morgan. He experienced a sudden rush of pity towards this resentful woman for the wrenching, endless loss she must have been experiencing.

Morgause had lost much during her forty-four years of life. She had been a young wife and mother of fourteen when her father had been murdered by Uther Pendragon, so she had been spared the indignities of rape suffered by her sister, Morgan. But, like Morgan, her rage against the High King was absolute. Her anger showed no signs of abatement, even though Uther had been dead for many years. She had been married as a child to a middle-aged man and plucked from the soft earth of Cornwall to live beyond the Roman Wall in a land of long winters and cheerless pragmatism. She had borne many sons to King Lot, all of whom had been strong and living, but joy had rarely touched her heart. Hatred had been instilled into her during childhood, first for Uther, who had treated her vilely anyway, and then, later, for Artor, her half brother, because he became Uther's heir. But hatred is a bitter draft, even for the strongest stomach. Perhaps she ached for laughter. Artor had no way of knowing, for she had never willingly opened her mind to him. And now the most loved child of all her brood was dead, in brutal and senseless waste, while in the service of her despised half brother.

Her youth had fled and only a husk of her spirit remained.

As Myrddion and Llanwith assisted King Lot to dismount, Artor offered his hand to his sister. Morgause accepted his aid, and he felt the delicate bones of her fingers in his light clasp. They were as cold and as brittle as the skeletal remains of a woman long dead. Her blue-green eyes were empty and unreadable.

"Welcome, sister. I beg that you accept my sorrow and shame for the death of your son, the noble Gaheris, who perished with great distinction to the honor of his house. I mourn with you for the loss of the fairest youth in all the tribes."

Morgause inclined her head in gracious acknowledgment but her eyes glittered for a moment with an emotion Artor did not recognize. A man more skilled with women would have identified the glaze of unshed tears.

"Gaheris was precious to us, so Lot and I have come," she answered him simply, as Artor offered her his arm. "We bear you no malice, brother."

Her fingers rested lightly on his forearm, and Artor observed that her hand was long and flexible, like his own. The nails were oval pink tips that dug into the fine wool of his sleeve just a little. Artor felt a shiver of deep presentiment, as if those delicate fingers turned into claws and struck at his unprotected heart. Yet he sensed that his sister spoke the truth. She was touched by his mode of dress as a public acknowledgment of Gaheris's value to the realm.

As the High King led her to a chair provided for her comfort, Artor considered Morgause and their long enmity. He admitted to himself that he had never cared to delve into either her character or her machinations. He had been preoccupied with the covert, subtle malice of her sister, Morgan, a woman of fierce intelligence and undying resentment. Now, Morgause seemed more substantial in her grief than her older sister, less empty and vindictive, more a white-faced Boedicca who was prepared to throw away everything for a moment of revenge.

Artor shuddered inwardly, under his mask of courtesy, at the power and empathy of his mother's blood, which had been passed on to all her children. In the keening, soundless grief of a mother, Morgause had awoken to her full self, and Artor realized with a pang that he was a little afraid of her.

All women can be a danger to us, Artor thought to himself. They work towards their ends in ways that men cannot understand.

Outwardly, Artor smiled considerately, and his eyes reflected his deep concern and his sympathy towards the regal couple. For all his vast girth, King Lot was a negligible force when compared with the power that radiated from the essence of his small, sable-clad wife.

Artor, Lot, and the other kings were soon seated, and wine and fruit were offered by young princes, all of whom had come to this war for their first blooding. Morgause accepted the offerings, and gazed into their young, ardent faces with thoughts of Gaheris firmly fixed in her mind.

The balding King Lot was seated a little higher than Artor, and his demeanor was no longer contemptuous and sneering. When he spoke, his voice was conciliatory.

"There has been bad blood between us in the past," the Otadini king began, his brow sweating slightly in his distress and chagrin. "And we have been made enemies by old resentments that should have been buried with those souls who were there at their genesis."

"Your words are wisely considered, and they do you credit, Lot. But I always understood your actions were motivated by loyalty to your family and to your tribe," Artor replied lightly, although his eyes conveyed the warning that lay beneath his courtesy. You may take these words any way you choose, you bastard, he thought to himself, remembering Lot's many attempts to usurp the throne of the Britons and enrich himself and his family.

Uneasily, Lot stirred his mounds of flesh within the confines of his chair.

"I ask that you accept that there is no longer any lasting enmity on my part, for the blood of my son has washed our quarrel away."

And that's the truth, Artor's inner voice added.

"Gaheris would have wished me to embrace his father," Artor murmured aloud.

"That is kindly said, my lord," Lot acknowledged, his eyes downcast.

Artor felt a twinge of sympathy for the aging king in his pitiful attempts at conciliation.

"I, too, am grateful for your kind message, and for the return of my son's remains, my lord," Morgause murmured softly. The queen held the eyes of her brother as she spoke, and the depth of her sorrow filled her own clouded eyes. Honesty emerged as well, and Artor sighed inwardly in sympathy with the woman. "I loved my son, Artor, even when he deserted his kin to follow your banner. I took pride in his fiery spirit, and I knew that he would win renown within your court. I believed you would never use him to further your ends in our quarrel, for you have always been gracious to our heir, Gawayne."

Artor read the unspoken question in her eyes.

"Sister, I did not believe the Saxons would harm Gaheris. I sent my emissaries to Glamdring Ironfist in good faith, but also in the full knowledge that they risked death. Such is a king's dilemma. But I never thought that Ironfist was so deluded that he would kill the son of an ally in his cause. I swear to the truth of my words."

"And I believe you," Morgause answered simply, and a single tear snaked down her still-smooth cheek.

Well done, Artor, the insidious voice of his colder self whispered in the convoluted corridors of his brain. He felt his gorge rise. In truth, he had considered the possibilities of treachery to the emissaries even before they had left Cadbury Tor, and so he must live with his personal guilt.

"We have come to join with you, for we intend to avenge these blows," Lot continued seamlessly. "We ask that you put aside our ancient quarrel and accept us as allies in this war. My people hunger to slay those dogs who killed their young prince. Personally, I have crossed the Roman Wall to kill them, each and every one, and I will continue to kill all Saxons forever, as long as those descendants of my blood hold the northern passes. On this occasion, Glamdring Ironfist has gone too far."

Myrddion smiled behind his hand, and wondered if Artor had not gambled on this very outcome when he succumbed to Gaheris's pleas to become one of the emissaries. Truly, Artor was a king of kings.

"For my part, distrust and past angry words between us are blown into the wind as of this day, Lot," Artor responded formally, for the gravity of the moment, and its opportunity, weighed heavily on the alliance he was about to form. "Gaheris was a courageous young man, but he also possessed *dignitas* and nobility in his nature. He died in defiance of Ironfist. And as he died, he shouted out their greatest weaknesses, faults that we will exploit. You may join with us, and your presence is welcome."

Through such deceptively simple words, Artor's force was swelled by one hundred and fifty additional warriors from the hot-tempered tribes of the Otadini, men who had carved a kingdom out of the mountains and the fertile plains, lands that had been prised from the blue-painted savages of the far north. With fire in their hearts, the Otadini had been victorious, and for all their strange accents and pale faces, they were men so skilled in the arts of war that their fellow Celts were cheered by this most important alliance. Where Lot placed his trust, all other northern tribes would follow. The Otadini could hold a grudge and a sword with equal skill, but, once given, their oaths bound them like iron.

Artor endured the shame of his own sins of omission, and told himself that the common good of his people demanded that he reign as a king, and not necessarily as a just man.

Morgause resisted every attempt to deflect her purpose to ride off to war with the warriors, and refused every plea that she should remain in the relative safety of Venta Silurum.

"I intend to watch each skirmish and each battle," she told her brother, and fire flickered in her pupils. "I wish to enjoy the death of every Saxon I can, with my own eyes. Through their deaths, I will free the spirit of my son and send him soaring to his ancestors on the souls of his enemies. And then he will waken with pride in the Halls of the Dead."

Artor repressed an exclamation of superstitious fear. What a terrible family we are, he thought, as he watched Morgause burning with maternal fury. Truly, women are far more cruel than we men credit. They would shatter the whole green earth for the sake of a child.

Artor promised Morgause that she would have her fill of Saxon blood.

She smiled coldly, well satisfied. There would be no mercy from her for those with Saxon blood in their veins. There were not enough Saxons in the isles to fill her need, or to assuage her endless, consuming grief.

The morning sun was high when the Otadini forces were welcomed into the High King's camp. Seabirds squabbled at the edges of the vast horde, fighting over scraps of food and hovering like birds of prey, eager for discarded morsels of bread from the camp kitchens.

Morgause stared at the birds' wicked beaks and their sharp black eyes. And she smiled, for she was entombed in a silent cone of portents.

Chapter V

MORIDUNUM

O ne week later, Artor's forces commenced their campaign
against the Saxons during a sullen, persistent rainstorm that
made men and animals miserable, and turned the earth into a churned
soup of mud under their hooves. The going was slow, as the main
force moved forward in troops of fifty mounted men while outriders
protected the foot soldiers and archers from sudden attack.

"Well, Artor, we won't be sneaking up on the enemy," Targo
sniffed, with all but the point of his nose muffled under hides. "Look
at that lot." He pointed behind them.

From their vantage point on a low rise, Artor could see mounted
men, baggage wagons, and the usual human flotsam and camp followers slogging through a slurry of deep mud. The long column struggled slowly through the muddy tracks that made up the coastal paths.
Behind it, the army left a wide scar of brown slush, a good six spear
lengths wide, that cut through the salt-toughened vegetation. Any curious Saxon looking down from the hills could hardly fail to see the
serpentine spoor of the Red Dragon of Artor.

"We leave a path, it's true, but I never planned to sneak up on
Ironfist. I want him to know I'm coming for him, so I hope he hears
of our numbers."

Artor's Battle Strategy at Moridunum

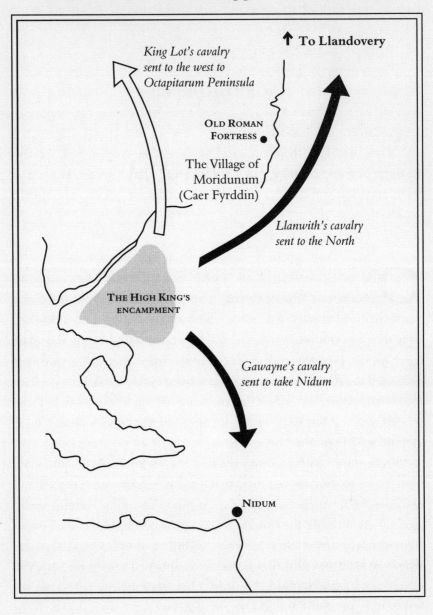

King Lot's cavalry
sent to the west to
Octapitarum Peninsula

↑ **To Llandovery**

OLD ROMAN
FORTRESS ●

The Village of
Moridunum
(Caer Fyrddin)

Llanwith's cavalry
sent to the North

THE HIGH KING'S
ENCAMPMENT

Gawayne's cavalry
sent to take Nidum

● **NIDUM**

"Shite, it's cold!" Targo sneezed gustily, sighed, and then hunched deeper into his leathers. "You'd have to be Saxon to choose to live in this country, and I'm far too old for campaigning."

"You can go back, if you wish, Targo," Artor replied.

Targo's nose quivered with indignation. "You'd send me away?"

Artor refused to rise to the bait, and stared out over the steadily moving baggage train, but Targo could see his master's lips twitch as he tried to control his laughter.

"Can you feel their eyes on us, lad? I've marched in Scythia through horrible country, just like this, and I could feel the knives that were aimed at my back. There are Saxons in those hills, and they're watching us."

"Let them watch all they want."

"So that's your strategy? You intend to march into country that's full of hostiles and let them dictate the game? I *know* I taught you to plan better than that."

Artor experienced a moment of dizzying rage that, fortunately, passed in a heartbeat. Targo was concerned, so he played the goading game. In a perverse fashion, Artor had learned to think clearly and logically because of Targo's patience. He owed the old man patience in return.

"When we reach the plains below the fortress of Caer Fyrddin, we will eliminate the local villages. It will be an easy task, given our numbers—and shamefully ignoble. Then, we shall sit on the plains, and we shall wait," Artor explained quietly.

"Just sit?"

"Of course. My plan depends on enticing Ironfist to come out of his fortress. We have about as much chance of success as we did at Anderida so long ago. But that attack was a lucky blow during darkness, and we had the advantage of surprise. If I attempted to take Anderida today with the same number of men, I would probably fail. I didn't know at the time how impossible that raid really was, and how fortunate we were to survive."

Targo forgot the cold and the drizzle that made his bones ache with a savage insistence. Artor had always had a knack for simplicity, deceptive and costly to the enemy, as uncomplicated ideas could often be. Artor would attempt to exploit Ironfist's human weaknesses, while exposing his own strengths as if they were flaws. At Anderida, he had divided his force. Two troops of cavalry had attacked the eastern and western gates, depending on Artor, Targo, and the Scum to negotiate a swamp in almost total darkness, climb the battlements unseen, and open the gates, all without alerting the guards of a superior force of Saxons. The tactic had been successful.

"Once we are settled into our positions, I propose to divide our force."

Targo half smiled within his damp and odorous nest. Here we go again, he thought.

"Divide them? Why?"

"We have passed Burrium and Gelligaer, the old Roman fortresses, and we are now heading towards Nidum. I intend to send Gawayne to winkle out the Saxons there, if only to please Morgause and her desire to taste Saxon blood. Also, Gawayne longs to kill someone for the sake of his brother, and he's not overly particular about the circumstances. At any rate, Nidum, at our rear, must be rendered safe to protect our flanks."

Targo nodded. Always ensure your rear end is safe.

"Gawayne will then become my forager," Artor continued, "and he will cheerfully denude the plains of Saxon reinforcements."

Targo nodded again. The use of cavalry in open country was a sensible option. So far, Artor was planning a safe, stolid strategy that any sound commander would use to achieve his aims. Targo waited for Artor's slant of originality.

"So what comes next?" he asked.

"I shall send Lot's warriors to the Octapitarum Peninsula at speed, and Llanwith will proceed to some gruesome place called Llandovery. At least, I think that's what it's called."

"You're insane!"

Targo's understanding of military strategy rejected the concept of dividing an effective fighting force into smaller, less effective units that were vulnerable to attack from an enemy force with a strong tactical advantage. The attack on Anderida had involved the division of forces that approached one site from different directions. But, on this occasion, Artor was proposing to send his cavalry all over southern Cymru, to the east, west, and north, while leaving his main force without protection.

"Ironfist will almost certainly mount an attack on our main force, and he could easily defeat them if they are unsupported."

"Normally I would agree with your assessment, and I have no desire to either lose or to die. Once I've sent my units to carry out the tasks I assign to them, I intend to sit and wait beside the river that comes down from the heights. We will have the water behind us on at least two sides and, from Ironfist's perspective, we will have nowhere to run and hide." Artor turned to Targo and challenged him with a gentle smile. "Each day, I will send Ironfist a freed Saxon with a gift. I'll also send a special, personal message from me that will enrage him."

Targo's horse stirred to nervous life as it sensed the sudden excitement of its old, timeworn rider.

"The purpose of my daily messages is to incite Ironfist to the point where he will charge out of Caer Fyrddin and attack me with what he believes is a superior force of men. I am gambling that his temper is as volatile as Ulf has described to us."

Targo realized that his protégé was gambling for dizzyingly high stakes.

"So it's likely that Ironfist will kill you," he grunted. "How do you propose to sit on the coastal plain and hold off hundreds of lice-ridden savages who all want your head? And my head, of course, will be an extra bonus to those barbarians."

"That's where Gawayne, Lot, and Llanwith come into play."

"But they aren't going to be at the river battle, are they?" Targo pointed out.

"I hope Ironfist forgets about them, or at least considers them to be too far away to constitute a threat. In theory, assuming that my smaller forces can hold this position, then Moridunum is *loosely* surrounded. But I intend that the three absent columns will return to the river and reinforce my command once the battle with Ironfist is joined."

He paused to assess the effect of his statement on Targo.

"Before you say a word, my friend, I am well aware that the three forces will take some time to return to my command and must ride at speed to join me. So, until they arrive and swell our ranks, I will use the Saxon's own tactic, the wall of shields, as my prime defense. With this in mind, I will strip my defensive force of its horses. These will be given to each of Lot's warriors so that they have a second mount to speed their return. They have the farthest distance to travel if they are to relieve my force, so they will need fresh mounts. Llanwith's column, and Gawayne's troop, can return in a relatively short time once they get a signal that their presence is needed. For our part, we must live or die on the courage and ability of our bowmen, who will be positioned behind my warriors at the edge of the river."

"I'm suddenly glad that old Pinhead is with us," Targo muttered. "I never mention it overmuch, but I once had to 'hunker down,' as the Romans called it. We were in Illyricum at a place that didn't even have a name, a little to the north of Herculia. The ground was dead flat and the barbarians were unpleasant. There were arrows coming in constantly, by day and by night."

"It's obvious that you managed to survive. What did your commander do? How did he protect you from bowmen and a surrounding force of savages?"

The two men moved off the low knoll and slowly walked their horses parallel with the main body of the army. Away from the press of pack animals in the column, the sucking discomfort of mud was minimized, and the rain had diminished to the odd sprinkle of drizzle. Targo emerged from his hide cocoon like a wizened and ancient turtle.

"All I can remember of my tribune is that his name was Sisto. He was an ordinary man without any particular intelligence, but I recall that he was stubborn and dour. He was told to hold the camp until relieved, so he planned to retain every square foot placed under his control and carried out his orders to the letter.

"We formed the fighting square after he had explained to us that if we broke, we were finished. We knew. The inevitable fate ahead of us stiffened our spines and strengthened our arms. We were packed tightly around our baggage train, and we used our shields above as well as to the side. Yes, Artor, you really must endure, without complaint. A fresh man must fill the shoes of every dead man, like clockwork. No wounded or dead can be abandoned to the enemy, because the savages will commit the most vicious atrocities just to weaken the resolve of your warriors. You must be prepared to die for something as useless as a baggage train or a dying man. You 'hunker down,' and you work on surviving the next five minutes, then the next hour, then the next day. This strategy is like a war of attrition to find out who has the strongest nerves." Targo cleared his throat and laughed in his croaking fashion.

"Sisto didn't particularly expect to live, but he was simply too stubborn to submit. We called him Old Sour Guts, but when we needed a boost of confidence, we only had to look at old Sisto, and he raised our spirits. He never smiled, and he never laughed, but his lack of passion of any kind meant there was nothing much to worry about—yet. We were still waiting for Sisto to tell us things were really bad when we were eventually relieved. Amazing, really, how much a commander can matter."

Artor understood the message in Targo's words. "The Saxons don't use bows often, and rarely do they give up the glory of hand-to-hand combat for the more sensible use of long-range weapons. No. If Ironfist does come forth, he'll surround us and try to batter our defenses down by brute strength."

"So we must hold our ground until Lot and Llanwith return to the battlefield," Targo said. "There's no help for it. Once you embark on this strategy, you must repel the Saxons until you are relieved."

"By which time," Artor concluded, "Ironfist's warriors should be enclosed in our net, and he will be like a ripe plum to pluck, to taste, and to devour."

"If we are besieged on ground of our choosing, then we'll be out of the rain but we'll have to contend with mud instead," Targo added encouragingly. "And I love mud. It slips the enemy up, and slows him down."

"You're the eternal optimist, Targo."

"But I'm still here, aren't I? And I'll be here after Moridunum. Wait and see. We'll crack them like lice."

As Artor rode down to call his captains together for their briefing, Targo sank back into his uncomfortable hides. The afternoon was giving way to an evening of poor visibility, incipient fog, and bone-numbing cold.

THE CELTS STOPPED their forward impetus at a small tributary of a river where grass and water were plentiful. In the ordered manner of all well-trained soldiery, the horses were watered first, and then tied to long tethering ropes that allowed them to graze under the sleepless eyes of the watch. Units of fifty men then organized fires, cover, and cookery, while on every vantage point, silent men on horses parted the shadows like wisps of smoke, and lights appeared like small red eyes where cooking and heating fires sent out glows of comfort.

Targo made his way to the heart of the host, where Artor's traveling tent was already raised and Odin was supervising a rabbit stew that he had somehow acquired on the march. Gruffydd was abroad in the hills, scouting and watching, and only old Targo seemed to be wandering without purpose.

The Roman thought carefully again about Artor's plan of action. Yes, it could work, as long as Celtic scouts were loose in the hills, either individually or in pairs. For any chance of success, the Saxon lines of communication must be cut, so the only messages that reached Ironfist were those that Artor wanted him to receive.

Targo tied a knot in the leather strings that secured his rainproof cloak to remind himself to suggest this tactic to Artor.

"The lad has the hearts of his warriors in his hands," the Roman murmured to himself as his eyes tried to penetrate the developing fog. "So he'll be careful to give them the will to hold their positions on the river. But it wouldn't hurt if I put the fear of Mithras into the Saxons at the same time. At least, it's something I can do on my own initiative."

When he spoke softly into the night, Targo never expected a response, so he turned white and his hand reached for his weapon when Luka silently materialized out of the fog beside his horse.

"Are you feeling sorry for yourself, old man?"

"Shite, Luka, you scare me shitless sometimes. And who are you to call me an old man? You're not so nimble yourself these days."

"I'm still younger than you are, Targo. If even half the tales you tell are true, you're older than Caer Fyrddin itself." Luka chuckled, a rolling laugh of amused friendship.

"Are you checking the dangers of the land, King Luka?"

"It's the habit of a lifetime," Luka replied economically. "What's Artor about?"

"He's sharing his suicidal strategy with Gawayne, Lot, and Llanwith. I guess you'll be with us as we stick our necks out obligingly in an invitation to have our heads severed from our bodies."

"I'll accept his strategy if Artor has planned it, for his mind is sharper than ten of Ironfist's axes. We may suffer losses, but I'd lay a wager that we'll not lose the final battle. Mark my words, old soldier. Artor dearly wants the head of Ironfist as a trophy, and his revenge will prevail even if we suffer massive losses in the process."

Targo felt his hackles rise in Artor's defense. "I'd swear you hated our king sometimes, Luka. How can you judge the boy so harshly? You've known him for as long as I have."

"Because I love him—and I believe in him. I see him as he really is, as a boy who didn't want to kill me when I tested his strength some twenty years ago. But, even then, I knew that he'd have filleted me if he'd had to, because he has always been ruled by his brain rather than by his feelings. Shite, Targo. You taught him that dying needlessly was stupid, and the only time I've known him to embark on a fruitless quest was when he wanted to return to Aquae Sulis to save Gallia. Perhaps he could have saved her . . . but if we had assisted him to do so, then he'd not be High King and we would most likely be long dead."

Targo drew his hand over his eyes. "I still harbor regrets about that incident, my friend," he replied softly. "I was the one who closed that door for him forever. Don't misunderstand me, though, because I'd do it again if I had to. Not for the Britons, and not for the people or the land, but because of my love for the boy."

"If there is collective guilt to be paid for what happened on that day, then we are all guilty and I should bear the lion's share. In my drunkenness, I was the one who blurted out that Artor was married, and that piece of news soon filtered through to Uther, may he scream in the Shadows for eternity. But, even so, we shouldn't blind ourselves to the real Artor. I serve him because he's human, and because he fights to win. He uses that mysterious and wonderful brain of his to puzzle out solutions to problems that are beyond us lesser mortals. He has been a formidable High King, but perhaps we should pity him, rather than glorify him. He can never know peace."

"After I've kicked his arse into the dirt more times than I can remember? No, Luka, I don't glorify him. I glory in him, and I'll go to my grave feeling the same way."

Luka's white teeth flashed out of the gloom in his cheeky smile, so ludicrous in the face of an aging autocrat.

"Then we'll agree to remember him as two different men, Targo. Shite, we're probably both correct in our assessment of Artor anyway, for a king must be everyman for his people. I'm glad I wasn't called upon to be the Warrior of the West." He smiled reflectively. "I married a sweet woman and, unlike Artor, no one cared whom I wed. I was fortunate enough to father sons. My feelings are my own so I am free to hate whom I choose, and love in the same way. I can be bad-tempered if I want to be, and no one cares a jot if I insult someone I don't like. Artor doesn't have that luxury, and he is forced to flatter King Lot and his poisonous half sister who have insulted him in every way possible for years, all for the sake of cementing an alliance." Luka pursed his

lips. "No, I don't want to be the Warrior of the West. Ruling my squabbling tribe is difficult enough."

"That's true, my friend," Targo agreed. He smelled the air like an
old hound. "I think he's about to turn us towards the south now until
we strike the sea."

"I never liked the water overmuch," Luka said crisply, and headed
off towards the tree line.

Targo watched as Luka slid into the shadows, becoming less than a
flicker of moonlight on the edges of the trees.

THE GREAT HALL of Caer Fyrddin lacked both height and dignity. The
Saxons had reused several Roman-built walls in its construction, and
had formed the rest of the structure from what trees were found on
the surrounding hillsides. The rafters of the hall were charred almost
black, the thatch was moldy and smelled of rot, while the straw on the
sod floor was filthy and lice-infested.

Bedwyr toed a heavily boned mastiff out of the way so he could
clean a rough table that was deeply stained with old ale, wine, and food
scum. Years before, he had learned to control a revolted stomach so
that the sights and smells of Caer Fyrddin no longer made his gorge
rise.

The young Celt had been raised in the hall of a minor chieftain of
the Cornovii tribe near the deep, velvet forests of Arden. At that time,
he had been a sturdy youth who had shown a talent for combat of all
kinds, although he was not overly tall for a warrior. His brown eyes and
even browner hair were set in a face that freckled so easily that, even in
his twenties, he still looked like a mischievous boy.

When he was eighteen, and had reached full manhood, he had
begged his father to give him leave to serve in King Llanwith's city
of Viroconium, where he knew he would see more of the world.
The Roman roads met at Viroconium, and Bedwyr hoped to catch a
glimpse of the great Artor and the legendary figure of Myrddion Mer-

linus. Mad for glory, Bedwyr convinced himself that, if Artor saw him fresh from sorties against the Saxons, he would be deemed suitable to serve as a warrior at Cadbury Tor, a wonderful place that Bedwyr could scarcely imagine.

As an adventurous and daring nineteen-year-old, Bedwyr was a joyous young man who loved to rove the Ordovice country, and even serving on the borders of the Demetae had been a thrilling and an exciting period of his young life. He had learned his woodcraft in Arden Forest before he was ten years old, and so he made the Western Mountains his own hunting preserve by roving on foot with a tread so silent that rabbits, birds, and fallow deer fell to the accuracy of his sling and his bow with ridiculous ease. Bedwyr was a gifted, lighthearted killer with an intimate knowledge of the terrain.

He never really understood the nature of the Saxon menace until his fate was sealed. The Ordovice clans had ruled the hills of Caer Sivii and Castell Collen so completely that the Saxons avoided their territory. Perhaps he would have retained his innocence far longer, or would have died before his time, if he had not gone hunting one late afternoon above the troop's base camp in a small, green valley near Castell Collen. His young compatriots were, as always, keen to eat whatever crossed Bedwyr's path.

His skill in the lengthening shadows was so well honed that he soon had a brace of coney and a fox that had been uncharacteristically rash. Bedwyr was searching for deer when he smelled smoke on the slopes above the valley camp.

He was drawn inexorably towards its source.

Bedwyr snaked through the underbrush directly above his camp with scarcely a rustle of leaves to betray his passage. The tents were afire and flames rose bloodily over the cooking hearth. The young man was trying to peer through the turgid smoke when the screams began, followed by a smell that made Bedwyr's stomach begin to churn.

The sharp stench of seared human flesh was hideous and unmistakable.

The screams were terrible, rising out of the lower valley with an awful, pain-fueled volume. Something twisted and contracted in the flames, but Bedwyr tried not to recognize the details of a man tied to a tree trunk as he roasted in the middle of the fire pit.

But there was no escaping the inhuman agony of those wailing, pulsating cries.

Bedwyr drew his knees up to his chest as he crouched under the low cover. The screams shivered up his spine and reverberated through his bones. Unbidden and unwelcome, the faces of his companions in the troop swam into his thoughts. Was the burning man Callwyn, or Octa, or Berrigan, or Melwai? Against his will, Bedwyr began to vomit uncontrollably so that he did not hear the slither of careful feet on the pebbled slope, or see the faint glitter of metal off to his right.

When his stomach could heave up only bile, Bedwyr managed to master his nerves, gather up the coneys and the fox, and rope their limp bodies through a cord attached to his belt. After checking for his knife and his bow, Bedwyr slid out of the low cover—straight into two very large Saxons. He barely had time to utter a small exclamation of surprise when a rock crashed against his temple and his wits deserted him.

When he awoke, he realized that his limp body was hanging over the rump of a horse, and he slowly became aware that his hands and feet were tied together under the belly of the animal. His tendons screamed from the strain and his head thudded in an insistent echo of the movements of the animal's flexing and bunching muscles.

Once again, he vomited bile weakly from his abused throat and stomach.

Just when he believed his muscles would tear from the agony of assaulted nerve ends and joints, a sharp knife cut him free and he slithered to the hard earth with an audible thump.

Winded, he stared up into the handsome, cold face of a tall Saxon youth. The young man spoke in a quick burst of what must surely have been Saxon, but Bedwyr shook his head weakly and shrugged his ignorance. The Saxon spat his impatience and reverted to bastardized Celt.

"Stand, dog!"

The knife cut the lashings at his ankles, and Bedwyr struggled to his feet.

"Look at me, dog! If you can keep up with the horse, there's a strong chance you will live. But I will cut your throat if we are forced to drag you."

A long rope secured his hands to the cheek straps of his horse's harness, and the animal was lashed into movement. Almost dragged off his feet, Bedwyr settled into a mind-numbing shamble.

At last, the leading rope slackened a little, and Bedwyr wiped his brow and temple where blood pumped sluggishly from a long, shallow wound. The horse's haunches quivered as they began to climb a long, low slope, and Bedwyr stared at the ground and concentrated on the position of stones, scree, and fallen branches. He was in no doubt that he would be killed out of hand if he fell.

Wordlessly, Bedwyr thanked his Christian god for his agile legs and whipcord muscles. Only his unshakable belief in his superb fitness kept him on his feet. Shrubs cut him, and gorse tore his legs. Stubbornly, he forced his exhausted muscles to propel him forward, one leg in front of the other, as each step became a word in a long, sonorous prayer to Jesu.

Stupefied, and drunk on the hypnotic rhythm of his stumbling feet, Bedwyr was barely conscious when the Saxons stopped. The dark silence was broken only by the sounds of labored, ragged breathing. The Saxon youth cuffed Bedwyr as he turned to check on his prisoner, and seemed disappointed that the Celt was still on his feet.

"Listen to me, dog! If you fall, then you die! If you live, you will be a gift from me to my lord, Glamdring Ironfist. Now, we run again!"

The youth rejoined his friends, and the agonizing journey recommenced.

The long night blurred into a series of muscle-killing bouts of running, punctuated by brief rests when Bedwyr did not dare to sit in case he could not rise again. At some point in the nightmare passage, his captor grudgingly gave him a few mouthfuls of water, and the cold draft cleared Bedwyr's head for a short time. His only sustenance was the long, unravelling prayer to his God, and the snatches of the Latin Host that he recited. One foot in front of the other! Again! Again! Again! Ignore the burning lungs! Ignore the pain of torn muscles! Run! Run! Run!

The first stains of dawn were reddening the sky when the half-light revealed a huge wooden palisade, built around a cluster of stone and timber buildings that hunched within it. Ragged huts huddled around the perimeter of the palisade, and fowls, mangy dogs, and half-naked children foraged for food or sunned themselves in the first light.

At the gates, Bedwyr hung his head as he leaned against the haunches of his running mate, whose nostrils were reddened with broken blood vessels. Once inside the forbidding walls, the Saxon youth cut Bedwyr's rope to the lathered horse and the frightened, exhausted animal was led away behind a squat building. While the youth rolled up his salvaged length of rope, Bedwyr heard the shrill scream from the horse as its throat was cut.

They'll eat him for the meat, Bedwyr thought to himself, with neither regret nor horror, too exhausted to care. The horse was better off dead.

Inside a smoke-filled, odorous hall, a huge, shaggy-bearded Saxon was seated, breaking his fast with coarse beer, some kind of oat cakes, and slabs of half-cooked meat. With smeared fingers, the man ripped the meat to pieces, and employed large, yellowing teeth to chew it to an oozy pulp. Bedwyr could see the whole process clearly, because the Saxon ate noisily with his mouth open.

The young Saxons told their tale of murderous cruelty in their own language and gesticulated often in Bedwyr's direction. They were obviously boasting to their master.

Then Bedwyr was dragged forward and cuffed to the ground in a crude copy of the full obeisance owed to a High King. Bedwyr was too exhausted to resist.

"Who are you, dog?" the master uttered in a guttural growl. "Where are you from?"

"I am Bedwyr, son of Bedwyr of Letocetum. I am a Cornovii."

The chieftain, whom Bedwyr later realized was Glamdring Iron-fist, looked vaguely at him. Bedwyr realized immediately that the Saxon had no idea who the Cornovii were, or where their lands lay.

Another rapid burst of Saxon words followed, which the Celt didn't even attempt to follow. Glamdring stared hard at Bedwyr with narrowed blue eyes above his muddy blond beard, while he continued to masticate methodically.

Bedwyr repressed a shudder and let his head hang low.

Glamdring made a decision.

"You're strong, I'll say that for you. You'll forget your outland name, and will be called Dog from this moment on. You belong to me. If you are a good dog and labor hard for me, you'll be fed. If you are not a good dog, you will die and your body will feed my pigs. Get a collar for him!"

Someone pressed a band of iron around Bedwyr's neck and a peg of metal was forced through the flange under his right ear. He was clubbed to his knees, his cheek lying on the table, while another Saxon used an iron hammer to pound the flange of iron closed. The metal scoured his skin, and Bedwyr knew that his neck would soon be bleeding where the collar rubbed against his flesh.

Another warrior thrust a short spear into the open hearth.

"You are now mine, Dog. If I die, so will you. And you will then serve me in Valhalla. Remember that my dogs are worth more than you are. They are Saxon dogs and they are fighters. You are a bastard Celt and were taken without striking a blow."

After that, Glamdring ignored him entirely. Dismissively, he threw bronze arm rings to the six young captors, who flushed to their hairlines with pleasure.

Prudently, Bedwyr remained on his knees, with his head sunk between his shoulders and his chin on his breast. In truth, he was ashamed. Although any attempt to escape would have brought death, Bedwyr regretted that he had been taken so cheaply when his friends had paid with their lives. He supposed that Glamdring and his fellows believed that he would be too cowardly to attempt escape. His heart began to beat with an ever-deepening purpose.

The warrior who was heating the spear eventually drew it out of the hearth. The point glowed a dull, sullen cherry red.

Glamdring nodded his approval, and several warriors approached and stripped the Celt to his loincloth. He would never see his tunic or leggings again. The warrior holding the spear approached Bedwyr purposefully. Bedwyr controlled his fear and his bowels with difficulty, while praying that he would not shame his ancestors.

His head was forcibly drawn back and his chest was exposed. The warrior pressed the red-hot weapon against the flesh above Bedwyr's right nipple. The flesh smoked and burned.

Except for the involuntary twitching of muscle, Bedwyr forced himself not to move. He had shut his eyes and concentrated on the crucifixion of his Lord Jesu, for if He could suffer such agony without complaint, then so could Bedwyr. Just when the Celt was sure he would scream, the hot metal was withdrawn, and Bedwyr fell to his knees, panting like an animal.

"Get yourself to the women in the kitchens, Dog. They'll put salve on my loving little bite. And remember, Dog, that you must be good and do what you are told, or you'll learn what real pain is."

For three years now, Bedwyr had done what he was told. Glamdring was his master, but any Saxon could order him to do their bidding.

His beard had grown and, although he tried to keep it trimmed with a blunt blade, it still turned into a ragged, matted bush. His hair was filthy and knotted although, when circumstances permitted, he would stand in the rivulet below Caer Fyrddin and allow the rushing water to cleanse his body.

In the months and years that followed his capture, Bedwyr's flesh became meager and whipcord strong. His muscles developed in response to the unceasing physical labor, and his clear eyes appeared downcast and deceptively docile. In the eyes of Glamdring's warriors and his women, Dog was a halfwit. Only the other house servants knew that Bedwyr was still alive within Dog's scarred body. Occasionally, in passing, he would murmur encouragement to a fellow slave, or exchange information culled from his duties in the great hall that he cleaned as vigorously as the Saxons would allow. He assisted the mastiff bitches to whelp, and the great, shaggy beasts loved him, especially one young male whom he called Wind because of its wiry grey coat.

The hall was Bedwyr's direct responsibility, and it was filthy. How the Saxons avoided pestilence defied reason, but perhaps even disease refused to take root among them. But Bedwyr intended to live and revenge himself on his captors, so he kept himself as clean as possible and took care of any cuts or bruises lest they fester and rot. One of Glamdring's women, less cruel than her sisters, had given him a salve for his burn, which he kept carefully and used for many months till the wound healed. He ate whenever he could steal food, even from the hounds and, despite a vague feeling of guilt, never shared with his fellow slaves. For Bedwyr, survival was everything.

As the years of pain and degradation passed, Bedwyr's faith began to die. The holy child of Christianity had sustained him on his journey to the fortress, but the darker gods of war salvaged his pride and strengthened his grip on life. In Bedwyr's jaundiced opinion, acceptance of suffering as a route to Paradise was a foolish affectation. Revenge kept him breathing, and the hope that Ironfist would one day die at his hands allowed the Cornovii to endure every indignity that was heaped on him to break his spirit. His Christian values were not dead, but they had merged with older, hardened beliefs that gave him a fragile reason to remain sane.

Over time, the Saxon chief scarcely noticed his daft servant with the insulting name of Dog. The slave was a familiar possession, like his favorite ale cup, which had become worn to the shape of his hand.

Now, as Bedwyr piled wooden trenchers into a wicker basket and rubbed the scarred surface of the table with a grimy scrap of cloth, a Saxon courier pounded on the gates of the fortress. Passwords were exchanged, and the messenger slid into the dark confines of the caer like an eel. Quickly, he was brought into the presence of the Saxon king. Since his capture, Bedwyr had become quite fluent in the Saxon language, but as he was rarely permitted to speak, Glamdring never considered that his slave had ears to hear, or a mouth to pass on secrets.

"A large force of Celts has moved up the coast under the banner of Artor's dragon, my lord," the courier reported. "They wear dull black so they are easily seen in the daylight, although the night conceals them."

The courier was an impressive-looking man. He wasn't particularly tall, but he was slender and well made, with hair that was very dark for a Saxon. Glamdring's eyes registered contempt for his visitor, whose blue eyes were the only clue to his northern blood. Even with all the dirt that caked his russet-brown hair, Bedwyr seemed more of a Saxon than this proud warrior.

"What are their numbers?" he asked in a cold voice, and the courier flushed.

"There are over five hundred cavalry, plus archers and foot soldiers, my lord. The baggage train is huge and they travel very slowly. They are prepared for a long campaign."

"So many? Artor is taking a risk, for his borders must have been picked clean."

"I saw the standard of Lot within the column. Your ally has broken his oath."

Glamdring chuckled quietly, and his courier took heart from his leader's indifference to the size of the host. For his part, Glamdring was pleased, for a large force was difficult to coordinate and was nearly impossible to maneuver. Artor would be impeded by the sheer size of his forces.

"The boy Gaheris assured me that Artor would come to exact his revenge, and that Lot wouldn't tolerate the death of his son. You bring me good news, very good news. Artor intends to fight us on our ground, and therefore on our terms. It's time we discovered for ourselves if this bastard is really the Warrior of the West." Glamdring had longed for the moment when he could finally test the might of Artor and his Celtic warriors.

While the courier and his master conversed, Bedwyr's concentration appeared to be wholly centered on his mundane domestic task.

"Call Nils Redbeard to me. You've done well, Cadall, and you may eat at our cooking fires. Afterwards, you will return to your post, and make sure that our scouts are ready to send me news of any changes in Artor's tactics. I expect to be told of all changes, no matter how minor. Artor is a successful leader and a skilled warrior, so he will have devised an effective battle plan."

"My life is pledged to serve you, my master," the courier vowed, and padded off to find the captain of the fortress.

Bedwyr collected his baskets and moved silently out of the hall. Quickly and thoroughly, he scrubbed the dirty plates in water drawn from the well and held in a large, roughly chiseled stone trough. The Saxons had grown careless of basic cleanliness, and no one noticed that Bedwyr used clean drinking water for his labors. He returned the slops back into the trough. The Saxons never seemed to sicken from drinking the polluted water, but Bedwyr permitted himself the enjoyment of this trifling triumph.

Bearing a leather bucket of clean water, he reentered the hall. The guards yawned and honed their weapons, ignoring his shambling presence. Bedwyr continued to clean down the tabletops while a litter of puppies charged his filthy toes and attempted to worry his bedraggled tunic hem.

Nils Redbeard entered the hall with a swagger.

The new arrival took his name from his fiery red hair and his potent temper. His ancestors were Jute, but he had been raised to hate the Celtic standard, and Glamdring Ironfist offered the only resistance to Artor's hold on the kingdom. Redbeard had embraced his master's viciousness and ambitions, and had quickly carved out a respected place for himself among Glamdring's warriors.

When he entered the hall, his pale eyes were hot and impatient.

The time for battle had arrived and he was eager to wade through Celtic corpses.

"You called for me, my lord?"

Glamdring glanced up, his crafty eyes intent on the eager face of his officer. "You have heard?"

"Aye. Our warriors are impatient to blood their weapons. When do we march, master?"

"When I tell you! Call in the warriors from the outposts. If Artor turns his eye on Caer Fyrddin, we must have troops to hold the fortress." Glamdring grinned like a fox. "And tell Valdemar to form an extra company to patrol the approaches to the caer. Their purpose is to nip at Artor's heels if he moves towards us."

Bedwyr dropped a small wooden cup that hit the edge of the table with a loud clatter. Both Glamdring and Redbeard looked at him.

"Isn't that right, Dog?" Glamdring demanded. "Dogs are useful animals to help us herd dumb beasts. That's right, nod back at me, Dog. Your friends among the Celts are dumb beasts if they think they can keep me penned up here in Caer Fyrddin."

Bedwyr grinned vacuously, and nodded so eagerly that his filthy hair shed dust and wisps of straw into the yellow light.

Both Saxon warriors laughed contemptuously and ignored the idiot.

Glamdring turned his attention back to Redbeard, and Bedwyr continued to mop and wipe, his open lips drooling thin strings of spittle.

"Lot's brat said we are incapable of learning from our enemies," Glamdring sneered, "but he was wrong, and now he's the one who's dead. The Celts use horses and are very dangerous where they can maneuver, but these hills are no help to his warriors. We'll borrow Artor's methods, and we'll use our young, unblooded warriors to make surprise attacks on his baggage train. You can choose those youngsters who show the most promise. Perhaps we can starve the bastards out so Artor will be the one to make the first mistake. Don't fail me, Redbeard."

"I'll not fail you, master."

"Then leave, for you have much to do."

Glamdring loved to talk to a captive audience, even if his bravado was only for the ears of a witless slave. With vile invective the master described how his warriors would take great joy in crushing Artor. He described in vicious detail how they would dine on the fruits of hit-and-run attacks against the baggage train, and how his archers, although Glamdring had but few, would use their longbows to pin down the fierce Artor.

"Are you afraid, Dog? You are nodding your head, so you are being a good dog. Now, bring Wyrr to me."

As Bedwyr hurried to find Glamdring's soothsayer, his heart rejoiced at the secret knowledge he now possessed. The Celts were coming at last. If his gods were kind, he would discover some way to reach them, and his long hatred could be slaked in full.

Chapter VI

THE ARDEN KNIFE

Bedwyr hurried through the muddy pathways of Caer Fyrddin to a small wooden hut that was isolated from the rest of the fortress dwellings. Although the structure was a simple construction of logs and bulrushes, it was rendered memorable by a series of severed, mummified hands, bound together with bronze wire, that hung, fingers downwards, before the doorway. In the mountain breeze, the hands clicked with the odd rattle of dried twigs. Avoiding the grisly totems, Bedwyr edged through the doorway of the sorcerer's lair.

Within the hut, the air was thick, sweet, and smoke-filled, for Wyrr was always cold. Dried bundles of herbs and other, less savory ingredients hung from the hazy ceiling, while pottery jars held oils and medicines. Other than an oddly carved chest and a simple pallet for sleeping, the overwarm hut was bare of any furnishings.

Like a ghost or a malevolent spirit, Wyrr loomed whitely out of the hut's darkness.

Glamdring's sorcerer was an aberration of nature in that he gave the physical impression of pale, wizened youth. His features seemed young, but when viewed closely, the preternatural wrinkles of old age were visible around his boyish eyes and on his cheeks. According to the whispers of the Saxon warriors, Wyrr had been born somewhere on the western coast of Cymru some twenty-six years before. Local folklore insisted that Wyrr's young mother had been struck dumb when she first beheld the silent infant, although no one remembered where this rumor had started. At any rate, the paths of Wyrr and Glamdring Iron-fist had crossed when the Saxon warrior was still an impressionable youth. Glamdring's women swore, in nervous whispers, that Wyrr had assisted his master to gain control of the western Saxon imagination and, in time, the position of thane. Certainly, Glamdring had manipulated the superstitions of his people and advantaged his leadership by shamelessly using Wyrr's influence. Men chose to step aside when the shadow of the little man fell across their path.

Wyrr had been fifteen when Glamdring first saw him, and the youth's face was young, unfinished in appearance, and sexually ambiguous. But, even then, Wyrr's skin showed a fine network of lines and blue veins. Wyrr's short stature was aggravated by swollen joints and bowed legs. From a distance, Wyrr appeared to be no older than ten years of age, but at close quarters he looked like an old man of ninety.

To add to the horrible fascination of his physical appearance, Wyrr was an albino. His skin was the luminous, fish-belly white associated with beautiful women and sickly old men. His hair was long and colorless. It was as if the gods had leached the vitality out of his tiny body before he was born, leaving behind a juiceless husk that was neither young nor old. His pale eyelashes and brows were barely visible; he grew no beard; and his small nubs of milk teeth gave his face a peculiar, half-finished look.

Whenever he walked in the daylight, Wyrr was forced to shade his eyes within the shadow of a thick cloak, for his irises were the same color as blood washed thin with water.

But if Wyrr lacked bodily strength or vigor, the gods had compensated him with superior force of will and a charismatic power that could be exerted over other, frailer minds. Doubtless, the child Wyrr would not have grown to his perversion of manhood without the temperament of a warrior and the cold cunning of an assassin. Although

110

fate had decreed that the albino was born to be a figure of fun, Wyrr was Glamdring's brain; he curbed the rashness and viciousness of the thane's behavior and replaced these flaws with a chilly intelligence. Wyrr and Glamdring, between them, made one formidable man.

Now, with fussy, childish steps, Wyrr preceded Bedwyr into the drafty, smoke-filled hall. His white robes scarcely stirred with either breath or movement. Unlike the hall and its master, the boy man was unnaturally clean for a Saxon, as if his health depended on an enforced regimen of hygiene. Bedwyr swore the little creature wore perfumed oils, for he trailed a reek of attar and costly nard.

"Come here, my friend, and share a cup of ale with me," Glamdring requested, his tone more conciliatory than the thane used with any other man or woman in the fortress. Glamdring was always careful of Wyrr's feelings and comfort, for the albino was the thane's most valued tool.

"Of course, master," Wyrr responded, in a voice that mimicked the thin, piping treble of a child.

"I go to war, exactly as we planned, Wyrr. And now I need your counsel."

"Of course, master," Wyrr repeated, seating himself carefully on the cleanest bench beside Glamdring.

"Will you throw the bones for me?"

This request, put almost humbly by the arrogant Saxon, was immediately obeyed. While Glamdring ignored Bedwyr's silent presence, Wyrr sensed the slave's interest, and watched the Celt under lowered, pouched eyelids with the flat scrutiny of a snake. Wyrr's lips parted in a sweet boyish smile, rendered chilling by his darting, purple-tinted tongue.

His heart pounding with fear, Bedwyr moved the litter of puppies into a quiet corner, then swept the soiled straw into a pile on the sod floor, ready for replacement.

"More ale, Dog," Glamdring ordered.

Bedwyr nodded.

When he returned, Wyrr was muttering under his breath and

swaying in time to unheard rhythms. Whether the sorcerer's trancelike
state was natural or feigned, Bedwyr had no way of knowing.

Wyrr cast the bones.

His crooning rose to a high crescendo, and then stopped as if a
blade had sliced through the sound. Theatrically, Wyrr's eyes snapped
open.

"Danger is close!" The childish voice hissed the sibilant and drew it
out into a thin, chilling glissade. "Too close! Much too close! Beware!"

You're a fraud, Bedwyr thought to himself. Unless you're referring
to me, you devil-spawned beast. In which case the danger to you is, I
swear, much too close!

The peculiar eyes widened until the pink irises were completely
surrounded with white. His indrawn breath quivered.

"Glamdring, my brother, everything depends upon your nerve and
your heart. Artor has come to kill you, and he gambles for high stakes.
You must match his will. You must match the man, or he will have
you at his mercy. If you would become High King, then you must act
like a High King."

"I don't understand, Wyrr." Glamdring's words were softly spoken
and, in Bedwyr's experience, uncharacteristically cautious.

"I see a shield wall, and a tall leader within the wall. The Saxon
way! I see it, master! The waves batter against the shield wall. And if it
fails, then all is lost. Fear is so thick that I can taste it. When the morning comes, the fear will be finished and the fate of Glamdring will be
set, like the knife that cuts through the wall. I can see the blade, where
the forest twines on its hilt. And the blade is the key. You must keep
the Arden Knife close by your side."

Glamdring recoiled in surprise. So also did Bedwyr. Both men
knew of a knife with a design of trees carved deeply into a handle of
bone.

"The blade is the key?" Glamdring repeated. "I own such a blade."

"Then keep it securely upon your person. Loosened, and free of
your hand, it will strike you a killing blow." Wyrr collapsed in a tidy
heap of white robes and hair.

Turning to Bedwyr, Glamdring issued his orders in a voice that was hoarse with urgency.

"Dog, go to my women. I gave one of them a knife with a tree motif on the handle. Filla has it. I want it back—and I want it now! And don't consider damaging it, Dog," Glamdring added with a cunning leer. "Nor would it be wise to bury it in my chest. It's mine, and will belong to no other man!"

As Bedwyr left the hall, Glamdring was already lifting the comatose Wyrr, holding him close to his breast like a beloved child, and raising a beaker of red wine to the sorcerer's pallid lips.

As he passed through the halls leading to the women's rooms, Bedwyr's heart beat to the refrain: "It's mine! The Arden Knife is mine! Mine! Mine!"

The blade had been taken from him when he was first captured at Castell Collen. Glamdring confiscated all the spoils of war and kept it as a curiosity. When Bedwyr had last seen the knife, it had been lying on the bench next to Glamdring's ale cup. The slave had almost forgotten its existence during the passage of three years.

When Bedwyr finally found Filla, the woman was unwilling to relinquish her gift. However, when Bedwyr warned her bluntly that Glamdring would simply take the dagger and then kill her if she made too much fuss in his hall, Filla became silent and sulky. In Glamdring's domain, women had no human status, being slightly below his dogs in importance but superior to his slaves. Throwing back her russet hair and sneering unattractively, Filla surrendered the knife to Bedwyr.

The knife was narrow-bladed and sharpened on both edges, and its lightness made it attractive for use by a woman. The handle was quite long, and the bone mounted in brass was heavily carved in a familiar pattern of intertwining trees. It reminded Bedwyr of his past, and the forests of Arden where he had learned to hunt as a boy. His fingers recalled every shape and decoration on the gleaming, ivory-white hilt. Glamdring claimed it as his own. Had the thane forgotten its history? Bedwyr knew that his face must show no recognition when the knife was passed back to the Saxon chief.

113

"You have my knife, Dog?" he snarled. "That's a good dog. Now give it to me."

Mentally ramming the Arden Knife into the center of Glamdring's chest, Bedwyr knelt and offered the dagger to his master on both open palms. The Saxon snatched it up and kicked Bedwyr away into the straw. The thane gloated over the blade for a few minutes and then thrust it into his belt, while Wyrr watched with impassive, unholy eyes that revealed nothing of what lay behind them.

Bedwyr's heart was heavy as he regretfully returned to his labors. If Wyrr spoke the truth, then his own hand had given a symbolic weapon back to the Saxons. Bedwyr felt his shoulders sag, and he raised the hands that had held his knife. He could have cursed their compliance aloud, had Glamdring not been within earshot.

A cold hatred overwhelmed his surging regrets.

What was a knife? It was nothing without a hand to hold it and a mind to guide its purpose.

I have the hands . . . and I have the mind, Bedwyr told himself. The knife has been mine for most of its life. The blade was made for me by my father, and my grandfather fashioned the hilt from the bone of a deer he had killed. Such a knife can never rightfully belong to a rogue like Glamdring. Wyrr's prophecy is false, and offers the Saxons either an empty promise or trickery.

Bedwyr felt the heat of his loathing for the Saxon race rise up into his throat. If he could, he would have torn the mountains down and buried the whole cursed race. And he would find some way to strike his blow and fulfill his destiny. He would be the Arden Knife, or his heart would burst in defeat. Artor had come, and all Celts must serve his cause if they were to rid the land of the Saxon scourge.

I will not fail, Bedwyr swore silently.

His eyes dropped back to his tasks, like any obedient servant of a powerful lord.

Bedwyr understood that the west was changing, even as he slaved for Glamdring Ironfist. He could see that Wyrr dreamed of a new order where Saxons ruled the whole of Britain, and Saxon language and culture swept away the past as if other races had never existed. King Artor had accepted the challenge to fight, just as Gaheris had predicted he would, and had come to lands where the soil was poor and grain was grown only in the topsoil that collected in the narrow valleys. From the Saxon perspective, glory could be won and, perchance, a throne. The death of Artor would expedite the Saxon domination of the land of the Britons, a disaster that Bedwyr could scarcely comprehend. Bedwyr observed how eagerly every Saxon male grinned and prepared his weapons, while their children played at battle games. The fortress was stirring out of its lethargy, and stores of grain and weapons were gathered into its storehouses from the surrounding farming communities.

After his work was done, Bedwyr curled up in the straw with the large, trusting hounds.

That night, as he exercised the dogs and fetched large slabs of dried horsemeat to feed them, he took pains to examine the fortress and its defenses with newly focused eyes. Previously, hopelessness had dimmed his perceptions, but he now had an incentive to be watchful, for Artor would need to know Caer Fyrddin intimately if he was to smash it beneath his armed heel.

More warriors than usual lay like large, untidy pelts before the fires in the forecourt. The simple, wooden barrack houses were full, and the sound of snoring rose like the sawing sound of bees—or pigs. But Redbeard had ensured that guards were watchful at the gates, and the watchtower contained two men who were dark silhouettes against the faint moonlight. Bedwyr was stopped several times as he wandered, and was asked why he was abroad. He was cuffed around the head when he tried to explain himself.

He also noted that many sides of dried meat were hung in underground storerooms, along with sealed sacks of grain, wax-sealed pots of honey, and fermented beer. The Romans had ensured that deep wells guaranteed plentiful water for the defenders, and the hillsides were honeycombed with rooms used for storage. As Bedwyr collected the horsemeat for the dogs, his sharp eyes missed little of his surroundings and nothing of the preparations taking place around him.

Artor had come. The night wind sang his name, and Bedwyr hugged his cold body and even colder heart with a bursting joy that was difficult to disguise. The Cornovii knew that his long captivity was almost over.

Outside, around the fires, a man sang tunefully of a shield maiden called Rowan who had been turned into a fair tree when her husband was killed. The song was sweet and sad, and, for a moment, Bedwyr was touched by the poetry that could live and bloom in the heart of Saxon life.

Then he thrust such blasphemy aside and brooded on his hatred. Although the Arden Knife lay close against the Saxon thane's skin, Bedwyr still owned it—steel and bone and twining trees—and now both he and his weapon thirsted for blood.

SEVERAL DAYS LATER, on a brazen day when the sun burst through the cloud cover and changed the color of the landscape to the sheen of hard metal, Artor came to a river that pumped its lifeblood into the ocean. The Celts made camp on its banks, with the pewter sea behind them.

"We have reached the end of our journey," Artor declared to Myrddion. "Here we shall fight the battle that will decide our separate fates."

Myrddion surveyed the sloping land that was thick with rank grass and soft with water.

"It's lousy terrain, Artor, but what can I say to you? You can see the perils for yourself. Your plan is audacious, and I doubt that I would have the nerve to carry it through. But, if it works as you expect, then the Saxons will be encircled in a band of iron. There'll be no escape for them." Myrddion frowned, and stared at his narrow hands.

"But if I fail, the Saxons will pick us off piecemeal," Artor finished for him.

"You're the one who must choose your ground, my lord," Myrddion said.

"The village on the river and the outlying farms are deserted,"

Targo said flatly. "There's no sign of the inhabitants. They've vanished into the landscape like ghosts."

Myrddion's face was sad and resigned. "I was born only a few miles away in that village on the river-bottom land. As far as I know, my cousins live there still. I suppose any Celts would be reduced to slaves under Glamdring's rule, or they'd have fled to the peninsula where Glamdring's arms can't reach them. I hope they remain safe and well."

Artor shot his old friend a narrow, surprised glance. Now that he strained his memory, the High King remembered Myrddion's tale that he had been born at Caer Fyrddin. But Artor had never imagined that this river land was his counselor's birthplace. The fortress was always the first place in his mind when Caer Fyrddin was mentioned. This land, caught somewhere between the sea and the river, was the Roman Moridunum, with all its accompanying echoes of doom.

Artor's eyes surveyed the terrain that was, for the most part, treeless. A small hillock rose above the river, its grasses even more thick and sharp than where they were standing. A single, dying tree, twisted by the winter winds, was slightly offset on its own low hillock barely twelve feet above the surrounding flatlands.

"There," the High King pointed. "The baggage train will take that high ground while our warriors defend the slopes and the firm earth below. We'll dig pits and trenches with spikes embedded in them to guard the approaches and direct Glamdring's warriors along the lines of attack that we want them to follow. We'll keep fires burning at all times for fire arrows and for cauterizing wounds, for the slaughter will be terrible. You, my friend, will organize the healers and the wounded at the center and, because we must, the bodies of the dead will be stacked before us and used to form a barrier to any final attack. Our warriors must continue to serve, even in death."

"Aye." Myrddion could see that Artor's plan had merit. But his own healing skills would be stretched to breaking point, as would the hearts of the Celts in such numbing, difficult terrain.

"I'd send Luka out with his scouts to drag in trees and strip this

117

area bare of timber," Targo offered, his old eyes intent on the copses of trees that separated the shore from the forest and the farmland behind it. "We'll need a good supply of firewood and materials for the pits."

"Aye. Give Luka my thanks in advance and ask him to strip the farms and village of everything of use," Artor ordered. "If any villagers remain, offer to pay for what we take. I'll not be a despoiler."

You and your scruples, Targo thought dryly, but he kept his private opinions to himself. "All shall be done as you wish, my boy."

"What is the river called?" Artor asked. "It isn't deep, but it's wide and fast flowing, and will repel any Saxons who attempt to ford it. It will be an effective ally to protect our left flank."

"I don't know its name—if it ever had one."

"Then I name this place Mori Saxonicus—the Dead Saxon River," Artor stated. "It's a bit awkward, but I'm not a mapmaker. Nor am I a poet."

"I don't care what we call it, as long as we win the battle," Myrddion countered.

In truth, Myrddion had decided that this campaign was as good a time as any other for him to perish, if die he must. If Artor failed, then Myrddion would be content to join his master. But if Artor was successful, and if he lived . . . well, perhaps he should then reconsider his mortality.

Myrddion Merlinus, once called Emrys, seemed far younger than his sixty-one years would indicate. Normally, a man of this great age was venerably ancient, toothless, and drowsing by the fire with wits that frequently wandered. Myrddion stood straight, his skin unlined and firm, with muscle and good health. A lifetime of nourishing food, careful cleanliness, and regular exercise had left the healer with a semblance of immortality.

But Myrddion was tired: bone-tired and weary of life. He had outlived all of the companions of his youth except for Llanwith and Luka, who were fast weakening with their advancing years. He had presided over the birth of his master and had then restored contact with him after twelve agonizing years, while the boy was raised in the place where Andrewina Ruadh and Lucius had hidden him. For one short moment, Andrewina Ruadh's joyous face swam through Myrddion's thoughts, accompanied by a trace of her perfume. A hollow seemed to open in his gut when he thought of her.

He had achieved his duty. If the Mother existed, and he sometimes doubted that she did, then he had paid his debt to her. For now, he could rest and be permitted the grace of dying.

But Artor was in great danger, here where the grey, salt seas met the white sands of the coast and the river pushed its brackish waters out into the main.

No, old man! She who must not be named still has work for you to do. But soon! Soon!

Myrddion relayed instructions from Artor to all the captains, and plans were put into effect to fortify the nameless knoll. While his army was still intact, Artor set both foot soldiers and cavalry to digging the trenches that he required. Selected bands of horsemen were sent into the foothills and returned dragging logs behind their beasts. A Roman redoubt was built and concealed, while lines of sharpened stakes were placed into positions that forced the attacking Saxon warriors to advance along predetermined paths. Nimble fingers were set to work weaving snares out of the long grasses, and still other horsemen were instructed to forage for rocks. The deserted village built on the foundations of a larger Roman settlement provided some brick, timber, and dressed stone, and abandoned and broken roof tiles were painful additions to the bottom of trenches. The younger men, and even the camp followers, collected smooth river stones for slingshots, while a fire pit was dug and put under cover to protect it from inclement weather. Pelles examined it, grinned a gap-toothed smile, and went looking for Myrddion to see if the baggage train contained enough pitch to meet his needs.

For three days the Celt forces sat in their camp by the river with the sea at their backs. On the third night, Artor called Lot, Gawayne, and Llanwith to attend him in his tent.

They came in the evening when the light still lingered, and it seemed that the long day would never be finished. The skies seemed to be very wide, while the setting sun touched the clouds with splashes of fresh blood. Even the pebbles on the white beaches seemed to be flushed with a thin wash of fresh blood, as if a man had died in the tidal waters and now, retreating waters had fouled the wet sand with the trail of murder. In a grim parody of a celebration, Artor's captains drank sweet Gallic wine and toasted Artor's emissaries by name. Lot's eyes were misted with tears as his son, Gaheris, was praised and the boy's memory was saluted.

Within his own mind, Artor invoked Licia as his talisman for the coming conflict.

"Tomorrow, our forces will divide," Artor began. "I won't delude you, nor attempt to convince you that my plans have no element of risk. My strategy is fraught with danger. Your three columns will be operating independently and you'll be remote from our defensive position here by the river. You must make Glamdring Ironfist's outly-ing settlements bleed freely to torment him. Your task is to strike at a number of strategic locations while my forces wait for him to attack my position here beside the river. I hope Glamdring will believe that my force is diminished to the point where he can make a decisive move. When he commences his attack, you must make a speedy return and throw an encircling line round his warriors with your cavalry."

"My pleasure, my liege," Gawayne stated flatly. "No man will survive where my warriors strike. Do you have orders for prisoners?"

"You will spare greybeards, women, and children wherever you can, but you must not risk the lives of any of your warriors in doing so. Young children must be allowed to live, Gawayne, for they are the future citizens of our nation and aren't old enough to bear lifelong grudges. All other decisions in the field are left to your discretion. Your goal is the total destruction of the settlement at Nidum."

Gawayne was essentially a simple man with an elementary, if steadfast, view of the battlefield. While he drew breath, he would not fail Artor, for his brother's sacrifice had bound him to the High King's cause for the remainder of his life.

"The most difficult task goes to you, Lot. Your command will proceed along the Octapitarum Peninsula to a fortified camp at a place called Castel Flemish. I have never seen this place, so your battle plan will depend on your assessment of its weaknesses. You must take the fortress, and it must fall to your force with speed, for you will have the farthest distance to travel when you return to our defensive position. We will be relying on your cavalry to encircle Glamdring's warriors and contain them inside the trap. Should the Saxon thane act as I expect, he will have stripped Castel Flemish to replenish his own troops before you even arrive at your destination. Glamdring's imprudence will make your task a little easier."

Lot nodded in assent. He understood that success or failure in the larger campaign hinged upon the revenge-hungry Otadini warriors that he led. Once Lot would have reveled in Artor's dilemma, but now the retribution he desired from Ironfist ensured that his vows to Artor would be upheld.

"Your men will be taking a full complement of spare horses to speed their return journey. They can rotate their horses and travel without having to rest their mounts. Your command will leave the bivouac tonight under cover of darkness, but try to be as noisy as you dare so that Glamdring will not be completely ignorant of our intentions. He must be forced to make false assumptions." Artor paused. "Are my instructions clear? Have I forgotten anything?"

Lot was confident that his warriors could take any Saxon fort, for the highlands were their natural home, and ferocity was bred into them through the privations of life in the frigid winters of their lands.

"Nay, Artor, I am content."

Artor turned to Llanwith. "Llanwith, old friend, your task is not easy. Your road lies north, and you must skirt around Caer Fyrddin until you reach Llandovery. Your orders are to strike at the Saxons in country that they believe is their safe haven, forcing them to look sideways at every tree and behind every rock. You have lost men in the past near Llandovery, so I assume you have personal knowledge of the terrain and an equally personal interest in the success of your task."

"Such a mission would be *very* personal, Artor."

"Then our battle strategy is decided. My plan is relatively simple: your men will attack his outposts, while I will send unpalatable messages to Glamdring Ironfist. He will not come out of Caer Fyrddin for some time, for he will not see any need. Even as we squat on this riverbank, I am sure we are watched, so I'll keep some cavalry to hunt out Saxon prisoners who can deliver my insults. I'm convinced that if I push him hard enough, Ironfist will eventually lose his self-discipline. And when he sets foot outside his fortress, my cavalry will provide an early warning of his march, before riding north and west to alert your forces and hurry you home. I'll hold the Saxon forces at bay until you arrive to relieve the main army." Artor stared fixedly at Lot, for the Otadini king could have the throne of the High King simply by being tardy in his response to Artor's need.

"I know what you risk, Artor," Lot stated. "And I understand the stakes. I've given my word, so I will come." He smiled at Artor. "A shield wall held by Celts," he said with dry humor. "They'll not expect you to do that, Artor, and they'll be overconfident when they come to meet your forces. Yes, I'll be back long before Glamdring is crushed, for my queen would never forgive me if she missed such a slaughter."

"I believe you, Lot. You were ever an honest man, for all that we held differing opinions, and I am happy to accept your word."

"But you may have to repel the Saxons for days, my lord," Llanwith muttered, cracking his great knuckles with worry. "Ironfist will come out from his fortress only if he outnumbers you, and we Celts have forgotten how to hold a single, untenable position to the death. What if Lot and I come too late?"

"Then you'll be responsible for our burial rites," Artor replied with an attempt at humor. "But Targo tells me that his Roman friends occasionally held impossible situations with little more than stubbornness and willpower. I will emulate them, and we will survive until your arrival." He smiled, exuding confidence. "Now, enough has been said."

Artor moistened two fingers and pinched out one of the oil lamps. The tent darkened.

"Tomorrow you ride, and Glamdring Ironfist will be forced to watch four fronts rather than one. Pray to your gods that we don't fail." Artor raised his cup and drained it in one smooth draft. "Until we meet in victory."

"In victory," the captains repeated, and upturned their empty cups on the table.

They filed out of the tent and returned to their waiting troops.

BEFORE FIRST LIGHT, the blackness was filled with the deeper shadows of men and horses milling around the dying campfires. Torches were lit and flared their phosphorescence over the black arms of the fighting men who slowly walked their horses in three different directions, carrying packs loaded with sufficient provisions to last for at least a week. The night was alive with the sounds of harness jingling and the dull thud of hooves, for Artor did not choose to hide his actions from the enemy. By the time first light came creeping up to the camp, the Saxons could see the tails of three columns moving purposefully away from the main body of the host.

Ironfist's spies dispatched couriers to Caer Fyrddin, and the game began.

Artor's harriers, under Luka's expert command, began to rove the foothills. They muffled the hooves of their horses, and their bodies were wrapped in black cloaks. If they saw a Saxon scout, they rode him down, and then shepherded him back to the main camp.

Three days passed in fruitful waiting.

Artor had set his men to work, shaping and preparing spare arrows, even if they didn't have sufficient arrowheads. The shafts alone, heated at the point over a fire, could still inflict damage on human flesh. And with a piece of fat-soaked lint attached to the point of the shaft, the archer had a fire arrow that could light the hidden pits of dead wood soaked in pitch that Myrddion had prepared as a defensive barrier. Ever the planner, Myrddion had anticipated the need to illuminate the field of combat during the depths of night, so that darkness would not benefit Glamdring Ironfist's warriors during any sneak attack.

Each evening, a prisoner would be selected from those unfortunates captured during the day. Those who spoke the Celtic tongue were drilled in the message they would be forced to deliver; if they spoke only Saxon, they would receive their instructions from Gruffydd in their own tongue. Then a blood-soaked bag was tied around their necks. Only Artor and Odin knew for certain what these bags contained, but it was clear that Artor was sending a message that could not be misunderstood by Glamdring Ironfist or his Saxon horde.

At midnight on the first night, the first Saxon was released on the edge of camp and sent to Caer Fyrddin with his poisonous message.

"Any sensible person would throw away the bag and take to his heels," Targo muttered as the Saxon disappeared into the darkness beyond the torches.

Luka admired the poetry and justice of Artor's actions. "If they don't carry the message to Glamdring, and he wins, they will be executed for treason. If they report to Glamdring, they risk being killed because they carried a message that he didn't want to hear. Either way, they cannot win."

"But our methods are just as barbaric as those used by Glamdring," Myrddion said sadly.

"Myrddion, old friend, sometimes you can be an old woman." Luka smiled. "What other choice does Artor have?"

"Oh, he has little choice, I agree, but I deplore the means by which we are smoking Glamdring out."

"Deplore away." Luka laughed. "I don't think Artor cares."

Artor did care, in the deepest part of himself. Sometimes, he hated what the king in him had to do. The slaughter of a man in the dead of night, even the least noble of the Saxons, weighed heavily on his already burdened heart, but he could not allow a hint of his self-disgust to show when Odin beheaded each spitting, cursing Saxon on the banks of the river. The corpse was consigned to the tides and the sea, but the head was bagged and sent to Glamdring. If Artor was disturbed by the orders he issued, he was not prepared to show his followers a weak and sickly face, for now was the time for courage.

SPIES HAD REPORTED the Celtic troop movements to Glamdring almost as soon as Artor divided his forces.

The Saxon chieftain sat in the gloomy hall that Bedwyr now cleaned every day. He worked unobtrusively, watching and waiting, trusting to Fortuna to give him a sign.

"What does Artor intend to do?" Glamdring puzzled. "Does he mean to starve us out? Can he believe that he can burn and pillage all of Dyfed and the Saxon villages?"

His captains looked bemused at their master's rhetorical questions and offered no advice, but Wyrr cautioned Glamdring to exercise patience. The gods would make all Artor's strategies plain in the days to come.

Covertly, Bedwyr watched Glamdring finger the hilt of the Arden Knife, reassuring himself that it still hung safely in its protective scabbard round his neck.

Glamdring is rattled. He's not the sort of man who has the patience to sit and wait, Bedwyr thought as he served horse stew in rich gravy to his master.

Glamdring cuffed his slave casually as gravy spilled onto his leg and disturbed his concentration on Artor's tactical moves. Bedwyr lowered his head and maintained his fragile control.

The next day, shortly after noon, the first courier loped up to the gates of Caer Fyrddin at a slow, tired trot. Terrified by his task, the captive had fully intended to flee, but one of Glamdring's patrols had discovered him only hours after Artor sent him on his way. The odorous leather bag, the staining of the courier's shirt, and his obvious fear had convinced the Saxon troop that Glamdring must be immediately informed of their discovery. The patrol had escorted the cringing warrior back to Glamdring's citadel.

Glamdring strode from the hall with a thunderous face when word reached him that one of his scouts had returned. A woman howled by the wall, and the still air waited on the thane's arrival. Bedwyr crouched at the great, wooden-planked door of the hall and listened with the panting hounds that rested behind him.

The scout was lathered with sweat and streaked with blood where the bag had leaked down his furs and his cloak. His eyes were pale pits of anger and fear. Glamdring snatched the bag from the courier and peeled back the leather to expose the countenance of the fleet-footed Wulf, a childhood friend. He clenched his strong teeth and demanded the message.

"To Glamdring Ironfist of Caer Fyrddin. I bear gifts in memory of Prince Gaheris, son of Lot, and of the emissaries who were slain by you in defiance of a flag of truce. We will watch from Hades as you hide in fear within your fortress while you collect more and more heads taken from your warriors. These tokens are all you will get from King Artor. Not one foot of Celtic earth will feel the imprint of your cowardly heel."

The scout stammered over the last words and flinched at the red points of light in his master's eyes.

"By the gods!" Glamdring cursed, but he kept his head. "Take this idiot out of my sight. Men who allow themselves to be captured are of no use to me. He can collect the wood for Wulf's funeral pyre instead."

The scout ran to obey his master; he had feared painful retribution and death from the thane, but, unaccountably, he had managed to survive.

Twenty-four hours later, another scout arrived bearing an identical bag. The message this man carried was briefer.

"Artor, High King of the Celts, is merciful, so he will permit you to live if you relinquish Caer Fyrddin. He scorns to send more such messengers; each will cost you a hundred warriors if you wait too long. You must decide—and you must make your choice very soon."

The scout blanched as Glamdring's cheeks flushed wine-red with temper.

"My lord," he stammered, "I brought the head of my companion back to his home to ensure he receives a decent burial. His body floats on the grey tide as we speak. I ask that you do not silence the mouth that brings these foul messages."

Wyrr padded up to Glamdring and hissed up at his glowering master.

"Think, my lord, for Artor always acts with a purpose. Does he wish to distract you with these vile slurs? Where are his other troops? Does he wish to blind you? You must think of these things, my lord."

Gradually, the red glow of rage dissipated from Glamdring's eyes, and he set the scout about the same task as his fellow from the previous day.

"Yes, you're right, my friend. I must think. Artor is playing games with me, but I won't fall into his traps." Glamdring's muttered words seemed designed more to convince himself than others, but Wyrr patted his arm affectionately to placate him.

Glamdring smiled at the small, misshapen wizard, and a shared moment of intimacy passed between the huge Saxon and the albino.

Bedwyr swore under his breath, but, as the hours passed, he saw that Glamdring's confidence was wilting perceptibly. Just before noon, Glamdring would start to pace up and down his hall, his fists would clench and unclench, while his wary eyes flickered towards the flagged yard and the view of the rocky path leading up to the fortress.

By the third day, Bedwyr began to realize that Glamdring was listening for the sound of a scout returning with another head and another message, and he smiled under the shadow of his beard. He did not believe that the thane had become a frightened man, but he sensed that Glamdring was disconcerted by Artor's tactics, and the forced inactivity was putting him on edge.

Bedwyr was aware that his own hatred for the thane was swelling as the Saxon's anger and frustration grew. Glamdring's nerves were fraying, and he displayed his anger with fists, sticks, and his boots whenever a slave, a woman, or even a dog crossed his path.

How long can you squat here, Glamdring Ironfist? Until the High King loses patience and comes to root you out of your hilly sty? And will you sit here like a fat pig avoiding the butcher's knife?

But no answers came to Bedwyr's silent questions, only a steady stream of bloody couriers.

When the fifth head was brought to Glamdring, his control snapped. As the scout uttered the hateful message in a quaking voice, Glamdring roared, and slashed at the poor man's throat without thought. The courier died in shaking spasms as his blood pumped out in an uncontrolled jet of bright red.

Surprised, Wyrr hurried towards his lord and tugged at his sleeve, but Glamdring held up one forceful hand.

"No!"

"Lord, think! Do not—"

"No, Wyrr! I have waited long enough. Even though our scouts have yet to discover the whereabouts of Artor's three troops, I'll wait for them no longer. Tomorrow, for good or ill, we march on Artor's timid Celtic army and we'll drive them into the sea. If they won't come to us, then we will go to them."

"Lord, this is not the way—"

"No!" Glamdring shouted, his brows drawing down in his ire. "I wait no longer."

Wyrr realized that he had chosen the wrong moment to speak.

That night, the darkness seemed full of eyes. Most men were silent as they honed and oiled their weapons into brightness. Their hearts were filled with a fierce joy, for the Saxons were fighting for their homes, as were the Celts. The women wept, as women always do when their men go to war. But Bedwyr was long past any sympathy for them. He thought of the Celtic women captives who had been enslaved, raped, and forced to live the most menial of lives within the fortress of Caer Fyrddin. Years of his own pain and humiliation filled his mind, and he longed for the death of all his tormentors.

Having made his decision to attack Artor's force, Glamdring suddenly seemed happy, relieved, and excited, and Bedwyr exulted in the thane's impulsiveness. The brute is overjoyed to be back in action, for he has hated having to sit and wait. Clever, clever Artor, to goad him into following a foolish course of action.

But Bedwyr feared that Glamdring's force of eight hundred fighting men was a frighteningly vast number for any army to face. It was entirely conceivable that the Saxon thane could overrun even the strongest defensive position.

As the darkness deepened, Bedwyr fretted that Artor would be attacked unwarned. Glamdring was unlike his fellow Saxons, for the man had no superstitious fears about making a night attack. Whatever plan the High King had devised could easily be imperiled by Glamdring's sudden, lightning-fast tactical changes.

"It's time for Dog to vanish so I can become Bedwyr again," the slave muttered into the straw of his pallet as he feigned sleep.

Long after midnight, the fortress began to settle after the initial feverish preparations for battle, and stillness enveloped the spirits of the men who sheltered within its walls.

Carefully, Bedwyr stirred in the straw. Until this last, desperate moment, he hadn't perceived any value in throwing his life away on the slight chance of gaining his freedom through escape. But now was the time for Glamdring's dog to flee and, if need be, to die as a Celt.

As silently as any beast stalking its quarry, Bedwyr slid from the hall, hugging the deep shadows of the walls. For three years he had watched the sentries change guard and he had studied the mechanism of the gate and knew the noise it made when it was opened. Two nights previously, in expectation that his time may have come, he had rubbed pig fat into the hinges and the metal flanges that held the bar in place, risking discovery to meet the necessities of a later, desperate plan. Now, slipping from one pool of darkness to the next, the Celt thanked his foresight and made his way ever closer to the watchtower overlooking the gate.

Bedwyr had no weapons other than his strong hands, and he knew that two men stood sentry duty on the walls. Around his neck hung a narrow ribbon of leather that had once carried a flat pebble amulet, but two pieces of stick now dangled from the ends of the thong, forming an effective garotte. Although shorter than he would have liked, it could prove an effective killing tool, if surprise was on his side. The only other protection at his disposal was a thick length of half-burned wood that he had plucked from the fire inside the hall.

Indeed, Fortuna favors the brave. And perhaps the affairs of great men are truly influenced by fickle chance for, as Bedwyr reached the base of the ladder, one warrior was freeing his clothing to urinate over the wall.

Before his nerve could fail him, Bedwyr ran at the ladder with the garotte clenched between his teeth and the makeshift club shoved into his belt. As he scurried up the rough wooden rungs, he was conscious of the scuffling sounds made by his bare feet. But he ignored the tell-tale sounds, for speed was his only ally.

As his head cleared the coarse-sawn planks of the platform, he was already freeing his club with one hand. One of the sentries saw him coming, but before the Saxon had an opportunity to rise and turn, Bedwyr struck him hard across the temple with his club. The Celt heard and felt the sodden crunch of shattering bone. Ignoring the other man who was trying desperately to cover himself and free his sword at the same time, Bedwyr manhandled the near-dead Saxon to the floor of the tower, and then swiped viciously at his fellow. He missed, and the second guard charged at him, his mouth wide open to shout the alarm. Bedwyr managed a backhanded blow with his club across the sentry's mouth. The man flailed his arms, reeled backwards, struck the edge of the platform with the back of his knees, and fell away into the darkness below the wall. The only sound from the desperate struggle was a distant thud and the faint clatter of dislodged pebbles as the man's body slid down the steep ravine that protected Caer Fyrddin on three sides.

Expertly, Bedwyr broke the neck of the unconscious guard, and then stood, breathing heavily but trying to mimic the stance and nonchalance of a bored guard.

Bedwyr's entire attack had taken less than one minute.

The minutes passed slowly as his blood cooled and he regained control of his breathing. Bedwyr was barely six feet above the ground but he was some twenty feet from the nearest warriors who were sleeping in various positions around banked fires. The distance had muffled the sounds of violent death.

Blessing his luck, and grateful for the element of surprise, Bedwyr waited until the silence was absolute. Then he wedged and lashed the body of the dead sentry so that he appeared to be standing at his post. Bedwyr's garotte now found a new purpose, as he used the thong to tie the limp body upright, by the throat, to the rough timber.

Bedwyr armed himself with the dead sentry's knife and sword, and peered cautiously over the edge of the parapet.

Only a curious mastiff had stirred in the hall, its superior hearing warning it that someone was awake and active. Bedwyr didn't fear the dogs, for he fed them and was familiar to them. The large animal lifted its nose to the air, recognized the scent of a friend, and wandered back towards the hall and warm straw.

Bedwyr sighed with relief, and then snaked over the edge of the tower and slid down the ladder without touching the rungs. Silently, on hard, bare feet, he reached the gate and began to lift the huge metal latch. His muscles struggled with the weight, but the well-tended wood and oiled metal rose smoothly to release the huge tongue from within its primitive frame. Fighting the gate with all his strength, he felt the whole mechanism slide free, and the gate began to turn on its huge framework.

A whisper of cloth on stone warned Bedwyr of danger, and he spun agilely to his left. A flash of light caught in the corner of his eye, and a small knife propelled by a desperate hand buried itself in the wooden gatepost where he had stood just a moment before. Without thought, and without compunction, Bedwyr withdrew the knife, stepped close to the cowled shape of his attacker, and clamped his free hand over the nose and mouth of the slight figure. A vicious twist of his wrist, and Bedwyr had his enemy's back turned to him, where the scrabbling, impotent hands couldn't touch him. The knife slid between his attacker's ribs like hot metal through butter, and Bedwyr buried the blade to the hilt and twisted it.

He released his hold and the dark form turned and started to slump. Two pale eyes widened until the whites were staring blankly up at him. Two pale hands scratched weakly at his tattered tunic and Bedwyr flinched away from the touch of the dying man. Wyrr, the sorcerer, opened his mouth as if to scream, but Bedwyr saw only a sudden rush of blood as the albino choked and fell.

Without waiting to check if the sorcerer was dead, the Celt kicked the pitifully small body out of his path, pushed on the gate, and ran off into the night.

"It's done! It's done! It's done!" Bedwyr repeated over and over again as he ran, careless of capture. Many miles lay between him and his master, King Artor. Blessedly, those weary leagues were mostly downhill.

Bedwyr fled as if the fate of the world depended on the speed of his escape. The night embraced his fleeing form, and only the more restless of the Saxon scouts stirred as the assassin sped past them on silent feet.

Chapter VII

GLAMDRING'S BANE

Gawayne surveyed the burning settlement with grim satisfaction. Old Nidum was neither affluent nor well defended, but it was a Saxon settlement. Initially, Artor had chosen to ignore its existence during his march to Mori Saxonicus, knowing that the small settlement posed no strategic power to harm his force, and, if circumstances decreed otherwise, action could be taken against it at a later time. Nidum had known that it was under threat, so its defenders had breathed a deep sigh of relief when the main body of the Celtic host had passed it by.

Gawayne had taken more time to achieve his task than he had initially intended. On his journey to Nidum, his troop had run into a band of thirty Saxon warriors who were traveling to join Glamdring's force at Caer Fyrddin and, although the scouting force was relatively small, it had taken a full day of desperate hunting before the Saxon warriors were eventually annihilated. On foot, and in open country, the Saxons would normally have been no match for fifty well-trained cavalry, but Glamdring's men had made a dash for the tree line and good cover, where they successfully defended themselves against repeated forays by Gawayne's cavalry. Eventually, Gawayne's losses amounted to five dead warriors and seven more wounded, before the last of the Saxons perished in a blood-soaked clearing within the thin line of trees.

If those bastards had managed to reach the forest proper before we caught up with them, we could have whistled for them for all the good our horses would have been, Gawayne thought nastily as he watched Nidum burn to the ground.

The citizens of Nidum had defended the settlement with hidden pits and traps sited around the stone-blackened Roman foundations. Gawayne gave a silent prayer of thanks to the Saxon predilection for destroying all Roman structures that were unfamiliar to them. Even though Glamdring had stripped Nidum of most of its fighting men some weeks earlier, those Saxons who remained were determined men. Gawayne was surprised to find that many native Celts were also among those who were trapped within the streets of the defeated city.

Gawayne had observed a small flotilla of fishing boats and coracles set off from the shore when his troops began to surge through the burning gates, and he wondered if those fleeing rats had been Saxon or Celt.

Celt, most likely, he decided. *To their credit, the Saxons don't usually run away from a fight.*

Then, despite his lingering anger at the death of Gaheris, he had felt a moment's admiration and pity for the Saxon race.

"This ground is all they have, so where can they run to if they abandon their homes?"

"You spoke, my lord?" Gawayne's second-in-command asked, his broad, young face puzzled and eager.

"Drive the defenders to the water's edge, and then offer them an honorable surrender. Any women and children are free to go without condition, and any males with Celtic blood are to be unharmed unless they strike a blow against us. They and their families may stay or go as they please."

"Are you sure that's wise, Lord Gawayne?" his sergeant asked, although the young man's admiration for Gawayne's magnanimity was written clearly on his open face.

"Give them my terms. If the Saxons refuse them . . . then you may kill them all." Gawayne gave the brutal orders regretfully, for there was little glory in wholesale slaughter.

Showing a rare insight into the plight of victims of war, Gawayne ordered that the Saxon women should be allowed to take what they chose from their homes before they and their children moved to higher ground and safety. By the end of the day, many Celtic families had simply melted away into the night, continuing a long pattern of passivity that the Celtic population of Demetae had adopted years before. Of the Saxon defenders only the indomitable, white-haired Thane of Nidum and a small group of aging warriors remained.

"There is no honor for any of us in your deaths," Gawayne said as he faced them on the shoreline. "I'm reluctant to revenge myself on you for the actions of Glamdring Ironfist in a battle that cannot be won."

The thane stood forth from the small band of defenders. His expression, in both body and face, was impassive. Although Gawayne was far from quick-witted, he decided that the thane had faced his fate squarely and was content with what the gods had decreed for him.

"We have no dreams of glory, my lord," he stated simply. "We know why Artor has come, and we offer no excuses for the actions of our thane. We are old men, and our only desire is to keep the last rags of our honor. I ask that you do not make my people suffer unnecessarily, simply because they are Saxon. One day, perhaps, my people will cast aside their traditions and embrace this land as their home, but I regret that I cannot forsake the old ways, even to save my own life. I beg that you kill us in open combat and let us die like men."

Gawayne thought hard, his sympathy engaged by the candor of the Saxon.

Only a fool would risk his warriors in such a fashion, and Gawayne was no fool. On the other hand, the words of the old chieftain had touched Gawayne's honor. Gaheris had been a man such as this, faithful to his oaths but not rigid in his thinking, a man who was capable of great generosity of spirit.

"If you will not lead your people away from this place, and if you will not permit me to allow your warriors an honorable departure, then I will fight you alone, to the death, so that the spirits of you and your men go to your gods with honor."

"My lord, you cannot do this," Gawayne's young sergeant remonstrated with his master.

"Of course I can," Gawayne replied, choosing to state the obvious. "I'm the commander of this detachment. I can do whatever I want."

Inevitably, Gawayne won the brief but savage battle. The old man lay dying at the water's edge, his chest pierced by Gawayne's dagger. As his eyes began to film in death, Gawayne asked the old man for his name.

"I am . . . Bandur . . . Sea Changer." The old man took one last, shuddering breath, and died.

"All honor goes to Bandur, the Sea Changer," Gawayne called, raising his sword and bloody dagger high above his head, and then the Celts slew the remaining defenders, quickly and with honor.

Gawayne gathered his men and they rode back to their encampment where the wounded awaited treatment.

The following day, Gawayne's forces were again on the move. Artor had instructed him to patrol the foothills, and the prince was eager to obey. Campaigns like the destruction of Nidum made him feel sad and unaccountably guilty, so he was pleased to shake its dust from the hooves of his horse. His forces hunted out Saxon villagers and warned all the Demetae Celts who could be found to avoid the main centers and roads. The Celts were as dourly sullen as their Saxon masters, and Gawayne was puzzled by their passive resistance. If he had ever believed that he would be greeted like a savior when he cleared the Saxons out of the hills, he now discovered the reality of Demetae thinking. For decades, the tribe had been pushed and prodded this way and that, without recourse to any natural justice. They had grown weary of the dreams and power struggles of strangers, and desired only the freedom to rebuild their homes and to farm their land. Gawayne's Celts were as strange to the archaic remnants of western glory days as the alien Saxons had been, and the western Celts would give no support to any warrior who was not one of the Demetae tribe.

Gawayne understood their plight.

The day was well advanced when an outrider heard the sound of gravel sliding from the hillside, a warning that someone was approaching from the east of Caer Fyrddin. Three horsemen were dispatched to intercept the man and bring him to Gawayne.

The Celtic warriors returned with a half-naked savage slung over the neck of one of the horses. The man was bound, hand and foot.

"Who's this pretty boy?" Gawayne asked sharply. "Where did you find him? It's obvious that you smelled him long before you saw him."

"He appeared out of nowhere, Lord Gawayne, right under the hooves of the horses as if he'd grown out of the ground. He speaks good Celt, but he's asking to be taken to the High King. I believe he could be an assassin."

The young Dumnonii warrior who spoke took the safety of the High King very seriously, for his tribe and the Durotriges clan both claimed Artor as their own. Gawayne grinned sardonically. Regardless of the origins of Queen Ygerne or Uther Pendragon, Artor was content to be simply Celt. In truth, Artor was more than half Roman in thinking, for his foster mother and his arms master both stemmed from that ancient, redoubtable race.

Gawayne looked down at the filthy creature. He had been allowed to fall to the ground. Stocky, rippling with muscle, but poorly nourished, the body of the man was grime-encrusted and lousy, from his matted hair and beard to his calloused, black toenails.

"Stand!" Gawayne demanded with scant courtesy. "Who are you? And where are you going? If you were seeking King Artor, then you're going in the wrong direction." His nose wrinkled as the stink of unwashed flesh assaulted his senses.

"I am Bedwyr of the Cornovii, taken alive from the land to the south of Castell Collen over three years ago. I was a house slave to Glamdring Ironfist, and I've escaped to carry news of Glamdring's defenses and strategies to King Artor. If I became lost, it is because I'm not familiar with this place."

Gawayne and his warriors stirred as the savage spoke, doubting that such a dirty creature could be Celt. Gawayne stared at the filthy, soot-darkened face, his distrust written plainly upon his freckled face.

"You may doubt me if you wish," Bedwyr said. "And I suppose I would do the same were I in your shoes. If you allow me to clean myself, and if you have something else for me to wear, then you will see that what I say is the truth."

"The air would certainly smell sweeter if you were clean," Gawayne responded. "But why should I believe you? Ironfist is capable of sending a spy to assassinate Artor under the guise of a freed captive. You'll have to be more convincing, my friend."

The man stripped off his ragged tunic with his bound hands. As he straightened, wearing only an equally dirt-encrusted loincloth, the warriors could see the slave mark on his shoulder and the iron collar round his neck. Deep scarring marked the flesh around the heavy metal. Gawayne recalled Gruffydd's scar, the twin to the cicatrice on the breast of this savage.

"Very well, I accept that you have been marked as a slave. But how can I trust a man who stayed in Caer Fyrddin for three years, and only now escapes from our enemies to join King Artor?"

"I bear news that King Artor must hear. As Glamdring's servant, I heard much, and even now his men pursue me. Don't hinder me, for he plans to attack Artor at the river mouth. Glamdring marches against Artor with a very large force, and they are determined to wipe Artor and his army off the face of the earth."

Since Bedwyr knew the location of Artor's camp, Gawayne calculated that his information was probably true. But a small worm of distrust still slithered its way into the thoughts of the prince.

"Why should you care? Don't you desire freedom and the chance to return to your family?"

Bedwyr spat on the earth, and anger flickered in his hazel-brown eyes. His lips parted, and Gawayne saw that his teeth were very white and sharp, as if Bedwyr had chewed on twigs and bones to preserve them.

"I won't rest or return to Arden Forest until the hive of Caer Fyrddin is scoured clean of the Saxon stink. For three years I've dreamed of choking the life out of Glamdring Ironfist, and I've stayed alive for the single purpose of revenge. Blood calls to blood, and a price is owed for the deaths of my friends who were burned alive near Castell Collen. When I flag in my purpose, I've only to remember those screams, and my hatred is restored and renewed." Bedwyr paused for breath and his wide, muscular chest heaved with repressed emotion. "You may doubt me if you wish, for any sensible man would, but don't block my path to the king. Only he can burn that filthy nest of savages. My hands can only kill so many, but the High King can slay them all."

The manic light in the eyes of the slave, coupled with huge knuckled fists that he raised in front of his face as if he was already tearing bone from bone, repulsed Gawayne. He hated the Saxons for their treachery towards Gaheris, but no one could doubt that this man was fueled by unhealthy lust for barbarian blood, and that nothing would deter him from his chosen path.

"Cut that slave collar from his neck," Gawayne ordered crisply, his decision made.

Other than to wince when a hammer and chisel freed his throat of the constricting iron band and set his blood flowing freely, Bedwyr made no sound.

"Take him down to the river," Gawayne ordered the three warriors who had discovered the slave. "You can give him a knife to shave his beard and shears to do something with that hair. But, just in case, you'd best keep him under close guard so that he can't attack you with your own weapon. Let's see how he looks when he's clean."

The river was icy, and Bedwyr shivered as he sat in the fast-flowing water and scrubbed his nakedness with handfuls of river sand. When one of the Celts threw him a knife and a small phial of oil, he dragged the sharp blade through his matted beard, cutting himself painfully in many places so that the water around him ran pink. Then he set to work with a pair of blunt shears on the mane of hair on his head. So matted were the tangled locks that Bedwyr decided to cut them off only an inch from his skull. He immediately gained a civilized appearance. Finally, clean and roughly trimmed, he lunged out of the water and stood, shivering violently, on the bank.

With a look of sheer bravado, he threw the knife into the earth between its owner's feet.

"I apologize if I have dulled the edge of your blade." Bedwyr bowed slightly, and grinned. "And I thank you also for the use of your oil. I'd not have removed three years of dirt without it, although I now smell of rancid fat."

"It's an improvement," the Celt guard, Alun, retorted.

The cavalryman passed him his tunic and loincloth, and Bedwyr pulled them over his wet body.

When he was brought back to Gawayne, no longer dripping but still chilled, the water and the hair cropping had wrought a minor miracle. Bedwyr's hair was now undoubtedly russet, and he had a disarming smattering of freckles over his nose and shoulders. The white skin where his beard had protected his face from the sun revealed a firm mouth and a stubborn jaw that belied the youth of the man who stood before the band of cavalry.

Bedwyr's body reflected the years of abuse suffered during his captivity. His nose had been broken, creating a slightly crooked appearance on his otherwise symmetrical face. The white seams of old scars covered his body, one laid on the other, especially around the ribs and the back. One of his smaller fingers had been broken, as well as several toes, and his torso and shoulders were covered with scrapes, bruises, and cuts.

Gawayne saw, and was half convinced.

"Tell me, Bedwyr, how were you captured?" he demanded.

And Bedwyr told him.

"I still don't understand why you stayed with Glamdring's warriors if you escaped so easily in this instance. If I doubt your honesty, it's because of your unwillingness to flee the Saxon fortress."

Bedwyr snorted. "Where was I to go? King Artor has only recently moved his army to this part of Britain, and, until now, there has been no haven open to me. I have cared for Glamdring's war dogs, but they would have happily hunted me down, for all that I slept with them and fed them. I've waited, and stayed alive, knowing that a time might come when I, Glamdring Ironfist's dog, could tear out his throat as I swore to do so long ago. I've been prepared to die for a very long time, for all slaves know that living is hard with such masters. But if I was destined to perish, then I wanted my death to mean something. I determined that I should direct a killing blow at the hearts of my captors and remain alive until Artor came."

"If you desire to kill Glamdring, you will have to stand in a very long line to await your turn," Gawayne retorted dryly.

"Nor was my escape easy. I sat quietly for years, enduring insults, blows, and starvation, so that one day I could take my chance to fly from Glamdring's tender care. In my escape, I was forced to kill two guards. I also killed Wyrr, Glamdring's sorcerer and his closest, most clever adviser. At least he'll never again whisper words of caution into the ears of his master. He was the intelligence behind Glamdring's brawn."

"Who is this Wyrr?" Gawayne asked. "We haven't heard of him."

"He was a vicious albino creature. He was clever and cold, but I killed him anyway. The knife I used to silence Wyrr's dangerous tongue was taken from me by your warriors. My lord, we're wasting time with these pointless questions." A sense of urgency gave an edge to his voice now. "I am only one man, and I'm easily slain if I should prove to be false. But Glamdring is coming against Artor, and he has amassed more than eight hundred men, and will raise even more warriors once the villagers begin to flock to his banner. Artor has enraged Glamdring beyond reason, and I was running to warn the High King when your men found me and brought me to you. Take me to the High King, Prince Gawayne, for I have not listened and endured my slavery for three years to see the Saxons win the coming war because Artor was kept in ignorance."

Gawayne thought ponderously for just a few more minutes. He remembered Artor's plan and made his decision. He directed his orders to the warrior whose knife Bedwyr had blunted at the river. As a fellow Otadini, Gawayne trusted him completely.

"Alun, take Bedwyr to Artor at full speed. Once there, you will wait for any message for me from the High King, and then you may return to my command. Use one of the spare horses for Bedwyr, and you can return his weapon. He looks famished, so give him some rations to eat as you ride to King Artor's encampment."

"My thanks, my prince." Bedwyr smiled. "Your trust is not misplaced."

"I hope not. Otherwise I'll find you, and I'll kill you!"

With efficiency and speed, Bedwyr and Alun were mounted and had departed within minutes of Gawayne's decision. Morosely, the prince watched the two horsemen disappear into the tree line. More than anything else, Bedwyr's riding skill convinced him that the Cornovii was no spy. The Saxons preferred to walk, scorning horseback, but Bedwyr was obviously a skilled horseman.

"Well, Artor will discover the truth of this man far easier than I could," Gawayne said aloud. "If Bedwyr found Glamdring's sorcerer to be exotic, what will he make of Myrddion and Targo?"

ALUN AND BEDWYR traveled at a steady canter. At first, they followed the track of Artor's army, so they moved swiftly. Then, as the light faded, they moved into the tree line.

The spring weather was still cold and Bedwyr was only lightly clothed, but years of privation had inured him to light rain and the chill of the night. When the horses began to weary, the two men walked. Bedwyr's horny soles were accustomed to the sharp flints and rough underbrush of the ground they traversed, but, even so, his bare feet began to bleed from slippage on the knife-sharp flints and slate. Although he gave the cuts and slashes little attention and walked on stolidly, he began to leave bloody footprints on the stone. Eventually, because discovery would be disastrous, Alun tossed him a length of old rag, and Bedwyr took the time to bind his feet.

The heavily wooded slopes of the hills rising out of the coastal strip appeared like stumpy teeth to Bedwyr, for he had been raised in Arden Forest. The whole dim greenness was silent, except for the cawing of the ever-present crows that had learned to follow armies a thousand years earlier. The young man's imaginative intellect filled the stunted woods with black, beady eyes that followed their passage. No stranger to the gloom of forests, Bedwyr felt at home in the dim, sea-green light, and gained confidence from the old trees that were twisted by the sea gales into strange, humanoid forms that rattled their leafy branches as the riders passed by.

Within four hours, they saw smoke rising above the tree line, and Bedwyr's ears caught the sound of running water, of a river, and the muted rumble of the nearby ocean.

The two warriors halted and dismounted to survey the terrain ahead of them.

Satisfied, Alun gathered his reins and remounted, indicating that Bedwyr should do the same.

"The smoke that we can see is from Artor's camp," Alun said, "but I can't begin to guess where Glamdring's men are. I can feel eyes watching us, and my back already feels the bite of an arrow. We shall have to ride for our lives from this point onwards, even if our horses die in the run. We go by the open road, so you must keep up. Hear me? I don't propose to stop if you should fall."

Bedwyr merely grunted, and settled his nervous horse. "Good. I'm sick of hiding. May the gods judge the justice of our cause."

Before Alun could take the lead, Bedwyr whipped his horse with his reins, and it sprang into a gallop.

The beasts bunched their thigh muscles and broke from cover, sending a flock of complaining crows flapping from the trees. Crouched over his horse's neck, Bedwyr urged his steed to greater efforts. The track was so muddy that he chose the slopes above the dragon's spore, with Alun directly behind him. A thin whistling sound came from the woods on their flank and a shaft hit the neck of his mount. The arrow was almost spent and caused the animal to check its stride only momentarily.

Bedwyr didn't hesitate, but plucked the shaft free. Blood welled from the slight wound.

He sank his heels into the ribs of his stallion, and the beast resumed its mile-devouring gallop. Other arrows fell around them, but they had been fired from an extreme distance and were spent. Other than one that grazed Bedwyr's cheek in passing, the shafts fell harmlessly away.

Even at full gallop, the two horsemen could see warriors on the fringes of Artor's camp stir like disturbed ants as they prepared to repel enemy riders.

"We are friends!" Alun screamed, and waved his free arm. "Friends from Gawayne! Make way! Make way! Gawayne! Gawayne!"

Several warriors planted their long rectangular shields in the mud, but Bedwyr and Alun paid them no mind and continued to urge their mounts towards the obstruction. Up rose the beasts, lifting their deceptively delicate forelegs to leap the line of shields. And then they were inside the camp, where grim men ran to surround them in a ring of cold iron.

Bedwyr dragged his horse to a shuddering halt, followed by a pale-faced Alun. Bedwyr stroked the bleeding neck of his faltering beast, threw the reins to a waiting warrior, and lithely leapt to the ground. The guards could see the bloodstained rags that bound his feet and the scars that covered his body.

"Have one of your men see to my horse's wound, for he's served me well and I'd not wish harm to him. And escort me to an audience with the High King." He smiled at the warrior with unconscious charm. "I bear tidings for King Artor from Glamdring Ironfist."

Artor had observed the mad gallop of the two horsemen as they approached the encampment. He recognized the second of the riders as one of Gawayne's Otadini warriors, and he had also observed the hail of arrows that had sped after them, reaching almost to the defensive wall of Mori Saxonicus itself. Myrddion stood beside the High King, counting the bowshots and estimating their number, for this skirmish was the first time that Artor's encampment had been under any attack, even one as feeble as this.

"There are at least six archers in the trees. They're probably in the branches, as the arrows are aimed downward," Myrddion stated. "I'll let Gruffydd know. He'll soon have them winkled out."

Artor nodded economically. "Who's the scarecrow on the leading horse?" he asked. "He rides like a man possessed. Bring him to me. We may need Gruffydd to translate if he's a Saxon, although why a Saxon would wish to enter my encampment beggars the imagination."

When Myrddion approached the strange-looking man, he was being shouted at by an enraged Luka, to whom he had thrown the reins of his horse.

"I'm not your stable boy, you impertinent scrag! And nobody speaks to the High King until I decide they'll be no threat to his person."

In his fury, Luka was even more obstinate than usual, and his eyes were mere slits in his dark, scowling face. The new arrival was going nowhere without his approval. On the other hand, the ragged warrior stood pugnaciously with his feet slightly apart and his hands planted belligerently on his hips. His jaw was thrust forward in an obvious challenge to the older man's authority.

"I've traveled on foot and by horseback from Caer Fyrddin. At some cost, I've escaped from the Saxon hive, and I can assure you that the High King will not thank you if you keep me from him." Twin spots of color burned on the stranger's sunburned cheeks and his eyes, more hazel than brown, threatened imminent bloodletting.

"Please, Bedwyr!" Alun pleaded vainly, and tried to pull him away from an increasingly angry Luka, who had half drawn his knife from its scabbard. "You don't know who you offend with your insults."

Bedwyr used his superior muscle to throw off the clutching hand of the taller warrior. "If he isn't King Artor, I don't care who he is. My message must not wait while dullards decide if I am fit to enter the presence of the great man. Yes, I'm ragged. And I'm dirty too, no doubt. And Prince Gawayne told me I smell, and I believe him. But Artor alone will know how to use the information I bring."

Luka pulled out his dagger with a venomous little hiss. "Whoever you are, I stand first in line, and I claim the right to add a second mouth to your throat. You insult Luka, King of the Brigante, and a member of the High Council of King Artor. No doubt you are hell-bent on offending anyone who gets in your way, but on this occasion you chose the wrong man to treat like a slave."

Luka dropped the reins with disdain, and Bedwyr flushed a little under his tan. Myrddion approached the young stranger on silent feet and made a small gesture to one of the warriors, who bent to retrieve the reins.

The horses were led away.

A little shame-faced, Bedwyr made a rather belated, indifferent bow to Luka.

"I offer my apologies, my lord, but my horse is wounded and my message has still not been relayed to the High King. I am impatient after years of inaction. Courtesy must wait on necessity as I must see the High King immediately. When King Artor has learned what I have to tell him, you may kill me any way you choose—if you can!"

"Sir, you are an impudent son of—"

Luka was robbed of any chance to instruct Bedwyr on his mother's chosen occupation by Myrddion, who cut into the discussion, raising his voice to drown out the shouts of the two men. Bedwyr was alarmed that Myrddion had approached so near to him unnoticed.

"Shut up, Luka! And you too, young man, whoever you are! You will keep a civil tongue in your head or Luka will cut you into ribbons. I am Myrddion Merlinus, and I come from the High King himself."

Bedwyr continued to struggle against Alun's restraining arms. In his anger, he scarcely heard the last part of Myrddion's message.

"He can try! Even if he *is* a king, he'll have to work hard to kill me off. And my mother was a decent woman, wife to a Cornovii chieftain. I'll not have her slighted."

"Enough!" Myrddion roared, using that particular gift of tone and volume that demanded instant obedience. "If ever a young man warranted my turning him into a toad or a snake, it's you, you dolt! Have done! Now!" He turned to Luka. "It's obvious that this cub had no idea who you are, Luka, so it's pointless to take offense. And shouting is unseemly for a king."

Luka looked chastened and sheathed his knife.

"You!" Myrddion pointed at Bedwyr. "Follow me!"

"I'm coming too," Luka insisted. "This bundle of rags is not to be trusted." He was spoiling for a fight; the whole camp had been on edge for days.

"Whatever you wish, Luka. But I suggest you leave your bad temper here before you see Artor. He's not in the mood. Try and behave like adults, both of you."

Myrddion strode off, disapproval evident in every line of his body.

"That's told us." Bedwyr grinned, and Luka found himself smiling as well.

"He takes the role of king's adviser and sorcerer very seriously," Luka explained. "You weren't very civil to him."

"Oh." Out of long habit, Bedwyr crossed himself in the Roman manner, although his faith was fractured. Luka's doubts about the young man's motives fell away, for Saxons didn't pretend to be Christian—ever.

Artor had seen the fracas from the knoll, and he was irritated. No word had come from Glamdring Ironfist, and the High King had begun to fear that his strategy was flawed. His temper was strained to breaking point, and his gaze was particularly cold.

Bedwyr had only to see Artor's remarkable hair and the king's great height to believe that all the rumors concerning his liege were true. He fell to his knees in the trampled grass and pressed his forehead into the dirt. His heart beat so quickly that he feared it would escape from his chest.

"My lord king," he murmured as he attempted to kiss Artor's foot.

"Rise, man," Artor responded gruffly and impatiently, clearly embarrassed by Bedwyr's homage. "Who are you? Clearly, you're not a Celt!"

Bedwyr drew himself to his full height of five feet seven inches, a respectable height for a Briton, although his king dwarfed him. His whole body bridled with insult.

"Sire, I am of the Cornovii tribe, and I was born near the forests of Arden in the north. My name is Bedwyr, son of Bedwyr, Chieftain of Letocetum on the Roman road to Viroconium. My family have been the guardians of Arden for time beyond time, and our stewardship of the forest is our greatest honor."

"My apologies, young man, if I have insulted you. But you must admit that you appear the veriest savage. Still, I was hasty and foolish, for Saxons don't ride near as well as you." Artor grinned suddenly and even his grey eyes warmed. "One day you may tell your children that you caught the great Artor in a fundamental error of logic."

Suddenly, as he basked in the warmth of the High King's charm, Bedwyr was robbed of his fluency. Confusion furrowed his brow, and devotion, and he would have abased himself again had Artor not physically restrained him.

"There will be no more bowing and scraping, for I hate all that fuss. Now, how did the Saxons capture you? From your look, I assume you were forced into slavery."

Bedwyr sighed and began the story of his captivity all over again. As he spoke, his eyes kept returning to the edge of the forest.

"I begged my father to send me to Viroconium, and from there, under King Llanwith's orders, to the border at Castell Collen. Saxons ambushed my companions, but I'd been hunting, and I managed to evade the terrible deaths suffered by my friends. I won't speak of what I saw the Saxons do to the Ordovice warriors, for I would rather hold those hideous memories in my heart until someone dies for it."

"Go on," Myrddion ordered.

"I was taken alive and was presented to Glamdring Ironfist as a gift. To reach his fortress, I was forced to run all the way to Caer Fyrddin without faltering. I succeeded, and became Glamdring's slave, his dog."

Myrddion mentally reviewed the distance between Castell Collen and Caer Fyrddin, and granted Bedwyr considerable unspoken respect.

Gruffydd was not so easily deceived by the cheapness of words. He walked round the younger man, his sharp eyes examining the scars, bruises, and scrapes that could be seen.

"Forgive me, Bedwyr, but the king must know of your wounds." And without warning, Gruffydd tore the young man's tunic from neck to hem so that it fell and pooled at his feet.

Of those present, Artor alone gazed dispassionately at the marks of violence on Bedwyr's body, overlaid by new scars and bruises. The mark of the slave collar was clear, and the scar tissue would never fade. The spear scar, twin to Gruffydd's own, was also very obvious on Bedwyr's chest. Then, the young man turned, so Artor and his advisers could see his back.

"Bring the boy something to cover himself, Gruffydd," Artor ordered impassively. "I can see that you were a slave, Bedwyr, and one of many years' standing. I'm surprised that you are alive."

Bedwyr frowned. "How could I die while Glamdring Ironfist still lived?"

When no one answered, Bedwyr lurched back into speech, no longer careful of his words and nearly weeping with anger.

"I am near to two and twenty, my king, and no longer a boy. I've seen too much, and heard things that shouldn't be heard. I am here to tell you of the words and deeds of Glamdring Ironfist so that you may grind him into his own filth. I know Caer Fyrddin intimately, for slaves are aware of everything that takes place within their prison, if they wish to remain alive. You may ask of me what you will."

"Then speak, Bedwyr, for I am listening."

Gruffydd returned, and Artor spread the rich woolen cloak his sword-bearer had brought across Bedwyr's shoulders with his own hands, a signal mark of honor that Bedwyr ignored in his passion and obsession.

"Glamdring has been waiting for more than a week, with his blood boiling. He longs to kill you in battle, but Wyrr, his sorcerer, counseled patience. Up until yesterday, that is. But Wyrr has been killed, and Glamdring will be upon you within hours. Wyrr was a dangerous man, for he calmed Glamdring's excesses of temper and guided the battle plans of the Saxon thane."

Artor raised one amber eyebrow.

"I killed Wyrr at the gates of Caer Fyrddin. I hadn't planned to murder him, so I can't take any credit for this lucky chance. He was an evil, stunted thing, but he was very clever, and he exerted great influence over Glamdring, who is a brute at heart. He was almost supernatural in his cleverness, and I suppose he had to hone his mind because his body was so weak and fragile. Without Wyrr's moderating influence, Glamdring Ironfist will come raging out of his hills and attempt to batter you into submission. The thane has no subtlety, just wild courage and fury."

"He can try." Artor grinned. He looked around him. "We'll teach the Saxons that we used the shield wall before we learned its true usefulness from our Roman enemies. We'll take Glamdring's primitive strategy and ram it down his throat."

A short while later, Artor seated himself on his campaign chair, which was so similar to the curule throne used by Caesar many centuries earlier. He began to issue his instructions, and servants and councillors alike scurried to do his bidding.

"Luka, you will review our defensive plans for this encampment. Obviously, we cannot rely on Glamdring attacking only by day, so make preparations for repelling a night attack. Targo has drilled the men daily in implementing the shield wall, which will be our prime tactical maneuver once Glamdring commits himself to battle. Hopefully, we will give our Saxon friends a lesson in battle craft."

Then Artor turned to a scar-faced, one-eyed man who was dressed incongruously in puce wool under a gilded breastplate.

"Pelles, the archers are yours to command. You will hold them in readiness behind the main line of our warriors, for they'll harvest the

Saxons before a single blow is struck. The baggage wagons will provide the height they'll need to comply with my wishes.

"Gruffydd, take seven men into the hills immediately after darkness falls and clean out that pocket of archers who are just beyond the boundaries of our encampment.

"Bedwyr, you may join Gruffydd's party once you have finished speaking to Myrddion. I assume you speak fluent Saxon?"

"Like a native, my lord," Bedwyr answered dryly, a little awed by Artor's crisp grasp of the situation.

"Myrddion, pick Bedwyr's mind clean of everything of importance about the layout of Caer Fyrddin and its defenses. You can also draw up battle plans for later consideration. The fortress will have to wait until we defeat its master. But once this battle is finished, I intend to attack Caer Fyrddin and burn it to the ground."

"Aye!" a chorus of obedience rang out.

"Now, tell me about Glamdring, Bedwyr. You were his slave, so you must know him better than most men. Can he defeat me? And, if so, how will he achieve his objective?"

"He has more than eight hundred tried and tested warriors, my lord, plus a number of able men who have been recruited in recent weeks. You have a little over two hundred warriors here, if my estimates are correct. Would that be a true assessment?"

Artor nodded.

"My opinion is that Glamdring cannot defeat you, for Wyrr is dead and the thane relied on him in every way. He'll try to bludgeon you into submission by attacking in force, but his impetus will be fueled by rage and the cruelty that multiplies within him, not by reason. The strength of his force will shake your camp to its foundations, and he will kill many of your warriors, but superstition will blind his eyes when he attempts to strike at your heart."

"Why?" Artor asked softly. He was impressed with this new ally, a young warrior with a mind completely unbowed by unrelenting abuse that would have broken a lesser man.

"The thane has placed all his trust in Wyrr's prophecy regarding the Arden Knife. Wyrr had a vision that this knife would be Glamdring's nemesis if he didn't hold the weapon close to his breast. Neither Glamdring nor Wyrr seemed to remember that the Arden Knife was my property, and that it was copied from a sacred relic of my tribe. The knife that Wyrr described was taken from me when I was first captured by the Saxon warriors, and it's been in Glamdring's possession ever since." Bedwyr smiled directly at his king. "However, what Glamdring and Wyrr didn't understand was that the Arden Knife is not a physical weapon that can be held in the hands and used to kill or maim an enemy. I, Bedwyr ap Bedwyr, am the Arden Knife! I am the heir to the forests of Arden, and I was born to be its protector." Bedwyr's face was stern and his eyes glittered. "And I, Bedwyr ap Bedwyr, will kill Glamdring before this campaign is completed."

Momentarily, Artor regretted the softness that had been beaten out of this fine young man, but, spoiled or not, Bedwyr was a particularly effective weapon that had come fortuitously into his armory.

"Then let us be about it. Killing weather is here, and the Saxons are coming to demand their share. Even the birds seem to know it." Artor smiled grimly at his assembled captains before turning to Luka. "Gawayne, Llanwith, and Lot must return immediately to this command. Send two determined couriers by different routes to each troop with their orders. I need them to return at speed, for I expect their commands to have Glamdring's force penned in within four days. Is that understood?"

There was no disagreement from Luka, or any further questioning from his audience.

"Come then. Gaheris is watching from Hades, and our swords are thirsty for Saxon blood."

The audience was over.

The camp boiled as the well-ordered machinery of Artor's army prepared for battle, and Myrddion began to pick Bedwyr's mind clean of his intimate knowledge of Caer Fyrddin. Then, at last, Bedwyr was free to find food and rest before he joined Gruffydd to hunt for Saxon archers in the hills.

"Artor always plans many steps ahead, Bedwyr," Myrddion told him before he went. "It could be worth your while to watch and to learn from a master strategist."

Night had fallen when Bedwyr joined Gruffydd and his small band of hunters as they slid into the trees beyond Artor's camp. They were dressed in Saxon clothing to confuse the enemy if they were discovered.

"We're hunting for Saxons, Bedwyr. I trust you have the stomach for it." Gruffydd bared his breast so that Bedwyr could see the old scar in the dim light. Bedwyr realized that fate had drawn them together at this unpromising place so that both men could lay their years of slavery to rest.

"It's a very good night to die, brother," Bedwyr replied. "So let us be about our lord's business. I am impatient to kill Saxons."

"Just be quiet about it," Gruffydd grinned wolfishly, "and you shall have your fill of them."

The night swallowed the whole group, and no sound warned that midnight hunters were abroad. Only the owls marked their passing, and, true to the Celtic goddess who ruled them, they did not warn the Saxons that death was abroad, and that it was eager for satiation.

Myrddion's Record of the Campaign
Against Glamdring Ironfist

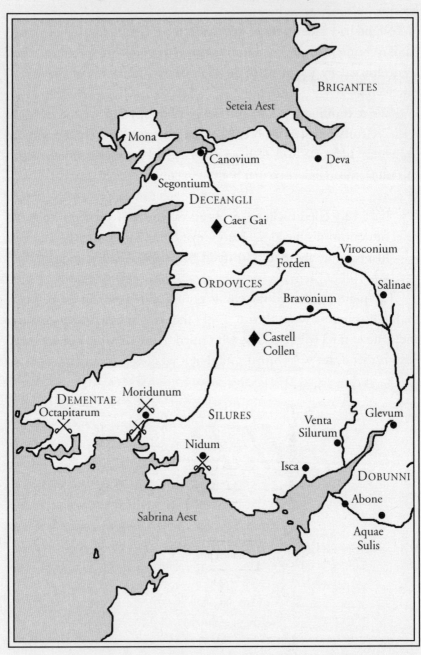

The Battle of Mori Saxonicus

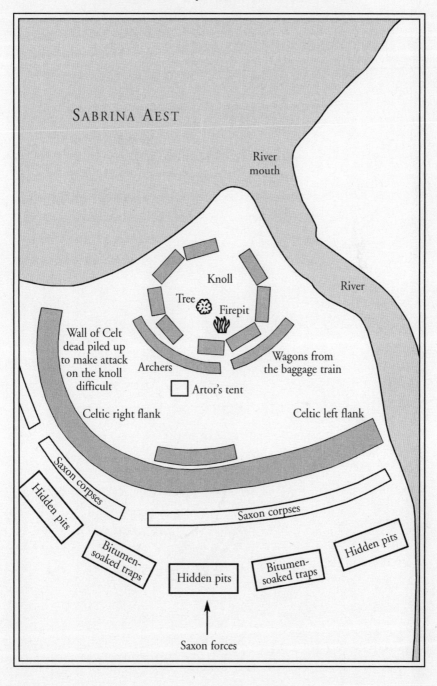

SABRINA AEST

River mouth

Knoll

Tree

Firepit

River

Wall of Celt dead piled up to make attack on the knoll difficult

Archers

Wagons from the baggage train

Artor's tent

Celtic right flank

Celtic left flank

Saxon corpses

Hidden pits

Saxon corpses

Bitumen-soaked traps

Hidden pits

Bitumen-soaked traps

Hidden pits

Saxon forces

Chapter VIII

THE RIVER WALL

Bedwyr waited, as still as a stone.

His patience was eventually rewarded by the noise of movement in a tree a hundred feet from him, more sensed than heard through the intervening distance. His acute night vision made out a dark, crouched figure that had appeared initially to be a bole in the thick trunk of the tree.

Bedwyr slid silently through the underbrush. Woodcraft had come back to him as naturally as breathing, so deeply was it ingrained in his nature.

At the foot of the tree, he rose to his full height. He could feel, and hear, an arrow notched and pointing at his breast.

"I have a message from Glamdring. Can I come up the tree to you?" he hissed in Saxon.

The man above remained silent. He was obviously confused and uncertain at the sudden appearance of a Saxon in these Celtic woods.

"Ironfist is coming to join us in a short while. Let me climb," Bedwyr hissed with greater urgency.

"Aye." The single word of agreement was sufficient to send Bedwyr clambering up the tree with all the agility of a boy.

The youth, who had wedged himself between three sturdy

branches, was little more than seventeen years old. He was a peasant, judging by his rough woolen clothing and lack of ornamentation.
When he saw Bedwyr's Saxon clothing, the boy's reservations disappeared, and the Celt felt a brief pang of guilt as he cut the lad's unsus-
pecting throat, immediately after the boy had revealed the hiding place
of the next bowman in the line.

Bedwyr carefully cleaned his knife on the boy's cloak, wedged his
body securely into the tree's fork, and took the dead man's bow and
arrows before passing silently onto the next archer.

After he had killed three men, Bedwyr returned to the rendezvous
point. His victims had been a boy and two aging men, testament to
Wyrr's tactics of using unpromising or useless fighting resources to
hide in the trees. Gruffydd and his men had also been busy, and had
contrived to find another seven bowmen in the forest. Finding the
Saxons had proved all too simple, and was almost too clinical to be
sporting. But their bows were long and surprisingly sophisticated, begging the question as to why the Saxons did not use these devastating
weapons more effectively.

"The Saxon peasants use their longbows as hunting tools rather
than fighting weapons," Gruffydd whispered to Bedwyr. "Its range
is remarkable, but the Saxon chiefs seem to consider such weapons
cowardly. We're fortunate that Glamdring isn't using a proper force of
trained bowmen to guard the approaches to our defensive positions,
for he could keep many of our warriors pinned down and ineffective with good archers, especially during daylight hours. And you, my
friend, might not have been so lucky when you charged headlong into
Artor's encampment right under their noses."

"Those bastards almost caught me when Alun and I made that
last dash for Artor's camp," Bedwyr hissed. "Do you see how far
we are from the shield wall? Those bows are a devastating weapon.
The force and range of their arrows makes our weapons fit for small
children."

"More to the point, Alun and the other couriers ride after moon-
rise. We have no time left to ensure that we've cleaned out these sod-

ding trees." Gruffydd swore with an old soldier's creativity. "If those riders don't get through, then we're sunk."

"I'm sure we found them all," Bedwyr whispered confidently, but, nonetheless, he peered into the dark treetops with eyes that strained to catch the slightest movement.

Bedwyr had no sooner stopped speaking than a horseman burst out of the encampment at full gallop.

It was Alun, riding to deliver Artor's summons to Gawayne.

As he passed a particularly thick copse of oaks, a bowstring sang and Alun slumped momentarily on the back of his horse. He clutched at his arm, snapped an invisible arrow shaft, and continued his headlong and dangerous passage through the darkness.

"Shite!" Gruffydd swore. "We've missed one of the bastards. Find him, Kennett, and don't be tardy about it."

He turned to Bedwyr.

"Bedwyr, take our spoils back to camp and inform Artor that we will remain here to keep the trees clean of Saxons for as long as we can. Tell him that Garun has seen fires in the hills, so the arrival of the Saxons is imminent."

"Take care of your head, old man," Bedwyr answered with a grin, receiving a painful, affectionate cuff in response. He snaked away into the darkness.

"That boy has a talent for the hunt," Gruffydd muttered to no one in particular.

Bedwyr was almost killed out of hand by a jumpy sentry as he slithered over a ditch and up into the no-man's-land that surrounded the Celtic force. Only quick talking, and the cluster of bows strung and carried over his shoulder, saved his head from a radical parting from his neck.

As he hurried towards Artor's tent, Bedwyr detoured to the smaller, but more exotic, quarters of Pelles, captain of the archers.

Although Pelles had no aristocratic pretensions, he loved ostentation and had earned the right to indulge his tastes through the force of his talents and deeds. Bedwyr almost laughed outright at a leather tent liberally painted and dyed with humorous designs of griffins. Inside, his quarters boasted a gilded lamp that hung from the central support, a profusion of fine wine jugs, goblets, platters, furs, and clothing chests that seemed incongruous encumbrances on a long campaign. However, in all fairness to Pelles, a folding table in the tent was laden with fine bows of different designs, feathers for fletching his arrows, and a small pile of arrowheads, all of which were shining and well tended.

Pelles was still awake. A battle was looming and the old campaigner was busy reviewing the disposition of his archers and the complicated methods of ensuring that their quivers were well supplied with arrows. Archers without weapons were so much dead wood in a battle.

Bedwyr marveled at Pelles's advanced age and his disreputable appearance. The old man had an impressive array of sword scars in addition to his blinded eye, which, fortunately, was not the orb he used to aim his arrows. He was dressed in fine wool edged with cloth of gold, a garb that was more ostentatious than anything Bedwyr had seen on Artor's tall frame. However, there was nothing clownish or laughable about Pelles, for all that he still carried the nickname of Pinhead. His years sat on him with a rich patina of experience, rather than age, and a ratlike intelligence shone out of his one brown eye.

"So you're the Celtic slave I've been hearing about," Pelles began with scant consideration for Bedwyr's feelings. "I wouldn't like to survive living with the Saxons for so long. You're either a man of great patience or you're a coward. Which one is it?"

"You be the judge, old man."

Ignoring the sudden red haze of anger in the bowman's one good eye, Bedwyr dumped ten longbows and quivers of arrows onto Pelles's folding table.

The bowman's mood changed immediately. He stroked the exquisitely laminated wood of a bow that was fully five feet long.

"The men who owned these bows are all dead," Bedwyr stated.

"I've heard of these beauties," Pelles murmured. He rose to his feet, all thoughts of insult now forgotten. "They're massive, damn near as tall as I am, and they must be a bugger to draw."

160

"I'm no bowman, I'm afraid, so I don't know." Bedwyr shrugged. "But the archers we killed were all boys and old men, so you tell me how strong you must be to use them."

Pelles drew back the gut string to its fullest extent and, for the first time, Bedwyr saw the half glove on Pelles's scarred hand and the fine leather arm guard that covered his whole lower arm from wrist to elbow.

"Damnation, but this bow is lovely to hold. The range must be incredible. And the Saxons have these? Why in the name of Tartarus don't they use them?"

"The men I killed were peasants, so perhaps a Saxon warrior considers the use of a bow to be lacking in dignity," Bedwyr replied, amused by Pelles's reverence for these sweetly shaped yew weapons. "It would mean killing from a distance. With one of these you can't get up close and sweaty."

"Then the Saxons are fools!" Pelles whispered as he stroked the bow with the same affection that he would bestow on a beautiful woman. "I'll have them—and gladly. Given time, every man in my ranks will carry such a bow. And they're made of yew!"

Pelles was still caressing the bows, marveling at their workmanship and muttering under his breath in excitement, as Bedwyr backed out of his tent.

Artor was also awake, for a glint of light showed through the flap of his tent. As Bedwyr attempted to gain entrance, he was almost gutted by Odin. Artor was forced to call the giant Jutlander off the supine Bedwyr.

"Gruffydd has ordered me to report that the woods are now clear of bowmen, but that cooking fires are burning on the nearest hills," Bedwyr said flatly, still a little awed by the speed and ferocity of the reaction of Artor's bodyguard. "He's convinced that Glamdring will be here within hours."

A wizened old man in a Roman cuirass sat up sharply from a straw pallet in a corner of the tent.

"Ironfist won't rest his troops, boy," the old man advised matter-of-factly. "He will want to surprise you before daylight. Perhaps his fires are designed to have you think he's still in the hills when he's actually closer to us than we expect."

"Aye, Targo," Artor replied thoughtfully. "I'd consider it myself if I were in his place."

"No, you wouldn't." Targo laughed abruptly. "Only a desperate fool would rush blindly onto alien ground."

Bedwyr rubbed his tired eyes. This ancient was obviously Artor's sword master, the man who had made his royal pupil the greatest warrior in the west. Truly, Bedwyr thought, there are legends to be found wherever I look in this desolate place.

"Lord Pelles has the Saxon longbows, my king," he said. "I left him caressing them as if they were beautiful young girls."

"That Pinhead!" Targo grunted. "No wonder he's lived so long. He has a fine palate for exceptional weapons."

"Excellent," Artor said. "You'd best get some sleep, Bedwyr, and Odin will find some suitable armor and weapons for you. Frankly, you stink in that Saxon garb."

Artor was, as ever, blunt and to the point when it came to battle matters.

Bedwyr washed in the river using oil and an old strigil supplied by Odin, who seemed able to magically conjure up any much-needed supplies at short notice. On the bank, Odin placed a rather worn cuirass, a helmet, and clothing. He had also found a serviceable rectangular shield, a Roman short sword, a whetstone, and a wicked, rather worn dagger.

Even in the dark, and in the chill of the brackish water, Bedwyr felt lighthearted as he sloughed away the last, lingering traces of his captivity. River sand scoured his flesh until it was as rosy and as clean as when he was first born. He scrubbed his hair and scraped away the first signs of his beard with his knife, specially honed for this duty. Although the Cornovii warriors normally wore beards, Bedwyr vowed to be clean-chinned like his king, although the thought of plucking his beard filled him with a frisson of horror.

Bedwyr scorned to use his discarded Saxon garb to dry his shivering body, preferring to tug on leggings, a woolen undershirt, and a leather jerkin over his wet flesh. For the first time since his escape from Glamdring's citadel, Bedwyr felt like a true Celt. Gathering up his cuirass, his Roman shield, and his worn weapons, he made his way to the nearest campfire.

Bedwyr knew he should try to sleep, but his weapons were strange to him. Odin later reported to Artor that the young man sat cross-legged near the dying fire and honed his weapons to razor sharpness, even the copper edge of his metal-clad shield.

Artor grinned. "There's nothing like a sharp shield edge rammed under the chin to give the enemy an instant jaw ache—if there's any jaw left."

Odin laughed, a rare response. The Jutlander had taken to chewing twigs and charcoal like his master, and his teeth were unexpectedly white behind his reddish beard.

"The lad has possibilities, Odin, but he is untested in battle. We shall see how he fares."

Odin nodded.

"Soon, Odin, soon," Artor murmured, and lowered his head onto his arms on the table. "Wake me at first light."

Around him, the camp seemed to be sleeping, but the eyes of many men looked to their weapons or attempted to pierce the heavy darkness. The hours of early morning had come, that time when warriors dream of death, and many of the men preferred to remain wakeful.

Without the disturbance or solace of dreams, Artor slept with the intensity and innocence of a child, with only Targo and Odin to watch his back for any hint of danger.

THICK FOG SHROUDED the camp, the river, and the strip of land between the sea and the forests. The saturated air was clammy, like a drowned man's touch, and Artor's troops felt the first stirrings of fear.

They suspected that Glamdring Ironfist's army could be upon them before the sun burnt off the mist.

Artor was awake and fully armed before first light. True to his promise, he had painted his face with blue woad and white clay so that a skull peered forth at the emerging day. He had ordered his standard unfurled, and it now stirred and undulated in the barely perceptible sea breeze that had brought the fog rolling down upon them. The men looked up at the rampant Red Dragon of Britain on its hindmost limbs, and took heart at the sight. Then they too painted their faces.

The High King strode, fully armed, towards the place where the shield wall would stand, with Targo and Odin dogging his heels. Wherever he passed, he ordered fires to be doused and men to hurry to their defensive positions.

Pelles had positioned his archers on the slight rise above the flat ground at the rear of the assembled force. Kneeling in rows, in the Roman fashion, they rested and waited, knowing that the prize of the first Saxon blood would be theirs. Pelles had set up his own smaller standard, a fanciful beast composed of many creatures, part snake, part horse, and part snapping reptile; his men took pride in being the children of the Chimera, as Pelles called his emblem.

At the rear, immediately behind the wagons, Myrddion and his healers were stoking their fires and making preparations for their role in the coming battle. Long tongues of metal were already heated to a dull cherry red within the coals, for only white-hot metal would cauterize a bleeding wound that imperiled life. The simples and remedies of his craft were laid out in pots in neat rows on the flat bottom of one of the supply wagons. Metal bowls, pincers, some evil-looking needles, and a large mortar and pestle were also close to hand. Fastidious as always, Myrddion had donned a leather apron that covered his arms, torso and legs. He knew that he would soon be bathing in blood, so his white hair was plaited away from his face in a long tail down his back. If he sorrowed already for the friends who would die, he refused to allow his sadness to show upon his serene face.

At the very edge of his defensive line, Artor's men massed. On

Targo's orders, the warriors had formed a living wall, with the tips of their rectangular shields buried in the soft sward and their bodies crouched behind them in the fashion devised by Caesar so many centuries before.

Targo issued orders that long spears were to be thrust between the shields so that any attackers would face a wicked forest of iron.

A second row of defenders stood behind the first. Their shields were tilted to protect the heads of the first line while still covering the exposed upper bodies of their bearers. Yet a third line of men stood behind these men and their shields were raised above their heads to form a solid wedge of wood and iron. Long ago, the Roman legions had named this tactic the tortoise for its impervious shell of iron.

"Rest!" Targo ordered, when he was eventually satisfied that the erstwhile cavalry understood the principles of siege warfare. "There's no need to tire yourselves out before Ironfist decides to make his entrance."

Artor stood bareheaded with Targo behind the third row of defenders. Luka was positioned on the left flank, with the river at his side. Artor had sent Odin to support Caius in securing the right flank. Their orders were to hold their position at all cost, even to the last man. Caius had grinned fiercely at his brother's orders, and Artor was disconcerted that something joyous glistened in Caius's eyes.

Never mind, Artor thought. If blood lust makes him a better commander, then I should be grateful for his services to our cause.

The ocean formed the ultimate barrier beyond their wall of iron, and the riverbanks were on their left flank.

"Well, my lad, we're as ready as we shall ever be," Targo informed his king with a satisfied smile. "All we await now is the arrival of our guest of honor. If he had any sense, he'd come through this damned fog like the Furies, hoping to catch us unawares."

"He wants us to know we are outnumbered, more to bolster his own confidence through our terror," Artor replied. "Even Glamdring Ironfist must have his doubts from time to time. After all, he is a mortal man, with the fears that afflict all leaders. We have one edge, courtesy of Bedwyr, for Glamdring has lost the advantage of surprise and that Wyrr creature who gave him such excellent counsel and balance."

"And where is our young assassin?" Targo asked cautiously. He still didn't entirely trust the Cornovii.

Artor pointed to the ranks of soldiers as they waited in a tight row, their bodies taut and their eyes constantly on the move as they probed the mist around them. Bedwyr had chosen to fight in the front row, at the very center of the line where the attack would be fiercest.

"That boy either yearns for death or he has a great deal of hate in his heart," Targo commented.

"The latter, I should think, for he'll bear the scar of that collar until death overtakes him. He hates near as hard as Caius."

"Hmph! I'd have thought him a better man than Caius," Targo retorted.

"I'm sure he is. And if he should live, I will make good use of him. The Cornovii have been constant friends, and it is my good fortune that I now possess the Arden Knife."

"Beware of hubris, my friend," Targo warned, his face creased with concern. "Bedwyr is a man, not a tool to be used and then discarded."

"I am. Every day. But for now, I'm beginning to wish that something would happen."

The pale sun rose weakly through the mist, but the thick air deadened all sound except for the seabirds who wheeled and screamed as they squabbled over shellfish on the pebbled beach behind them.

Suddenly, a scream gurgled out of the dense whiteness. It was abruptly cut off.

"One of our friendly visitors seems to have found a pit," Artor said softly.

"Hold firm in the ranks," Targo barked, although he took care to keep his voice low. "God rot this fog. I can barely see the first defensive line."

"The sun is beginning to rise now, Targo, so we should soon have better vision."

A stiff breeze suddenly rattled the standards. Luka's green serpent coiled and uncoiled on the left, and the eagle of Caius spread its brazen wings on the right. Abruptly, in that moment of chance that all warriors welcome, the sea breeze freshened and the cloying mist was blown away into rags of leprous grey air.

A vast horde stood massed only one hundred yards away.

"To your positions, you sons of whores!" Targo screamed, and Artor's trumpets repeated the order.

Artor turned and raised his gloved fist.

"Pelles!" he roared. "Make the Saxons bleed! Remember the innocents of Y Gaer!"

The first row of bowmen stood, drew their bowstrings back to their fullest extent, and sent a withering volley of arrows into the massed body of the Saxon host.

Without even pausing to see the damage caused by their arrows, the first row knelt and the second row notched their arrows and fired on Pelles's orders.

Likewise, the third row fired in their turn.

"Cease fire," Artor screamed.

The hail of arrows had done a deadly service, but the damage was mostly superficial. The first volley had caught Ironfist's men unawares, and many had fallen in that initial withering rain of bolts. The second volley had caught those warriors too callow or too stupid to raise their bull hide and metal shields, but the third volley had simply skewered the warrior's defensive shields.

At the end of the fusillade, some fifty Saxons either lay still on the ground or writhed like broken-backed snakes in their agony.

"Well, that's a few less to kill," Targo said callously.

Artor grimaced. "I think there's probably another eight hundred or so to go."

"Artor!" roared a stentorian voice out of the press of Saxons that were now separating into long ranks of hulking warriors. "Whoreson! Interloper! Today you die! I, Ironfist, am here with a promise of death."

"Don't respond, Artor," Targo hissed.

"Do you think I'm in my dotage, old man?"

The Saxon warriors crouched into their fighting positions, their
axes and swords bright in the strengthening sunlight.

"Do you mean to skulk behind your warriors all day, Artor?"

The shouted words roared over the whimpers, curses, and moans
of the wounded.

"We will take your miserable shield wall and hang it about your
necks."

"You talk too much, Ironfist," a voice yelled from within the ranks
of Artor's wall. "Where is Wyrr? In what hell does he await you?"

Glamdring howled, extended one arm, and one wing of Saxon
warriors suddenly charged directly towards Artor's left flank.

"That sounded like Bedwyr. He knows how to sting Glamdring,
for he's sending his men straight towards the pits." Targo chuckled
mirthlessly.

A dozen Saxon warriors were killed as they fell through seemingly solid ground onto the wicked, sharpened stakes. The rest of the
attackers changed course, as Artor had intended, and continued their
assault on the center of that flank, right at the point where Artor's
defenses were deepest. The High King could hear Luka shouting over
the screams as the Celts used their spears to cut down the maddened
Saxons.

"Let Hades take them, Pelles," Artor roared, and the trumpets
sounded in unison. The Celts on the left flank enclosed themselves in
their iron shields as Pelles's men peppered any exposed Saxon breast,
head, or legs.

Glamdring attacked the right flank immediately in a direct frontal
charge, but the pits were found quickly, and a vicious engagement
commenced. Artor gave the order to fire, and Pelles's second line of
archers wheeled to cover the right-hand side of the defensive position.

Then, with a rush that made the ground shake, Glamdring led the
bulk of his troops straight through the middle to strike the very center
of Artor's defensive line.

They struck with the force of a wave, but the line managed to hold.
If one man fell, the man behind him stepped into the breach, and,

periodically, Pelles was ordered to send off a volley of fire arrows that had a withering effect on both friend and foe as concealed traps of pitch were lit. The tortoise maneuver saved the Celts from all but superficial injury, but the Saxons were soon running red with wounds or twisting in cloaks of flame.

But they would not disengage.

Like the tide from the sea that strikes against rocky headlands, the Saxons came again and again and yet again. Each Celtic loss was irreplaceable, but Glamdring spent his men like a drunkard wastes wine, in the full knowledge that he had the advantage of numbers. In the front line of defense, Bedwyr drove his sharpened shield up into several unprotected chins and felt the blood lust rise in him as arterial spray covered him from head to foot. If a man died beside him, he scarcely noticed. He stabbed with his spear until the shaft broke, and then he used the axe of a fallen Saxon with equal ferocity.

He hadn't watched the pig killers practice their skills for three long years for nothing. Now he swore at the Saxon warriors in their own tongue, maddening them with insults until knife, axe, or sword found an opening.

Then, as suddenly as his attack had begun, Glamdring called his men out of bowshot and back into the tree line.

Artor detailed two messengers to determine the casualties from the right and left flanks. He could see, well enough, the damage that had been wrought to his center.

"We will move back six spear lengths and pile the Saxon dead before us like a wall, leaving a corridor for the enemy to maneuver," Artor ordered brusquely. "Those warriors who are wounded are to be put out of their misery. No mercy! Glamdring's next attack will be a full frontal tactic to try to break our center, so make them climb over the corpses of their comrades in order to reach us."

Targo hurried to oversee the orderly movement of troops.

He soon organized the noncombatants into teams to remove the dead and the wounded. The Celtic dead were piled like cordwood to form a wall before the baggage train, a last line of defense, if needed, and protection for the healers working feverishly to provide succor for those wounded who could be saved. Like a well-oiled machine, Artor's army moved to obey, without question, without fear, and without qualm.

While Myrddion was hard at work with the bloody business of saving life, Pelles's men scouted among the dead for Saxon arrows. Meanwhile, Celts killed all wounded Saxons without compassion, taking care to stay out of arm's reach of each warrior. Saxons didn't die easily, and even a fatally wounded man would try to take an enemy with him into the darkness if he came within striking distance.

In the front line, Bedwyr eased his cramping muscles and checked his weapons with one eye cast towards the distant tree line where the Saxon host was sheltering. Beside him, a Brigante warrior cursed as he found a chip in his sword.

"Hades, shite, and damn all Saxons!" the warrior cursed with a lamentable lack of imagination. A rough piece of cloth angled across his face covering his cheekbones and nose, although the coarse dressing was much stained with blood.

"I've damaged my father's sword on a Saxon head," the Brigante muttered, disgust evident in every word and facial expression.

"Ah, but is the Saxon dead?" Bedwyr replied dryly as he cleaned his own blade with a strip of cloth torn from his tunic.

"Yes! But I caught the edge of his helmet when I swung. Sod it!"

Bedwyr examined the Brigante more closely. His woven cloak and pin, a massive golden ring, and a torc of considerable artistry marked the warrior as a man of note.

"You're bleeding," Bedwyr stated economically.

The Brigante swore again and untied his makeshift bandage. Across the tanned young face, a long, deep wound ran on a slight angle. The flesh gaped, especially on the cartilage on the nose, and Bedwyr decided that this warrior was a man of hard discipline to ignore the pain and slow seep of blood from such a wound.

"Well, Scarface, I suggest you ask the healers to stitch that Saxon love tap together, or it'll be poisoned by all this shit," Bedwyr's free hand pointed to the slurry of mud, blood, vomit, and feces that had turned the clean earth into the killing fields that surrounded the shield wall.

The Brigante cleared his throat and spat bloody sputum onto the soiled mud.

"Aye! It's stupid trying to kill Saxons when my nose is half off. Hold my place in the line, Arden Knife. I'll return before the Saxons find the nerve to come at us again."

Then, as an afterthought, he held out his sword hand in the ancient symbol of brotherhood.

"My name is Melwy of Verterae, and I'm proud to stand beside you."

Conscious of the honor offered to him, Bedwyr wiped his sword hand on his bloody tunic and gripped the Brigante's proffered hand and wrist.

"They'll be calling you Melwy Scarface from now on, I'm thinking, my friend. Aye! I'll hold your place in the line for you while Lord Merlinus gives you a new nose."

Both men laughed and Melwy ambled away, still ruefully examining his damaged blade.

As he sat in the mud and honed the edges of his sword while waiting for the next attack, Bedwyr marveled at the camaraderie of the battlefield. Men fought and suffered together, and the diversities of tribe, status, and wealth became mere affectations in the brotherhood of death.

Then Bedwyr forgot Melwy Scarface completely.

Artor had commenced the battle with two hundred and fifty effective warriors in his reduced command, apart from the fifty archers and another thirty noncombatants. A small group of camp followers, fierce women who followed their men onto the battlefield, assembled slings, stones, and even knives for the time when they would be needed. The High King had lost sixty men on the shield wall, a loss he couldn't sustain with every attack. The Saxon dead were now piled six feet high, but Glamdring's massed army seemed as large as ever as they recovered in the shelter of the trees.

Artor sighed. Three days was a very long time.

"Have no doubts, boy," Targo muttered as he pulled a strip of rag over a superficial wound on one arm. "I've slowed down a bit over the years, else I'd not have been touched. The battle goes well, Artor. We have lost one of ours to two of theirs in these first probes, but soon it will be one of ours to three of theirs. Your tactics have worked so far, boy, so you must have faith. Lot and Llanwith will come, and we will still be here to welcome them back into the fold."

The High King bit his lip. So far, he had not even had an opportunity to draw his sword, and he deplored the need for good men to die while he issued orders in relative safety.

He walked among the men and explained his plans to his warriors. If they could endure for two more days, Glamdring Ironfist would be caught in a destructive web of sharp iron. He would be finished, and they could return to their homes and a life of peace and plenty.

"I won't lie to you and say that this siege will be easy," he told them. "We could lose this battle, because we are gravely outnumbered. But I refuse to believe that Celtic hearts are less stubborn and disciplined than Saxon might. Let Glamdring batter against our defenses; we will not crumble. When the Saxons come again, I will fight with you if someone will lend me a spear and a shield."

"No, lord, no," one warrior called out. "You must control the battle, or we will all perish. We can hold. We *will* hold!"

Artor bowed his head in homage to the man's courage, and told his warriors how privileged he was to lead such exceptional patriots. He also explained Bedwyr's use of the sharpened shield edge as a weapon, and, after viewing the Cornovii, sticky with Saxon blood from head to toe, the waiting soldiers took out their whetstones and commenced working on the edges of their own shields.

Then, in the afternoon, shortly after each man had consumed his rations of stale bread, a heel of cheese, and clean water, the Saxons began their next attack.

Glamdring had been busy developing a new strategy. Perhaps the words of Gaheris had come back to haunt him, for this time his warriors were not at the point of the attack column. A line of peasant archers moved warily through the long grass to a point just out of reach of Pelles's conventional short bows, while the warriors of Glamdring's main force remained along the tree line just out of arrow range.

A fusillade of Saxon arrows struck the shield wall with such force that they almost passed completely through the wooden shields.

"Hell's kitchen!" Targo swore. "Those longbows are the work of a demon."

"Then it's handy that we have ten of them," Artor replied. "Pelles," he shouted to the commander of the bowmen. "Select your best men to use our longbows. Move them forward so that they are in the lee of the Saxon bodies. They can use them as a shield to pick Glamdring's archers off one by one. The Saxons are in the open and should be easy targets. Get to it."

Pelles took one of the bows for himself, and nine other exceptional archers were issued with the remaining weapons. Rushing forward to the protection of the barricades, each stood, unleashed an arrow, and then ducked back into safety.

Most of the arrows had not been pitched correctly and simply buried themselves harmlessly in the earth, but Pelles's aim was true.

The other archers quickly adjusted their trajectories to match the aim of their leader.

"That Pelles is worth his weight in gold ingots," Targo crowed as two more Saxon archers fell to the ground.

"Save it for later, Targo. Here they come again."

And so the whole, grim reaping of death began again. The battlefield had become a struggle of wills, of attrition, as both sides suffered losses, but the flower of west Saxon manhood was sacrificing itself on soil that was churned into red mud.

During the height of the battle, Artor heard a high-pitched whine, and something struck him hard under the arm in the narrow gap between his cuirasses and his shoulder greaves. He staggered backwards with the force of the blow and saw a feathered shaft protruding from the side of his shoulder.

"Dear Mithras!" Targo gasped. "You're hit!"

"Snap off the shaft and adjust my cloak over it. It doesn't matter if you hurt me. My men must see that I am standing with them."

Targo obeyed, although the wound made a strange sucking sound, and Artor was very pale. Targo gestured to Pelles, who summed up the situation in a glance. Ten pairs of eyes scanned the ground beyond the struggling morass of men until Pelles notched an arrow, lifted the longbow, and fired, all in one smooth action.

Targo watched the flight of the arrow and saw a rough-clad Saxon fall back against the wall of Saxon dead, skewered neatly through the throat by Pelles's shaft.

Targo grinned savagely and stood beside his king as he tried desperately to stay upright.

"At least the bastard who shot you is dead, but there could be others charged with doing the same thing. If you are killed, then we all lose. Can I call for Myrddion?" Targo begged.

"No. Not yet. My men will lose heart if I leave the field of battle, and, if that happens, Glamdring will defeat them. If the standard of the Red Dragon is fated to fall, it will not be because I ran from the field of combat at the first scratch. Let them try to kill me."

"Very well then, boy," Targo agreed. "But at least let me take some precautions."

A young messenger was acting as a courier between the two flanks of Artor's army, and Targo intercepted him, whispered in his ear, and sent him to Pelles.

Once he had heard the message, Pelles waved his arm in acknowledgment, and two of his archers with longbows scaled the mound of Celtic dead. Their task was to scan the field with arrows notched and ready to fire at any Saxon bowmen who should target Artor.

Meanwhile, the High King concentrated his scattered wits on the melee before him. Although breathing was difficult and his chest was one long protest of pain, he did not have the luxury of time to allow his wound to affect his control of the battle.

"Double the line, Targo. And send the first line forward by one step. The Saxons will be caught between the wall of their own dead and our warriors and won't have room to maneuver."

Targo looked out at the desperate struggle. He sensed that the will of the Celts was beginning to buckle.

"But—"

"Do as I say," Artor shouted over the screams of dying men. "And then order Pelles to hit the Saxons with every arrow we have. There is to be nothing held in reserve. Now!"

Targo had no choice but to obey. Perversely, when they were told that Artor wished them to advance one step and then hunker down into the Tortoise, the weakest men found extra strength. Those warriors who had time to look behind could see Artor, proudly standing in the open on a slight incline of ground. He seemed unafraid of the enemy weaponry. The warriors believed he had consummate faith in their abilities, and so their spirits responded to his trust.

Caught in a narrow defile, the Saxons died under the withering rain of arrows from the Celtic bowmen until Glamdring was forced to order his warriors to retreat to their positions along the tree line.

Both armies took the time to lick their wounds.

"Move all my warriors back by six spear lengths," Artor panted. "And collect all arrows and weapons as before. Then rebuild the wall of Saxon dead so that it has a different opening leading into our barricades. We must make them pay for every life they take."

"You are sorely wounded, sire," Luka murmured. The young messenger had told him of Artor's plight, and he had hurried back from the left flank during a lull in the battle.

Artor fixed him with his flat and impenetrable eyes.

"Luka, get back . . . to your . . . position."

Luka could see that every word hurt Artor, yet he fled from the scorn in the king's eyes. There was no sign of softness or weakness in the Artor of thirty-eight years of age, and not one corner of his heart was unguarded. Even an old friend like himself must serve in the role that Artor had planned for him.

"You look at me as if I was a monster, Targo. But who will hold you all together if I don't do it? Those whom the gods would destroy . . ." Artor's voice trailed away.

"They first make mad?" Targo shook his tired old head. "I don't think so, my son. The Greek who coined that ancient truism didn't know you. The gods love you, Artor, mad or not, as they never loved your father. And we love you too."

The last words were uttered in a bare whisper that, in his pain, Artor did not hear. He stood, four square upon the rising ground, until the afternoon gave way to early evening and the men were permitted to rest, to eat, and, in turn, to sleep.

"Will you see Myrddion now, my lord?" Targo asked.

Artor sighed and permitted his shoulders to slump.

"Yes, I will see Myrddion now."

Chapter IX

A SEASON IN HADES

Myrddion's small kingdom was a kind of hell. The stench of the dead was a persistent itch in his nostrils, not sharp and sweet yet, for death was still young, but wet and heavy, like an empty sickroom after the patient has died.

Men lay on makeshift pallets in the circle of the wagons. Glassy-eyed with poppy juice, they bore wounds of varying severity: the bloody stumps of amputation by sword or axe; the gut-piercing wounds of arrows that stank like death already; and the delirium of head wounds that few men survived. Those who bore lesser wounds had already rejoined their fellow soldiers, bearing their bandages, stitches, and slings like heroes. They would rather kill again and again before they joined the living dead of the knoll.

Myrddion and his healers worked on tirelessly. While his leather apron was covered in dried and fresh blood, his fastidious hands were clean, for he had noticed many years earlier that dirty hands hastened putrefaction. He had ordered regular supplies of boiled river water, trusting that water from the brackish tides would be clean. Similarly, every rag used on a patient was washed before it touched another man, just as Myrddion himself laved his hands before he touched a new patient. Men still died, but other men swore that the devil's spawn saved more lives than he lost.

Myrddion was holding a dying man's hand, pretending to be his father, offering a harmless lie as comfort, when Odin assisted Artor into the circle of the dying. Myrddion's face blanched at Artor's extreme pallor, but his voice did not cease its soft, country cadences as he talked about the lambing on the morrow, and the young calves frolicking in the upper meadows. The eyes of his patient had the pinpoint pupils of poppy juice, and he soon fell asleep, lulled by his father's talk of ordinary, familiar things.

Myrddion extricated his hand gently and kissed the closed, fluttering eyelids. The young man smiled as he dreamed.

"Will he live, Myrddion?" Artor asked quietly as the healer joined him and plunged his hands into clean water.

"No. He's been disemboweled. He will die by morning regardless of what I do. If the gods are kindly he will dream through the night, at least as long as the poppy lasts, and I promise he will feel no pain."

Myrddion's serene face was infinitely sad and Artor began to truly understand what his chief counselor achieved on the battlefield. If a dying man needed a lover, a friend, a wife, or a parent, Myrddion took their place. He said everything that was needed to bring peace and heart balm to the sufferers, and allowed brave men to die wrapped in the arms of loved ones who were far away. Although he never struck a blow, Myrddion Merlinus had the grace and the gravity of a hero.

Artor's head began to spin, and he almost fainted.

"Come, Artor," Myrddion ordered, as he immediately took the younger man's weight. "I have a clean pallet just for you. Let me see what you have done to yourself."

Artor recoiled from Myrddion's touch.

"No. I cannot lie with these men. I cannot be ill, for too much depends on tomorrow's battles. Take out the arrowhead and wrap me tightly. Come what may, I must be seen to be in command when dawn lights the day."

Myrddion smiled gently with complete understanding.

"If you are dying, Lord Artor, I will tell you so. If you are not, then you will do what I say. Odin, strip your master to the waist."

For once, Odin evaded Artor's febrile hands and obeyed Myrddion. The cuirass was removed, followed by the leather jerkin, and both men's faces paled as they saw the deep staining of Artor's woolen undershirt. When his chest was bared, the stump of the arrow was revealed.

"How are you breathing, my lord?" Myrddion asked gently.

"It hurts, but the air still goes in and out," Artor replied with grim humor. "No, Myrddion, I do not have a sucking chest wound, but talking is painful."

Myrddion examined Artor's back and pressed lightly on the swelling muscle under the shoulder. Despite his clenched teeth, Artor cried out and his face greyed even further. Targo was sure his master would faint, but Artor struggled to remain in an upright position.

"Well, Myrddion? You promised me the truth."

"The arrow has passed almost completely through your body. I must cut into your back to draw the arrowhead out with the shaft attached. I think you may also have broken your shoulder bone—which accounts for the pain—but, no, this is not a sucking lung wound. That injury would have resulted in your death."

"Then start cutting. I must return to my post."

Myrddion laughed lightly. "No, my king! You are now in my hellish little domain, and I consider your wound serious. Yes, I will patch you up so you can join your troops at dawn, perhaps, but unless you have a wish to depart this earth, you must consign your body into my care. At least for tonight."

"Shite!" Artor swore, for Myrddion rarely lied, and never to him.

He nodded to Targo. "Take my place in the line, Targo," he said softly. "Tell any warriors who ask that Myrddion is sewing up a minor wound, and that I will rejoin them at dawn."

"Me? I've never been in command before. You know how I feel about officers."

Artor clenched his teeth as Myrddion explored the wound around the arrow shaft.

"Do as I bid you. Immediately!"

"Shite, boy! Me? An officer? I've avoided that responsibility for forty years or more."

"You became an officer on the day I became High King, so don't argue with me. Just obey the orders you've been given." Then Artor grinned. "Remember, if you make a mistake, you're dead."

"By all the gods!" a disgruntled Targo snapped as he moved slowly out of the circle of suffering.

Myrddion continued to probe at the small entry wound on Artor's shoulder.

"I'm going to hurt you now, Artor. You may use the poppy juice if you wish, but I'd rather you were awake to let me know if I strike some vital spot. Odin will hold you down, and I need you to grip this strip of leather firmly between your teeth. Biting through your tongue is the last thing I need to happen."

Artor shook his head firmly. "There'll be no poppy juice. We'll do it your way, old man. Just don't let your knife slip, for I fear that Odin wouldn't understand."

Odin and another healer held the king upright on the pallet, his arms firmly imprisoned by his side. Still another burly man sat on the king's legs, while Myrddion secured the strip of leather inside Artor's mouth.

"This hurts me more than it hurts you," Myrddion joked, and made a fast incision into Artor's back with a narrow, razor-sharp blade.

Artor's whole body bucked with the shock of the sudden pain.

"Hold him fast," Myrddion ordered, and the blade sliced through flesh and muscle once again, this time deep into Artor's back. The king's brow was thick with a cold sweat, and his teeth bit deeply into the leather. It was only Odin's massive strength that kept him motionless as Myrddion used a fire-cleansed skewer to probe the open wound.

"Aaah!" he cried. "I've found the point of the metal."

As Myrddion probed deeper into the wound, Artor's eyes rolled back in his head and he slipped into unconsciousness.

"Good! Now we must work fast."

Myrddion's fingers were slick with blood, but he did not attempt to clean them. Instead, he thrust his thumb and forefinger into the wound, parting tendons and muscle physically as he prepared a path through which the arrowhead would pass.

Then, standing directly before his king, the healer willed himself to carry out the task that was now before him.

With a tightening of his whole body, and with his left hand flat on the shaft, he punched the broken stump of the arrow shaft deep into Artor's shoulder.

Odin watched in horror as the arrowhead appeared out of the back of the High King's shoulder; he would have struck at Myrddion, but the healer's eyes quelled him with a glance.

Returning to the exit wound, Myrddion fixed the arrowhead firmly in a pair of large tongs. Then, with a great flood of blood, the healer pulled the arrowhead and the broken shaft clear through Artor's shoulder.

From both wounds, fresh blood pumped fiercely. Odin would have covered the chest wound, but Myrddion slapped his hand away.

"Don't touch him with your hands if you truly care for our king," he said sharply. "The flow of blood will cleanse the wounds and can make our work easier."

Only then did Myrddion pause and wash his hands.

Myrddion's personal assistant, Fynn ap Fynn, was at his master's side immediately. "I need fresh cloth, Fynn. It must be clean and un-touched. And I need the bottle of salve and the glass jar in my horse bag. Hurry!"

Fynn, the son of Finn Truthteller who had been apprenticed to Myrddion Merlinus when he was little more than a boy, was a forty-year-old veteran of many battles. Fynn had served the healer and the

High King since boyhood, so he knew what Myrddion needed before the old healer had decided for himself. Now, he hurried to obey, for he understood exactly what was required.

Fynn went quickly to one of the supply wagons where neat boxes of clean wood held the battle supplies intended for the healers. With clean hands and a pair of tongs, he extracted folded cloth, which he brought back to Myrddion. Then, he fetched a pottery jar with the Roman numeral X marked upon it. Other jars, with different numbers, rested in nests of straw.

Myrddion's other satchel also sat on the seat of the cart. Hesitantly, as if he was intruding into a private room, Fynn rummaged through its neat compartments until he found a precious glass jar. His task completed, he returned to Myrddion and the royal patient with a mumbled apology for his tardiness.

"No, Fynn, you've done well. Now, watch carefully. If anything should happen to me, this is what you must do."

The healer then swabbed the wounds clean and poured some of the contents of the glass jar into both wounds.

"This is apricot brandy," he told his assistant. "I use it to kill those humors that cause wounds to rot."

He paused to survey his work. The wounds bubbled and hissed as the liquid began to bite into them.

"Now mix the herb poultices on two clean pieces of cloth," he added, almost as if speaking to himself. "But don't use your hands to mix it. There's a clean wooden spoon in the jar. Good. Very good."

Myrddion gingerly inserted one piece of vile, green-covered cloth over the frontal wound, and then placed the other on the incision in Artor's back.

"Now, wrap him in fresh linen, and bind it tightly. The pressure will help the fragments of bone to knit and will keep the poultice in place. Use as much cloth as you need. I'd rather use too much than too little."

He glanced across at the Jutlander, who was absorbing the surgical process with an awestruck expression on his face.

"You may clean your master now, Odin. But don't touch his bandages. Cover him, and keep him warm. All else is in the hands of Mithras."

Odin commenced the process of cleansing his master's torso of blood. When he had completed this task, he wrapped Artor's upper body in a length of new wool, and then sat with Artor's head resting back against his chest.

As Odin held his king in his embrace, he sang a tuneful outlander song that seemed, somehow, to ease the hearts of restless, agony-wracked men in Myrddion's makeshift hospital.

Myrddion and Fynn went back to their grim nursing tasks.

Odin watched as other men died, and noted that it was always Myrddion's fingers that closed their eyes. Other patients came limping into the circle, and it was Myrddion's hands that cauterized their wounds with hot iron, Myrddion's gentle fingers that smoothed thick salve onto the smoking wounds. Those who could walk away bowed in gratitude to the white-haired healer as he sewed wounds together, embraced the dying, and eased the passage of the dead.

The sky was still pitch-black when Artor awakened, his eyes dazed with pain. Myrddion was immediately by his side.

"What hour is it?" Artor muttered in a hoarse voice as he struggled fitfully to get away from Odin's embrace.

"It's nearly an hour before sunrise. Had you not woken naturally, I'd have been forced to bring you back to consciousness. I gave you my word, Artor."

"I thank you, my friend. Can I dress now? The warriors must see me abroad."

"The arrow is out, Artor, and I've cleansed the wounds and applied poultices. You were lucky, for that arrowhead was wickedly barbed. I could never have drawn it back out through the point of entry in your flesh without inflicting lasting damage to you."

Myrddion pressed a small barbed arrowhead into Artor's nerveless fingers.

"It's time now to see if I am still a healer," he added, as he called

183

Fynn to bring the apricot brandy and the salve, along with a supply of fresh bandages.

Artor shivered as the night air touched his flesh, but Myrddion assured him that the wounds showed no sign of heat.

"But we must be certain, my lord," and he poured more of the potent liquor onto the flesh, where it foamed against the edge of the wound.

The High King cried out in pain, but the cool poultice offered immediate relief. The process was then repeated on the incision in Artor's back.

Prewarned this time, Artor clutched the arrowhead and his amulet and bore the pain as manfully as he could. When he was bandaged and wrapped once more, Myrddion offered him a cup of some brackish tea, a brew that Artor eyed suspiciously.

"The sky will soon lighten in the east, my king, and you must perforce return to your duties. I have placed a little poppy juice in that herb tea, but you will not fall asleep from the little I have given you. You may feel a little distant from your pain, but it's just enough to allow you to heal and yet maintain command of the battle. Trust me, my lord, for I don't lie to you."

Artor managed to grin, and then swallowed the vile-tasting concoction.

"Now, let Odin feed you, but you are to have no wine, mind. Eat red meat if you can, and pad your cuirass before you don it. I will send more of the tea before noon. Have no fear, for I am certain that we'll see Caer Fyrddin fall together."

The besieged camp was a hotbed of speculation, for some men swore that the High King was dead, a rumor made believable by the presence of Targo at the sentry fires. The old legionnaire swore to the doubters that the High King lived, but fear swept the ranks with a sour odor of its own, the acid-green stink of defeat.

When the sun commenced its slow rise over the horizon at first light, Targo ordered the men to stand to and take up their positions. They obeyed, but their shoulders were bowed and their eyes were shifty under their helmets. Targo feared that some warriors might run when the Saxons appeared.

A ragged cheer began in the center of the camp and swelled even higher as the tall figure of Artor moved casually towards the shield wall.

"Artor! Artor! Artor!"

The cry rang out until the carrion birds feasting on the dead Saxon bodies rose in a cloud of black wings. Pale, a little drawn around the mouth, but undoubtedly alive, Artor walked on his own two legs, in full battle armor, to stand in his accustomed place on the knoll.

As the noise stilled, Artor spoke to the men. Those who could not hear him had the message relayed until the last one hundred and twenty men on the wall, the wounded and the hale, heard the High King's orders.

"We came to bring justice for the murder of our emissaries of peace. We came to drive the western Saxons into the sea and to end years of war. Now is the time of reckoning. This day will be long, but we are the Army of the Dead, are we not?"

Their throats were now raw, but the men shouted back the single word, "Aye!"

"We brought clay, charcoal, and woad with us to paint our faces. Let us do so today, so that the enemy will see skulls under every helmet. Let them gaze upon us and be afraid."

Again, the cheering and affirmations of loyalty were shouted until even the gulls ceased their eager hunt for fresh human flesh.

Then Artor smeared white clay upon his own pale face, leaving circlets for his eyes and his mouth that followed the contours of the bones of his face. Charcoal taken from the fire pit created a black outline around the eye sockets, nose cavity, and mouth, and woad darkened the flesh within to a color so dark that it was almost black. Odin lifted his golden helmet and placed it over Artor's bound hair, and a skull looked back at him in the pale first light.

The men cheered wildly at the sight of their king's face, and men painted each other with the form of the skull. They found their black cloaks and shrouded themselves in sable and called out towards the enemy lines.

"We are the Army of the Dead. You may try to kill us if you can!"

Then Artor's depleted force waited for Glamdring's warriors to return.

Targo joined his master, and relief shone from his aged eyes.

"Thanks be to Mithras that you're still alive and standing. Only a High King could stiffen the spines of the men on a day such as this. We protect such a small pocket of land, so pray that we can hold till night falls."

"We will hold," Artor replied distantly, and Targo saw that the shark's eyes of his king were even colder than usual.

"The wound was minor then?" Targo asked, more to break the preternatural silence than out of any curiosity.

"Just don't make me laugh, and don't allow me to move too suddenly," Artor replied with something like his old humor.

"Thank Mithras for that. Here they come!"

The Saxons fought savagely through the walls of their own dead and battered themselves against the shield wall. Skull faces looked back at them, and even the most determined Saxons began to feel the first frissons of superstitious fear.

Against all reason and odds, Artor's line managed to hold.

The Saxons came again at noon, and Pelles's men used the last of their scavenged arrows on the massed Saxons before the shield wall took the shock—and more. As smooth as a deadly dance, men fell and were replaced even while their bodies were being passed backward. The Saxons fell in their scores, and their bodies were piled up against the defensive wall.

Later, as darkness fell, the Saxons retreated to their own lines.

The shield wall was now alarmingly thin, and Artor knew that his Celts were almost done. Their losses were still slight compared with those of the Saxons, but there were very few Celts who did not carry a wound of sorts, and the shield wall had slowly been pushed backward until it was now at the foot of the knoll. If Llanwith and Lot did not come on the morrow, then Artor's army would be annihilated.

Artor was amazed when a cheerful Pelles joined him in his tent atop the knoll. The one-eyed archer threw himself onto a stool and sighed cheerfully as he rested his swollen feet.

"We keep collecting some of our own arrows back, so we will have something to throw at them tomorrow," he told his master. "But now I seem to have more archers than my arrow supply can meet. I thought I'd offer you twenty of my boys to put into your line, for it seems hellish thin to me."

"Why are you so cheerful, Pinhead?" Targo snapped. "By any estimation, the situation here is quite grave."

"Tomorrow is as good a day to die as any. I expected to meet my end years ago, and I'm still here. I'll trust to Artor's luck, for he's always been a good bet in the past. Remember the loot we collected at Anderida? Shite! That was one hell of a battle. But this place? Mori Saxonicus? They'll be telling tales of the shield wall when you and I have been dead for a hundred years." He smiled across at the old Roman veteran. "And I wish you wouldn't call me Pinhead. My son wouldn't like it."

Targo gaped. "What woman would have children with you? You're hardly the prettiest warrior in the army."

Pelles attempted to look affronted, but his humor shone through his muddy eye.

"I've got a woman and two children under twelve, a boy and a girl, so no more use of Pinhead, old soldier."

"Let's hope your daughter doesn't look like you, my friend."

With Artor's heartfelt praise to warm him to his scuffed, black boots, Pelles left shortly afterwards to return to his archers. He was immediately replaced by the High King's foster brother, Caius, who asked for admittance to the tent.

Like Pelles, Caius too was sanguine. He had borne the brunt of the fighting and his loss of men had been horrific, but Caius seemed oblivious to the blood and destruction that had taken place around him. If anything, he appeared feverishly confident as he gave his report to Artor.

Blood had drenched Caius's black cloak so that it hung in stiff folds from his shoulders. The steward's arms and hands were clean, for Caius was as fastidious as Artor, but his boots told a story of bloody mud, spilled brains, and all the ghastliness of hand-to-hand fighting. Artor noticed, distantly, that Caius's good humor stopped short of his eyes.

"Whew, brother! You'll bear some interesting scars from that wound. You must be the luckiest man I have ever known."

Caius peered carefully at the wound and watched Myrddion work with a morbid interest until Artor became uncomfortable under the avid stare of his brother.

"Should Llanwith and Lot fail us, Caius, I will be sorry to know that you will not see your children again," Artor said to distract him. "And I will regret the tears that Ector will weep for you."

Caius snorted. "He'll weep for you, perhaps, but not for me. My mother's blood still lies between us like a wall of stone. And Julanna and the children will hardly miss me. Gods, they barely know me. I've spent years in your service, brother, but I'm not complaining. Still, I've enjoyed these many years with you, which is odd, considering I have always rather despised you. I wish it wasn't so, and it doesn't mean I want you to die. Quite the contrary, in fact. Unfortunately, I cannot help my feelings. It's purely a matter of jealousy, I suppose, but you have achieved so much, and I have so little to show for my efforts at achieving glory."

Artor's face reddened and his jaw clenched. "You have a wife and children to sing your praises when you go into the Shadows. When I pass on, there will be none who will care, apart from those few among us who are my true friends. And I can count them on the fingers of one hand. You've allowed yourself to resent a memory of the past and of what might have been, rather than a flesh-and-blood man."

The king looked deeply into the eyes of his foster brother, as if he could tear apart the veil of containment that made Caius an enigma.

"Besides, Caius, men speak of your courage and your skill in battle with admiration. You obey orders, even impossible ones like those you have carried out during the last two days. Whether you care for me or not is immaterial to me. You are a valued ally and a gifted steward. What more do you want?"

Caius's eyes dropped so that Artor couldn't see his thoughts. Everything you have, brother! Everything! The love, the respect . . . everything!

Caius laughed ironically, and Odin rose threateningly from his position at Artor's back.

"You can call off your dog, Artor, for I could never do you any harm. I know that I am nothing without you but an empty bag of piss and wind. I simply want you to know that I have always attempted to serve you as well as I could, and I choose to speak the truth on what might be my last night."

"I understand and I'm grateful, Caius. I intend to ensure that we continue to speak our thoughts in the future, for honesty is of more value to me than any amount of praise or false love. I have always considered you to be a fine leader and a gifted warrior, for all that you believe yourself to be inadequate. At any road, I still consider it is premature to consign ourselves to the darkness of death tomorrow."

Caius snickered, and the sound had no humor in it, only threat. "Yes, there are still Saxons left to kill, I suppose. That's some consolation, I admit. Sleep well, Artor, and I'll pray that your luck holds." He turned and slid out through the tent flap.

Myrddion stood back and admired his handiwork. He noticed the pain in Artor's eyes, and set to work grinding another cup of herb tea in a bowl of stone, using a pestle of the same dense, grey material.

"That man will cause you trouble yet, Artor," the older man whispered. "Caius still makes my flesh creep, but this day has been full of horrors. He's right, you know. For all that he has risen high in the land and has proved his worth a thousand times, the Severinii will always stand behind him in my mind. He's also correct to be jealous of you, for your men do love you. But they have no feelings for Caius. They obey him and they respect him, but nobody loves Caius. There is something in him that repels most men. I suppose he is to be pitied."

Artor flinched a little. "His father still loves him, regardless of what Caius thinks, and I also feel some affection and pity for him. I'm not sure why exactly, but he is the only close link I have with my childhood . . . with old Frith . . . and Mistress Livinia . . ." Artor's voice trailed away and Myrddion feared that his master might weep under the triple pressures of physical pain, the duties of command, and the terrible burden of waiting. Knowing that tears would shame his king, Myrddion discreetly turned his back and poured hot water onto his concoction. When he again faced his king, a cup in one hand, Artor was composed once more.

"Drink this, my lord, and rest. The night will be short enough, and Odin will watch over you."

"Caius is as he ever was: a tool fitted to my hand. I've always known that he is best used in battle, where his tendency to cruelty is called courage. I only fear for him in times of peace."

"Drink, Artor. Odin will wake you if Ironfist should determine to attack during the night. As the kingdom stands, peace will be a long time coming, so Caius will be safe for many years."

Myrddion slipped out of the tent and returned to his dying charges. Terrible as his duties were, the healer knew that they were not as arduous or as soul-destroying as the burdens that were carried by his king.

Artor slept, and the night gave way to a red and glowing sun in the eastern sky.

GLAMDRING IRONFIST FUMED and raged as he tried to rest in his campaign tent.

He kicked his favorite woman out of his sleeping furs, and threatened to behead the first Saxon to call the High King by name.

"Artor! Artor! Artor! All I hear is that cursed name. Those rotting Celts with their skull faces should all be dead, and I swear they will be carrion for the birds before tomorrow ends. But where is Wyrr, now that I have need of him?"

Glamdring knew that his request was rhetorical. He had stood at the gates of Caer Fyrddin and howled over the body of his adviser. None of his Saxons had dared to move or speak because the red light of madness was in Glamdring's eyes.

"Who has done this thing?" he had howled. "Who has killed my Wyrr? Find the murderer for me, and I'll flay him alive before I burn him. Find him!"

Glamdring's warriors had glanced at each other, lost and confused. Only Nils Redbeard had had the courage to step forward from the huddle of warriors and tell the truth to his master.

"Both of our sentries have been killed, along with Lord Wyrr, and the slave called Dog has gone. We believe that Lord Wyrr surprised him as he was escaping through the gates."

"Dog?" Glamdring's muddled thoughts focused on the one certainty that emerged from the chaos of his imagination. "Dog did this? That idiot who cleans my hall has killed my most loyal and most valuable servant?"

With each word, Glamdring's rage intensified so that spittle stained his beard and his knuckles stood out whitely as he clutched the hilt of his sword. His warriors flinched away from him, while Nils Redbeard lowered his eyes and prayed to his gods that his master would permit him to live.

"Yes, my lord. I've tortured one of the servant girls who had been friendly towards him. She knew nothing about him . . . except that he had learned to speak and understand our language. I'm certain that she spoke the truth, for I broke her fingers and toes, one by one, and she would have told me anything at the end. She had no idea that he planned to escape."

"Kill her! Kill all the Celt house servants, for I'll not fear to sleep in my own hall. Put their heads on poles above the gate as a warning that Glamdring Ironfist will not tolerate disobedience. And put all the guards that were on duty tonight to the sword—publicly! They have failed in their duty to their tribe."

The bloody executions had scarcely blunted the edge of Glamdring's rage.

Even now, a snickering voice echoed in his mind, taunting him and reminding him that he would be a failure without clever little Wyrr to guide him.

But Wyrr was now worm food.

Glamdring fingered the carved bone hilt of the knife that hung round his neck. "But I still have the Arden Knife," he whispered aloud. "And Wyrr was certain that no hand could touch me unless it held the Arden Knife. So my luck will hold to the very end."

But Glamdring was grimly aware that his original force had been reduced to only four hundred fully fit men capable of following him into the next battle. His wounded numbered a hundred or so, but, because Saxon warriors were reluctant to retreat during a frontal attack, they rarely survived the fearsome injuries that were inflicted upon them. To be struck down usually meant death for the Saxon warriors for they were never lacking in courage.

Today would be different, for Glamdring suspected that the Celts had also suffered huge losses. The Saxon chieftain could comfort himself with the knowledge that his depleted forces were still larger than Artor's original army, many of whom were off on a wild-goose chase as they harassed small settlements that were of no strategic importance.

The end was in sight, for how could the cursed Artor hold his narrow strip of land much longer? The Celtic king was in a hopeless position, and Glamdring Ironfist would bear Artor's head back to Caer Fyrddin and set it on a pole before his hall with all the other Celtic slaves.

"The crows will pick his skull clean, and I'll find Dog! For him, I will create a special, more fitting death."

But the sea wind brought the smell of corruption back to Glamdring on the early-morning air. His own dead had been stacked into piles by the Celts and had been formed into barricades that slowed and frustrated his attacks. Even now, a miasma of death snaked through the Saxon camp, sapping the will of his warriors. Glamdring recognized that the Celts must be surrounded by Saxon dead as well as their own, and that the stench emanating from the battlefield must live with them, night and day, waking and sleeping. But they still held their shield wall in place, and they refused to give an inch when the Saxons engaged them in combat.

"May the gods make that whoreson rot," Glamdring swore.

But of all the reverses of the last few days, the loss of Wyrr was the deepest blow. Only Glamdring knew how important that preternaturally aged stripling had been in his thoughts and in his strategies.

In temper, he hurled his ale jug across the leather tent, where it shattered on the hard earth and filled his nostrils with the reek of sour beer.

"The foul Dog!" Glamdring cried aloud in disgust as he recalled his erstwhile slave and the damage that had been inflicted on his campaign. "He will die a thousand deaths, mad with pain, if I ever lay my hands on that animal. But before he dies, I'll give him to my women."

Glamdring knew that no worse punishment existed, for women, especially those who had lost loved ones in battle, surpassed men in cold cruelty. They would keep an enemy alive to extend his suffering long after a man would have put him out of his misery.

Yes, he would give Dog to the widows of Caer Fyrddin.

What would Wyrr have advised? The thought went through his mind, now that he had decided on Dog's fate.

For two days, Glamdring's forces had faltered at the shield wall used by Artor's defenses. And it was becoming increasingly obvious that another direct assault was unlikely to succeed. Perhaps an alternative strategy would be more effective.

Glamdring Ironfist might have been an ignorant man, but he wasn't stupid.

The answer to his problem came to him immediately, and he hastened to dress himself. In a fever of impatience, he plunged out into the predawn darkness to rouse his captains.

"We attack in the dark, immediately, as soon as you can wake our warriors and send them on their way. The Celts will be asleep, expecting us to come at them at dawn. If we are silent, we will have surprise on our side and will be able to negotiate the barricades without those infernal bowmen picking us off at will."

Glamdring's captains nodded and grinned. Their thane had been abstracted of late, and his irritability and uncertainty had helped to fuel a sense of hopelessness that swept through the troops as they fruitlessly attacked the Celtic positions. Now the old Ironfist was back, bursting with energy so that the air literally crackled around him.

The captains dispersed to alert their troops. Night birds watched with large, luminous eyes as the Saxons began to creep out onto the stretch of open land that separated their bivouac from the Celtic positions.

From a tall tree, Gruffydd awoke with a jerk as a careless foot snapped a twig a short distance away. For the last three nights, Gruffydd and his companions had watched the Saxon camp, killing any unwary warriors who wandered away from their fellows to relieve themselves. Using the cry of a night bird as an alarm signal to his men, Gruffydd slid down the tree and began to crawl on hands and knees through the deepest shadows to their prearranged meeting place.

He was joined by his fellow lookouts within minutes.

"The Saxons are planning a night attack, and they've started moving already. Artor will be caught abed unless he is warned. You, Kennett, will take my place as leader of our little band while I carry the message to the High King."

"They'll discover you as soon as you begin to move, Gruffydd. If you try to outrun them, you'll need to break cover. And if you do move onto open ground, you won't stand a chance."

"I'm no longer young, Kennett, and I've never much cared for succumbing to the ills of old age, so shut your teeth and carry out your task."

He embraced Kennett quickly, and then began to move resolutely in the direction of the Celtic lines. At first, he kept to the shadows of the tree line, but, finally, he broke cover and sped silently with the uncanny sense of the trained spy.

Dressed in black, Gruffydd knew he wasn't easy to see, so, as he outstripped a troop of Saxon warriors heading towards Artor's flank, he began to shout a warning to the Celt defenders.

"Awake! Awake! The Saxons are coming! Man the shield wall! Awake! Awake!"

Gruffydd could hear the sounds of Saxon pursuit immediately behind him, and saved his breath for running. The darkness protected him from accurate bowshot or from spears, and he knew that only close contact with a Saxon warrior could bring him down.

He ran until he thought his heart would burst.

At the first line of Saxon dead, he slowed momentarily to detour along the narrow passageway between the walls of bodies, and a young Saxon almost caught him. A groping hand clutched at a trailing fold of his cloak. He managed to slip out of the garment, leaving the Saxon holding its sable folds.

"Awake!" he shouted breathlessly. "Awake! The Saxons are coming! Awake!"

The spy threw himself over the last line of corpses, and tumbled over a stiff swollen hand. Thrusting aside a sudden superstitious dread, he scrambled to his feet and pounded over the fifteen feet into the blackness that had settled over the Celtic camp.

"Make way! Sword-bearer Gruffydd! Make way!"

His lungs were heaving as he fell against the wood and iron defenses. Hands grasped him and manhandled him through the lines as if he were as light as chaff, while the three lines of the defenses re-formed and thrust their spear butts into the earth in preparation for the coming Saxon charge. Gruffydd saw no sign of panic in the Celtic ranks, just the skull faces of tired men, their red eyes ringed with dark woad shadows against the smeared chalk on their faces.

Artor loomed out of the darkness, Odin at his heels. Gruffydd realized for the first time how close the shield wall was to the knoll where the baggage train created a natural circle.

"It's good to see you in one piece, Gruffydd," Artor murmured.

Gruffydd squinted up at Artor's pale face, only partly lit by the lowering moon. He had never seen his king so pale under his tan, and he wondered if Artor was wounded. If so, Artor's stature and mien gave no clue to his condition.

"Pelles!" Artor called, and the little man came running. "Unless you can fire arrows in the dark, get your men to the wall where they can act as a fourth line of defense. I doubt your men can miss a shot from close range, even if they can't see what they're aiming at."

"I obey, my lord. My men are keen to see some blood. They take it hard that they've suffered no losses after so many good lads have gone to the Shades on this sodding plain. They'll acquit themselves well."

Artor grinned. "Take care, Pelles. You're the last of the Anderida Scum, and I'd take it amiss if you risked your head unnecessarily. Perhaps I'd start to lose my luck."

Pelles winked his one good eye and grinned. "There's no chance of that, lord. I've known for many years that the better you plan, the luckier you become. Only you would have had the foresight to position Gruffydd where he could warn us if Ironfist tried for a night attack. Your luck will hold, but Llanwith and Lot had better hurry."

A shudder of sudden contact ran through the lines in front of them. The Saxons were throwing themselves at the Celtic line in a frenzied attack in almost pitch-black darkness.

"Shite! I'd best hurry!" Pelles cursed, and ran back towards his bowmen.

"Gruffydd, call out the noncombatants, the wagon teams, the smiths, and any healers who can be spared. You can even call the women if they can use a slingshot. But the line must be held!"

Artor's eyes were distant. "Come, Odin. It's time the king added his sword to the battle. Targo, you stay put and keep me informed of everything I should know."

"Sire, I've obeyed you for fourteen years and followed you from one side of our lands to the other, but I'll not stand back and wait to die. I may be old, but I still know how to kill."

"As you wish!"

Artor waded into the second defensive line alongside his warriors. As a man before him slumped over his weapons, Artor took up the warrior's shield and drew his massive sword, ignoring the sudden agony that leapt along his shoulder and chest.

Around him, men's eyes flared and the cry went up, "The king is with us! Artor! Artor!"

Mechanically, with Odin at his back, Artor straddled the wounded man and used his sword like a scythe. Where it struck flesh, it cleaved to the bone, and through the bone, and the Saxon warriors fell back from its deadly swathe.

Another Saxon appeared, almost over him, and Artor's blade was fully extended. Before the axe of the savage could fall on Artor's unprotected head, Targo's short sword pierced his throat and the man fell to the ground.

The Saxon warriors attacked in wave after wave of huge, dim shapes that thrust and hacked at the Celtic line as they appeared out of the darkness. Gradually, the enemy became more visible as the sky lightened, and Pelles's archers fired over Artor's head, striking down the Saxons before they reached the line.

But still the enemy came, in endless, desperate tides, and Artor knew that the line was near to breaking.

"Back!" he roared. "Fall back to the knoll! For the west! Fall back to the knoll!"

The Celtic warriors fell back in disciplined ranks, fighting for every foot of earth. The Saxons sensed victory, but as the Celtic line constricted, it thickened, and the defenders were now fighting on firm earth, rather than ground that had been churned to mud with blood, entrails, and dying men. Still, as the sun rose in a red orb over the tree line with the early-morning dawn, Artor saw little to bring him comfort. With their backs to their own piled dead, the shield wall had nowhere else to go.

From above them, the air was suddenly thick with a fusillade of stones that struck with deadly results and, even if they missed their mark, Saxons flinched away from the aerial attack and were distracted from their task. On the piles of their own dead, wild-eyed women swung slings round their heads and screeched like demons, cursing and crying in their rage and battle lust.

"The women! Gods love them!" Targo muttered, as he hacked away at the knees of Saxon attackers. Above the small form of his servant, Artor smiled as he used his shield in imitation of Bedwyr as he sliced another Saxon across his unprotected jaw.

Artor could even hear the screams of noncombatants as they called on their gods for courage. One smith cleaved the shield wall briefly as he wielded a bar of iron that had been heated to bloodred brilliance in the fire pit. As two Saxons reeled away from him, clutching their eyes, the smith stepped back behind the shelter of the shields once again without even noticing a gaping wound across his thigh.

Artor's sword was thick with blood and gore, but, even though his fingers slipped on the cunning pommel, the great blade seemed to possess a life of its own. The reflected light from the rays of the sun ran down Caliburn and transformed it into a grim, blazing tongue of light.

Then, as Pelles's archers found themselves pressed against the heaped and rotting pile of corpses, a horn began to blare from the west, answered by another from the north.

"At last! They've come at last," Artor yelled, as his sword arm continued to shear through the bone and muscle of his enemies. "Lot and Llanwith are here! Fight on, men of the west! The cavalry have come."

As his last words sounded out, Artor's despairing warriors found a new reason to raise their swords. The horns sounded again, and Targo repeated Artor's words, joined by Odin and others, until the whole shield wall was chanting as they killed and were themselves killed in turn.

"The cavalry has come! The cavalry has come! The cavalry has come!"

Out on the plain, Glamdring saw the massed cavalry as it burst from the trees behind him, and he screamed in impotent rage as the audacity of Artor's gamble struck home.

Still more horsemen were pouring over the river crossing, their horses swimming strongly through the wide estuary. Glamdring could see that his forces were caught in a pincer movement between two formations of cavalry. Artor's strategy was masterful, and Glamdring accepted, numbly, that he was caught in a fatal trap through his own impatience and stupidity.

Another horn sounded from the east, and Gawayne was upon the rear of the Saxons. Glamdring saw it all, the defenders now beginning to step forward where they had previously retreated, the Otadini surging out of the river with their axes and swords swinging, and behind him the implacable warriors of the Ordovice tribe.

Trapped! There was nowhere to go. Glamdring Ironfist screamed his defiance at the sky, while the warnings of Gaheris reverberated through his head. "You never learn . . . you never change . . . you never learn."

The Saxon thane realized that his only course of action was to abandon the field and to seek the safety of Caer Fyrddin.

"To me! To me! To me!" he shouted. "Retreat! Retreat! Fight your way through to the woods."

As the Saxon force began to fall away, Artor lowered his bloody sword, for his abused chest and arm muscles were no longer strong enough to bear the weight of the huge blade. He pressed his hand beneath his leather jerkin and discovered that Myrddion's bandages were now saturated with blood.

"Order the men to rest, Targo. They have achieved miracles, and the west will remember this great battle as long as these isles endure."

He turned to face his sword-bearer.

"Take Caliburn, Gruffydd, and clean it well for it has served the west yet again." He gazed around at the nauseating bloodbath. "But first, before we take pleasure in victory, we must take care of our wounded."

Down on the plain, Lot and Llanwith were making sport. Cavalry against foot soldiers was an unequal struggle in any battle, but now, after three days of vicious fighting, the Saxons were weary and desperate to escape. Those who were still fleet of foot formed into small bands and fought their way through the horsemen to scatter into the forest like woodsmoke. But many of Glamdring's men were cut off, and they were quickly mustered into small groups where they were encircled and hacked to pieces at the pleasure of the Celtic relief columns.

Queen Morgause watched the carnage from a low mound overlooking the battlefield, with only a token guard to protect her. She hungered for Saxon blood and drank in each desperate attempt by the battered Saxons to flee from the battlefield.

Over the screams of the many small skirmishes taking place, she heard the exultation of the Otadini warriors in their fierce battle cry.

"For Gaheris! For Gaheris! For Gaheris!"

In the privacy of her cowl, Morgause wept, and was at last content with her revenge for the loss of her son. Her heart swelled with grief and triumph as she rode through the weary lines of the Celtic defenses and nodded a greeting to her brother. But she didn't pause until she reached the top of the knoll, where she dared Myrddion's wrath by gloating over the living, the dying, and the dead. She gazed over the piled Saxon dead, more than a spear length in height, and smiled slowly.

The wall of Celtic corpses was a perfect position from which to observe the massacre of the few remaining Saxon warriors, and Morgause watched from horseback like a black basilisk or funerary sculpture made from granite.

Myrddion was revolted by the queen's obvious pleasure in the carnage. Her spirit seemed to feed on the pain inflicted by her husband as he took revenge for the loss of their son. Myrddion would have ordered her out of his small kingdom, but he glimpsed something in her eyes below the gloating and the blood lust, something that was vulnerable and lost. He turned away from her, his stomach churning. He knew that she was doing lasting damage to her mind and to her soul.

Indeed, until her death, Morgause was never again a woman of power. Something essential to her spirit was extinguished on the battlefield beside a nameless river. The queen lived and ruled for many more years, but she had become a fair husk dressed in black-edged robes who was unable to savor the true taste of living.

"We pay for our pleasures and our revenges," Myrddion murmured aloud.

"Lord?" his patient asked, his eyes mere pinpoints under the effects of Myrddion's last jar of poppy juice.

"My apologies, boy. I was merely trying to make sense out of an enigma, but I suppose it's an impossible question I ask of myself. Now . . . your arm will always be stiff, but at least your fingers will still move at your bidding."

As he finished stitching the wound and wrapped it securely in clean cloth, the healer glanced back at the queen. She remained a black shape against the blue sky, and her form was so still that she scarcely seemed to breathe.

"May the gods have mercy on you, Morgause," he whispered softly towards her. "For you will pay for what you have desired on this day."

And so the backbone of the western Saxons was smashed. The red morning was followed by an even redder day, and the Mori Saxonicus seemed to run pink with a flush of diluted blood. Crows and ravens feasted well on the stripped corpses of the Saxon dead before Artor ordered that the heaped, corrupted flesh should be burned in large communal graves to reduce the possibility of disease.

For his part, King Lot searched in vain for the body of his son's murderer. Glamdring Ironfist had escaped, and the whole, bloody campaign would be for nothing unless the Saxon thane was found and executed. Lot ranted and swore vengeance, but Queen Morgause turned towards her half brother and read his intention in his adamantine eyes.

"Fear not, husband," she said tonelessly, "for Artor will not permit Ironfist to live."

Even Lot blanched at the sight of his queen's frozen face.

Artor ignored his sister and focused his attention on the field of battle and the last Saxon stragglers as they were slaughtered. Then he turned to Targo.

"Find that young Cornovii, Bedwyr, and bring him to me. We go to Caer Fyrddin, and I need his knowledge of the fortress."

The small group of warriors who had survived the battle of the shield wall was left to guard the wounded, and to burn the corpses of the warriors who had perished.

Waiting only to have his dressings re-bound, Artor was soon on horseback, leading the cavalry to Caer Fyrddin and the remnants of the Saxon horde that sheltered there.

And Bedwyr, the Arden Knife, rode with him.

Chapter X

CAER FYRDDIN

Bedwyr had survived the terror of being in the first line of the shield wall for a miraculous three days and five battle waves. Men touched him for luck after the first day, since he was covered with blood from head to toe but had not received a single scratch. At the end of the second day, they averted their eyes from his glazed face out of superstitious dread, for his eyes burned with the heat of madness in his smeared, skull-like face.

During the night attack, Bedwyr had fought like a man possessed. The very smell of Saxons turned his stomach and inflamed his rage. The real Bedwyr did not exist in that charnel house that was the first line of defense; he was Dog, and he was repaying every blow, every slight, every wound upon his companions' bodies, and every scream that their flame-blasted throats had made.

When the battle was over and the Saxons were in full retreat, the young man gradually returned to his senses, and he was appalled at his actions during the fighting.

He stank of blood, both fresh and dried. He reeked of death, and his shorn hair was stiff with something he did not care to name. Revolted and half maddened by what he had seen, Bedwyr bolted to the river to lie in its shallows. Even here, he could see the waters were fouled with diluted blood and the remnants of corpses that bobbed in the wavelets along the shore.

He trudged across the river mouth to the sea, his booted feet crunching over the sand and pebbles. Once there, he stripped off every stitch of wet clothing. In the salty water, he allowed the waves to suck at his flesh as it peeled away the detritus of death that fouled every crease of his body. Naked, he lay at the tideline, his limbs moving flaccidly with the surge and the tug of waves. Soon, he found himself lulled into a type of waking dream where he was back among the trees of Arden.

"Hoi?" a rough voice rasped out. "You! Bedwyr! You're wanted!"

Bedwyr refused to stir. All he could tolerate was the movement of the sea, as gentle as the comfort of his mother's arms.

Dirty, booted feet splashed into the shallows beside him. Unwillingly, Bedwyr opened one eye.

"Leave me alone," he moaned.

"I can't, lad," Targo replied kindly, his eyes shadowed with sympathy in his stubbled face. "King Artor wants you, and he isn't known for his patience. When a High King calls for our presence, we mortals obey."

"I'm going nowhere," Bedwyr stated quietly, but his eyes scanned Targo's looming figure, and he seemed to regain some sanity as the old soldier smiled down at him.

"Glamdring Ironfist has escaped the battlefield, and will find refuge in Caer Fyrddin. This campaign isn't over, so we've no time for rest or rejoicing. You know the fortress intimately, as you boasted to us, so you're needed, lad, and you will come, even if I have to drag you into Artor's presence."

"There's no chance of that, old man. I outweigh you and outreach you."

Targo's pleasant tone hardly changed. "I won't have to do anything. But Odin will, and he outweighs and outreaches you." Targo pointed to Odin, who stepped forward and blocked out the sun.

Bedwyr sighed and struggled to his feet. "I have no choice, do I?"

"Not a lot." Targo smiled. "I heard you fought well at the wall."

Bedwyr's face collapsed, and Targo realized that the young man was on the verge of weeping.

"You've never been in a battle before, have you, lad?" Targo put one sinewy arm round the shoulders of the young man. "I thought not. This battle was nearly as bad as it gets. Over six hundred men have died here in just three days. Even a seasoned warrior would be shaken by such an ordeal, but you're new to it. One day you will wake up and think that it was all one dim, half-forgotten nightmare."

Odin helped Bedwyr to dress in his soaking clothes, which were, at least, cleansed by the river water.

"Try not to dwell on it, lad." Targo attempted to comfort the young man. "Most warriors carry horrors with them, but we seem to put them into the back of our minds until we need some information that we've learned from them." He clapped Bedwyr on the back. "I think Artor will ask you to accompany us back to Caer Fyrddin. He knows that if he doesn't kill Glamdring now, he'll have to return in a few years' time and go through the same killing fields again. It's best we get the job finished, once and for all."

Artor had already determined that half of the cavalry complement of the forces commanded by Lot and Llanwith would be sufficient to take the fortress at Caer Fyrddin and defeat the remnants of Glamdring's forces. The foot soldiers had earned a rest, uninterrupted sleep and care for their wounds. The remainder of his cavalry would see to the burning of the Celt and Saxon corpses, and construction of a cairn to honor the Celtic heroes who died at the mouth of the river.

At least the Celtic rations and supplies wouldn't run short, for their losses had been horrific.

Lot and Llanwith had both achieved their respective objectives, and Artor knew that Glamdring would receive no reinforcements from the Saxon villages, only refugees.

Luka would be given command of half of Lot's cavalry and the remnants of those warriors who had fought at the shield wall. Their task would be to move the wounded and noncombatant troops back to

Venta Silurum in slow stages, as well as escorting the spoils of war that had been taken from the Saxon bodies at Mori Saxonicus.

Caius was already taking inventory of the heaped Saxon weapons, torcs, golden pins, and finger rings as Artor departed for Caer Fyrddin. As the High King passed on horseback, his foster brother grinned at him as if their conversation in his tent on the eve of the last-ditch battle had never taken place.

Artor's previous reluctance to attack Caer Fyrddin was no longer relevant. Its walls might be strong, its water and stores might be plentiful, and there were ravines that guarded three of its four sides, but unless Ironfist could man his ramparts with troops, Caer Fyrddin would be taken eventually. With the confidence born of waging a successful campaign, Artor's cavalry took their time as they climbed the first mountain that loomed over the river valley, and smoked out isolated pockets of Saxon resistance as they rode.

On the first hill that gave an uninterrupted view of the river and sea, and the hills behind it, Artor found evidence of a once thriving community. The ruins of Roman walls, domestic houses, and buildings given over to commerce edged the cracked remains of broad streets.

"What they cannot use, these Saxons destroy," Artor said sadly. "I suppose this is all that's left of Moridunum, where Myrddion was born. Perhaps it will rise again, and race will come to matter less than the land on which men and women live."

"Look, Artor. Over there." Targo pointed towards the slopes of a hill on the western outskirts of the ruins. "See? I'd swear that was once a Roman theater. Even Glamdring couldn't destroy it entirely."

"Bedwyr." Artor turned to the young man. "In what direction lies Caer Fyrddin from here?"

The Cornovii pointed to the north, towards a misty crest that lay beyond low hills. The distance, it seemed, wasn't far, but it was mostly uphill.

That night, Artor required Bedwyr to draw plans of Caer Fyrddin again and again in the dirt. Artor absorbed every item of information he could extract from the younger man about the sheer cliffs that breasted the walls, the single wooden gate guarded by the watchtower, the hall, the well, the piggeries and the cow byres, the barracks for the fighting men, and even the deep grain stores located in the foundations of the old Roman fortress.

"Caer Fyrddin would have defied us for years if Ironfist had chosen to sit tight. It guards the whole river valley."

"But your plan winkled him out of his citadel, Artor," Lot said.

"A great deal of the credit for that must go to Bedwyr for robbing Glamdring of his counselor. Although I never met him, Wyrr appears to have been a potent weapon, and his absence gave us a great advantage. On such random chances do the fortunes of war hang." Artor looked thoughtful. Memories came back to him of Anderida, his first successful battle. "Bedwyr, does Glamdring guard his back?"

"I don't understand what you mean, my lord." Bedwyr scratched at the stubble of russet beard that already blurred the clean lines of his lower face.

"Is it possible to climb the cliff faces?"

"Not Anderida again," Targo complained, quick to understand the king's thinking. "I hate heights even more than mud and swamps."

Llanwith laughed at the memory of the suicidal trap that Uther Pendragon had set for his son so many years before.

King Lot simply looked puzzled.

Still none the wiser, Bedwyr attempted to picture the steep cliffs that encircled the ancient fortress.

"Not really. Of course, there are old sewers under the fortress."

Artor raised one expressive eyebrow, and Bedwyr hurried to explain.

"The Saxons razed the original Roman outpost to build their halls and to develop their own system of defenses. But the old sewers used by the Romans became a garbage dump in the lower reaches of the system, and were used for granaries and storage areas closer to ground level. The original sewers open out directly onto the sides of a cliff, about halfway from the bottom. Don't ask me how they ever worked, for I don't know. I don't think Glamdring even realizes the stone channels are there."

"How do you know about the sewers, Bedwyr?" Artor's voice was patient but his eyes were very sharp.

"I never gave up searching for an escape route during the time I was a prisoner, especially when I realized that Glamdring had ceased to notice me as a human being. I discovered I could go anywhere in Caer Fyrddin as long as I was careful. One day, as I was trying to find a way out of the fortress, I crept down into the foundations. I found the stone sewers, and I managed to discover a path that ran through them, but they finished with a sheer drop down the side of a cliff face. Stealing rope wasn't an option, because such items were carefully guarded. At that time, I didn't consider that route would be of any use to me. It was a very long drop to the ground below."

"Were you afraid of falling?" Artor asked bluntly.

Bedwyr blushed to the roots of his ginger hair. Then he paled under Artor's scrutiny, and his voice, when he did try to explain, was cracked and hesitant.

"I'm afraid of heights, Lord Artor."

Targo began to laugh, until he realized the young man was in deadly earnest.

"I kept trying to find rope that was long enough for my needs, but I was always glad whenever I was unsuccessful. God knows what I'd have done if I'd had to climb down a rope into nothingness. I suppose I'll never know now. Oddly, I don't mind climbing up, especially when I can't see the ground. I climbed the watchtower at Caer Fyrddin in a fearful rush, so I didn't have time to be afraid, and I've climbed trees since boyhood. I don't understand why I was too frightened to climb down the cliffs from the sewer, and I'm ashamed of the fear that kept me in that hideous place."

Artor touched Bedwyr fleetingly on one shoulder. "You made amends for it at the shield wall, lad, but I had to know why you never used that route to escape."

Targo and Odin exchanged sympathetic glances, but Artor's expression remained stern.

"That particular foible must soon be overcome, Bedwyr. While I might sympathize with your experiences, I don't have time for your fears. Could the cliff be climbed to the point where the sewer outlet comes out if we could lower a rope down from inside the tunnel?"

"Possibly." Bedwyr blanched. "But I'm not thrilled at the prospect."

Artor sat quietly and sipped wine. Lot and Llanwith watched him think.

"Gruffydd? I want you," Artor called.

Gruffydd appeared silently out of the gloom. "You bellowed, my lord?"

Artor paid no heed to Gruffydd's humor, but King Lot was affronted by the sword-bearer's familiarity.

"Do you still think you can pass close scrutiny as a Saxon? I imagine Glamdring will accept any and all volunteers at this moment. His force must be reduced to a bare one hundred men, but even that small number could pose a problem for an attacking force."

"If entering his fortress will lead to victory over Glamdring's forces, then any risk is acceptable," Gruffydd responded. "Otherwise, we'll be back fighting the bastard within a year or two."

"Sadly, that's true. Do you feel the same way, Bedwyr?"

The young Celt's heart lurched. "Gruffydd might enter the fortress as a Saxon without any real difficulty, but Glamdring will recognize me as his dog even if he only has time for a cursory glance. He will know of my arrival as soon as I enter the gates of his fortress. It was me, after all, who killed Wyrr, so he must long for my death." He looked at Artor. "I will go if you ask, my lord, because it's preferable to climbing a rope over a long drop, but I'll need an excellent disguise. I know I'm in the best possible position to find my way through the sewers, but if I'm discovered, then so is Gruffydd."

"Don't fret, Bedwyr," Artor rejoined conversationally. "We're still many miles from Caer Fyrddin, so we'll talk again tomorrow."

Bedwyr was beginning to realize that the High King rarely acted on impulse. In many ways, Glamdring and Artor shared the same traits of pride, charisma, and the ability to command, but Artor's mind was cold and it was ruled by logic. He would willingly sacrifice his closest friends if the Celtic nation required their blood, but his sorrow was real and lasting. His responses were chilly, unlike those of the mercurial Glamdring, but, most telling of all, men loved Artor, even as they died for him, because he asked no more of them than he expected of himself. Bedwyr had no doubt that if Artor had been fluent in the Saxon tongue, he would have been the first man to attempt entry into Glamdring Ironfist's citadel.

During the following afternoon, the Celtic forces ambushed five Saxon warriors and dispatched them quickly. Artor ordered their bodies to be stripped and their rough clothing cleaned of all traces of blood.

"Did you ever hear of the Trojan horse, Bedwyr?" Artor asked at the campfire that night.

"No, my lord," Bedwyr replied, confused as usual by the leaps that Artor's agile mind made with such ease.

"It was a trick used at a place called Troy in a battle that occurred many, many years ago," Llanwith told him. "Long before Rome was even a collection of mud huts, Troy was the greatest fortress in the known world."

Bedwyr looked nonplussed.

"Many years ago," Artor explained, "a man called Homer wrote that the ancient Greeks once attacked the city of Troy in a war that was fought over a woman, of all things. Homer's army carried out a siege that lasted many years and employed an enormous army of warriors, but the city proved to be impregnable, and the siege couldn't force the Trojans to surrender. Eventually, a clever warrior in the Greek army called Odysseus built a huge wooden horse, an animal that was sacred to Poseidon, the god of Troy. They left the wooden horse outside the gates of the city." He smiled at his assembled warriors. "Then the Greeks sailed away over the horizon."

Lot frowned. "So did the Greeks simply give up?"

"Not quite, Lot. Odysseus had left twenty men inside the horse. The Trojans dragged their gift into the city, and celebrated what they believed to be their defeat of the Greeks who had retreated in their ships. Odysseus and his men waited until the Trojans had drunk themselves into a stupor and then crept out of their hiding places. Some of the Greeks opened the gates to the city to allow their returning comrades to enter, while the rest began to slaughter the population." Artor made a throat-cutting action with one hand. "There is an old saying that still warns us to beware of Greeks bearing gifts."

"So Bedwyr and I are to be your Trojan horse," Gruffydd said.

"In a nutshell. And three more Saxon-speaking warriors should join you, for we captured sufficient clothing to disguise five warriors." Artor looked at Bedwyr. "Obviously, your red hair will have to go. If we can't dye it, we'll have to shave it, eyebrows included. And no beard, of course. You will also wear a long coil of rope wrapped round your waist under your clothing. The extra padding will make you look portly, which will help to disguise you. Once you negotiate the sewers and find your way to the opening in the cliff, you will lower one end of the rope down to our warriors, who will be positioned below."

He paused, and Bedwyr nodded his understanding.

"My warriors will then attach it to a rope ladder, which you will pull up to the opening in the cliff. You must attach it to a secure object inside the sewer entrance. When the rope ladder is in position, it will be a simple matter for my warriors to enter Caer Fyrddin through the sewers. Glamdring will have no means of knowing we are entering under his feet."

"It's an excellent plan," Llanwith said. "The perfect Trojan horse strategy, but do you have a rope ladder that's long enough to use?"

"I don't climb well," Lot complained, patting his large paunch as he spoke.

"Would you climb the ladder for the memory of Gaheris?"

Lot nodded, swallowing a lump in his throat.

"Farryll, Camwy, and Lucan all speak Saxon fluently," Gruffydd remarked. "So that makes five of us."

Artor smiled. "Then it's time for you to have a very close haircut, Bedwyr. Glamdring has never really looked closely at you, has he?"

"No. To Glamdring, I was only Dog. But he will recognize the mark of the slave collar."

"Only if he sees it." Artor carefully considered the outward appearance of the young Cornovii. "I'm certain we can make you look like a different man if we disguise your clothes and your hair. And, of course, your scars."

"Of course," Bedwyr echoed faintly.

He realized he was going into Caer Fyrddin regardless of his misgivings, so he acquiesced glumly. As he had said earlier, entering the fortress in disguise was far preferable to climbing a rope ladder over a yawning chasm.

WHEN CAER FYRDDIN was within easy riding distance, Odin shaved Bedwyr's head with a razor-sharp blade. His growing beard was removed as well, and Odin rubbed a little coal dye into Bedwyr's russet eyebrows. Bedwyr felt distinctly odd. From somewhere, Artor had produced yards and yards of sturdy woven rope that, once wrapped round Bedwyr's waist, gave him a very plump appearance and completely changed his body shape.

He was a new man.

Once the five spies had donned their Saxon dress and armor, picked up their circular shields and donned the distinctive Saxon helmets, even Bedwyr had to admit that they were unrecognizable as Celts.

Artor smiled down at his young charge. "Your task is to enter the citadel and report to Glamdring that our force is two hours away from Caer Fyrddin. While you're carrying out this errand, we will position a small number of warriors close to the cliff below the sewer outlet. Once you have lowered your ropes to them and the rope ladder is secured, the need for subterfuge will be over. Can you master your hatred of Glamdring until then?"

"Aye. I can pretend to fawn at his feet if I can cut his throat at the end," Bedwyr replied sardonically.

"Good."

The following morning, five disguised Celtic warriors found themselves loping up the long track that led to the fortress at Caer Fyrddin. They were seen long before they reached the walls, and when they reached the shadow of the watchtower, they were acutely aware that longbows were trained on them.

"Glamdring appears to have learned a valuable lesson about the effectiveness of his bowmen," Bedwyr hissed.

"I'll do the talking, and you remain silent," Gruffydd whispered. "It's possible that Glamdring might remember the sound of your voice."

"I am Cerdan Shapechanger, and this man is Modrod of Forden," Gruffydd called out to the Saxons on the ramparts. "And these three oafs are our servants. We have eluded Artor's outriders and we bring news from Castell Collen. Let us in! Artor's cavalry are not far behind us, and his main force is only a few hours' ride from Caer Fyrddin."

In spite of the Saxon appearance of the five warriors below them, the men on the watchtower were taking no chances.

"Wait. We will call for the master."

"Better and better," Gruffydd mumbled sarcastically in Saxon.

While Gruffydd and his companions cooled their heels outside the fortress, Bedwyr noticed that the village huts had been hurriedly abandoned. Obviously, Glamdring had ordered every living soul into the fortress to swell the ranks of the defenders.

Above the gates, heads stared down at him with empty eye sockets. With a wrench, Bedwyr recognized face after face, the Celtic slaves of Caer Fyrddin, beheaded and rotting on poles. He pointed upward with one dirty finger.

Gruffydd laughed uproariously, and muttered at Bedwyr through his mirth. "Laugh, you idiot! Someone will be watching on the wall for our reactions."

Bedwyr managed a weak grin. "They were my fellow captives, every one of them, and they've been slain down to the last child."

"So laugh, Bedwyr!" Gruffydd insisted. "Glamdring will answer for his sins the sooner, and no one has been left alive to betray you by accident."

Bedwyr made a great play of nudging another of the disguised men, and pointed out the youngest head, a child of fourteen.

"He'll pay for little Gannett," he said under his laughter.

Llanwith had briefed Gruffydd on the fall of Castell Collen, so when Glamdring appeared on the wall, Gruffydd was able to give an accurate account of the rout. As Glamdring nodded on several occasions, it seemed likely that the thane already knew the details of the sacking of the northern fortress. Bedwyr was grateful that Artor had left little to chance.

"Repeat your names." Glamdring shouted from above. "Who are you, and what do you want of me?"

"We are Cerdan Shapechanger and Modrod of Forden. These other men are my servants." Gruffydd paused to ensure that anyone within earshot heard his voice. "We've been avoiding Artor's cavalry for days, but they're now only a few hours' riding from Caer Fyrddin. My family lived near Castell Collen, but my kin are now dead and we came to take our revenge when the battle commences here. All the west knows that only Glamdring Ironfist still resists Artor of the south."

Glamdring swelled a little at Gruffydd's flattery. He pointed a horny finger at Bedwyr. "And what of you, Modrod of Forden, wherever that is? Why have you come to me? You seem well enough fed."

"My wife and children are dead, my fields have been burned, and Artor's men have put my slaves to the sword." Bedwyr made his voice as high pitched as he could. "I may be plump, but my arm is strong, and I pledge it to the service of Glamdring Ironfist."

Some worm of doubt must have wriggled in Ironfist's memory.

"Take off your helmet, Modrod."

Glamdring inspected Bedwyr carefully from his position atop the watchtower.

Bedwyr was now grateful for his recognition of the heads of his fellow servants. Anger helped him to stare into Glamdring's eyes without fear. Determination squared his shoulders and raised his chin in defiance, which Glamdring mistook as a desire to revenge himself on the Celts. After all, Dog would never have looked his master in the eye.

"You're hairless for a Saxon," Glamdring stated bluntly. "That's unusual for our people. How did you get your bald head?"

"Illness, great thane. Hairless I may be, but my heart is Saxon! If you don't need our swords, we will go to a place of safety. We'll have done our duty, for we have warned you of the arrival of the bastard Celts."

"Don't be hasty, Modrod. In time of war, strange faces and circumstances breed distrust. The caer welcomes your extra swords, so you may enter as welcome guests."

One problem negotiated, Bedwyr thought silently to himself, and limped through the gates into Caer Fyrddin, a place that was little changed from the night when he had fled its slavery.

"You may eat with us after you have rested," Glamdring called from his position on the ramparts, his eyes never leaving the new arrivals as they passed into the confines of the fortress.

THE MEAL THAT evening was almost Bedwyr's undoing.

The hall was so filthy that Gruffydd feared food poisoning. The fire pit pumped thick smoke up to the soot-stained ceiling rafters, and the walls were greasy and stained where men had leaned against the wooden planks.

Long food-crusted tables and benches ran the length of the hall, while Glamdring and his chief officers sat at a shorter table that spanned its breadth at the head of the hall. Gruffydd and the other Celts sat as far as possible from the high table. They ate quickly, and drank little.

Warriors stabbed at the greasy swill of meat with their knives, careless of the gravy that stained their beards, and the whole room stank of spilled ale. The Saxons amused themselves by casting their bones over their shoulders and occasionally giving meaty treats to the hounds. It was one of the hounds, the young grey mastiff called Wind, that almost betrayed Bedwyr. The dog remembered him, and made a great fuss of him by licking his hands and leaping up to place his huge paws on Bedwyr's shoulders.

"You have a rare talent with dogs, friend Modrod. Do they always offer you their friendship?" Glamdring was joking, but a trace of suspicion lurked in his muddy blue eyes.

"I've bred animals since I was a lad, my lord. I swear I can train the most recalcitrant pup into a useful fighting dog."

Glamdring whistled, and the grizzled head of his deerhound rose over the end of the table.

"Let us see what you can do with old Grodd here," Glamdring challenged. "He allows no one but me to feed him."

Liar, thought Bedwyr. Grodd had been fed regularly by most of the servants whenever Glamdring tired of caring for his dogs, although Bedwyr doubted that the thane had even noticed.

Holding up a succulent bone, still dripping with fat, Bedwyr called the dog by name. At first, Grodd looked at him with hostility, and growled at the strange human before him. Glamdring began to laugh. But the bone was tempting and Grodd warily approached Bedwyr. When it was close enough to pick up Bedwyr's scent, the dog remembered shared scraps and allowed Bedwyr to scratch its ears before it snapped up the bone. The Celt feigned the near loss of a finger in the process.

"A fine beast, thane. I can see why you take pride in him."

Glamdring was mollified. "It seems you are indeed talented with animals, Modrod. Let's hope that you're as capable with Celts."

The ale flowed and Bedwyr conspired to spill as much as he drank, knowing he would need a clear head for the task before him.

Another difficult moment was narrowly avoided when a serving woman almost dropped her ale jug when she recognized the hazel eyes of Bedwyr. She had managed to avoid death because she was half-Saxon and had been forced to share Glamdring's bed since she was eleven. No one had considered that she was Demetae and might resent her servile place in the caer. Bedwyr saw her look of consternation and recognition, and pulled her towards him and onto his lap before she could utter a word. Gripping one large breast in his hand, he forced her to kiss him and then began to nuzzle her ear.

"Smile, woman! Do not betray me if you value your life."

She smiled nervously as Bedwyr ripped open her tattered gown and fondled her breasts while Glamdring, ever observant, laughed crudely with his captains. When Bedwyr bent to kiss her nipples, he whispered again.

"Lock yourself in the kitchen tonight, and, with luck, you and your children may survive the night's events."

"Leave her, Modrod!" Glamdring ordered from his elevated table. "She's just a serving wench and not worth much, except that she's carrying good ale. If you want a real woman, there are Saxon widows here who'll share a riding with you like you've never known."

Glamdring held his horn cup out for the girl to fill, her breasts still bare in the firelight. The thane twisted one nipple cruelly with his left hand, and she gasped with pain. Then, as she hurried away to refill her jug, she gave Bedwyr a brief, enigmatic smile.

"My thanks, lord thane, but I've always had a taste for servile woman flesh. There's something about fear that gives a man . . . that extra spice."

Glamdring laughed and agreed, and the evening passed on.

Eventually, feigning drunkenness, the five Celts made nests for themselves in the straw by the doors of the hall, while those Saxon warriors still able to walk returned to their barracks.

Gruffydd marveled at the confidence displayed by Glamdring. In spite of the warning that danger was on his doorstep, life within the fortress continued on as if the Saxons were at peace.

Our task is made easy, Gruffydd thought sardonically. Defeat at Mori Saxonicus has taught Glamdring nothing. He is prepared to risk his remaining warriors against Artor's vengeance without so much as an extra guard at the gate. The man is a fool!

As Bedwyr pretended to sleep in the verminous straw with the pungent-smelling Wind pressed hard against his side, he marveled at how quickly his circumstances had changed. He had laid out this same pile of straw only a week earlier, and now he was here again, planning to bring Caer Fyrddin down around Glamdring's head.

"It's time to go," Gruffydd hissed.

Five men and a huge mastiff rose to their feet.

"Must we take the beast?" Gruffydd pointed his knife. "It could get in our way."

Bedwyr was appalled. "Wind is my dog, and I'll keep him for myself. I raised him from a pup, so I'll vouch for his temper. If possible, I'd prefer that all the animals should be kept alive. The Saxons usually treat them far better than they treat humans."

"Oh, sod it then! Just don't let that great lump get in the way. Lead on, Bedwyr."

The great hall was still, except for snorers and the shifting mounds of dogs. Bedwyr had only to whisper a command and the beasts returned to their sleep.

At the head of the group of five men, Bedwyr led the way, holding a small, flaming torch. Gruffydd brought up the rear, lighting the darkness with another small torch. The men edged their way through the narrow, muddy passages between kitchens and sleeping quarters until they reached a sloping compound and a dark doorway with worn steps leading downward into stygian blackness.

"These are the granaries," Bedwyr whispered, and began to descend.

Through the wicker baskets, and the leather and wooden storage bins, Bedwyr picked his way until, behind a heavy wooden box filled with miscellaneous pieces of ironmongery, he revealed a low stone opening, curved at the top. It was barely three feet high.

"From here on, the passage tends to get smaller and smaller as we move along."

Wind balked at entering the dark hole at first, but soon scrambled after Bedwyr when he realized that his master might abandon him again. At the rear, Gruffydd swore pungently as he crawled through after the other men.

The stone passage widened after a hundred yards, so they could walk, albeit bent over. The walls were covered with decades of encrusted filth and old, dried slime, and Gruffydd tried hard not to imagine the waste from latrines that had fed into this channel over the years.

At least we can be grateful that the sewers are no longer in use, he thought grumpily.

Down and down the sewer went, narrowing sometimes until Bedwyr was forced to remove the rope so he could wriggle through the restricted space. The oppressive feeling of tons of earth and stone above them made the Celts feel like men long buried, and their bodies were fouled by decades of waste.

They spent an unpleasant hour crawling.

Then, as suddenly as they had entered the sewer, they reached its end. A small crack of moonlight appeared at the end of the sloping tunnel, and the five men found themselves at a rubble-strewn exit hanging dizzily over empty air.

As Bedwyr cast his eye around the cavernous opening, he noted that the Romans had built these sewers out of smooth dressed stone and the living rock of the mountain. But, at one time, those canny engineers had recognized some weakness in the defense of their fortress, and had contrived to set bars of iron deep into the stone, probably to prevent a persistent enemy from attacking their unprotected backs.

Most of the iron bars were rusted through or broken by the passage of time, but two metal stanchions at the very edge of the exit were still firmly embedded in the rock floor. Fearing danger in using only one, Bedwyr used both stanchions to secure the rope.

Gruffydd dropped a large pebble into the black void below.

A hissed curse came from the darkness far below, and Gruffydd grinned whitely at Bedwyr.

"I think I may have hit someone on the head."

The rope was lowered and the men retreated back into the sewer. Soon, there was a tug on the line, and Bedwyr pulled it back up to the sewer entrance with the rope ladder tied firmly in place. Within minutes the ladder, too, was secured to the iron stanchions.

Bedwyr patted Wind's large square head, and prayed that the ladder was long enough and would hold the strain of the men's weight.

The rope sang and strained as it took up the weight of the first climber. In the sewer entrance, the five men watched, hearts in mouths, as the metal bent a little, but the bars held.

Then Odin, the heaviest warrior by far, crawled into the sewer entry.

One by one, other men followed. Artor stared at Wind with mild curiosity. The mastiff bared his teeth for an instant, but then dropped his massive head submissively.

"Is that your dog, Bedwyr?"

"Yes, my lord. I'd consider it a favor if you spared the Saxon animals when we take the fortress. They are superb beasts and are magnificent hunting and fighting animals. I promise you that they are the one true skill of these Saxons. They've been bred to be man killers, but they are noble creatures nonetheless. If we ever bred such animals ourselves, we could train them to be useful to our cause."

Artor grinned down at Bedwyr's earnest, worried face.

"Did you feed them when you were a slave?"

"Yes, my lord."

"Would they obey you?"

"Yes, my lord." Bedwyr nodded his assurances to the High King. "One further matter, my lord," he continued. "There is a female slave in Caer Fyrddin who is only part Saxon. She has not betrayed me, and I promised that she and her children would be freed. She's lucky that her head didn't become a decoration for the gates of Caer Fyrddin, as did those of the other Celt slaves who were here when I killed Wyrr. These slaves have been ill used for years, and she considers herself to be beyond hope. I ask that you spare her if you can. I have told her to lock herself in the kitchens, and I would hate to see her suffer because of me and mine."

"Very well, Bedwyr," Artor replied. "After all, she does have some Celt blood in her veins."

It took several hours for a hundred men to enter the fortress. The stanchions were only strong enough for one man at a time to climb the rope ladder. Against all the odds the old iron stayed firmly within the rock.

The remnants of Artor's forces, under the commands of Llanwith and Lot, would be in position to pour through the entrance gates as soon as they were needed.

"Lead the way, Bedwyr," Artor ordered. "Odin will be directly behind you, followed by myself. I will follow Odin because we are the two largest men and will have the most difficulty passing through the tunnels."

In any event, both men nearly became wedged in the narrowest sections. When they finally clambered into the relative comfort of the storage room, both Artor and Odin had decided privately that never again would they commit themselves to such an ordeal.

Artor immediately turned to Bedwyr. "Where are we now?"

"The warriors' quarters are to your right as you leave the store-room," Bedwyr explained, drawing in the dust of the stone floor. "There are at least a hundred men quartered there."

"Odin. On my command, take fifty of our men and capture the warriors' hall. Kill them, and keep killing them until such time as all are slain or they agree to throw down their weapons. We don't have sufficient numbers to take prisoners until the battle has been won and the fortress is secure. Is that understood?"

"Yes, my lord."

Artor turned back to Bedwyr, who continued.

"At least twenty more Saxons are asleep in the great hall with the dogs. Although they are drunk and should not put up an effective fight, the dogs might cause some problems as they are trained to kill and to hunt."

"Where will Glamdring be?" Artor asked in a soft, dangerous voice.

"Ironfist will be with his women, here." Bedwyr stabbed his make-shift map with one dirty finger. "But he may have kept his personal guards close by, now that he's under threat from your forces. The watchtower will be well guarded, and those men must be killed if the gates are to be opened. There are other guards on the ramparts, but I doubt they will be of any significance."

Artor nodded. "We will have the advantage of surprise so the battle should be over swiftly. Fortunately, there's no way that Glamdring can obtain reinforcements. I will command the main force of twenty men and will secure the great hall, while you must select five men to search for Glamdring and his personal guards. Your task is to capture Glamdring and kill those warriors who are with him. No mercy."

Bedwyr nodded in understanding.

"Gruffydd. You'll take the remainder of our force and capture the watchtower. At the earliest opportunity, detail men to open the gates and allow Llanwith and Lot to enter the fortress with their warriors." Artor gazed round at the assembled group of captains. "Is the plan agreed and understood?"

"Aye!" their voices chorused.

Within thirty minutes, the Saxon defenders were captured or killed. Most chose to die in a final act of defiance.

Accompanied by Lot, Llanwith swept his cavalry into Caer Fyrd-din and cut a swathe through those warriors who escaped the charnel house of the great hall and the warriors' barracks.

Of the dogs, only Grodd chose to die. The animal's skull was cleaved in two by a blow from a great axe as he attempted to defend his master.

When a surprised and naked Glamdring was discovered in bed with his woman, he was immediately surrounded and kept away from his weaponry. He was at Bedwyr's mercy.

The serving woman was freed from the kitchens, and the rest of the female slaves. At first, they cowered and wept, fearing the usual fate of women taken in war, but Artor remembered his vow and they were herded into the Great Hall. He determined that no innocent female would suffer if she had been forced to labor in the Caer Fyrddin fortress.

Glamdring's women and the other camp followers of the fortress were another matter entirely, and would be forced to suffer the fate of those females who are, ultimately, the spoils of war. The Saxon children were herded together to be relocated into the west to endure slavery or adoption.

The Saxon thane wasn't permitted the dignity of dressing. Bedwyr kicked him from his bed, naked and bemused, while Gruffydd silenced the screams of his woman. Bedwyr pulled Glamdring's head back by a handful of greasy hair and tore the Arden Knife from round his neck. With the knife pressed to his throat, he was forced to stumble to the hall, his naked feet slipping on spilled blood and his shriveled manhood the subject of several ribald jokes.

"You are not so boastful now, little man," Bedwyr sneered, and Glamdring shook his muddled head as he tried to recognize a voice that teased at his memory. "You're just piss and wind, aren't you?"

"Who are you?" Glamdring demanded. In truth, the thane had never feared death, only failure.

"Don't you recognize your faithful dog? My, my, Glamdring Jellyfish, didn't you think that I'd return and bring the army of Artor with me? You have always been thoughtless without Wyrr to tell you how to think!"

Naked, Glamdring stood in his great hall, furious and struggling. But then he realized that Bedwyr was taking pleasure from his fruitless efforts. He closed his teeth with an audible snap and, although the cords stood out on his neck from the effort, he squared his shoulders, raised his head, and kept his lips shut.

The Celts surrounded him and the few Saxon warriors who survived in a ring of iron.

For all his impotence, something noble enlivened the savage stolidity of Glamdring's face, the same nobility that a wild bear or a boar could possess when it fought the dogs to the death in the full knowledge that it would die anyway. Bedwyr hardened his heart and stroked the scar round his neck.

Artor walked forward, his hair freed from under his helmet, and his great height dwarfing even the bulk of Glamdring. He stared down into the bearded face of the man who had chosen not to bow, and whose eyes remained filled with implacable hatred.

"You killed my ambassadors under a flag of truce at Y Gaer. What is your excuse for this breach of honor?"

"What honor do Celts and cowardly curs possess? This land is ours now, and you are the usurpers. We've lived here for generations, invited by your King Vortigern. I am a descendant of Horsa and I claim my right to these lands."

"If you had chosen to hear my terms, this land would still be yours." Artor actually sounded regretful. "I was prepared to offer you an honorable truce between equals, accepting your right to the land your forefathers won. You and I are Britons, as is Lucan, for all that his grandfather was a citizen of Rome." Bedwyr pointed casually to one of his companions, who had posed as a Saxon in order to enter the citadel. "He speaks Saxon, just like you. In fact, you welcomed him into your fortress. He is a Briton, and proudly so. King Lot has the bloodlines of the Picts, and they ruled this land when all our ancestors lived in mud huts and crawled on their bellies. Had you accepted that you were a Briton first and a Saxon second, hundreds of men would still be living and breathing. The fault, Glamdring Ironfist, is in your prejudice and your false pride."

Glamdring spat at Artor, who merely stepped aside. Artor looked sadly at the naked man, still so powerful and unashamed by his nakedness.

"You were a worthy adversary, but you would have been a better ally. When will your people ever learn? When will they see these mountains, the open plains, and the green fields for what they are? A gift to us from the gods, especially if we could live in peace and harmony together."

"Never!" Glamdring bellowed in his rage. "I am the heir of Vortigern. This is my earth. You may kill me if you wish, but it will change nothing."

Artor sighed. "Vortigern was Celt, Glamdring. Celt! Don't you understand? No, you don't. So you speak like a fool and a brute, for what you cannot use, you debase or kill. But a wise man knows that cruelty will strike back at him a hundredfold." He gazed at his captains who surrounded him. "Behold your enemies."

Llanwith stepped forth. "You have killed any Ordovice warrior who strayed into your lands. You showed no mercy. You blooded your young men by torturing our guards on the borders. You stole our women and brutalized them. I demand your death."

Glamdring spat at him.

King Lot stepped forward. "You are fortunate that my queen is not with me, for she would demand that the Celtic women flay you alive. I was your ally, yet you killed my son because he would not break a blood oath. A better and a wiser man would have set my son free for the courage he showed. I demand your death!"

Gruffydd stepped forward. "Your warriors killed my family, and I was enslaved." Gruffydd tore off his woolen undertunic to expose the spear scar. "I bear the Saxon mark. I've brought many good Saxon men to their deaths because of you and your blood-soaked father. I also demand your death."

Finally, Bedwyr bared his shaven head. He faced Glamdring with the dog, Wind, by his side. "You called me Dog, and you taught me how to hate. I watched my companions die horribly, and then you enslaved me. I cleaned your muck, learned your speech, and was forced to kill your sorcerer, Wyrr. I am Bedwyr, of the Cornovii, born near the forests of Arden, and I will hate you forever for your brutality." He smiled triumphantly at Glamdring Ironfist. "I also demand your death, because I, Bedwyr ap Bedwyr, am the Arden Knife."

Finally, Glamdring's composure broke and he cursed and screamed, his rage turning his face red and his eyes beginning to fill with small dancing fires. He refused to accept that he had contributed to his own destruction because neither he nor Wyrr had placed any value in the worth of a slave.

"If I should die, then let me die in combat," he demanded. "I will fight any one of you, or all. It matters not to me."

"You didn't allow Gaheris the honor of death by combat," Artor stated uncompromisingly. "For what you did to Gaheris, you shall be fed to the crows, as was he, without the boon of honorable disposal of your remains."

Glamdring struggled in his bonds.

"For what you did to Gaheris, and to Cerdic, and to all those noble warriors who died because of your treachery at Y Gaer, you will be executed like the felon you are."

Artor gazed directly into the eyes of Glamdring.

"Your hands will be removed like a thief, and you will die where you now stand. After your death, the hands that caused the death of Gaheris will be presented to his mother, Queen Morgause, to do with as she chooses. May your gods have mercy on you in the Shades of death."

Artor nodded to Odin, standing alongside the screaming Glamdring. King Lot himself held the rope that tethered. Glamdring Ironfist's hands together. With a vicious heave, the Saxon's arms were extended in front of him on a tabletop.

"Now!"

Artor's voice was steady, and his face expressed nothing but the contempt he felt for Glamdring.

Bedwyr turned away, sickened despite himself, as Odin used one mighty blow of his axe to remove Glamdring's bound hands above the wrists. Glamdring howled in shock, pain, and impotent fury.

One of Lot's officers collected the grim relics and placed them in a leather bag while Glamdring stared at the stumps of his arms. He watched as his lifeblood pumped away into the straw.

"For the sake of Gaheris, and his memory, your head will be displayed on a pole and taken through these lands until the crows eventually pick it clean at Cadbury Tor. You would have done the same to me, if our positions were reversed. I find no sensibility or decency in you, only the instincts of the beasts, so I will not spare your life. To exist, handless, would be too cruel a punishment, and I am not a man such as you. So I, Artor, High King of the Britons, have said. Let it be done!"

Glamdring bowed his ashen face until his hair fell forward and obscured his features. As he rapidly bled to death, he fell to one knee, almost as if he finally offered a Saxon form of homage to the High King of the Britons.

He had finally come to the realization that Artor could be merciful.

Odin took one more mighty swing with his axe, and removed the head from Glamdring's body. Taking a spear from one of his men, the Jutlander impaled the head and raised it aloft, to the cheers of the assembled Celtic warriors.

"Glamdring's body will be tossed outside Caer Fyrddin, where the carrion shall feast on it. You will then strip this pesthole of anything of value. All children and those Saxon women who will submit shall be taken into the south land, where they will begin a new life. Bedwyr will take Glamdring's hounds. All else that remains shall be razed to the ground."

And so the Saxon fortress at Caer Fyrddin was reduced to ashes and rubble.

Far away, in an oxen-drawn cart of wounded men, Myrddion saw a plume of black smoke in the west. As he watched, he recalled each of Artor's campaigns with a pang of regret. Even now, after all this time, more men were dying to ensure the safety of the Celtic nation.

Myrddion pressed his temples where a sick headache was beginning to center in spiking, radiating pain. There were so many wight-haunted places, and it was so hard to remember them all. Magnis, Lindum, Pontes, and Causennae, where the Roman roads ran straight and true; in the hills below Ratae and on the river out of Vernemetum; the places ran together in his head in a long, grim procession of wounded men, amputations, and ugly deaths. He could still smell the cremation fires of Vindomora, when winter gripped the north in a fist of iron and the Saxons and blue Picts had almost broken Artor's line, until he drew them onto the ice that his sappers had spent days weakening and then disguising. Oddly, Saxons did not swim.

Myrddion struggled to remember the names. Navio had been terrible, deep in the forests that covered the slopes of the mountains. Saxons and Celts had hunted one another in a spiteful, long, and futile autumn until the Saxons and the Angles had retreated to the land beyond Lindum. And then, before they could lick their wounds and regain their strength, Artor had gathered his scattered troops, given heart to tired men, and led them in a grueling forced march in pursuit of their enemies. At a nameless ford, the Celts had made the river run red with enemy blood.

Of course, early in the years of struggle, the Saxons had poured out of Anderida, where the whole, fearful campaign had begun, but Artor had won great victories at Anderida Silva and east of Noviomagus. Still, Anderida remained a Saxon stronghold, guarding the narrow seas to Gaul and, one day, even Artor's great strength couldn't halt their slow, inexorable advance. The barbarians extended their walls and their sphere of influence around Anderida as each Saxon summer came and went. Myrddion was a realist, as were the citizens of Noviomagus, Portus Adurni, and Clausentum. One day, when Artor was no more, Anderida would set fire to the south.

"Lord of Light, Myrddion in the heavens, foster father and namesake, I beg you to help my master," Myrddion whispered. "The High King doesn't understand that a fragile peace may be more destructive than any number of bloody engagements. For who can quiet the cruelty of man when his enemies are defeated?"

But the seer smiled painfully at his qualms, for deep in his wise and guarded heart, he rejoiced at the magnitude of the Saxon defeat. Yes, the tales would spread like wildfire, and grow in the telling.

And so the twelfth, and the last, great campaign of Artor's wars against the Saxons was won, and the legend of Camlann had begun.

Chapter XI

THE WOMAN WITH
YELLOW HAIR

Six months after Artor had returned in triumph to Cadbury Tor, the earth was locked tightly in the grip of late winter weather. Although the fields still lay under a thin coverlet of snow and frost, farmers were already trying to break the sullen soil into furrows to plant for the coming summer. The fruit trees were bare of leaves, and animals foraged for what grass still lived in the cold hollows, supplemented by fodder that had been scythed the previous autumn.

The skies were grey, and were rarely blown clear of the cloud cover that would allow only the shadow of a pallid sun to shine through. Raptors wheeled in the skies as they chased rabbits or other small creatures clad in their winter coats. Cadbury itself was slippery with black ice, and elderly folk were forced to tread carefully on the rough-flagged pathways lest they fall. The whole landscape was a symphony of shades of grey, punctuated by the black tracery of trees and the dark foliage of oaks and pines. Beauty dwelt there, and peace, so that the villagers raced on the frozen ice and rosy-cheeked children played incomprehensible games in the naked trees without fear.

Glamdring Ironfist's skull had long been picked clean, but it still stood over the wall as it peered, with empty, gaping eye sockets, at the villages and fields that he had intended to destroy. Truth to tell, even in such a brief time since the sacking of Caer Fyrddin, the Saxon was rarely remembered, except as a "boggle man" to frighten small children. Violence and murder are ultimately futile in the face of the vast demands of the land.

Artor sat in his great hall and arbitrated between dissatisfied or warring villagers, and if he was often bored by petty arguments and squabbles over boundary walls, he never permitted his serene face to show his feelings. No matter what decisions he made, the people declared that he was the greatest king that the world had ever seen. Artor knew that sound common sense solved almost everything, and that he was no Solomon but a plain man who understood the issues of the common people.

The throne room was much as it had been prior to the Battle of Mori Saxonicus, but Artor had insisted on several new additions. From the ceiling, the torn and bloody standards of Artor, Pelles, Luka, Caius, Lot, and Llanwith were hung from large iron stanchions. Their tattered, stained appearance declared their hard use and venerable history.

At the other end of the hall, Artor had ordered that the battle standards of his enemies, of Katigern Oakheart, Glamdring Ironfist, and the other masters of the Saxon west, should be hung. These banners were also bloodstained and stiff with dried mud; some were rent from end to end and still others had been burned at the edges.

The White Dragon of the Saxons and the Red Dragon of the Celts snarled at each other across the long hall.

On a small table at Artor's right hand lay a fine box made of hazel wood that had been harvested from a dead tree branch. It contained a scrap of cloth, once white, but now brown with dried blood. Artor had sent warriors to search for the flag of truce at Y Gaer, and this fragment was all that could be found. And so Artor cherished a relic by which he would remember the sacrifice of the patriots who had served him so well. Whenever his courage was wanting, or his growing cynicism told him that his efforts were for nothing, he simply had to grip the hazel box to recall that he was required to show duty unto death.

By comparison with many of the Celtic kings, Artor's court was spartan, but its cleanliness, the bright hangings, the mosaic before the dais, and the stained banners had a power and sophistication more potent than gold, heavy carvings, or ornate paintings.

On this day, two visitors came to the High King's court. The first man was a courier from King Leodegran, the rather pompous ruler of the Dobunni, who shared the soft lands south of Sabrina Aest with the last of the Roman cities. Leodegran planned to visit Cadbury Tor in all state within the month, and he planned to bring his only daughter, the fabled beauty, Wenhaver.

The courier was well pleased with Artor's graceful words of welcome, and with the promise of good food and a warm bed before he would have to return to Corinium, where Leodegran was holding court. Ever courteous in matters of protocol, Artor gave the courier a single band of fine silver in thanks for his pains.

Inwardly, Artor groaned. He was well versed in the machinations of tribal princes with daughters of marriageable age, and loathed the facile social duties of a High King and the juggling for power of those who would stand at his side. Nor did he believe that Leodegran's visit was wholly a matter of courtesy. For several years, Artor's advisers had insisted that he owed his kingdom a wife and an heir, so that the bloody mess preceding his own coronation should not be repeated.

The king knew he had to marry some time, but he was sick of having eligible girls thrust under his nose. They were always too young or too old, too beautiful or distressingly ugly, or so giggly or ambitious his flesh began to creep.

Wenhaver was reputed to be of exceptional beauty, but he needed more than a lovely face to give him happiness. Artor remembered the pleasures of his marriage to Gallia with fondness and idealism, although her features had dimmed after the passage of so many years. What he did remember was a woman who shared his life in all respects.

231

Every detail of his life was discussed thoroughly, shared in loving communion with his wife, just as she shared her life, her thoughts, and her fears with him. In Gallia's arms, he had been free to be afraid. And, after all these years, her loss still left him with a hollow pit in his stomach and a dark hole in his heart.

What princess, raised to rule a regal household and bear aristocratic children, could be the partner of his thoughts and deeds as Gallia had been? Even as he finished his graceful speech to the courier, he fingered the small female figure that hung on a golden chain round his neck, and recalled the feel of Gallia's breasts and silken flanks.

Gallia had been real and true. The princesses and daughters of lordlings who were paraded before him were neither, for these girls were playing for very high stakes. Regardless of her character or her appearance, the young woman who became High Queen would carry her family with her to prominence. Unwillingly, Artor admitted to himself that the successful female must, perforce, hide any flaws or personal misgivings behind a compliant, passive face.

Therefore, if one girl was much like any other, Artor decided to choose the female who possessed great beauty and power, and whose father would become an ally, certain to augment the king's endless need for money and men to secure the fortresses along the Spine. The mountain range would keep the Saxons out of the West while the citadels were manned and strong. Therefore, the High King's marriage was a necessary tool in the maintenance of the kingdom.

But common sense is cold comfort when a man has known the rare communion of spirits that he had shared with Gallia.

Gallia had died so long ago; Artor had worn her marriage gift from Frith for almost longer than Gallia had lived. Frith had found a small knot of hazel wood in the forest that had been shaped by nature into the form of a tiny, pregnant woman. In the absence of Gallia's dead mother, and in the Roman custom, Frith had removed the young girl's birth charm from her neck on her wedding night and replaced it with this small fertility charm.

Artor had never removed the charm since Gallia's death.

Dear Frith—slave, mother, and adviser—had died as she protected Gallia. The swords of Uther Pendragon's warriors had cut her down as she tried to reach out to her mistress, but Frith hadn't journeyed alone into the darkness of Hades. She had buried her bronze hairpin through the eye and into the brain of one of their assailants, killing him instantly. Whenever Artor stroked the little amulet, Gallia's gaiety and Frith's steadfastness gave him courage.

The second visitor walked casually into Artor's hall as if he owned it.

As soon as the murmur of the crowd alerted Artor, he looked up and saw a familiar, exotic figure striding confidently towards the throne.

Gareth, Frith's grandson and steward of the Villa Poppinidii, had come to Cadbury.

In a hall of dark-haired people, Gareth stood apart. His ash-blond hair was unnaturally long and was bound with a long bronze pin at the base of his neck. Gareth bowed, and the High King recognized Frith's hairpin in the young man's hair. When Artor was a child at the villa, he had played with that sturdy, unadorned spike of bronze when he was little more than a toddler. The king felt strangely dislocated to see this simple object in the hair of a warrior. Memories of Gallia and Frith overwhelmed the king, so that his nod to Gareth was a little slow for true courtesy.

Gareth saw the pain in Artor's eyes and took no offense. After all, Gareth was one of the few men who knew that Artor had been married and had fathered a child.

Gareth was now thirty years of age and powerfully built. While he was not as tall as Artor, he towered over most of the men in the great hall of Cadbury Tor. His golden skin, his blue-green eyes, and his pale hair were an obvious inheritance from his grandmother's barbarian blood. Artor was prepared to swear that Jute blood ran through Gareth's veins.

Myrddion gently touched Artor's shoulder to gain his attention.

"May I suggest you cancel the rest of the court until tomorrow,

Lord Artor? Gareth would not have come from the Villa Poppinidii unless he was pressed by some urgent need."

Myrddion's voice was such a low whisper that even the closest warriors could not have heard his words. The wise man knew that Gareth had loved Gallia, and that he now cared for Licia, Artor's unacknowledged daughter. The young man's business must be important for him to leave Artor's child.

Artor nodded in agreement, and lifted the heavy dragon crown from his head.

The crown had lost none of its visceral appeal and beauty with the passage of twelve years. On Artor's bronze curls, the rampant golden dragon, with its wings reaching up to a point above the High King's forehead, was a sight to inspire awe. Even now, placed on the side table beside Artor's hazel box, the crown winked with the luster and mellow beauty of heavy, buttery gold; garnets; and large, simply cut citrines. Scaled with the stones from his mother's earrings and Uther's horde of ill-gotten gems, Artor's crown was a statement of inhuman might ennobled by great craftsmanship.

"The High King's court is closed for the remainder of today, and will reconvene tomorrow," Myrddion announced in a voice that echoed through the great hall. The king nodded courteously to the disappointed petitioners who were agog with curiosity. With a buzz of surprise and eager surmise, the citizens, both highborn and lowly, filed out of the great hall, staring covertly at Gareth as they passed him.

"Come with me," Artor ordered Gareth, as he rose and left the hall, trailed by Odin and Targo, who was forced to use a cane to assist his ancient hips.

As the High King strode through his domain, Gareth had ample opportunity to examine the tall figure of his lord. Superficially, Gareth could discern few physical changes in Artor's form since he had first seen him in the stables of Villa Poppinidii eighteen years earlier.

The king wore his formal robes of fine wool, some of which were dyed red and others bleached to a snowy whiteness, with his usual casual elan. His outer robe was secured at the shoulder with a large, wheel-shaped brooch that was decorated with a continuous, sinuous band of pure gold. His underrobe was pristine and left bare his strong calves so that Gareth could admire his soft half boots of brain-tanned pigskin. No costly jewelry hung from his ears, neck, or fingers, except for his thumb rings and a single ring on his index finger. Gareth sighed with admiration.

Artor's face, however, had changed, albeit subtly, and Gareth pondered over this as he walked abreast of Targo in his lord's wake. Two deep creases between the brows spoke of concentration and worry. The king's eyes had always been a chill, northern-grey color, but humor and an acute interest in other people had warmed them during his youth. But now the High King's eyes had become unreadable and glacial. Only someone who had worshipped Artor all his life would recognize the faint signs of disillusion that drew down the corners of his mobile mouth. Fortunately, humor still lurked in those well-shaped lips, and promised that the lad who had been called Artorex hadn't totally perished in the transformation from boy into mature man.

No words were uttered until they reached Artor's personal apartments. The king's mind raced with a host of unpleasant possibilities, but he dared say nothing until they reached his private, secluded room, where all truly secret business was conducted. He dismissed his guard, and ushered Gareth, Targo, Myrddion, and Odin into his inner sanctum.

Artor's private rooms were masculine but opulent. The furnishings included a finely carved table, built by a clever Brigante craftsman, where the king wrote what decrees were necessary. His favorite curule chair was comfortably cushioned, and the wall had fitted niches where he kept his many scrolls. Other chairs were scattered through the room, and there were cushions on every bench to soften the hard wood. Small panes of glass from Italy, the size of a human hand, were set into a narrow, arrow-slit window to keep the cold winds at bay and yet allow light into the room. A golden wine jug waited for Artor's hand, and bronze platters of fruit and nuts tempted his appetite.

Once Artor saw to the comfort of his guests, he asked Gareth why he had come to Cadbury Tor.

"Master Ector has received a good offer for Licia's hand in marriage, my lord. You know the boy, at least by note, for he is Comac ap Llanwith, of the Ordovice. He is the youngest son of King Llanwith."

The High King started, and his eyes became hooded. Suspicion snaked in his mind like a subtle poison. Gareth was perturbed by what he read in the king's face. Did Artor truly distrust King Llanwith, one of his oldest friends?

"Does this Comac know who Licia is?" Artor demanded flatly. His eyes were colorless and as empty as glass.

"No, my lord. King Llanwith hasn't told the boy, believing that his friendship with you would be compromised. Licia and Comac met when King Llanwith visited Ector as a family friend. Although Licia is young, she knows her own mind, and she has set her heart on Comac."

"She's far too young!" Artor protested like an old man.

In truth, Artor hadn't even considered that Licia was now a woman and was of marriageable age. The passage of time had been stilled for Artor when he considered his daughter; and she was frozen in time as little more than a toddler. No man would be an appropriate lover for the daughter of Gallia. He had rarely held Licia in his arms, so thoughts of her loving another man filled him with horror. That she would risk the perils of childbirth caused hot blood to surge to his head.

"She is fourteen, my lord, as you well know. Livinia is to be married in the spring, and she's only a year older than Licia. I'm afraid that where one of those girls go, the other follows."

"Oh, is that so?" Artor asked narrowly. "Caius hasn't mentioned anything to me about the matter. Who is Livinia to marry?"

"My lord, Caius is not yet the pater familias of the family, and Master Ector makes these decisions. He has arranged a match between Livinia and the grandson of Branicus, the Magistrate of Aquae Sulis. It is a very good match, but it's not as favorable as Licia's choice. Should Comac's older brother perish, then Licia will become a queen."

Artor flushed to his cheekbones. His jealousies and bad temper were an insult to his foster father. Ector loved Licia as truly as Livinia Minor, his own granddaughter. Common sense began to reassert itself in Artor's mind. Licia had to marry someone and, in Llanwith's household, she would be safe.

"If Ector approves of Licia's marriage, I suppose I have no right to throw barriers in their path. I will send a bride gift that is more than fitting. Does that make you happy?"

Artor was very near to sulking, but Gareth refused to take offense.

"There is one other matter, Lord Artor, although I don't quite know how to broach it, for I suspect it will make you angry."

"Spit it out, Gareth. You may as well tell me now and get the matter over with."

"Comac has expressed a wish that Licia should be called Anna for all public ceremonies. His people would frown upon a Roman name for a member of their royal family, although Comac would continue to call her by her given name in private. I should also mention that Comac believes Licia to be your half sister."

"What?" Artor was stunned by this revelation. "Do other people gossip about such a connection with me?"

"Yes, my lord, they do. And, for this reason, King Llanwith has agreed to the match for the sake of Licia's continued welfare. He believes that if a connection with you becomes widely accepted, even if it's wrong, it would place Licia in some danger. If she is in the bosom of King Llanwith's court, she'll be safe forever."

"But why do people in Aquae Sulis make the connection with me? I don't understand."

It was a matter about which Artor had given no thought. For once, his ability to predict a turn of events had failed him.

"She is a perfect female image of you, my lord, except for her eyes. I've watched her as she has grown, and have always recognized the resemblances between you. Out of respect for you, no one has suggested that she might be your daughter, but all the citizens of Aquae Sulis are aware that Master Ector's foster daughter has high connections. This marriage seems to solve everything, my lord, and she will be happy whether she is called Anna or Licia or both."

"The marriage seems to be for the best, Artor," Myrddion broke in hastily, not only because he sought to nullify Artor's disapproval, but because Llanwith had discussed the problem with him several weeks previously. Knowing Artor's blind spot concerning Licia, Myrddion had been unsure of how to broach the topic with his master.

Targo was more practical. "You'd not have liked anyone to bed her, Artor, but Gallia would have been glad of such a match for her Licia, and you should be happy as well. Llanwith has been your friend for many years, and marriage between his son and your Licia is an honor for both of you."

"Very well." Artor was exasperated and out of sorts. "The match is sensible, even if I hate the thought that she is now a full-grown woman. Very well. Let us drink to Licia, or Anna, or whatever name is chosen for her. May she bear many strong sons."

The men drank sweet wine and tried to ignore Artor's mood, which was still morose.

"Will you attend the wedding, my lord? Ector would welcome your presence, for a dream came to him that foretold his death, and he wishes to say his final farewells to you."

Artor stared at Gareth, who forced himself to endure the king's fearsome eyes without flinching. Gareth had known Artor since he was a boy, and he had always seen that piercing grey intensity for what it was. Artor was thinking and calculating.

"No, I won't attend the wedding. To do so would be to draw gossip straight to Licia's person. We shall let the world believe her to be my half sister if they so wish. It is conceivable, if I use my imagination, that Uther could have got a child on some maidservant before his death, and that Master Ector would foster the child. But, should I attend the wedding, I give legitimacy to Licia, and that would make her, and any son she bears, targets for unscrupulous villains. I'll trust to Llanwith and his heirs to do their duty."

Gareth nodded his understanding of Artor's instructions, although his face reflected his dissatisfaction.

"You think me uncaring, Gareth? I'm not, I promise you. I will leave Cadbury for the Villa Poppinidii in five days' time, and will offer my felicitations to the family before Licia weds. As for Master Ector, I am disturbed that he should believe himself to be near death. He is my father in all but name, and now I understand why he has exercised his responsibility to select husbands for Livinia and Licia before his eyes close for the last time. I owe everything I hold dear to him, so of course I will come. Myrddion will let it be known that Master Ector is failing."

"Of course, Artor," Myrddion murmured.

"My lord," Gareth broke in, his heart in his mouth. "I request that you allow me to hold you to your promise."

Gareth saw Artor's eyes shift sideways momentarily, as the king tried to remember what he desired of him. Then Artor's brain thrust up the memory of their conversation which had taken place in the Garden of Gallia over six months earlier.

"Aye. Once Licia is wed, you may come to Cadbury Tor and join the guard. Odin will instruct you in battle craft until you have mastered the skills of a warrior. Mind you, Odin is not up to Targo's standard, but the old man cannot bend and stretch the way he once could. No doubt he will help Odin from time to time—in his own inimitable fashion." Artor grinned like a young boy again. "He'll have you leaping fences in no time at all. And he will also be making numerous, dire prophecies about your mortality."

Targo laughed, exposing what few teeth he still possessed.

Myrddion glanced surreptitiously at Targo. In the deepest, most honest part of his heart, Myrddion fretted that Artor would eventually be cast adrift as those few persons he loved were lost, inevitably, to death. The old warrior was failing; Mori Saxonicus had been the last time he would exercise his battle craft. Soon, Targo would pass into the Shades, and Artor would know another irreparable loss in the fabric of his life.

Gareth rose to his feet and bowed in homage to his lord. "I ask that you allow me to retire, King Artor, so I can contemplate the achievement of a dream. There are no words that can sufficiently express my thankfulness."

Once Gareth had left Artor's inner sanctum, the mood in the room became more relaxed and natural. Although Gareth was an old acquaintance, Artor was reserved with persons whom he didn't wholly trust, especially in those matters that had been troubling him since the Battle of Mori Saxonicus.

"Now that my last duties to Ector and Gallia are almost complete, the time is approaching when I must consider a suitable marriage for myself." He turned his gaze to Myrddion. Artor's expression was fey and reckless, causing Myrddion to undergo a brief moment of panic. "What say you, my friend? Which woman of your acquaintance would bring the strongest alliance for the crown of the Britons? Personally, I don't care who shares my bed as long as they are fertile and compliant. You shall have to choose for me."

Myrddion blanched, and the other men looked horrified. Only Targo chose to speak, having the license of great age as protection.

"Have you gone soft in the head, Artor? You may marry if you wish, of course. In fact, it's your duty to beget an heir to follow in your footsteps. But Myrddion shouldn't be forced to choose your wife. What if the match goes horribly wrong? Oh, I know you won't care, but he will. He'll blame himself if he brings trouble and pain to you."

It was now Artor's turn to color. "Forgive me, Myrddion. It was wrong of me to make such a foolish suggestion, and I'm sorry for any insult I gave you. My only excuse is that the world is topsy-turvy today, and I'm feeling a little lost."

He paused.

"I agree. I should choose for myself, but I don't believe that I can find love again, and never in the political hurly-burly where the position of queen would elevate one of the tribes to eminence. I am a commodity, to be fought over and flattered. I doubt the suitable women in the realm care a jot for me."

Artor rarely admitted to human weakness or fears, so Myrddion readily accepted his apology. The few visible flaws in Artor's character were why Myrddion loved his king so well.

"I can only advise you, my lord. In fact, Leodegran's daughter seems eligible enough, but I've never seen her, or had the opportunity to gauge her suitability. Unfortunately, it's likely that even you will be denied that privilege until your wedding day, for, as you are well aware, the nuptials of kings are matters of alliance, rather than love."

Artor grinned his wry approval of Myrddion's summation of the situation.

"Then this Wenhaver could become my new bride. After all, how bad can the girl be? Organize it for me, will you, Myrddion? Check the girl personally and gauge her suitability. And then force Leodegran into offering a significant bride price if you're satisfied with her. That bastard has always been tardy in provisioning my warriors and paying my taxes, when the whole world knows that his lands are rich in copper, tin, grain, and even gold. If he wants Artor for a son-in-law, then he can pay through the nose for the privilege.

"Oblige me by traveling to Corinium and looking the girl over before I'm saddled with a visit from that pair. If this Wenhaver is suitable, we can agree on a bride price and sign suitable treaties when Leodegran visits us in state. If not, perhaps they'll stay away. Dancing attendance on a girl barely full grown is very tiring."

Myrddion bowed his head in acquiescence and examined his master from under his lowered brows. Artor's face reflected nothing but boredom. Myrddion sighed.

Despite himself, Myrddion grinned. Leodegran was a pompous ass, and Myrddion would enjoy the haggling, especially as he held all the strategic power in the palms of his narrow hands.

"And Gruffydd is off to Venonae to see his brat, the babe Nimue. Cadbury Tor will be quite bare of company, unless you plan to go wandering off somewhere, Targo."

"I will go with you, Artor. I have a desire to see Ector and Licia before the Villa Poppinidii changes forever. Even though Caius may

241

be steward to the High King, he'll make changes at Aquae Sulis when Ector has gone that these old eyes won't care to see."

"What's your opinion of Gareth, Targo?" Artor asked casually as the meeting of friends stirred to depart and leave their king to his rest.

"Gareth does have the look, doesn't he, Odin? Perhaps he'll make a worthy warrior, even if he's coming to the craft a bit late. At least he can ride a horse, which makes him more competent than our last pupil."

"Will you never forget, old man?" Artor laughed, and the room was suddenly warm in the balm of the High King's pleasure.

WITH SMUG, UNCRITICAL approval, Wenhaver stared at her reflection in a silver mirror. The new veil was exactly the right shade of blue to suit her eyes. The Romans certainly knew the tricks of dying fabric, and her father had paid dearly for this piece of azure gossamer, especially purchased for her visit to Cadbury Tor. She sang as she pirouetted around her untidy room, clutching the length of delicate cloth to her breasts.

"He will want me! He will fall in love with my beauty on sight, even if he is very old. And then I will be Queen of all the Britons."

Leodegran had taken his daughter in hand one month previously after learning from a Cadbury courtier that the High King planned to marry. Leodegran had rubbed his hands together in pleasurable anticipation, and blessed the day that he had invested in several well-placed spies within Artor's court. As he was a born horse trader, Leodegran knew how foolish it would be to presume that Wenhaver would capture the High King's heart. However, his greedy spirit also knew his value to the throne of the west. Even if his daughter had been plain, she had an excellent chance of succeeding in this particular political maneuver.

When he explained to his daughter the importance of their visit to Cadbury, Wenhaver had preened and sulked by turn until her doting father had promised her a slew of new robes, dresses, hair adornments, and gems, all as fair bait to capture the eye of the High King.

And now, two legendary nobles were visiting Corinium to assess the appropriateness of Leodegran's daughter.

"I can convince these silly old people that I will be an excellent queen," Wenhaver decided with an uncritical glance in her silver mirror.

"Mistress?" her maid asked, and Wenhaver realized that she had spoken her thoughts aloud. Her cheeks colored with chagrin and anger, and the servant flinched away from her mistress's displeasure.

"I will wear the yellow shift this evening, Myrnia. And take care that it's uncrushed. Father has summoned a seer to read my fortune, and I'll not look a fright in front of him."

The servant bobbed her head in acknowledgment, and inwardly cursed that she should bear the responsibility of making the yellow shift presentable. Wenhaver was notoriously careless with her clothing, and left the finest fabrics in untidy piles wherever they happened to fall. Then any hapless girl who tried to remedy the damage had the skin stripped from her back.

Wenhaver was very young to be such a celebrated beauty, but Leodegran had been so proud of his small girl child that he had shown her off to his guests from the time she could first walk and talk. Gifted with unblemished golden skin, clear blue eyes, and plentiful golden hair, she had been a perfect, delicate child.

The young woman had only grown in beauty over the years and had been so cosseted, spoiled, and flattered that Wenhaver had come to believe that physical appearance was everything and that her wishes superceded the needs of everyone else in Leodegran's house. She never counted the cost of an item, nor cared for the feelings of others, because she had been encouraged to believe that she was ideal in every way.

Nobody liked Wenhaver overmuch, except King Leodegran, but then she was his daughter.

In fact, Leodegran was mostly to blame for the excesses of his daughter. He had married a beautiful girl merely sixteen years ago. Leodegran furrowed his brow in concentration as he dredged up her name out of the four wives and countless concubines, mistresses, and casual inamorata who had littered his path in life. Yes! She had been called Sybille, and she had huge, aquamarine eyes that were really the only part of her he had ever noticed. She had borne Wenhaver, her first and only living child, sighed quietly as if her work was over, and then died without fuss.

Leodegran grinned. Sybille had been the perfect wife, all things considered. He loved fine food, good wine, elegant clothing, and all the comforts of the senses. In short, Leodegran worshipped at the altar of physical appearance and sensation. Yes, Sybille had been perfect. She bore his lovely Wenhaver and then "went away."

Nobody liked King Leodegran overmuch either.

When evening came, Wenhaver permitted herself to be dressed, and a band of beaten gold was positioned to restrain her golden curls. The yellow shift suited her coloring, and Wenhaver added a necklace, several bangles, and two thumb rings of the same metal to accentuate the effect. Like a child with too many baubles, she tossed her box of jewels onto her table and rooted through the scatter of ornaments to thrust rings onto every finger.

Myrnia was secretly amused by Wenhaver's ostentation. Her own mother had been serving woman to a Roman lady, and, as a child, Myrnia had marveled at how one single, well-chosen gem could enhance the lady's style and grace, qualities that Wenhaver wholly lacked.

Much pleased with herself, Wenhaver swept into Leodegran's eating room with much swirling of fabric and tossing of her yellow curls.

Leodegran was wealthy and he enjoyed the luxuries of that wealth. He was large, portly, and fair in hair and features. His face had once been masculine and handsome, but now he was fleshy, and his cheeks and nose were ruddy with broken veins. He, too, was dressed with much outward display, so he saw nothing amiss in his daughter's attire.

The woman who sat quietly at the table at his left hand was a study in contrasts. She wore black, broken only by panels of charcoal in her undershift, so that darkness moved about her as she walked. Her hair was unbound, signifying her single status, and was streaked liberally with silver that, oddly, made her black hair even darker and more lustrous. Her face was pale and narrow, her eyes were downcast, and the few lines on her smooth countenance were the only visible betrayals of her age, which must have been closer to fifty than forty years. Although she was already very old for a woman, her hands were unblemished and ringless. In fact, her only ornamentation was a band of filigree gold of great price across her unlined forehead and a necklace at her breast that was shaped like an open eye. The prism of the pendant was a single large topaz that winked in the torchlight as if it was alive.

The woman made Leodegran uncomfortable as her eyes bored into his, while her monosyllabic answers to his attempts at gallantry made him feel gauche and unsophisticated. Unnerved, Leodegran was inclined to find fault, and Wenhaver was his first victim.

"You're late, daughter. We have long awaited your arrival."

Wenhaver pouted, and her eyes swept over the strange woman who sat at her father's hand with such ease.

A dowdy creature, she thought. But the filigree brow band caused her a twinge of envy.

"We only wait on a seer, Father. Of what account is such a person that I should come to you carelessly dressed?"

Wenhaver had been encouraged from birth to speak her thoughts, unfettered by reason, kindness, or common sense, and Leodegran's brows drew into his aquiline nose with displeasure and embarrassment.

"The seer, as you refer to her, is here. We are privileged this day to eat with the Lady Morgan, half sister of the great Artor, and daughter of Ygerne, the fairest flower of the Britons. She has come specifically to meet you, so mind your manners."

Now, under her false smile of shy greeting, Wenhaver was truly sulking. She was a practiced actress, so her pretty apologies gave every indication of honesty, but, under the artless expression, she was furious.

She noted that the woman, Morgan, was ancient, and as for the seer's mother and her fabled beauty, little of it showed in the daughter.

In her formative years, at the cruel bidding of Uther Pendragon, Morgan had learned patience as well as cruelty, and the old monster had also taught Morgan the value of good intelligence. Like Leodegran, her brother, Artor, and even her sister, Morgause, she used a spy in every court in the west. And Cadbury's secret watcher had sent word to Morgan that the High King was likely to wed at last.

Remembering a very old prophesy she had made in the villa outside of Aquae Sulis when she and her brother were still young, Morgan wondered if this scion of a corrupted and idle tribe was Artor's bane. Did this child bride have enough capriciousness under her beauty that she could weaken everything that Artor had built? Would she prove to be his feet of clay?

Morgan had hurried south, had ridden day and night, sparing neither her personal guard nor the horses, when she received word that Myrddion Merlinus planned to visit Corinium on the orders of the High King.

Now, seated across from a girl woman whose beauty was heart stopping and whose eyes were mercenary, Morgan pondered how best to warn the child that Myrddion's instincts were the sharpest in the west. Wenhaver must dissemble, and the spoiled little bitch didn't know how.

As for her father, Leodegran was plump, vacuous, and well meaning under his dyed hair and salivating interest in food and women. He must be persuaded to protect his daughter from her worst excesses if she became queen, and this epicure had no power to protect a cat from an aging mouse. Artor would behead Wenhaver and find another wife, if the silly little slut overreached herself.

By and large, simpering into Leodegran's faded blue eyes with feigned admiration, Morgan decided that the Dobunni king was the most pressing of her worries.

But he was just a man, after all, and an old goat at that. He could be induced to dance to Morgan's music, just in case he was needed in her complicated game of meddling and malice.

Satisfied, Morgan swiveled her attention to the spoiled beauty who raised one eyebrow at her in disdain. No one could teach Wenhaver subtlety but perhaps self-interest would teach her how to lie.

"No, my dear, I do not share my mother's beauty, do I?" Morgan stated without preamble. "Not like Artor, my half brother. But I am not old either, whatever my hair might say. I was born with the white streak of prophecy at my brow, and it simply deepens with time."

Morgan's voice was beautiful and finely accented. More disconcertingly, Wenhaver felt as if the older woman had looked deeply into her brain and picked out her innermost, most shameful thoughts, ready to expose them to the light of day. Morgan's lightless eyes trapped Wenhaver's with her own, and the seer smiled in a particularly unpleasant fashion.

Wenhaver shuddered.

"I apologize again for my lateness, Lady Morgan, and if I was rude, I'm sorry for that, too," Wenhaver managed to say with some sincerity. "I am afraid I am flustered and am not myself. The whole world has heard of your great skills, and I would never have dreamed that one so lowly as I should be singled out by you to demonstrate your art." Wenhaver curtsied deeply as she spoke, and lowered her telltale eyes so that Morgan couldn't see the false flattery in them.

Morgan laughed, her mirth like the tinkling of silver bells, and Wenhaver was forced to watch her father being seduced by Morgan's charm. She fumed inwardly as she reclined on her couch and picked up a tiny knife with a hilt shaped like a hummingbird.

This bitch knows exactly what I think.

"Every word, child. I understand every word," a voice whispered in her head, and Wenhaver dropped her eating knife.

It's all in my imagination, Wenhaver thought desperately.

And Morgan laughed again.

The meal was opulent, and rich in sauces and fine meats. Morgan ate sparingly, refusing the Spanish wine and choosing water instead. She ignored Wenhaver entirely, and set about capturing Leodegran with anecdotes about Uther Pendragon, Artor, life at court, and the oddities and peccadilloes of the great ones. Her wit was sharp and unkind, but humorous for all its bite, and Leodegran was not a kindly man anyway. In sharp contrast with her chilly responses before Wenhaver had joined them, Morgan was now the great lady, even coquettish as she pressed Leodegran's puffy hand with her slender fingers.

Irritated, ignored, and thoroughly outclassed, Wenhaver noticed that Morgan dyed the tips of her long white nails with henna, and patterns of great intricacy had been painted onto the still-young skin of her elbows, disappearing erotically into her shift. Leodegran could not take his eyes off Morgan, and Wenhaver could almost read his lascivious thoughts.

"If I want him, I will have him, child! I do as I please!"

Wenhaver was just beginning to believe that the mocking inner voice came from her own jealousy, but then Morgan laughed once again and lifted her fathomless eyes to meet the angry blue irises of Wenhaver. She smiled at the girl with the same sweet falsity that Wenhaver had struggled to master.

"Dear Leodegran, I do believe that Wenhaver grows impatient. We will talk later, alone if you wish, but I fear I must do my duty by your house and discover Wenhaver's future."

Leodegran's chest swelled, probably from thoughts of the erotic pleasures that were to come. Morgan was no doubt a woman who was well versed in the skills of the sleeping chamber, thought Wenhaver distastefully. She was beginning to wish that she could flee from the room.

"Give me your hand, child. Let me read the lines."

Wenhaver complied, but she flinched rudely when she felt the cool, reptilian touch of the seer.

"You will live for many years, child. And during your long life, you will experience only a gradual loss of your beauty. At the end, you will hide yourself in a convent, rather than permit the world to know how fate, and your own decisions, have contributed to your ultimate ugliness."

"I thought you were supposed to predict pleasant things," Wenhaver cried, almost in tears at the thought of such a future. "I don't want to be old, and I don't intend to become ugly."

"You may call on me when your beauty starts to fade. For I have a glamour that will trick any man. You have only to ask."

Mollified a little, Wenhaver asked whom she would marry.

"Why do you think I am here, Wenhaver? Even now, Myrddion Merlinus rides to Corinium to broker the marriage between you and the great Artor. Yes, you will become High Queen of the Britons, if you are very, very careful."

Wenhaver pulled away from Morgan's fingers and clapped her hands with glee.

"I will become the queen, and beloved, and all shall look upon me and marvel at my beauty."

Morgan fixed the girl with her extraordinary eyes. "Do you wish to know more? I can tell you more of your future if you are not content with what I see in your hands."

"Yes! Yes! You must tell me more," Wenhaver urged.

Leodegran looked smug.

Morgan drew out a fine strip of delicate leather and bound her eyes.

"Artor will not love you, no matter what you do. His heart was given to another woman a long, long time ago, and he will measure you by her, and he will find you wanting. In time, he will come to love a plain woman who is lovely within."

"Was his first love so beautiful?" Wenhaver snapped, her petulance rising dangerously.

"She was fair enough, but she was good, and clean, and loving. These are the qualities he admires in a woman, as you will discover, and he will search in vain for similarities between his first love and yourself. He will find another as his fires slowly die, but even then, happiness will elude him."

"I will make him love me," Wenhaver pouted. "I will!"

"You will fail, child. But others will be drawn to you as moths to the flame, and the great and the noble will worship at your feet."

"Well, that's not so very bad, is it, Father?" Wenhaver responded.

Leodegran beamed. He could already imagine the deference given to him by the tribal kings.

"Of course, you will soon be eclipsed by the Maid of Wind and Water, but, fortunately, she doesn't care to compete with you," Morgan continued. "When that time comes to pass, you must beware that you do not show your hand too plainly, or Artor will cast you out."

"He would not dare," Leodegran rumbled pompously. Already, he could imagine the prestige of possessing such a powerful son-in-law and the bounty that would pour into his hands as a result. He repeated his challenge to bolster his courage. "Artor would not dare to insult the Dobunni."

"Artor dares anything, for he is all-powerful. You must take care, Wenhaver, for you could burn at the stake for the edification of the people if you misjudge your situation."

Wenhaver blanched. The thought that such a fate was even possible was beyond her comprehension.

"You will, however, hold the keys to the kingdom in the years to come. But nothing is certain. If you are imprudent, Artor might take decisive action to remove you from his life. If you successfully carry out your role as queen, you will be remembered down through the misty years of time, and a thousand years will not dim the memory of your fabled beauty. You will also be vilified over the ages, but you will not care for that. You will always love what you cannot have, and have what you cannot love. But immortality is worth a little sacrifice, is it not, girl?"

Wenhaver bridled slightly at the scorn in Morgan's eyes. "I will be queen, and I'll be remembered forever. What else matters?"

"Why, nothing, my child, and it's certain that the Celts will never forget you." Morgan smiled at Wenhaver.

Wenhaver never stopped to consider the ambiguity in Morgan's words. She wasn't particularly intelligent and had never experienced the clever manipulative skills and half truths used by courtiers.

"I must stop now, for I am tired and feel the need to rest," Morgan said softly, and then smiled seductively at Leodegran. "But only for an hour or two. Perhaps we will speak later, my lord."

"Of course," Leodegran answered in a voice suddenly thickened with lust and a frisson of delicious fear.

Leodegran took beautiful young servant girls as, and when, he chose, but Morgan promised sexual delights that would drown his senses. He bowed to the seer as she rose from the table and walked away. The darkness was trapped in her fine woven shift and in her extraordinary hair.

As she moved silently into the apartment that Leodegran had given her, Morgan permitted her polished, expressionless face to smile. The ambitious were so easy to manipulate, and, by her reckoning, Leodegran and his daughter were likely candidates for elevation to the Throne of the West. But, if Myrddion saw through the silly little minx, their loss really didn't matter. The Fey had visited the court of the Catuvellauni King, Cadmus, now resident at Bannaventa on the edges of Arden Forest. Driven out of Verulamium, Londinium, and Durovigatum by the Saxon advances, Cadmus would sell his daughter, Rutha, to the highest bidder, despite his Christianity.

Morgan considered two other kings with suitable daughters who were more than eager to take Leodegran's place if the Dobunni king failed to convince Myrddion of Wenhaver's suitability.

Back in her apartment, Morgan cast the bones, and then flinched when she saw what the future truly revealed. But patterns of hatred become old friends if they are clutched to the bosom for decades.

The seer saw a ship tossing on a wild sea, and she understood that she was about to embark on a journey into the west. Behind her, all the great Britons were dead and burning, even her sister, while Cadbury Tor was deserted, the buildings merely shells for the wind to play in.

A yellow-haired woman, grown grey and old, prayed on her knees in a nunnery, and Saxon strength drove all the goodness from the rawness of the earth.

Then, in the mists of the past, she recalled Artorex's beautiful face and heard her own portent: "Beware of a woman with yellow hair, for she will lead you to ruin."

Then Morgan saw her own face in the bones. Her preternatural youth had finally submitted to time and she had become an aged crone, fit only for frightening children. To the north, in the forest shield, Artor's children's children grew tall and strong, while she left nothing behind her but the miasma of fear.

"Is it worth all the suffering?" she asked the bones, and for once they answered her.

"Of course not. You will destroy Artor's body, but unfortunately for your peace of mind, his spirit cannot be broken."

Later that night, she taught Leodegran new and erotic secrets of the bed until he would happily have offered her marriage if she had been willing. By the time the night was done, Leodegran promised her everything she desired, and, while he had a sharp, convenient memory, Morgan would remind him of his duties as a father when needed. But for all the bodily pleasure she gave the king, and for all that she strove to feel something of meaning, Morgan knew that her own soul was dead.

Chapter XII

THE MAID OF WIND
AND WATER

Gruffydd's heavy body pushed through the half-opened leather curtains and into the kitchens of Venonae, carrying a pile of gifts. The familiar comforting smells of hot water, burning wood, cooked meat, and human sweat mingled pleasantly to greet his entrance.

How quickly the years had passed, Gruffydd thought, since he had first brought the infant Nimue to be cared for by the chief cook of the Venonae garrison. Although she had never borne a child of her own, Gallwyn had proved to be an excellent mother and Perce, the kitchen boy, had grown to be Nimue's staunchest companion and foster brother. When Gruffydd came to visit, he always felt as if he was returning to a second family.

"Where are you, Gallwyn?" he called, a little alarmed at the quiet. "For shame, woman! Lazing about at this time of day when the venison is beginning to burn."

He laughed gently at this old joke, but a quick glance at the chaos in the usually ordered hearth stopped his mirth. For twelve years, Gruffydd had become well versed in the ordered frenzy of the kitchens, so a protracted silence and the fact that a large pot of stew was about to boil over on the hearth unnerved and alarmed him.

Using a gloved hand to swing the cauldron out of the flames on its long, hooked arm of wrought iron, Gruffydd dumped his cloth-wrapped gifts on the scarred tabletop and began to explore.

First, he found three kitchen girls huddled together by the wood-pile. They were weeping, with their reddened, coarse hands clenched over their tearstained faces.

"It's Mistress Gallwyn. She's sick, and she's near to dying," one of them moaned.

Clearly, someone had to take charge in the kitchens, and twelve years at Artor's back had prepared Gruffydd for almost any calamity.

"You won't help your mistress by burning the garrison's food," Gruffydd shouted at the maids. "Get to work. The bread oven is cold, there's no kindling, and the stew's boiling over. Hop to it."

"Perce is cutting more wood now," one of the girls wailed.

"Then we can thank the heavens that everyone hasn't gone wandering off." Gruffydd pointed to the oldest woman in the group. "What is your name?" he asked brusquely.

"Jena," the woman replied timidly, her voice trembling and uncertain. "Sir," she added as an afterthought, for the whole world knew that Gruffydd was sword-bearer to the High King.

"Jena, you are now in charge of the kitchens until you hear otherwise. And you will be held to blame if there's no food for the tables upstairs."

The servants scuttled away to complete their chores.

Gruffydd strode straight to Gallwyn's sleeping compartment, a burrow too small to bear the grandiose title of a room. The curtains were drawn tightly shut.

"Gallwyn? Gallwyn? What ails you, woman?"

A tall, slim fury exploded through the curtains and drove him back with hard blows to his chest from delicate, clenched fists.

"Nimue! What are you doing, child? What has upset you? You know me. It's Gruffydd."

Gruffydd gripped Nimue's wildly beating arms by the wrists and took in the wide-eyed, terrified expression on her face.

"She's not to have any noise! And she has to be kept quiet, so you'll not disturb her!"

Irrelevantly, Gruffydd noticed that Nimue's growth had come upon her, and now they stood eye to eye.

"You must allow me to see her, my dear," Gruffydd ordered softly. "I'll not upset her, I swear. If she is ill, we must make her better. Now tell me what has happened."

"I don't know!" Nimue wailed. "She was laughing with me as we peeled the carrots, and then she seemed to choke . . . and just dropped to the floor." Tears flowed unbidden from the young girl's eyes. "Her lips are all blue."

"You'd best ask one of the kitchen hands to make some herb tea for her. And sweeten it with some of that honey that Gallwyn loves so much. But first, send a messenger to bring the herbalist to this room as fast as he can get here. He will know what to do to help her."

Gruffydd had seen his own grandfather die in just such a fashion when he was little more than a lad, and he was suddenly afraid.

He steeled himself to pull back the curtain to Gallwyn's narrow alcove. What was he to do if Gallwyn should die? What would become of sweet Nimue?

The child was fourteen, and her terrible birth, cut from her mother's body under a willow tree, had done her no lasting harm. But Gruffydd remembered Morgan's prophecy when Nimue was only a week old: she would become a fearsome creature if she wasn't loved, and, in time, Nimue would steal away the mind of the kingdom. Thanks to Gallwyn's love and earthy common sense, neither dire prediction had come to pass.

Gruffydd took a deep breath, forced a broad smile to his lips, and swept back the curtain.

Gallwyn was resting on her pallet inside the tiny room. She was sitting almost upright on a pile of cushions that had been placed behind her to ease her breathing, but her appearance was that of one who was already dead. Nimue had accurately described the blue tinge around Gallwyn's lips, and Gruffydd knew that something vital had failed inside the body of his old friend.

"Gallwyn?" he whispered softly. "Can you hear me?"

"Of course I can, you daft bugger," the old woman wheezed painfully. She opened her faded hazel eyes. "I'm glad you came, Gruff. Even if you are too late."

Every word seemed forced out of her heaving chest with an effort.

"Nimue is fetching the herbalist to see if he can help you," Gruffydd whispered, and smiled, although he felt a lump begin to grow in his throat. "She is also bringing some herb tea with your favorite honey, so I expect you will soon be feeling like your old self again."

"No tea will help me, Gruff. I know I'm dying, and I don't think it is far away."

"Then don't talk, sweet Gallwyn. Rest now, until you are stronger." Gruffydd could have wept, for he could see the film of death even now as it began to cloud Gallwyn's sharp old eyes.

"I'll be resting soon enough. But now is the time for some straight talk. I'm dying, aren't I?"

"Probably, Gallwyn." Gruffydd offered no false hope. "But some people survive this illness."

"Not me."

She rested for a minute and closed her heavy eyes.

At that moment, Nimue returned with a wooden bowl of some fragrant liquid rendered almost viscous with honey. Coaxed to take a sip, Gallwyn obeyed meekly, and a little color came back into her pallid face, but the work-roughened hand that Gruffydd held was slack and cold.

"Nimue, my lovely, you are to listen to the words I say to old Gruff here. And you are to obey him in all things. Promise?"

Nimue would have promised anything, and did.

"Gruff, we've been friends since you put my girl into my arms, is that not so?"

"I'd never argue with you, Gallwyn, for I know I'd lose."

A trace of her old humor returned when her other hand attempted to smack his face. The pretended blow was as light as a caress.

"Someone's got to take care of my little girl if anything happens to me. Someone's got to see her safe."

Gruffydd could see that Gallwyn's eyes were leaking tears. He was shocked, for the ruler of the High King's kitchens had never been seen to show weakness.

"No!" Nimue wailed, and began to sob in earnest. "You cannot die, for I won't let you."

"Bring me some more tea, child," Gallwyn ordered gently, and Gruffydd knew she had forced herself to drink every drop in the cup. "Make me some more, for I feel better than ever."

As soon as Nimue departed, Gallwyn turned her pleading eyes to Gruffydd.

"Promise me that you'll take her, Gruff. The dogs are sniffing around her already, and I'll not be here to help her. She'll end up like her mother if you desert her."

In her agony of spirit, Gallwyn had gripped Gruffydd's tunic with her good hand, but now her strength was beginning to fail her, and the hand fell away. Gruffydd heard how her breathing was slowing, and he placed his lips next to her ear and whispered to her as, slowly and agonizingly, the old woman began to slip away into the Shades.

"I'll keep Nimue by my side, whatever happens. I promise. I'll ask Artor to make her his ward, and then I'll find her a good husband to protect her. These things I promise you, old friend, so you may die in perfect peace."

Gallwyn's eyes were closed when he raised his head, but she was smiling. As Nimue pulled aside the curtain and saw her drained face, she dropped the cup of hot liquid and threw herself down beside Gallwyn. She wept into the old woman's shoulder like a small babe.

Eventually, Gallwyn simply stopped breathing and died in her foster daughter's arms, almost as if the clockwork of her body had irreparably broken.

Nimue was inconsolable. She refused to leave Gallwyn's corpse for the rest of the day, and sat weeping and rocking her body, no matter how Gruffydd tried to comfort her. The girl only stirred when she was told that Gallwyn must be wrapped in a shroud for burial.

"No," she stated flatly. "Gallwyn wanted to be burned. She told me many times that she didn't want to go into the cold, wet ground. She said she would hate it, so I won't let anyone do that to her. You can't put Gallwyn into a hole in the mud."

"I promise you that we won't bury her, Nimue. I promise. But she must have a shroud. Did she have a favorite dress?"

Nimue wiped her reddened eyes and then used both hands to tear down the brightly woven curtain.

"She loved this length of cloth. I'll sew her into it if you and Perce will find wood for her funeral pyre."

As the child found Gallwyn's precious needle and a length of rough thread, Gruffydd asked her if she would need help to move Gallwyn's corpse.

"No. I will move her myself. It is my duty to wash her and prepare her for the fire." She spoke with an unconscious pride.

Gruffydd patted his foster daughter on the shoulder and kissed her on her forehead. "You're a good girl, Nimue. Gallwyn was very proud of you."

Somehow, during the grim day that followed, the kitchen workers contrived to ensure that the inhabitants of the fortress were fed.

Meanwhile, Gruffydd and Perce spent their time gathering wood in preparation for the funeral pyre. Together, the two men dragged logs into a rough platform and packed dry moss and kindling around its base. Then the whole pyre was soaked in a jar of oil that Perce had purloined from the storehouse in the fortress.

When construction of the pyre was completed, the household servants took turns, when their duties permitted, to gather pine boughs and sweet-smelling grasses to dress Gallwyn's last bed. Nimue completed her last offices for the only mother she had ever known, and Perce and Gruffydd bore the corpse to the pyre with relative ease, considering the distance. Gruffydd had always believed the cook to be a large woman but, as she lay in his arms, he realized that she was only as large as a twelve-year-old boy.

She always seemed bigger than life, so I never really noticed how short she was, Gruffydd thought sadly. It's difficult to imagine that I will never see her smiling face again.

Once Gallwyn's body was placed on the pyre, Nimue pressed a bunch of wildflowers, bound with a length of her own silver-blond hair, on the very center of the shrouded shape. Gruffydd added a length of fine linen that he had brought for Gallwyn as a present, and a treasured leather armband that had been given to him by his own mother.

Then, before a small but grieving cluster of mourners, Gruffydd pressed a lighted oil lamp into Nimue's hands.

"She loved you best, child. Send her to whatever gods she served."

At first, the wood was slow to burn, but then the oil caught and flames leapt high into the coming night, wreathing Gallwyn's remains in flickering fingers of orange, red, and rose. The smell of burning pine logs and needles almost masked the distinct odor of human flesh as her body shriveled and burned. Perce, Nimue, and Gruffydd remained at the fire until the whole platform collapsed in a pile of smoldering ash, and then the two men led the weeping girl away.

In Gallwyn's sleeping alcove, they found that Jena, full of sudden self-importance, had ensconced herself on Gallwyn's pallet.

"Get out of this room, you bitch," Nimue yelled. "Get out! Gallwyn's ashes aren't yet cold, and you're trying to steal her possessions. I'll rip every hair out of your head if you don't move your sorry carcass out of her room."

"It's mine. I'm the head cook now," Jena whined at Gruffydd.

"You may have it tomorrow after Nimue leaves this place," he growled at Jena's sullen face. "Then you can sleep wherever you like. And if you have anything in your pouch that is not your property, you'll give it to me immediately. If you refuse, and I find that you have stolen anything from Gallwyn's room, you will be flogged."

Jena shook out the roughly woven pouch that was tied round her waist. A small silver-gilt mirror and Nimue's bronze hairpin fell onto the tiny table that took up much of the small sleeping cubicle.

Nimue flew at Jena like a sleek white cat, claws and teeth bared in rage. Only the combined efforts of Perce and Gruffydd managed to avert serious injury to the older woman.

Jena rose to her feet, clutching her bleeding face where Nimue's nails had torn the flesh.

"You barbarian cow! You cursed whore! You've even got the serpent mark to show you're the daughter of a stinking, barbarian slut."

Gruffydd's large and calloused hand slapped her sharply across her bleeding cheek. His eyes, which had been merely irritated until now, were suddenly hot and bloodshot.

"Shut your filthy mouth, woman. The High King himself ordered the tattoo to be placed on Nimue's leg to show that she is his. He will not take kindly to your description of the Dragon of Britain as a barbarian serpent mark, nor to your calling his ward a whore and her mother a slut." Gruffydd took hold of the terrified Jena by her homespun shift and shook her. "Now get out and return to your place with the other servants. Whether you remain in charge of the kitchens remains to be seen. But I suggest you think over what has happened today and return at a later time to make your peace with Nimue."

The round-eyed cook ran from the tiny cubicle.

Gruffydd turned to face Nimue. "It's time you attempted some sleep, young lady. We must ride from Venonae at first light."

The tired child was compliant, and Gruffydd left her to join Pelles and his captains of archery, who had returned to the frontier town after the victory at Mori Saxonicus. He drank too much ale, and when he finally fell asleep, he was far too drunk to dream.

THE NEXT MORNING, Gruffydd's temper was not improved by a thudding hangover. He drank copious drafts of fresh water, and then set about finding a horse for Nimue. He managed to purchase a surprisingly cheap little mare. He checked the mare's legs and physique carefully and could find no obvious fault with the animal, but the look of triumph on the shifty horse trader's face when the deal was struck told Gruffydd that the beast had some sort of defect.

"You'd best watch this horse, Nimue. That greasy trader thinks he's put one over on me; I don't like his attitude at all."

"Well, I think she's a beautiful creature," Nimue crooned in the direction of the large dun-colored horse. "I shall call her Gallwyn—or perhaps Whinny, since Gallwyn is not really a suitable name for an animal."

Nimue was fighting hard not to cry again, so Gruffydd strode away to load his pack animal. He found Perce already fulfilling that task, and beside Gruffydd's old horse stood a wall-eyed donkey.

"Going somewhere, Perce?" Gruffydd asked roughly. "Where did you get that donkey?"

"I'm off to Cadbury, Lord Gruffydd. I've dreamed of going there all my life, so now I'm going. I'll walk there if needs be. As for Betsy here, I just found her."

"Why, Perce? You're twenty-five years, at least, which is far too old to take up the sword or the bow. What can you possibly hope to achieve by going to Cadbury Tor with us?"

Perce glared mulishly at Gruffydd. "I want an opportunity to show that I'm capable of more than just cutting wood and washing out the cauldrons. You know the way to Cadbury Tor, and I don't, so I intend to go with you whether you like it or not."

The High King was fond of saying that no possible weapon should ever be overlooked, so Gruffydd decided to let Artor decide if he could use the boy. The lad's willingness and apparent good intentions seemed genuine, and Gruffydd was loath to dash his dreams.

Nimue joined them and they stood beside the cold ashes of Gallwyn's funeral pyre. The morning breeze sent spirals of silver dust into the air to be dispersed over Venonae and the land that surrounded it.

"She'll be happy here in these lands where she worked for such a long time," Nimue said sadly, then dropped her horse's reins and walked carefully between the charred wooden supports of the pyre.

Something caught her eye, and she fell on the object with a glad little cry. She slipped it into a simple bronze locket that had been her last gift from Gallwyn.

Gruffydd had a suspicion that Nimue had found a fragment of Gallwyn's bone. He had paid two peasants to collect any bones that the conflagration hadn't devoured and beat them into dust so that Nimue wouldn't be upset by the sight of any of her foster mother's remains. They had apparently failed to complete their task efficiently.

The idea of cherishing such a grisly object was repugnant to Gruffydd, but Nimue had strong instincts of love and a great dam of passion within her. If some remnant of Gallwyn's life gave her the strength to face a lonely and uncertain future, who was he to be her critic? Gallwyn would not have cared. In fact, Gruffydd knew the old cook would have been secretly pleased that a part of her person would lie above Nimue's heart.

"Well, Perce," he said, "if you are to ride to Cadbury with us, you can forget your creature comforts for at least a week."

"What creature comforts?" Perce retorted gaily, his face wreathed in a wide grin. Unlike many peasants, the young man's strong and healthy white teeth enlivened his face.

Then Gruffydd turned his attention to Nimue, whose delicate face was torn between sadness and excitement.

"And you, my girl, must wear a covering over your head and shoulders while we travel. You'll burn to toast and develop a fever if your skin cooks, and then where would we be?"

She carried out his bidding and covered herself. Her extreme fairness would attract unwelcome attention from all the young males for leagues around, so her continued health wasn't Gruffydd's only consideration.

Barely half an hour from Venonae, the dun mare began to pirouette and dance in an attempt to unseat its rider.

Gruffydd instantly understood the problem.

"Hand me the reins, Nimue. And then you must hang on to Whinny's mane for dear life. She is trained to toss her new rider, and then return to the stables of her old owner. We must lead her with brute force until she becomes used to the fact that she has left her old home forever."

Nimue obeyed instantly, and Gruffydd quickly lashed the reins to the pack carried by his own horse—just in time, for a moment later, Whinny succeeded in tossing the girl off her back and onto the hard ground.

Without concern for her grazes and bruises, Nimue leapt to her feet, gripped the sides of the iron bit that ran through the horse's mouth, and pulled downwards with all her strength. Perce contributed his part with a whippy branch that he used on her flanks. Between them, they forced Whinny to follow in the wake of Gruffydd's mount.

For some miles, the mare fought them, squealing in protest, and Gruffydd promised himself a long, hard conversation with the offending dealer when next he returned to Venonae. He was beginning to think they would make better time if they just let Whinny go when at last the horse surrendered and began to plod along as if she had never caused them any difficulties at all.

The journey settled into a humdrum string of days in the saddle and nights lying under the stars, and Gruffydd had leisure to examine his new charges more closely.

Nimue was beautiful, in an odd, alien style. Her hair had never been cut, except for the hank at the front that had been used to bind Gallwyn's funeral flowers. For the long days of travel, she wore it plaited into a thick rope that hung well below her waist. In color, her hair was a rich silver-blond, as rare as sunshine on a midwinter's day. Even Gareth's striking pale hair did not match the silken glory of Nimue's coloring, and her very white skin added to her memorable face. In marked contrast, her eyebrows were dark and feathered upward, giving her face an icy, Otherworld appearance. Her eyes, framed by long, dark lashes, were the deep, gentian blue of the north, and revealed a lively intelligence and curiosity, honed by Gallwyn's tutelage. The cook had ensured that her charge could read a little and knew her numbers.

No wonder the young men are sniffing around her like randy dogs, Gruffydd thought with dismay.

Even without the dragon tattoo on her leg, which accentuated the delicacy of her bones, there was something wild, unnatural, and wholly erotic about Nimue's appearance. She was tall and slender, which wasn't unusual, given her Saxon or Jutlander ancestry, and her long legs and narrow feet and hands gave her a sensuous, almost serpentine grace. Her beautiful, full mouth smiled often, and she could use her mobile brows to pull comical faces that kept both men laughing.

She looks as if she could insinuate magic into a man's soul, Gruffydd mused as he gazed at her by the campfire, but she's just a little child at heart.

Then Nimue grinned at him, and even the aging Gruffydd felt his heart stagger a little in his chest.

As for Perce, Gruffydd discovered that he liked the young man, now that he was finally coming to know him better. In all the years that Gruffydd had visited the kitchens of Venonae, Perce had been just another servant, always hard at work, and always with a simple smile on his freckled face.

On closer examination, Gruffydd realized that Perce's boyish, tow-colored hair and guileless blue eyes hid a nature that was as stubborn as the donkey he was riding. Perce had come to Venonae as a child, and had been given the backbreaking tasks of wood cutting, scrubbing, and washing to earn his food. He had completed every menial task without complaint, believing that at Venonae he was one step closer to his dream of becoming a warrior.

Such patience and good humor spoke well for the young man. And he was strong. The formidable muscles on his arms and shoulders were a testimony to years of cutting down old trees for kindling and lifting huge iron cauldrons in the kitchens. Most men with dreams would have become embittered during the long years of dreary toil, but Perce retained an internal joy that put a spring in his step and a natural, quick smile on his face. The lad's needs were simple, and his thoughts were imbued with hope. He was going to Cadbury, and anything was possible where Artor, the High King of the Britons, rested his head.

The strange little group traveled the long, weary miles from the mountain country of the north to the Great Plain where the Giant's Dance stood, and then to Cadbury Tor. The children, as Gruffydd thought of them, were lost in wonder at each new sight, from the Roman roads to the ancient monoliths that reared up out of the deep grasses in the silent places. The pair chattered and fought like siblings, and one of Gruffydd's chief fears was laid to rest. Perce loved Nimue completely, but in a brotherly fashion, for he had played with her for years and kept her out of the way in the busy kitchens in those times when Gallwyn was hard at work.

When Nimue and Perce first spied Cadbury Tor from a distance, they were almost struck dumb with wonder.

The land around the tor was quite flat, and the hill seemed an unnatural thing, a tall mound that had been constructed by giants at the beginning of time. The ramparts encircled the hill, rising ever higher like the spiraled curls of a giant apple skin that had been cut by a skilled kitchen maid. Atop the hill, a stone church sat, thick-walled and square, close by a great wooden hall that was surrounded by the living quarters of the High King and his court.

Below the tor, a flourishing town was growing quickly. Stables, blacksmiths, potters, bakers, jewelers, physicians, traders, and free-born servants labored and bred in new split-wood-and-thatch houses, all of which were a little grander and more spacious than those that existed in Venonae and Venta Belgarum.

"It's like an ant heap," Nimue exclaimed in a voice full of wonder. "But the High King lives at the very top, unlike the ant queen, who lives deep underground. How wonderful! Look, Perce, there are cows, and pigs, chickens . . . oh, so many animals. And they are so fat! And the grass is so green and sweet." She threw her hands in the air like a little girl, leapt off Whinny's back, and then fell down into a thick carpet of clover, rolling and laughing in the soft greenery and ignoring the aggressive hum of angry bees.

Fortunately, the tor was still some distance away, and only a brace of amused farmers were there to see Nimue's antics.

"Remember that you are a young lady, Nimue, so you shouldn't shame Gallwyn with your foolishness," Gruffydd admonished her. Yet, through her enthusiasm, he saw the wonder that Artor had wrought through fresh eyes. Fields of grain, orchards, and meadows flourished in profusion around the township. An ample number of streams fed the crops, and the verdant groves of apples, pears, nuts, and peaches filled the air with the smell of nature in all its glory. And deep beds of clover sweetened the honey.

From a distance, Cadbury was an ordered miracle.

These marvels did not cease as they approached their destination through orchards, pastures, and grain fields. The field hands appeared healthy and smiling, and every man they passed doffed his cap, pulled on his forelock, and cried, "Hail to you, friends. Welcome to Cadbury and the court of Artor, High King of the Britons."

Artor was revered. When the High King had returned to Cadbury after the devastating carnage of Mori Saxonicus, men and women had knelt in the dust and abased themselves as he led his troops up the road leading to the tor. When he had tried to remonstrate with the citizens for their devotion, they had wept and thanked him for ensuring their safety. Later, he had spoken in the town forum and begged the people's pardon for the loss of so many dead fathers, husbands, and sons. Artor had expected quiet misery; instead, he was faced with a sad triumph, for the womenfolk held their loved ones fortunate to have died for their people in the greatest war of the age. Artor had never really understood the people's homage, but Gruffydd recognized their devotion, having been the child of peasants before he had become a slave. He knew that Artor offered hope of a secure future during dangerous times. Even more important, he offered ordinary men and women a beloved leader who would never desert them.

After the battle of Mori Saxonicus, Artor was truly worshipped by the Celtic peasants. The united kings had smashed the western Saxons so totally that hardly a man in the northwest claimed Saxon blood. In the east, Saxon settlers were licking their wounds until they regained the strength to mount another Saxon summer, but, for the present, peace had come to the land. It promised to be a time of plenty.

MYRDDION MERLINUS HAD ridden to Leodegran's court with mixed emotions. Undeniably, a married and settled Artor with a compliant wife and intelligent sons was needed if the Britons were to continue to enjoy this period of peace and plenty that the High King had won for them.

On the other hand, Artor was beloved by many male friends who wouldn't easily make way for a mere woman. Nor did Myrddion believe that any female could capture Artor's padlocked heart. Jealousy and strife seemed the certain outcome of any marriage where love was involved. Only a marriage of convenience offered any chance of lasting felicity.

The town of Corinium did not appear particularly impressive. It had no wall, a mute tribute to Roman rule, and possessed many of the characteristics of a Latin city without the accompanying grandeur. However, once inside the walls of its great hall, Myrddion soon realized that a sybarite ruled the Dobunni people.

Wall hangings of imported fabrics covered the bare walls, adding an overlay of rich color to the stern strength of roughly dressed stone. The wall paintings were almost obscene in their subject matter, and all the benches in the great hall were cushioned with fabric that was richly shot with threads of gold. On one bare wall, an old Roman fresco of pigmented gesso was prominently displayed. It depicted a golden-haired Apollo driving his gilded chariot across the sky to the admiring joy of his sister, Diana, dressed in silver garments and complete with her bow. The room was odd and mismatched, but it was amazingly opulent.

For three days, Myrddion had enjoyed the dubious pleasures of oversauced food that gave him indigestion and the doubtful company of an indolent buffoon. Still, Myrddion decided, Leodegran could be far worse. His wealth was legendary and, Midas-like, the Dobunni king turned everything he touched into gold. His indolence and shallow nature made him a compliant prospect as a father-in-law, and Leodegran was unlikely to meddle in affairs of state.

Yet the opulence around him stifled Myrddion's senses. Artor had given him carte blanche, an onerous and mildly frightening prospect, but, compared with the weights of duty and loss of freedom that Myrddion had thrust upon Artor so many years ago, this small responsibility hardly mattered.

Did he set any store in Leodegran's lavish promises? None at all! Did Myrddion care what type of queen Wenhaver would make? Probably, but Myrddion set little value on women as a sex. Perhaps Morgan had understood that this prejudice was the scholar's greatest weakness.

A lengthy banquet stretched before Myrddion, and he would have made his apologies if he hadn't been a creature of ingrained courtesy.

Resplendent in imported brick-red cloth edged with gold thread, Leodegran hurried to meet and welcome Artor's most trusted adviser into his home. The entire Celtic nation knew that Myrddion Merlinus had only to whisper in the High King's ear and Artor would listen. Leodegran's swift words of fulsome praise and fawning respect repelled Myrddion.

Against his instincts, Myrddion had come to a decision that very afternoon, so now he must endure Leodegran's feast and the Dobunni king's flush of success and joy. Myrddion wished he was content with his decision, but the old scholar was a sufficient realist to understand that no one was good enough for Artor in his eyes. Leodegran was malleable and so his daughter was less important than the dowry and the strengthened alliances that she brought with her as bride price.

As Leodegran droned on and on about the great honor bestowed upon his house, Myrddion was already planning his explanation to Artor.

"Look the girl over when the Dobunni come for their state visit to sign the nuptial arrangements. If she's not to your taste, then reject her. You *are* the High King!"

Myrddion snorted, causing Leodegran to stop his fulsome praise in surprise. As manipulative as ever, Myrddion had provided his conscience with an excuse if his precipitate decisions went awry. Myrddion was, at bottom, an honest man.

May the gods help us, he thought to himself. Here is the very worst example of the Roman influence in Britain. Leodegran is Celt enough to be proud, and Roman enough to love hedonism and sophistication. But he can never be trusted, for self-aggrandizement is the only force that drives him. Hades only knows what his daughter is like.

Morgan had chosen to warn Wenhaver about Myrddion Merlinus before the seer rode away among her servants, bent on some mysterious errand known only to herself.

"Myrddion is far too clever for you, Wenhaver. If in doubt, be silent and compliant, for if he speaks against you, Artor will never call you his wife."

"He's quite old, isn't he?" Wenhaver replied. "Really old gentlemen always seem to like me. They call me 'poppet,' and they beg for kisses from me."

Morgan's laugh had an ugly, grating sound. "Myrddion is old, but he's not in his dotage, so don't bother to try your tricks on him." She was undismayed by Wenhaver's stupidity, for a foolish girl is far more easily led.

Wenhaver tossed her golden head and pouted, her bottom lip protruding unattractively.

Morgan frowned. "Don't wear that pout when you are with Myrddion. It makes you look quite plain . . . almost unattractive."

Clever, clever Morgan.

Wenhaver dressed with some care before she was ushered into the presence of Myrddion Merlinus. As befitted a maiden, she wore the softest pink, only a shade above white, but sufficient to highlight the blush on her cheeks, artificially applied with carmine, and the blue of her eyes was accentuated with just a touch of the hideously expensive lapis lazuli powder. Myrddion was wise to the use of female cosmetics, but he admitted to himself that Wenhaver gave all the surface appearance of being a quiet, obedient, and sensitive young lady.

For her part, Wenhaver summed up Myrddion in a single glance. She would never be clever, but she was shrewd enough to recognize that the aging man before her had once been more beautiful, in his own way, than she would ever be, and was quite immune to the allure of physical appearance. If she was to use him, she would be forced to find another ploy. Perhaps Artor can be induced to grow weary of him, she thought as she curtsied so low that her head almost touched the ground.

Myrddion's graceful words of thanks, coupled with his lavish and eloquent praise of her dress and hair, were accepted as her due. She smiled innocently and murmured artless words of appreciation. Myrddion also smiled, but unaccountably he felt the hair rise on his arms.

Leodegran had been uncharacteristically subdued during these introductory niceties. Myrddion had wasted little time in setting out the terms of Wenhaver's marriage to the High King, and Leodegran was still absorbing the bride price he would have to pay. He wondered how he might find a route round the excessive demands that his daughter's wedding would make on his purse.

"Felicitations, my daughter," Leodegran finally said expansively. "King Artor has asked for your hand in marriage and I have agreed to his terms. Myrddion and I have settled on a date two months after we visit Cadbury Tor, so I suppose you will require new and lavish clothing for the ceremony. Fortunately, we shall have some time for fripperies in the interim."

He took her by the chin and kissed her on her smooth forehead.

As became a gently born female, Wenhaver said everything required of an innocent girl, proclaiming her lack of worth, and expressing her fears that she would disappoint a man of Artor's superior tastes. Her expression was as guileless as she could manage, but the sharp-eyed Myrddion spied some glitter of self-satisfaction beneath her blue gaze.

Soberly, Myrddion rode away from Corinium two days later, having been treated to interminable feasting, hunting, and other, more exotic amusements that gave him no pleasure at all. Wenhaver seemed vapid, beautiful, and profoundly stupid, and the occasional slips she made when the conversation did not revolve around her person and her needs betrayed an atavistic selfishness. On one occasion, a serving maid stumbled into Myrddion's path as he returned to his sleeping chamber. He had helped the young girl to her feet, and, although she had quickly turned her head away, he had been appalled to see five deep scores on her face from cheekbone to throat that had been caused by wickedly sharp nails. He knew instinctively that Wenhaver's pretty little talons, tipped with henna, were responsible. Evidently, she had a penchant for inflicting pain.

In Wenhaver's favor was her youth, her great beauty, and flashes of charm that Myrddion observed when the girl wasn't trying to entrance him. She was so achingly youthful, so like another woman that Myrddion had loved before he had grown into a cynical man, that the scholar found himself believing that she could be shaped into a more noble purpose than vanity or pride. Artor was a conscientious and fair man. He could mold the girl into the queen that she was capable of being, if the High King exerted patience and kindness.

Myrddion hoped that Artor would see the child beneath her sophisticated, brittle facade.

I'm being cowardly, Myrddion thought sadly, but the problems of tempestuous females were beyond his understanding or his patience.

He would have regretted the bargain that had been struck but he told himself Artor was a match for any spoiled beauty. All that was required of the maiden was fertility and loyalty and, if she failed in any way, Artor had the power to remove her. Wenhaver would soon learn that Artor was not a man who danced attendance, even on the fairest woman in the land.

• • •

THE VILLA POPPINIDII was abuzz with frantic activity as the aged Ector, his excited servants, and a mildly distracted Julanna prepared for two weddings that were to occur within a scant two weeks.

In Aquae Sulis, summer had come at last, and wildflowers filled the fields, competing with spear-point shoots of barley, rye, and wheat. Fruit trees were beginning to blossom and the chocolate-brown earth had the fecund, ripe smell of new and exuberant life.

Artor and his usual retinue arrived without fanfare, but, in the mysterious all-knowing ways of simple folk, the villagers awaited him where a smaller road forked towards Sorviodunum. Newly green branches, flower buds, and hazelnuts, carefully collected where they fell because of their holiness, were thrown before the feet of the High King's new destrier, Coal having been retired to the villa after the battle of Mori Saxonicus.

The adoring faces of the villagers embarrassed Artor as they gazed up at him with whole-hearted worship and awe.

"Artor!" they cried. "Welcome to the High King."

The king pulled his black horse to a halt and dismounted. Many familiar faces from the villages were here to greet him and celebrate the coming festivities. Even pensioned-off farm workers from the Villa Poppinidii, men who had known him when he was a boy called Lump, offered their tributes. To all well-wishers, he gave individual welcomes, asking the names of those he did not know, and remembering incidents of credit from the lives of men and women from his youth.

The peasants kissed Artor's hands, his feet, and the hem of his cloak, and he didn't have the heart to rebuff their simple declarations of patriotism and affection. Many years earlier, Lucius of Glastonbury had warned Artor that a man is never a hero in his own town, but here Artor enjoyed the adoration of ordinary people who had known him in his early life.

As always, Ector embraced Artor at the time-scarred doors of the villa. Ector's face lit up at the sight of his foster son, but his pleasure faded a little when he realized that Caius was not among the retinue. Ector's embrace was as fervent as ever, but Artor could feel the old man's bones beneath his withered flesh. Artor's heart mourned already for the loss that would inevitably come.

"My dear boy, you are quite unchanged. Welcome! Welcome! My steward will see to the comfort of your friends and servants. Meanwhile, come to the scriptorium and share a good, red wine with an old man. You, too, Targo, my friend, for I see that you are near as infirm as I am, and I long to speak of the old days that only we three can remember."

Talking all the way, Ector led the two visitors to his favorite place, the wood-lined scriptorium where Artor had read surreptitiously in the darkest parts of the night and impressed his master with his grasp of Latin.

Another young man, who bore an uncanny likeness to Gareth, brought wine, cups, and tiny plates of dried fruit, stuffed delicacies, and nuts into the warm old room and assisted both his master and Targo to sit on comfortable stools, well padded with woolen fleece for softness and warmth.

Once the young man had bowed low and closed the door, Artor raised one quizzical eyebrow at Master Ector.

"That young man is Garan, Gareth's youngest brother. He's been training to become steward for a good two years, for you surely know that Gareth's heart is set upon joining you at Cadbury Tor. Gods, I'd join you there myself, but time has imprisoned me in this lovely place, and my lady would miss me if I left for even a day."

Artor was glad when Targo, who had been toasting his feet on the warm tiles, interrupted the small moment of gloom with his usual cheerful bluntness.

"I understand just how you feel, old friend. My days of easy traveling by horse are done. The mind is eager and young, but the flesh refuses to obey, so I'm thinking that I am looking on the Villa Poppinidii for the last time. Oh, to be young again!"

"I try never to look backward," Ector replied with a smile. "All of my happiness is here, and I'm glad my two girls will be well settled before I join my lady."

His face changed, and shadows crossed his faded blue eyes like dark clouds passing across the sun.

"I see that Caius is not with you."

"He is my steward, and acts in my place at Cadbury," Artor explained. "But he will be here for Livinia's day of triumph. He sends his love and congratulations on an excellent match."

Ector smiled regretfully. "Caius said no such thing. The villa is merely a convenient country house in my son's life, to be visited only when he is tired of his duties with you at Cadbury. No, don't color up, Artor, and don't look so guilty. Caius has never cared for the villa since my sweet lady died. Every corridor reminds him of his sins, and the boy prefers to run away rather than face the truth in his secret heart. I'm an old man, and I have grown weary of making excuses for our only son. We cosseted him, Livinia and I, and we blinded ourselves to the flaws in his character. I know what my son is, and I thank you for your long years of guardianship over him."

"Ector, there is no need—"

"We may be honest now, Artor." Ector placed one gnarled and swollen-jointed finger over the king's lips. "Unfortunately, I can leave you nothing of the villa, but I have these scrolls that I have always intended should be yours at the appropriate time. That day has come, so I will order them packed away to return with you to Cadbury. What Caius doesn't see, he won't miss, and I'll sleep well knowing that Lady Livinia's ancestors didn't collect these scrolls in vain. The land that you and poor Gallia were given is still your own, and the title is in the name of little Licia. You may be sure that Garan will care for it with as much devotion as Gareth has done in the past."

"What can I say, master? I will miss you when you go to your ancestors, for this villa is my only true home, and you have been a loving father to me, the only one I ever had."

"I wasn't always the best of fathers to you, Artor, and I regret my lack of warmth when you were a boy. Yet I have learned to love you, and I hope you have forgiven me for my indifference."

Artor flushed with embarrassment. "You ensured that I had a full belly, useful labor and play, a woman to love me, and an education. What more could a kinless foster child expect? And I ran wild, as I recall, yet I was never badly beaten or mistreated."

"It's very kind of you to make an old man feel better, very kind indeed," Ector muttered, and brushed away a couple of old man's tears. "Your loveless childhood has often preyed on my mind."

"You have been my father for all my life, Ector, and I would have been proud if you had sired me."

"Shite, Artor, you'll have me in tears in a moment," Targo broke in with his usual irreverence and gap-toothed grin. "What would your enemies think if they discovered you were as sentimental as the next man?"

Targo saw that Artor's usually veiled eyes were clear and un-guarded here in the villa's scriptorium, as he drank in Ector's essence in the full knowledge that he might never see the old man again.

"You don't need to mourn for me when I go to the Shadows, for my lady Livinia is waiting impatiently for our reunion. When Caius eventually dies, Livinia Minor and her husband will own the Villa Poppinidii, for I have made my wishes clear to the magistrate, and to Drusus, his son. Our simple way of our life will continue, and I will die happy."

Wordlessly, Artor embraced the old man's frail form, and felt the fluttering of Ector's ancient heart through his breast.

Ector struggled to his feet.

"Now is not the time for sadness. Our girls are to be wed, and the sun will shine in the next two weeks as it has never shone before. I know you will not be present for the nuptials, so tonight we shall enjoy an early bridal banquet and we shall be happy with our lot. Come! We shall bathe, then rest, and tonight we will make merry."

Targo grinned evilly. "Are your wine stocks still good? I've never developed a liking for ale."

"My friend," Ector replied, "on this night you may swim in beautiful Falernian wine that I managed to discover in the storehouse of Gallinus. Let us drink a toast to the finest girls in the land of the Britons with the best wine that has ever been fermented."

"I'll gladly drink to that!"

"I have planned a feast for tonight that will rival anything but the bridal feasts themselves," Ector added with satisfaction. "We'll dine on oysters swimming in periwinkle sauce, soups made from the finest fish, shellfish, and eels that can be found, whole glazed boar stuffed with doves, squab, jellies, and a cornucopia of sweet delights to make my old arms master believe he has died and gone to the abode of the gods. We shall gorge, Artor, on the finest that Aquae Sulis can offer."

"You spoil me, Ector. I swear I grow fatter with every night I sleep beneath this goodly roof." Ector slapped his foster son's flat belly in jest.

"You've never overeaten in your life, my boy," Targo said with a smile. "For tonight, forget that iron control you always exercise and let us make merry until the morning comes."

Targo and Ector slapped each other carefully on their backs and looked well pleased with themselves.

Artor and Targo eased their aching muscles in the baths while Ector continued with his duties in the villa, and then the High King commenced his daily sword practice in the villa's exercise yard.

"Damn, boy, you're still so very good," Targo praised as he watched Artor move gracefully through the old choreographed patterns of killing. "Your new wife will have no complaints of your strength or your staying power."

Targo's ribald laughter lightened Artor's heart a little, for this night was for celebration. He dressed with great ceremony and care, and, with his magnificent hair unbound, he was a wondrous sight in fine wool and cloth of gold that reflected the dancing firelight. Odin had brought two finely carved timber chests from the packhorses, and they waited in the atrium until Livinia Minor and Licia joined them at their feast.

Julanna was justly proud of her girls. Livinia Minor had become a beautiful dark-haired maiden, with rosy cheeks and a form that was now womanly and lush. When Artor presented her with his gift, she colored sweetly and kissed his cheek. She showed the natural grace and dignity of her grandmother, tempered by Julanna's sweetness of spirit.

The girl exclaimed over the fine woven cloths and the glass goblets from the Middle Sea. As she delved deeper and deeper into the box, more and more marvels came to light. And then she found the necklace and earrings of rare Scotti pearls that were the grey color of Artor's eyes. The contents of her box would make Livinia Minor a hostess of distinction, even in sophisticated Aquae Sulis, and her smile of delight was all that Artor could have desired.

Licia, on the other hand, was very like Artor with her amber hair, her fine but strong-boned face, and in her unusual height and slenderness that made every movement a graceful dance. The eight months that had passed since he had last seen her had transformed her from a child into new womanhood, but she was still young enough to be excited as she opened her box.

Artor had lavished all his love on the gifts for his daughter in her moment of celebration. Golden wine cups, flagons chased with the dragon motif, long lengths of wondrously dyed fine fabrics, a kitchen cauldron of the finest iron, and jewels and ornaments to tempt the heart of any girl were stroked and admired. At the very bottom of the box, a small bag of silver mesh held a golden chain, and a similar container concealed a dragon knife fitted for the smaller hand of a woman.

"My lord king," Licia breathed as she lifted the golden chain out of its small silver bag. "This gift is magnificent."

Hanging upon the chain was a burl of wood, small in size, but smoothed by years of use. It was perfectly formed in the shape of a little pregnant female.

"But this is yours, my lord," Licia protested. "I cannot accept such a gift."

"*You* cannot accept it . . . but Anna can," Artor replied, and smiled at the young woman. "For it belonged to her mother." His grey eyes were aglow with happiness.

Licia smiled and drew the knife from its scabbard. "This dagger is the twin of your own knife, Lord Artor. Wherever I go from now on, I will have no need of protection. Aye, it is a beautiful weapon."

"All I ask is that one day you will give it to your first son, in remembrance of me."

Her face became serious at last, and her warm amber eyes embraced him. "Am I really your sister, my lord? I have heard the rumors, and I am not a fool. Such regal gifts as this could only come from kin."

Artor placed his hand on his wildly beating heart and looked at his daughter longingly, his whole soul visible in his yearning eyes.

"Your personal safety demands that you have not been told the details of your birth." Artor smiled affectionately at the young woman. "Perhaps Llanwith will tell you the truth of your birth one day, but I cannot do so. These baubles are only expressions of love and admiration. I wish you well throughout all the days of your life."

The girl reached up and kissed his cheek. "I thank you, my lord, even though I don't quite understand what you are saying."

Artor pondered her words. Had she guessed at the truth? In Licia, he saw the mirror of his own contained face, but her features were more animated and joyous because life had not worn away her faith in all things good. He hoped with all his heart that time would keep her protected from the travails he had suffered during his younger days.

The feast that evening was all that Ector had promised, but for all their boasting, Targo and Ector were both safely in their beds long before midnight. Artor sat by the fountain and breathed in the scent of wild roses, jasmine, and rosemary. The stars were white lights in a velvet summer sky and the wind stirred Livinia Major's tree with a gentle susurration of leaves. That night and in the days that followed, Artor knew a peace that had been absent since he had left this safe and lovely villa to become High King of the Britons.

• • •

When Artor, Targo, and Odin left the Villa Poppinidii, they looked back at the quiet pastoral scene one last time and filled their eyes with the view of the mellow stone and brick structure on the hill. Each man saw the peaceful scene through different eyes, but each acknowledged in his heart that it was probable he'd never sleep under its roof again.

Targo watched the birds as they wheeled and dipped, eager to pirate new shoots from the budding fruit trees. Their speed and grace reminded him of the men he had killed and the women he had bedded. Rome was a memory so faint in his heart that only its heat and the smell of pressed olives still stirred his senses. Like the birds, he had alighted at Villa Poppinidii and found sustenance and a home within its old walls with their familiar order and beauty. Like the crows, he had rested for a time, feasting on the rich pickings of its verdant fields, before braving the excitement and freedom of the Old Forest. In response to the fates, he had followed Artor, prepared for ruin if need be, and instead had found honor at a time when he had ceased to believe that he was worthy of the word. His heart sang with thankfulness, and he knew that he was fated to lie with old Frith and Gallia when he finally crossed the River Styx. Artor would understand that he must close Targo's eyelids with copper coins to pay the Ferryman and scatter his ashes at Cadbury Tor, but Targo would be happy if the priests gave him Extreme Unction on his deathbed. Targo had a long list of sins on his conscience, and a clever man takes care to cover all the possibilities, both pagan and Christian.

Artor saw a far-off falcon hovering on the high winds. He recognized the dark tree line where the Old Forest began, and his heart was lost to the strangeness he had experienced years before when he found himself within its confines. If he tried, he could imagine the ivy-covered chimney of the house that had once held such brief joy for him. He hoped to find it again one day, but like the raptor on the wind, he knew that he was a solitary creature, too used to the company of strong men to willingly give his heart to anyone who demanded emotions from him that had withered years earlier.

He stared at the villa and watched as a young lad carried leather and wooden buckets to the stables. He remembered his other, younger self, and wondered if he could ever have been content in this haven of tranquillity. On the whole, he doubted it, and perhaps even Gallia would have grown old and bitter had he followed some other king to the battlefield, again and again.

"All things have a purpose, but we can never understand the master design," he said aloud, and Targo looked at him with frank derision.

"The only thing wrong with you, my boy, is that you never savor the moment. You must always be off to the next experience, the next idea, and the next problem, so you miss the quiet days that give us the greatest pleasure. Let's just sit here for a moment while my damned leg isn't aching, and enjoy the sunshine. That should be enough for any man."

Artor smiled, and nodded, but his eyes turned upward to the falcon that was circling lower and lower, having spied some creature that it could capture with its hooked talons and strong, curved beak.

I'm looking forward to the next experience already, he thought, as the bird swooped to make its kill.

Chapter XIII

THE MAID AND THE MISTRESS

Cadbury was bustling as Gruffydd, Perce, and Nimue rode through the crowded township and up to the first great gate of the fortress. The guards on the wall knew Gruffydd well, for the sword-bearer was a man of whom legends and songs were already sung.

As the small party made its slow way up the spiral path to the summit, Gruffydd's patience was pushed to its considerable limits, not so much because of its steepness but because of the slowness of Perce's spavined donkey. Nimue had cast off her makeshift straw hat and cloak in the sunlight's warmth. Her hair was half undone and framed her face like a crown of silver; her elfin face was alight with excitement and mischief.

Few of the men who lined the ramparts could tear their eyes away from her, and some whistled or made offensive suggestions about Nimue's relationship with Gruffydd. The sword-bearer merely impaled them with a vicious stare, causing them to look away and lapse into chastened silence. Perce wanted revenge for the insults, but Gruffydd somehow kept his temper and forced the boy to move upward and onward to their destination.

Nimue was sufficiently female to preen—just a little.

Now that Cadbury was upon them, Gruffydd doubted his wisdom in bringing either of his two charges to Artor's fortress. Perce had been a moment of whimsy on his part, but Nimue? He had promised Gallwyn that he would guarantee the girl's safety, and, short of spiriting Nimue off to a cold welcome from his wife in Venta Silurum, Cadbury was the best alternative.

Nimue was too beautiful, too clever, and too naïve to be left unprotected. Artor had marked her with the dragon symbol when she was barely two weeks old, and then had completely forgotten her, leaving Gallwyn to care for and raise the babe. Gruffydd had no choice, for only Artor could decide her fate.

When Caius strolled out at the last log gate, and made similar lewd suggestions about possible uses for Nimue, Gruffydd halted his horse, instructed the children to keep moving, and addressed Caius.

"I take offense at your suggestions, my lord. If you'd care to look, you'd see the mark of Artor on the child's right ankle and leg. I'm surprised that you have forgotten her, because the High King decimated your troop to avenge the death of her mother. She is the child of the willow."

Caius whitened, leaving twin spots of embarrassment on his cheeks. Caius did not care to be reminded of those far-off days when he had been shamed. He was now well past his fortieth year, and his body had grown portly in the exercise of his duties as Artor's steward. Even in the short time since the battle at Mori Saxonicus, the king's foster brother had earned prestige through his genius for making money, and he fully intended that his life would remain as comfortable as it now was.

"All that happened a long time ago, Gruffydd. I had forgotten the brat still lived. She's a beauty, I'll say that for her, but the king's new bride may not welcome another beautiful woman at Cadbury."

"New bride? What do you mean?"

"The kings have prevailed upon Artor to marry. He must beget an heir, or the kingdom will endure the same nonsense that occurred when Uther Pendragon died. My brother doesn't seem to care whom he marries, so Leodegran has become the lucky father-in-law. That sluggard is fortunate to have a daughter of the right age, appearance, and pedigree."

Gruffydd was taken aback but quickly recovered.

"That's excellent news, Lord Caius, for the king should be married. Has he met this beauty?"

"No, Gruff, that's the joke of it all. Artor says he's too old to care. In fact, he's younger than me. And *I'd* care, believe me!"

Caius laughed naturally, and Gruffydd found himself surprised once more at how engaging Artor's foster brother could be when he put his mind to it. But Gruffydd had always judged men and women by their actions rather than their amiable expressions. Even now, Ector was presiding over the marriage of Caius's daughter in the household of the Villa Poppinidii because Caius was too busy with other interests to attend the wedding. In Caius's view, daughters did not count; his lack of a son irked him constantly.

"Your charges are out of sight now," Caius pointed out. "I trust that caring for that lass will be an enjoyable burden, my friend."

"Yes, my lord. Good day to you."

Caius simply nodded, and Gruffydd galloped his horse in pursuit of Perce and Nimue, who were still riding upwards, squabbling about which direction gave the finest view from the tor.

So Artor is to marry, Gruffydd thought speculatively. Artor had resisted marriage for many years, but now, as he settled into the beginnings of middle age, Artor's advisers had obviously forced the High King to see political reason.

The fortress of Cadbury was boiling with servants in their best livery, rushing to and from the great hall to other buildings on the paved summit of the tor.

Leodegran's arrival is obviously being eagerly awaited, Gruffydd thought, as he kneed his horse towards the stables, instructing his young charges to follow. Then the two young people were instructed to unload their beasts and follow Gruffydd to his quarters.

"I will ascertain whether Artor will see you," Gruffydd said doubtfully as he observed the ordered chaos of Cadbury from the wooden shutters of his room. "Clean yourselves as best you can, and then don your finest clothing. The king is a man of unusual perception and he will not judge you well if you are dressed like servants. I'll go and find out what he expects of you."

Before making his way to Artor's quarters, Gruffydd entered a comfortably furnished room at the far end of the servants' wing. There, before a fire in a stone hearth, sat the ancient Targo. He was wrapped in furs and looked as disreputable as ever.

Targo had now accepted that his arthritis was a problem. He had been an elderly man when he had trained the young Artor in sword craft, but now he was ancient and seemed to be little more than an untidy bundle of sticklike bones, a hairless skull that he kept shaved bare, and a pair of black eyes that sat deeply in his head. Artor was utterly faithful to those whom he loved, and now that Targo's body was no longer of any practical use to his master, he was allowed to rest in an apartment as luxurious as that which was being prepared for Leodegran. Targo continued to stand at his master's back as a bodyguard, and Gruffydd knew that Targo was still capable of spitting an assassin on his short sword, no matter what the personal cost might be. Artor would never shame his old tutor by putting him out to pasture. Besides which, Artor enjoyed talking to the old man, and the sword-bearer's simple heart honored his lord for the consideration he gave to his loyal retainer.

Targo peered up at Gruffydd with eyes that were glossy with the beginning of cataracts. As he caught sight of the red-grey hair, Targo recognized his guest immediately.

"Back so soon, Gruff? My master gave you two months' leave to visit your grandsons, and you're back far too early. Did you have trouble on your journey?"

"No, I had no trouble, but I acquired two youngsters along the way, and I don't really know what to do with them."

Targo relished news and was sorry to hear of Gallwyn's death. He remembered Nimue as an infant, and Gruffydd's description merely piqued his curiosity for more gossip.

"Bring the girl on a visit at some convenient time. I often wondered whether she was worth the lives of those innocent warriors who died when Artor decimated Caius's troop. She must be a full-grown woman by now."

"She's beautiful enough to restart even your old heart, Targo. But I warn you, there's something wild about the girl, for all that she's loving and . . . well . . . she's just a sweet little thing."

Targo snickered and poured wine into a bronze goblet. Gruffydd noticed that Targo's shaking hands spilled some of the wine.

"After such high praise from you, I look forward to meeting this paragon who has caught the attention of the unassailable Gruffydd."

Then Gruffydd described Perce, and the young man's ambitions, his strengths, and his endless, almost unnatural patience.

"He's far too old to be trained as a warrior. He's twenty-five if he's a day, but he holds to his dream regardless of what I say."

Targo laughed outright, and then his face suddenly collapsed into a coughing fit that made Gruffydd very worried about the old warrior's state of health.

"Bollocks, Gruff," Targo sputtered. "You and I know there's no real age when a warrior is fit for training. Yes, it's best when he's young for there are no bad habits to beat out of him. But it's what's in the heart that counts. Even now, Odin trains Gareth, and Gareth is thirty. Artor will know if this Perce is suitable immediately he sets his eyes on the man, for all that he's engrossed in thoughts of this stupid marriage with this Wenhaver creature."

Targo sounded so peeved that Gruffydd was alarmed. The old man stalked around his chamber with something of his old vigor, although he favored one leg and pressed a swollen-fingered hand to his hip.

"It's probably just an old man's fancy, Gruff, but I remember that witch, Morgan. She told us many years ago that Artor's second wife would destroy the kingdom, and I'm beginning to grow superstitious in my old age."

Gruffydd snorted at the very idea that Targo would believe in anything he couldn't see, touch, hear, smell, or taste.

"What did Morgan say that worries you so much?"

"She told us that Artor should beware of a woman with yellow hair. At the time, no one at the Villa Poppinidii took the threat seriously because we didn't know then how often Morgan's predictions would prove to be correct. And how many golden-haired women appear naturally among the Celts?" He paused. "Shite, Gruff, I worry about my boy. Morgan has always meant him harm, and, by all reports, this Wenhaver has yellow hair."

"Artor's no fool in the game of love, Targo. You know that better than anyone, and I'd not care to stand in her shoes if she ever upsets him."

Targo slapped Gruffydd's back in gratitude, and they resumed their original conversation.

"I'd like you to bring the boy to me after Artor makes his decision. Perhaps there might be something that these old hands can do to help him with his ambitions. It would be an interest, mind, and I can't promise any success. From what you say, the boy may be a clod."

"Your reservations are understood, Targo. I'm grateful for any help, because I like young Perce. He reminds me of how I felt when I was young."

Targo chortled and then slumped back into his chair as another coughing fit shook him.

"You? Young?" he said when he could speak. "You were never young, you old reprobate. You and I were born old."

Gruffydd looked closely at the mercenary, his eyes troubled. "Are you well, Targo? Because I must say you don't look it. I'd be sorry if anything were to happen to you."

"I am well enough, old friend. Mori Saxonicus was a bit too much for me, but I'd not relinquish one moment in that charnel house for an added decade of life. I've no plans to rust away through idleness, I'll tell you that for nothing. Besides, my boy still needs me, so I'm good for a few years more. But I take your concerns in good heart, Sword-bearer. We're neither of us too pretty now."

"You never were, Targo, I'm sorry to tell you," Gruffydd quipped, much heartened by Targo's explanation.

The old warrior looked happy and content as Gruffydd eased his way out of the comfortable, overwarm room.

Gruffydd's status gave him quick access to a rather distracted Artor, who was sampling and discarding various sumptuous tunics presented by a tailor from the town of Cadbury. Artor seemed grateful for the interruption and swiftly ordered the tailor to take his leave and return later.

Gruffydd explained his early return once more, and confessed his quandary over Nimue and the kitchen boy, Perce.

"May I call them into your presence, my lord? You'll be able to decide what should be done. The boy is a particular problem as he is determined to become one of your warriors. I've tried to dissuade him, but he won't be deflected. I've discussed his situation with Targo."

"Hmmnn!" Artor grunted, and lifted his leonine head.

Gruffydd noted that the High King's remarkable hair had recently been cut at the shoulders so that the curl was accentuated. Artor's one vanity had been his remarkable hair, so Gruffydd wondered if the shearing of his plaits spoke of a radical change that was taking place in Artor's thinking. Somehow, the idea wasn't comforting. Also, the High King had grown a close-clipped beard that gave his face gravity but spoke of a mental severing from his Roman youth. The lines around his eyes and mouth were scarcely evident after his many years of struggle, and his body was as fit and as healthy as ever.

"I should also offer my felicitations on your coming nuptials, my lord," Gruffydd added. "I hope that you sire many sons."

"Don't you start on me, Gruff. I had to marry sometime, so this Wenhaver woman will do as well as any other girl. Leodegran will hold his part of the northern frontier the firmer because of the marriage agreement, so don't delude yourself that I have fallen in love with her at my advanced age."

"I didn't wish to suggest that your decisions were anything but your own concern, my lord."

Artor laughed. "I will speak with your orphans. Some excellent warriors died to avenge the honor of Nimue's mother, and I admit I'm curious to see how she has turned out. She was also responsible for your services to me, my friend, which was a princely gift from one so young."

Gruffydd nodded his head in gratitude for the king's kind words.

"You can also call on Myrddion to attend me while you're about it. He plans to be absent during the arrival of King Leodegran, and I won't countenance his defection. He's having second thoughts for some reason, and he's feeling guilty as a result."

"Master," Gruffydd replied, and backed out of the king's presence. As usual, he wished that Artor was less candid around him, as the king's confidences were dangerous for the continued good health of an ordinary man.

In the corridor, Gruffydd found two servants and delegated their separate tasks to them. He then leaned against the wall and waited for Nimue and Perce to join him.

Odin found him first.

The giant Jute had become civilized during the years of Artor's reign. He wore shoes and had given up furs during all but the coldest weeks of winter. But he was still enormous and utterly committed to the personal welfare of Targo and Artor.

"You're back," Odin said with a wide smile. "That is good. Targo has missed you during your absence."

"And you didn't?" Gruffydd teased.

"I have, I have," Odin replied with his usual seriousness and honesty. "Yes. I have missed you a little, my friend."

"I am honored, Odin." Gruffydd laughed, and the warrior looked puzzled. "I missed you, too."

Nimue and Perce entered the corridor at this point. They were squabbling as usual, and Gruffydd found himself feeling quite avuncular.

Nimue had cleaned the worst of the mud and dust from her person and was dressed in a gown of unbleached wool that should have been ugly and gauche. But she had released her hair from its plaits and combed the silver blondness until it fell like a great, waving curtain over her shoulders and down her back. The bronze necklace she always wore disappeared into her neckline, and her slashed fringe was held firmly in place by her mother's barbaric bronze pin.

Even Odin drew in his breath at the sight of her, especially when she pirouetted and he caught a glimpse of the dragon tattoo above her worn leather sandals.

"The babe!" he said in wonder. "The wise woman and the seawife."

"Pardon?" Gruffydd asked, but Odin pressed his lips together and stared at Nimue until her cheeks reddened.

"Do I look nice, dear Gruff? I wish I had a better dress, but I'm sure the High King will understand."

Her gaiety was infectious, and even Odin's lips twitched, a considerable achievement since the whole world knew that the Jutlander had no sense of humor. Alongside her, a cleaned and shining Perce, dressed in simple homespun, only managed to appear more awkward than usual.

Gruffydd realized that Nimue had the power to eclipse any woman and he began to fear for her well-being, for he was all too conscious of the jealousy and vanity that existed among the women at Artor's court.

They knocked at the doors leading to the king's apartments, and Artor bellowed for them to enter. Nimue and Perce abased themselves before their king with that unmistakable awe and reverence that cannot be counterfeited. As she bowed, Nimue's hair fell over her shoulders to the floor in a silken ripple of silver, and it was at this point that Myrddion Merlinus entered. The healer was long past even the pretense of youth, but he still stood straight and slim in his black garb, his hair as silver-white as the mane of Nimue.

"Rise, my children," Artor ordered. "And come closer so I can see you." He turned to Myrddion. "What do you think, Myrddion? Was she worth the lives of ten men?"

Nimue raised her eyes, and her dark, feathered brows frowned a little at Artor's tone. Her northern eyes sparked with the beginnings of temper. She stood up straight, a slim and beautiful Valkyrie in her commoner's gown, but the biggest fool in Cadbury would know instinctively that she was far from ordinary.

Myrddion Merlinus stood like a dullard, his face wholly blank and his mind wiped almost totally clean. He had always understood that sexual attraction can be sudden and inexplicable. After all, he had fallen in love during his callow youth with Flavia, the daughter of Flavius Aetius, who possessed the potential to become a disastrous and dangerous woman. But since he had learned the dangers of affection at the bloody hands of Uther Pendragon, Myrddion had chosen to excise women from his life. Over the years, he had experienced brief periods of lust, for no man can wholly control the atavistic, primitive demands of human nature. He had slaked these feelings with willing women where there was no chance of emotional entanglements.

Now, a pair of ice-blue eyes fringed with dark eyelashes, and pale pink lips that were artlessly full and glistening, almost robbed the elderly man of speech. When he had remembered to breathe again, Myrddion felt a long, hot flush that began somewhere below his heart and rose up his face to be lost in his silver hair.

She's a child, and she must be near to half a century younger than I am, he thought to himself. Shame suffused his cheeks again. There's no fool like an old fool!

Abruptly, Artor called him back to the king's quarters in Cadbury Hall, and his doom.

One look at Myrddion's face, and Gruffydd felt a shiver run through his belly.

"I'm sorry if I seem flippant, child, but I speak my mind," Artor stated, fully aware that Nimue was affronted.

Nimue was not cowed, but it was to Myrddion she turned.

"Please, my lord, what is flippant? If I know, I may answer my king properly."

Myrddion was immediately captured by the direct honesty of her eyes. He shook himself mentally and carefully explained the meaning of the word.

"I thank you, my lord." Nimue nodded in understanding. "I will not forget."

She turned back to Artor.

"Sire, your question was not flippant, for taking the lives of men is a serious matter. And yes, I am worth ten innocent men. The logic is inescapable. You ordered their deaths in order to punish my enemy, and you are the king. Your orders are always just, so my worth is as you decided. As to whether you have received any benefit worthy of the lives of those men, I do not know, for Gallwyn didn't tell me."

Artor looked at Myrddion, who was staring at Nimue with both speculation and something else that Artor couldn't quite recognize.

"The girl appears to have an exceptional grasp of logical reasoning," Myrddion said conversationally to Artor. "Especially when you consider the manner of her raising."

"Lord?" Nimue interrupted, her brows now drawn together in anger. "I beg your pardon, but I won't hear a bad word said about my dear Gallwyn. And you've wronged her. She taught me my letters and numbers, and she taught me not to lie or to steal. She was good, so my *raising*, as you call it, was good too."

Artor was obviously amused. He bowed to Nimue, who blushed right down to her slender throat. Many girls lose their beauty for a moment when they color up, but, on Nimue, the rosy flesh enhanced and embellished her fine skin.

"I apologize if I have hurt your feelings, Nimue, but I am a simple, rough soldier, and I have missed the company of women for many, many years. In fact, your character reminds me of my foster mother, Livinia, although she was far more tactful than you are, my child."

Gruffydd observed that Nimue's agile brain was filing away a number of questions, especially the nature of tact.

"Oh, gods!" Artor suddenly remembered. "Do you still wear your tattoo?"

Nimue gave Artor a lopsided smile, and, with a hint of patronage in her sweetly curved mouth, she slowly nodded her head. After all, she could hardly have removed a tattoo of such size without leaving considerable scarring.

She lifted the hem of her dress and showed the dragon, its wings stretching almost to her knees.

"Well, you wear my mark, so it's fitting that I find something at court for you to do. Would you wish to serve the queen when she arrives at Cadbury Tor?" Artor assessed Nimue's extraordinary beauty and immediately reconsidered his offer. He realized that no woman, especially a beauty such as Wenhaver, would welcome Nimue as a servant, for she would be a constant challenge to the queen's status in his court.

Myrddion cleared his throat. "My lord, if I might make a suggestion? For some years I have felt the need to train an apprentice to carry on my work when I am no longer capable of serving you. This young woman is sharp, as you said yourself, and she already has the rudiments of learning. She could be of great use to you after my time has come."

Artor stared at his old mentor with quizzical and measuring eyes. Myrddion had trained many apprentices, both male and female, in his chosen craft of healing. In this case, the healer's offer was peculiar, for Myrddion was being uncharacteristically hasty in his decision to share his knowledge with this young, untrained girl who had nothing in her favor but a lovely face and a certain degree of native cunning.

Does the old man feel a flutter in his heart at last?

Then Artor rejected this solution, for Myrddion was far too careful to succumb to either love or lust on such a short acquaintance. His old friend was simply being generous in giving an orphan girl a trade and a place in a hostile world.

"That'll be long in the future, my friend, for I am convinced you hold the secret to eternal life," Artor joked. "But the idea is good, regardless of your reasoning, so you may keep her if you wish. But

Nimue must agree, for Cadbury will gossip, and she will bear the brunt of any curiosity or resentment. No one will dare to question our decisions, but she'll be an easy target for the court's interest. Besides which, Myrddion, not many young people would choose to putter around with your potions, your poisons, and the bloody business of healing. Nimue might not agree . . . and as she has reminded me, she is worth ten good warriors."

Nimue's eyes gleamed dangerously, but, wisely, she chose to be silent.

Both men looked at Nimue, who nodded her acceptance with an enigmatic expression.

"Now, boy, what shall we do with you?" Artor examined Perce closely by walking round the young man as if he was a horse being inspected for sale.

Perce stood quietly and deferentially under the king's scrutiny, his honest face shining in happiness simply to have found himself in the presence of the High King.

"I intend to become a great warrior, my lord," he stated. "One day, I will be the finest of all those warriors who serve you."

"You aim high, kitchen boy," Artor stated blandly. "Do you have any skills?"

"No, my lord. But I will learn fast, and I'll work hard. With your permission, I intend to ask Lord Targo to assist me in achieving my destiny, just as he did for you. I only ask for a chance to begin my training."

Gruffydd winced. Perce was presuming a great deal, and the High King could tear down his dreams in an instant if he cared to take offense at the words of a mere kitchen boy. While Artor approved of measures that gave the old man an interest, he would resent any task that could affect Targo's health.

As the boy waited for the king's decision, a trumpet call sounded in the far distance and Artor moved over to a window and pushed open the wooden shutters.

"Damn!" he swore. "Leodegran is early."

"Lord, perhaps Perce might become Targo's servant?" Gruffydd broke in. "I have spoken to my old friend and he's indicated to me that he likes to feel useful. At the same time, this boy would happily care for the needs of his master. You are aware that Targo weakens daily . . ."

Distractedly, Artor waved a hand in agreement, although his forehead was furrowed at the mention of Targo's ailments. "That arrangement will suffice, at least for the present. For now, I must change and prepare to meet my guests, as Leodegran's party is already at the first gate. Damn!"

Yet Artor understood the fears of an ambitious young man, so he smiled encouragingly at Perce and charmed the kitchen boy forever.

"One more thing before you leave my presence," Artor added. "Your name reeks of the kitchens. You must change it if you wish to serve me as a warrior."

Perce nodded seriously.

"You will see to quarters for Nimue, Myrddion, for she's now your apprentice. I place her under your personal protection. Gruffydd, Perce is your responsibility, so you will make sure that he chooses a more appropriate name." No trace of sarcasm tainted Artor's words. "Make the necessary arrangements with Targo for his training if this young man believes he can become my finest warrior and a hero of the Britons."

Nimue and Perce hurried away, but Gruffydd couldn't resist pausing at a long arrow slit to look at the procession snaking its way up the circular road leading to the top of the tor.

At the head of the procession, Leodegran rode on a showy, dappled grey horse and wore a king's ransom in gold and gems over robes of awe-inspiring luxuriousness. Behind him, in the midst of brightly clad maids and ladies, Wenhaver was demure on a steed of purest white. The horse's mane had never been cut and the glossy hair had been plaited so that now it fell in waves across the powerful, arched neck of the beast. Cleverly, Wenhaver had chosen to wear ivory while her maidens were clad in flower colors, ensuring that she stood out within their vividness like a pale, elegant lily in a field of wild blooms. Like a small golden-blond doll in fine and costly raiment, Wenhaver sat easily upon her dainty mare.

A long baggage train accompanied the visitors, laden down with many wooden chests in which Leodegran and his daughter had packed enough clothing to dress all of Artor's court. Armed warriors with drawn swords protected one wagon whose wheels bore evidence of a very heavy load. Inside the wagon, Artor's dowry lay snugly within chests filled with straw.

The retinue was large, even by Leodegran's standards. It finally halted in the forecourt of Artor's hall, which was cheerfully decorated with colorful banners and filled with liveried servants and warriors who gleamed in gold, vivid shades of blue, and garlands of flowers.

Gruffydd could see that Wenhaver was very pretty, slightly plump, and somewhat disgruntled. As she was helped to dismount, Gruffydd watched her stand on the foot of the warrior who offered her assistance, and his heart sank. Although she apologized with a heart-stopping smile, Gruffydd wasn't deceived. That's all we need, he thought, a sulky little bitch who likes to hurt things when she's in a bad mood.

Wenhaver swept away, lifting her heavy skirts from the dirt of the flagstones. She looked up and caught Gruffydd's eyes for a moment, and he was shocked to see that her face was sullen with resentment and dislike. Clearly, Cadbury held no charms for its new mistress.

"ALL THE WORLD must smile, for the High King is about to wed," Myrddion murmured as he set Nimue to practicing her Latin with chalk on a smoothed piece of slate.

"Isn't it exciting, lord. I've never seen a really important wedding, so I shall consider it an essential part of my education. What shall I wear?" Nimue grinned unself-consciously, and Myrddion suddenly felt very old. "The day is so beautiful," Nimue went on. "I saw servants out early collecting baskets of flowers, and it seems a pity that such lovely things will just wither and die once they are cut. When I marry, all the flowers will be growing in pots."

"Much like the garden you have planted in my window and on any flat surface in my rooms. How can I be taken seriously as a manipulative and wicked demon when my rooms are full of daisies, and geraniums, and . . . whatever!"

Myrddion sounded a little peevish, so Nimue kissed his hand with a mixture of nonchalance and coquetry.

"My lord?" she asked, under demurely lowered eyelids.

"You think to tie me up in knots, suck out my brain through my nose, and then leave me to perish in lonely old age," Myrddion joked.

Nimue was immediately contrite, and her remarkable eyes impaled him with her obvious sincerity.

"You could never be old, my lord," she said without hesitation. "You are the cleverest man in the kingdom, by far. And the handsomest," she whispered softly, as she contrived to keep her face bland.

Two months had passed since Leodegran and his only daughter had arrived at Cadbury to pay tribute to Artor and to finalize the arrangements for the wedding. During their visit, they had feasted, hunted, and surveyed the house of the High King. Then, with the advent of high summer, they had departed so that Wenhaver could see to her bridal clothes and her preparations for the wedding, leaving Leodegran to ponder on the contracts he had made to purchase a kingdom for his daughter.

As the last of the Dobunni retinue left the Cadbury pastures, there was a collective sigh of relief from all who had attended them. Throughout the brief visit, Wenhaver had acted with impeccable and distant courtesy in public, allowing the crowds of Cadbury to be captivated by her beauty and apparent refinement. But the denizens of the tor knew better. Away from the adoring crowds, and out of the cold view of the High King, Wenhaver sulked, threw tantrums, and turned her apartments into a stew of valuable broken glass, torn dresses, and spilled cosmetics. Cadbury was cold; Cadbury lacked refinement; servants didn't bow low enough, and, most irksome, a woman of extraordinary beauty was already ensconced within the fortress.

Inevitably, Wenhaver hated Nimue at first sight. She was fond of saying to all and sundry that Nimue was obviously a witch's child foisted on the High King for nefarious reasons she could not name, but the lowliest servant knew how she raged at Nimue's beauty, even though they never mixed socially.

"She's unnatural, Father, and I don't want her here," she complained to Leodegran before they left Cadbury.

Leodegran sighed. "Perhaps she'll be gone when we return for the wedding," he replied hopefully.

As fond as he was of his only daughter, Leodegran found Wenhaver's tantrums tiresome. And, on occasions, he considered that her more ridiculous demands were frightening because she exposed a grasping miserliness in her nature that even he, in all his indulgence, found repugnant.

"Fortunately, she'll soon be Artor's problem and not mine," he muttered to himself.

"You need hardly ever see the girl, Wenhaver," he soothed. "She is the apprentice of Myrddion Merlinus, so she is kept very busy and would never attend Artor's court."

"But the man has Artor's ear. The High King should be guided by his wife, not by some devil's spawn who is too old to be useful."

Wenhaver was enjoying a massive sulk.

"Let me give you a word of advice, daughter. Don't try to insinuate yourself between your husband and his friends, for, believe me, you will lose the battle and you will appear to be a very foolish young girl. Please, refrain from attempting to tell him what to do. Artor is the most powerful man in the west, and you are but sixteen years old. The court will laugh at you, and you will become an object of ridicule." He paused. "But if you can present him with a son and heir, he will be far easier to manage."

"Ugh!" Wenhaver shuddered. "Artor may be handsome and very strong, but he is so unbearably old!"

"He's not *too* old, my girl. Rumor has it that there are a large number of warriors in his personal bodyguard who have the same hair and features as all the Pendragon clan."

Gruffydd held serious doubts as to Artor's wisdom in accepting the sly little baggage as his wife. He could see that she was spoiled beyond bearing, rude to all persons she deemed to be her inferior, and dismissive of the splendor of Cadbury Tor. Where were the warm woolen curtains to cut out the drafts? Where were the golden cups and the fine linens? Why did Artor not trade for glass vessels from Gaul for a civilized table? And every maid in Cadbury was clumsy and useless. She would bring her own servants with her when she came back for the marriage.

So the underclass of Cadbury Tor, the servants of the fortress, dreaded her return and cursed the sight of her when the long procession made its way through Cadbury's forecourt two short months later.

Her quarters were bright with flowers and perfumed with luxurious oils, but Wenhaver dismissed these efforts to make her feel welcome. She complained that the bed was too soft, and the narrow windows needed shutters to keep out any night chills. It was useless to explain that painted screens would shield the most fastidious lady from errant breezes. The servants bowed, agreed with her every outrageous whim—and hated her. But around Artor and the lords of the court, Wenhaver was the perfect woman. Even though she was barely sixteen, she had been raised to understand the caprices of powerful men. Artor was flattered, deferred to, blushed over, and, in short, treated like the master of the universe.

All in all, it was a pity that the High King didn't recognize a masterful piece of acting. In fact, he barely noticed Wenhaver at all. She simply did not impinge on his thoughts. Men of Artor's age require more of a woman than pretty pouts and a plump pair of breasts. The demands of the body, the itch to possess soft flesh, could be scratched anywhere. But as Artor had learned the hard way, legitimacy was everything. Yes, she would do, as long as she bore him a son to continue the Pendragon line of succession. But if the girl looked for romance, she would find only disappointment.

Her first meeting with Artor had been a revelation. Leodegran had warned his daughter that the High King was not a man to dance attendance on the emotional needs of a woman and was not likely to be particularly flattering in his manner. On that first visit, when a warrior had helped her to dismount, she had been in a bad mood. The journey had been long, her back ached fiercely, her clothing was too tight, and she told herself that standing on the warrior's foot had been accidental. She was tired!

Her doting father, with exaggerated flourishes, had introduced Artor to his daughter, and she had fallen into a deep, graceful curtsy. Then she waited to be assisted to her feet. And waited. And waited still longer. She looked up and saw King Artor's face, stiff, disapproving, and all too aware. He had seen what she had done.

But Wenhaver was unused to being called to account for her actions. Besides, as far as she was concerned, the marriage bargain had been struck and she was betrothed to the High King of the Britons. Such political agreements are not easily broken, and certainly not for the injured toe of a mere servant. With a flush of embarrassment on her cheekbones, Wenhaver rose and extended her hand to Artor to be kissed.

"My lord," she murmured, as he took her fingers by their very tips and lowered his full lips to kiss one of her rings, taking care that he did not touch her flesh.

"My lady," he replied with exaggerated courtesy.

And so the betrothed couple met and measured each other, and were not impressed.

At rare moments, Artor very nearly disliked Wenhaver. The crowning incident occurred when he took her to meet Targo, his one true link with his beginnings.

"Must I go, my lord?" Wenhaver had complained. "I'm not comfortable with old people."

Artor was forced to remind himself that she was the same age as Gallia when they had first wed. Wenhaver saw his lips twist with distaste, and she realized that she had made a mistake.

"Yes, you must," he insisted. "Targo was my teacher, my friend, and my bodyguard. He is entitled to respect from you."

Artor's tone left Wenhaver very little choice in the matter, so she determined to give the High King no further cause for complaint—at least until they were safely married. Then that nasty old man could be pensioned off to some far-off spot where she would not have to endure his presence. Wenhaver already had a growing list of changes that would be introduced once the wedding had been consummated.

The meeting in Targo's apartments did not go well. Wenhaver was distant and cold, and wrinkled her nose at the mingled smells of old man, liniment, and ale that permeated the rooms. Artor was not pleased, and Wenhaver's subsequent attempts to curry favor with Targo fell very flat.

The old Roman read her character accurately from the moment she arrived. He was too old and too irascible to dissemble, so he teased her unmercifully with some particularly crude comments, even for Targo, who had heard every vulgarity in the civilized world.

Showing rare common sense, Wenhaver avoided Targo's traps and merely smiled with honeyed sweetness. Targo showed no signs of leaving Wenhaver be, so Artor shook his head ruefully at his mentor and took her away.

Targo grinned evilly. "Artor will regret his ties to that little harridan, young Percivale. You mark my words."

Percivale was the name that Perce had chosen for use at court. He had discussed the matter with Targo, and they had agreed to wait for a suitable occasion to obtain the High King's approval for its use. But, in the meantime, Targo's use of the name gave him much pleasure.

"Did I ever tell you about the only person who came really close to killing me?" Targo sighed pleasurably. "She was the sweetest, softest woman I ever saw. She had a very long knife and the advantage of surprise. Almost got me, but I managed to kill her first. I cried for weeks when she died."

Perce stared at Targo with frank disbelief. "You'd never cry over a woman, lord, no matter how much you loved her. Lord Artor, perhaps, if he should perish. But a woman! I may have been a kitchen boy, Lord Targo, but I'm not a child to be tricked with pretty stories."

"Are you accusing me of being a hard-hearted liar, boy?" Targo growled.

"Well, not exactly, lord," Perce began, his face reddening right down to his collarbone. "You're not hard-hearted, but I just can't imagine that you'd weep for someone who failed to destroy you. You're exaggerating, Lord Targo."

"Humppff!" Targo replied. But under the gruffness, he was pleased that his pupil didn't lie, even to mollify him.

Perce was so happy in his labors with Targo that he felt his heart would burst with joy. Targo no longer had much skill with the sword because his joints were twisting from the bone disease, but he'd forgotten more about combat than most men ever learned. One look at Perce's open, freckled face, and the way the young man moved when he held weapons in his hands, was enough to remind the old man of the young Artor, before the exercise of power took over his life.

Now that Targo's hands were slowly turning into twisted clubs, Perce shaved the old man each morning. His infirmity also required Perce to assist his master to bathe, followed by a morning meal where Perce would seek out the choicest titbits from the kitchen to assist the old man's digestion. After this task, Perce's duties were completed, so Targo could begin to teach the rudiments of swordcraft to the younger man. Even without an armed sparring partner, the lessons went well, for Targo's legs still moved, albeit stiffly, and his skill was such that Perce rarely found an opening and touched the old mercenary. Perce's drive to excel was so strong that he practiced tirelessly, except for when his duties to Targo called him. In a surprisingly short time, Targo could no longer evade Perce's wooden sword. As Targo had done for Artor so many years before, Perce took to sleeping on a simple pallet across the door of the old man's room.

On several occasions, the High King tripped over the lad during late-night visits to see his old friend.

"What's he like, Targo?" Artor asked the old man one night, while an exhausted Perce lay sound asleep outside the entrance to the room.

301

"I wish you had a thousand of him. There are some who are born masters, and some who become masters. Perce is of the latter breed. He's a good man, clean through, and I'd know. He mops up after me like a mother. Damn these hands! Who'd have thought in twelve months my knuckles would swell and my fingers would twist until I can't hold a sword?" Targo's brow furrowed, and a single tear ran unheeded out of one eye. A little more than a month before, he could ride, but something had given way inside his head and his strength was diminishing daily.

Artor saw the single tear and repressed an overwhelming feeling of sorrow for his friend of so many years.

"I have to be shaved and bathed like a babe. Damn, but you'd never believe how often we use these sodding things." Targo waved his ruined hands at his master. "I hate the weakness of old age, for all that Perce never makes me feel like a burden. He says that it's a privilege to serve a man of the legions. Perce doesn't lie, so I know he feels it's worth his while to clean up my puke and shit without complaint. In a few months, my body has become more finicky than that of a child. I can't eat what I used to, and good red meat fair curdles my innards. I'm an old man, and I've lived way past my time, so I should be grateful to be still breathing. But I feel it, my boy, no matter how hard I try to pretend that I'm still useful. May Mithras bless Perce, for he helps me feel like a man again."

Artor wrapped his arms round the frail old shoulders and held Targo close.

What could he say in comfort, when all Targo described was the truth? Instead, he rocked the old man as he would a mother, a father, or a lover.

Perce had woken and watched from his pallet, glad that neither man knew he was awake.

"You're still of use to me, Targo. When the nights are cold and Gallia is a distant memory, and when I know I can never acknowledge Licia's future children, then I feel the gorge of Uther rise in me like some waiting venom. At these times, I come to you to find the old Artorex in your eyes, and these thoughts make me happy for a little while."

Targo broke their embrace. "I wish I *had* been your father, boy. Though you'd be a damn sight shorter than you are now."

Both men laughed briefly.

"I would like to ask for Odin's assistance for two hours a day to train my boy in the use of weapons when he is exercising with Gareth. I can work on Perce's brain, but Odin can give him the skill and the battle sense. I can assure you that Perce will become a warrior, and I ask you to accept him as such for me. Consider him my very last gift to you."

Artor bowed his leonine head, and then gripped Targo's malformed old paw in his warm hands.

"You may have whatever you desire, Targo. You may have Odin, Perce, or the whole kingdom if you will it. As long as you are prepared to stay with me."

"Nothing is forever, Artor, you know that. But of one thing I am certain. I believe that Perce should take my place when I am gone to the gods."

"If he is that good, I will certainly consider it. But no one *can* take your place, my friend. No one! Who'll remind me that I'm mortal, once you have gone to the Shades?"

"Shite, boy, they'll line up to prove you're mortal!"

After honest laughter, both men sat silently and stared into the fire for a long time.

"Am I doing right by marrying this Wenhaver?" Artor asked eventually. "I don't much like her."

"I suppose you have to marry someone, and this one will do well enough if you treat her as if she was spun gold and pander to her vanity. But I'd never trust her, boy. She's as shallow as a puddle on the roadway."

"I hear you, Targo," Artor answered with a boyish grin.

"And she'll be as muddy as a puddle on the roadway if she takes it into her silly head to get stirred up," the old man continued.

"And she's likely to trip me up if I don't watch where I am walking," Artor added.

"You've got it, lad. Aye. But you were ever a quick study, just like my Perce." Targo glanced with affection to where his servant was still feigning sleep.

"I'll become resentful of Perce if you keep going on about his virtues. You know what my father was like."

Artor was only half joking, and Targo knew it.

"Ah, but you'll always be the closest to my heart. And you must be the one who'll light my funeral pyre."

"Cease such talk," Artor admonished Targo gently. "Your time hasn't arrived yet."

"But it's close, Artor. I can feel it coming."

ON THE LATE spring morning when the High King of the Britons was to wed, Artor tried to conjure up some of the joy he had felt twenty years earlier when Gallia had come to him, all in crimson, with field flowers in her hair. But he simply felt forsaken, like a man who has outlived his time.

The previous day, a letter had come from Aquae Sulis—expected, but hard to endure nonetheless.

The courier who had brought the fine scroll bowed so low that his back bent like a good longbow. Artor gave him a handful of coins in thanks, took a deep breath, and broke the wax seal that kept the scroll tightly wound.

The Latin script was very pure and inscribed in a beautiful hand.

To Artor Rex, High King, and brother by marriage.

Ector, your father, has died. He slipped quietly away in his sleep, so I thank the gods that he suffered no pain. My lord was happy and at peace, having completed his promise to you and having watched the marriages of his beloved granddaughters.

Do not reproach yourself, my lord, that you only saw him occasionally. He took such pride in you, and in the trust that you placed in him, and he was constantly warmed by his memories.

He was content to pass into the Shadows, for he believed with his whole heart that his loved ones were awaiting him beyond the veil. He often spoke of how he would embrace Gallia and Frith in your name when he joined them. He took joy at the thought of death and rejoining his beloved Livinia, so we shouldn't grieve for him.

I have sent word to my husband who has decided to be present when Ector goes to meet the gods. Ector has chosen inhumation, and wishes to lie in the Garden of Gallia with the sarcophagus mounted under a granite bench so that visitors can sit in the sunshine and contemplate the beauty of the world in which his remains will lie. He believes that he will hear and feel them and their joy. I have found a stonemason who is already working on Ector's memorial. I have decided that a simple line of Latin should be carved on one side, away from the weather:

ECTOR WAS A TRUE FATHER, HUSBAND,

SON, AND WARRIOR

HE WAS A MAN

Have I been too sentimental? Will his spirit go into the Shadows joyously under such an epitaph? I will be guided by your advice, for you knew him better than any other man.

I had hoped to send you his felicitations on your wedding day, for Ector was glad that you had decided to end your long period of mourning. Ector understood that love of the living takes precedence over any respect owed to the dead.

I wish you happy and will always remember the debts I

305

owe to you. My friend Gallia would have been so very, very proud of you.

The Villa Poppinidii goes on, as it always will, so do not fear for us.

From Julanna, matriarch of Villa Poppinidii.
Scribed by Sisiphus, servant of Branicus,
Magistrate of Aquae Sulis.

Artor had wept a little, and then gave the news to Targo. On his last night unwed, the High King and his old arms master had recalled Ector's many words and deeds over a fine flagon of red wine, so that the High King awoke the following morning with a pounding headache and an empty feeling somewhere below his ribs. He dressed with care, eyes downcast, and with a temper fraying with regrets and memories.

The day was inauspicious and he dreaded its end.

Targo insisted on attending the marriage ceremony, so Perce dressed the old man in his best finery, and then transformed himself into a fitting accessory to accompany a person of such distinction. He assisted his master to the church, then purloined pillows to ease Targo's aching joints on the hard wooden stools that had been commandeered from the priests. Perce ensured that they arrived early, so that Targo could point out every person of importance to his servant before the ceremony began, when the young man must take his place with the other servants along the outer walls of the chapel.

All the lesser kings from throughout the land had come to Artor's wedding bearing gifts of competitive ostentation and uselessness. Artor was amazed at the variety of objects presented by his peers and viewed the silver platters, golden buttons, ornamental sheaths, eating knives, jeweled gloves, precious nard, and even a pair of golden-soled sandals with amusement.

Among the guests, Targo noted that Llanwith was almost wholly bald and was accompanied by his son and grandson, who looked so much like the old king that Targo had no difficulty in pointing them out to Perce. Fortunately for Artor's peace of mind, Comac and his new wife, Licia, had chosen to stay at home, for Licia remained in mourning for her grandfather. Artor listened to Llanwith's descriptions of their match with obvious pleasure.

King Luka had arrived alone. He was now quite bandy-legged from a lifetime in the saddle, but Perce gazed at him with open-mouthed respect when Targo described his role in the weapons training received by Artor. The three travelers were fast assuming the gloss of legend.

"Oh, the years have flown by, my boy. So fast. You must remember all that I tell you of the past, or else it may be lost forever."

"I will remember, master," Perce vowed, and as he did not write, he decided that he would ask Nimue to keep Targo's memoirs for him.

"Ah, now there is King Lot. He is known as Lot the Fat. And the woman with him is Queen Morgause, who is Artor's half sister. She's a stupid, vicious woman who hated Artor for many years. But she made her peace with her brother after Artor avenged the death of her son, Gaheris, who was murdered by Glamdring Ironfist a little time past."

He smiled in remembrance of the death of the Saxon thane.

"And the crone in black is Morgan, sister of Morgause. She's a witch, and is sometimes called the Fey. She is clever and vicious, and she has hated Artor forever for what his father did to her family."

Perce looked blankly at Targo.

"You'll discover the discord that lies between Artor and Morgan at a later time, my boy. For now, you must simply be careful to avoid the woman. She'll use you to hurt my Artor if she recognizes an opportunity to do so."

Targo smiled as he recognized other guests, and they bowed to him in turn.

"The fine-looking man is Gawayne, eldest son of King Lot and Queen Morgause, so he is King Artor's nephew and a genuine prince. Technically, I suppose, he is Artor's heir. He is also the best swordsman in Britain. I forget just who is who among his brothers, they all have similar-sounding names. Morgause is a silly creature, but she chose to remind the world of Gorlois, her dead father, when she named her sons. She is, at best, an obsessive and stupid cow."

"She can't be that stupid if she manages to rub everyone's nose in her birthright every time her sons are named," Perce whispered.

"Good lad," Targo responded. "Most people don't realize what she's doing."

"And there's Nimue," Perce added happily; the two friends were too busy with their respective masters to see each other often.

Myrddion entered the church and sat discreetly behind the kings. His black clothing, his silver hair, and his scarcely lined skin, now pale from years in his library, made him an arresting and distinguished figure.

But Nimue, his apprentice, eclipsed all other women in the church. She wore her extraordinary hair loose, as befitted her status as a maiden. She wore grey, in keeping with her position, but no color could have suited her ethereal beauty half so well. Her skirts swept the ground and her arms, ears, and white throat were bare of ornament.

She spotted Perce in the press of celebrants and gave the boy a smile of such extraordinary brilliance that it set her face alight. More than one pair of male eyes followed her to her seat behind Myrddion, and more than one young man found that his jaw had dropped unattractively open.

"How Queen Wenhaver will hate her." Targo grinned in amusement. "Myrddion is the nimblest mind in the kingdom, so he'll keep her safe."

"What do you mean, master? I don't understand. Why would anyone hate Nimue?"

Perce was so obviously innocent of lust that Targo found himself determined to have a long talk about sexual matters with the boy.

"Nimue is exquisite. She's also blind to how good she looks to any man with functioning balls. That artlessness just makes her more alluring, and, for the ruthless men among us, she will always be a walking invitation to rape."

Perce snorted.

"What does that rude noise mean?" Targo snapped at the young man.

"She'd kill anyone who attempted to force themselves on her. I saw her once bury that hairpin of hers so deep in an archer's thigh he couldn't walk for a week."

Now it was Targo's turn to laugh. "She wasn't aiming at his thigh, was she?"

"He moved at the last moment. Otherwise he'd be—"

"Castrato," Targo finished for him.

Perce nodded.

Targo glanced down the path as more guests arrived. "Here comes the Bishop of Venta Belgarum. I can see that he's managed to grow quite plump." Targo smiled as he recalled the fine fare and excellent wines that were the accepted lot of the priesthood. Such suffering they were forced to endure in the service of their god!

"Right, off with you, lad. I'll see you after this sodding alliance is cast in stone."

Perce was often confused by Targo's mode of speech as, indeed, were most of the courtiers of the king's favor. The old man could utter such vulgar crudities that Perce was glad that no ladies were within earshot. Yet when he chose, which was rarely, Targo spoke like a lord. His intelligent mind had collected elegant words and phrases over a lifetime. Now, when he cursed and swore, Targo seemed to be trying to recapture the young self who had joined the Roman legions. Perce understood Targo's dilemma because he came from the same poverty, and had learned the same language at his mother's knee. The difference between them was that Targo had spent his youth killing, and Perce had not. The younger man was very religious, which Targo was not. In short, Perce had the opportunity to learn all that Targo knew, without having to spend a lifetime hiring his services out to the highest bidder.

Perce pushed and shoved his way through the throng of servants to an advantageous position, where he could observe the entire proceedings.

Shortly afterwards, King Leodegran entered the church with his daughter, who was dressed in gold and deep red with her golden hair unbound and curling. Every finger bore a ring, and so many bangles and bracelets adorned her wrists that the gold chimed oddly as she moved. Her face looked extraordinarily smug, an expression that detracted from its natural beauty.

The bride and her father walked slowly down the aisle. Caius, in his role as steward of the High King's household, called on the great men of the west to stand in the presence of the High King and the Bishop of Venta Belgarum. King Leodegran and Wenhaver took up their positions before the altar, and Artor entered the church from behind the altar. He wore white, unleavened by any color at all, in mourning for Gallia and the felicity of a marriage that he had known so briefly. He was heavily adorned with gold, in his crown, his torc, his armbands, and a shirt of ringed mail dipped in the precious metal so that the sun turned him into a nimbus of light. Behind him, Gruffydd bore the huge sword, Caliburn, by the hilt.

Artor's eyes skimmed over Caius with some disdain, for they had argued briefly that morning when his foster brother had postponed his journey to Aquae Sulis until after the wedding feast.

"Your absence will force Ector's ceremony to wait for your arrival," the High King had muttered. "I wish I could marry by proxy, and attend his last rites out of respect for our father. This feast is not important to me."

Caius bowed in feigned agreement, but his eyes were distant.

"Brother, my father would expect me to ensure that your wedding was perfect in every way. When all my tasks are done, then I will be gone. By all reports, Julanna is managing well with the help of Livinia and Branicus."

And you resent it, don't you? Artor thought acidly.

But now wasn't the time for argument and, perhaps, Julanna would welcome more time without her husband.

Artor could feel the huge, comforting presence of Odin, who stood behind him and Caius, in his size an exclamation mark of power.

It won't be too long before Perce will stand alongside Odin, Targo thought to himself. I can surely last that long before I go to meet the gods.

He glanced over at the rigid back of Morgan, where she stood almost directly in front of him. Under the blackness of her robe, every muscle was stiff and angry.

"That poor woman will never forgive Artor," Targo murmured aloud, ignoring the odd disconcerted stares of the other guests near him. "I doubt she will ever find peace till the day she dies."

The wedding itself took very little time, and was conducted in the businesslike tone of a treaty, as in reality it was. The Mass that followed was longer, although many of the guests did not embrace the Christian god and so did not take part in the ceremony. Targo was surprised to see that Perce unobtrusively made his way to the end of the queue and accepted the host from the bishop's own hands.

Then, anticlimactically, the ceremony was over. Perce supported Targo as the old man slowly shuffled away, for Targo wished to attend the feast and needed to rest beforehand. As they left the church, Targo caught at Myrddion's arm in passing.

"My lord," Targo said, with his usual disreputable grin, "I have a hankering to meet your apprentice. You have kept her so busy, she has had no time to visit even Perce. My lad and Nimue have been friends their whole lives. May she attend on me before the feast?"

"You old lecher," Myrddion grinned, in a manner wholly unlike himself. "As it happens, I would prefer her out of Wenhaver's view for a time, so your invitation solves an urgent problem for me. I must wait on our High King and his bride, and the queen has taken an unreasoning dislike to my little Nimue."

Your little Nimue? Targo thought, astounded. But he had not reached his advanced years by rushing headlong into unconsidered speech.

"My thanks, Lord Myrddion," he said simply.

Myrddion separated Nimue from an admiring gaggle of young warriors and pointed Perce and Targo out to the young girl.

311

"Targo is the King's oldest friend. He is Perce's mentor, and he wants to meet you. You can flirt with these young warriors at any time."

"Thank you for rescuing me, Master Myrddion, for I find them excessively stupid."

"They frequently are, my dear," Myrddion stated dryly. "Be quick, or you will miss them."

As Nimue glided away with her skirts whispering over the stone of the church forecourt, a woman slid beside Myrddion and lowered her veil.

"The dragonlet is very fair, is she not, Lord Myrddion?"

"Morgan! Why must you creep around like the monster in a children's story? Yes, Nimue is very fair, and she has many of the qualities of a young dragon." Myrddion watched as the girl's slim grey figure disappeared into the wooden palace in the wake of Targo and Perce. Then he turned to face his old enemy. "Time has not been kind to you, my lady. I always warned you that revenge and hatred would eat away at your soul."

Despite the sting in his words, Morgan's eyes were regretful. She acknowledged the truth of his words by nodding briefly towards him.

Morgan's face had become a travesty of her once striking beauty. Her raven-black hair was now heavily streaked with white. Her skin was still soft, but in the harsh light of day, her features were creased in lines that narrowed her nose, pinched her nostrils, and turned her red lips into an inverted crescent of disappointment. Her unhealthy pallor was accentuated by a new tattoo that outlined her lips in blue and barred her forehead.

"There is a word for old enemies who know each other so well that they are almost friends," Morgan said softly. "I don't recall the word, but I feel that way about you, Myrddion."

As she spoke, Myrddion noticed that she had sharpened her teeth into points.

"They are called *fools*," he answered curtly.

"Then we are both fools, Lord Myrddion, for we are already part of the legend of Artor. I know that you will finally achieve your heart's desire, for I see it in your face and in the darkness behind my eyes. What will I receive? I wonder. The goddess does not grant the seer the power to discern her own fate."

Myrddion took Morgan's yellowing claws in hands that were still strong from years of riding and unmeasured hours of writing.

"I'll let you into a secret, Morgan. It's one I have never told any other person before you. I sometimes see beyond the veil, or I think I do. I have seen a vision that tells me that you will die in exile, and you will bless the moment when you draw your last breath."

With a sudden feeling of guilt, he dropped Morgan's hands.

"I'm sorry, Morgan, for I had no right to tell you of my dream. I don't even believe in such rubbish. If I have caused you pain, then I regret it, and I offer you my apologies."

"Remember what I said about old enemies?" Morgan smiled, a grisly reminder of the beauty that lay in the bones below her haggard face. "None but you, Myrddion Merlinus, would dare to touch even the hem of my robe, least of all my body. Be wary that you do not become a fool like me, for I have come to believe that a kingdom is not everything. I have made myself into a creature that frightens children and adults both. And it's certain that only habit continues to fuel my hatred. Gorlois died so very long ago, but ancient vices are sometimes all we have left, so I find myself warning you of your fate."

Myrddion had never underestimated Morgan's power, regardless of whether it was born of observation or intellect or magic.

"Then tell me the worst," he said.

"Two women will destroy Artor. And both are here in Cadbury," Morgan stated absently and without malice. "I cannot maintain my rage as I once did, for the kingship was a worse punishment on Artor than any petty cruelty I could have devised."

"You were always wise, Morgan." Myrddion felt unaccountably comfortable with the witch woman, and was oblivious to the stares and superstitious dread with which the departing guests viewed them both.

"You must know that your Artor will be the greatest of men, so you have not given your youth away for nothing," she added. "When the stars fall, and all we know is forgotten, Artor will be remembered. We, too, will become creatures of myth, as insubstantial as ghosts, because we were a part of his life here on earth. Some men were born for burdens, and one of those men is Artor. Some men were born for tears, and Artor is also one of those men."

Myrddion stared deeply into Morgan's eyes, now almost green with foresight.

"And what was I born for?" he asked casually, although his heart tightened with tension.

"That would be telling, old enemy, wouldn't it?" Morgan smiled, and slipped away to be swallowed by the departing throng.

Myrddion watched as she left, feeling relieved and a little disappointed. All men wish to know their future, especially if it is pleasant and filled with happiness. But Myrddion would have been the first to admit that no one wants to learn the day and manner of his death. In that regard, he was no different from any other man.

He made his way to Artor's side. He bowed deeply to the High King and inclined his head to Queen Wenhaver. She tapped her feet with annoyance.

"Please accept my felicitations on your wedding day, my liege. It is widely believed that you have married a woman of great beauty and prestige, who will bring acclaim to your court."

"My thanks, Myrddion," Artor said shortly. "But do stop bowing and scraping, for you know it annoys me." He had been in Wenhaver's company for ten minutes and could already feel his temper fraying.

"You make Cadbury a place of beauty by your very presence, my queen," Myrddion continued, ignoring Artor entirely.

Wenhaver hovered between smug acceptance of the compliments and the feeling that she was being patronized.

"You have an unusual apprentice," she sniped, her spite evident in the tone of her voice. "Whatever made you take on such a strange, barbarian creature, Lord Myrddion? Many people believe her to be a witch."

"I accepted her as my assistant because of her intellect and the logic of her thoughts, my queen. Few women have such incisive minds, and fewer still are gifted with the ability to overcome their personal feelings and see the truth in most situations. If others call her a witch, perhaps it's because she manages to see into their secret hearts and thoughts. Besides, Lord Artor's family has witches of real potency, unlike Nimue."

Myrddion was a polished statesman and his courtesy was faultless, but Wenhaver recognized that she had been slighted, especially when she saw Artor's amused smile. And there and then, she determined to do Nimue whatever harm she could to avenge this insult to her honor.

"You are far too clever for me, Lord Myrddion," she simpered.

His eyes darkened with contempt.

"Please excuse this old man, I need to rest before the pleasures of your wedding feast. May I extend my wishes that the gods bring harmony and fruitfulness to your marriage?"

"You may," she replied. And to show her displeasure, she contrived to bow to Artor's friend a little lower than custom required and with exaggerated flourishes that were insulting, and a parody of courtesy.

As Myrddion walked away, he considered how foolish he had been to ignore his initial reservations; he should not have offered her father a marriage contract that committed the High King to this unmanageable woman. She'll see us all in the thrall of the Saxons for the sake of her stupid, pointless vanity, he thought, as his booted heels echoed on the flagstones. "And the mistake was mine. I was too eager to find the west an heir."

Meanwhile, Nimue was enjoying herself hugely in Targo's luxurious room. She drank ale with the old man, a shocking thing for a well-brought-up girl to do, but, as Nimue told Targo artlessly, she had been raised in the kitchens where ale was safer than water.

Nimue nodded. "Gallwyn always told me that unless you can see for yourself that the water springs cleanly from the ground, it can be poison to drink it. Ale is always safer than water."

"Your Gallwyn was a woman of great good sense," Targo responded. "I've seen a whole army shitting out their guts because they drank unclean water." The old man eyed Nimue curiously to see if his language had offended her.

She merely laughed.

"So, show me this tattoo of yours. I saw it when Odin put it on your leg when you were a babe, but you were barely two weeks old at the time."

Nimue bared her fine-boned ankle and raised her skirt.

"See here." Targo traced a part of the dragon's head and body that was almost serpentine in nature. "That's the work of Morgan, the witch. She called you her little serpent. She ordered Gallwyn to deliver you to her quarters. She wanted to use you as a weapon against her brother."

"The High King?" Nimue was agog. Gallwyn had never told her of Morgan and the witch's attempt to place a tattoo of her own design on her leg. "This Morgan must be very wicked. I think I must meet the woman."

"Don't antagonize that hellcat." Targo was alarmed. "She's a dangerous woman, Nimue."

Nimue merely smiled. "But so am I, Targo. And it seems we have unfinished business, she and I. She will find that I am no one's tool."

The martial light of battle that had suddenly appeared in Nimue's eyes made Targo nervous.

"At any road," he went on, "when Artor learned from Gruffydd of the abomination on your ankle, he arranged for Odin to change Morgan's tattoo from a serpent into the design you now know."

Nimue smiled and traced the dragon's head, its wings, and the claws that mounted up the length of her calf.

"The tattoo must have taken a very long time."

"It was all done in a single night, my child." The old man smiled apologetically. "Ah, but it hurt you, and Odin was fair weeping by the end of it, even though Myrddion gave you a drop of the juice of poppies to dull the pain. Poor Odin had to do the entire job quickly, you see, or Morgan would have changed the design once again."

Perce brought Targo a cup of fragrant herbs and assisted the old man to drink.

"Well, I like my dragon. No one else has such a mark on them, and while you may say it is Artor's dragon, that is not true. It is *my* dragon." Nimue softened her defiant words with a brilliant smile.

"Ah, but you're a grand lass, Nimue." Targo grinned at her through the stumps of his teeth. "My Artor would've done far better to be shackled to a girl like you rather than that whey-faced Wenhaver."

"You're upsetting yourself, master," Perce said anxiously.

"No, I'm not upsetting myself. I'm speaking the simple truth," a grumpy Targo replied.

Nimue reached over and patted his age-spotted hand. "The question is moot." She smiled at Perce. "There, I finally got to say that word. Do you hear, Perce, how intelligent I am beginning to sound?" She turned back to the old man. "I wouldn't marry Artor even if he wanted me."

"And why not?" Targo was rather insulted.

"I think he already loves someone else. I want to be the only one for my man when I choose to marry," Nimue replied simply.

Targo grinned at her. She was a quick one, and sensitive, that was certain. But could she survive the kind of court that Wenhaver would create? Did she have the strength and the guile to walk in a nest of vipers without being stung?

Targo told her his thoughts, and she laughed even more gaily than before.

"I walk with Lord Myrddion. Ten men died for me, and I survived my mother's murder and the cold of the river. Let the vipers beware, for I will crush their heads under my heel."

Targo looked deeply into Nimue's eyes, and saw there a capacity for rage and ruthlessness that Wenhaver lacked entirely. He felt a little afraid of this exquisite child.

"For the sake of all of us, child, I ask that you don't harm Artor in the process. He saved you, girl, so that you could grow up safely within Gallwyn's love, and he punished the man who murdered your mother.

The prophecy that Morgan the Fey placed on you said that you would steal away the mind of the kingdom. I would be disappointed if you were the one who ultimately destroyed what Artor has built."

The thought of harm to his king was so unsettling that Targo began to tremble. Nimue knelt before him and held both of his hands over her heart.

"I'd never do that, Targo. I will never deliberately harm my king, for I owe him my life. And I pay my debts. Look into my eyes and see the truth of what I say."

Targo was convinced. He could see nothing there that could disturb his dreams or trouble his thoughts.

"Is Myrddion kind to you?" he asked. He spoke a little gruffly to hide his embarrassment.

"Kind? No, nor would I desire him to be merely kind. He trains my brain to see the world as it really is, to read Latin, and to apply logic. He makes me practice for hours, just as you make Perce repeat sword positions for hours, and I love it. I wish each day were longer so I could learn more from the best scholar in all of the west."

Her fierce loyalty made Targo smile.

"The best, Nimue? That is high praise indeed."

"It's deserved. No one has worked more selflessly to secure Artor's kingdom. Nobody! He has dedicated his entire life to the task."

"And now he is burned out, just like me," Targo teased in a mock-serious voice.

"He is not!" Nimue retorted with a flash of anger, and Perce would have intervened had Targo not waved him away. "He is handsome and strong. Myrddion is still fit, and he rides a horse far better than many warriors. He is quick-witted and he makes me laugh, especially when I hear the games he plays with the stupid and the self-important. My master is not old, for all that he sometimes thinks he is."

Targo heard a tone of regret in Nimue's voice that caused him to wonder if, perhaps, Myrddion had met his match at last.

"It's time we all rested, child. Banquets are endless, and this old man can only face such an ordeal with sleep beforehand. Now, give me a kiss to remind me of what it was like when I was once a handsome young soldier."

Nimue complied willingly. "I think you're a naughty old man who has had more than your share of lasses in your day," she retorted evenly, in a fashion definitely unbecoming of a well-bred young lady.

"Without doubt, my dear, the numbers are beyond count. But for now this old body must be content with dreams of you."

"How nice," she replied, and danced out of Targo's room.

"Myrddion Merlinus doesn't stand a chance," murmured Targo.

"Pardon, master?" Perce asked.

"I was just thinking out loud, boy. We old men are reduced to such silliness."

Perce helped the old man into his bed. Targo closed his knowing eyes and fell into a light, old man's doze. The afternoon drew out, and the whole citadel waited, for Artor had wed and Cadbury was about to change.

In the kitchens, the servants and cooks toiled over a meal of un-precedented gastronomic magnificence, and even the fortress's dogs fed on the scraps thrown by the servants into the midden. But only Perce saw the danger from the crows, rooks, and ravens that stalked through the scraps in the rubbish pits and darkened the sky when they were disturbed by the intrusion of a servant boy with a bucket of slops. The birds had their own tale to tell—and they knew, with the scaven-ger's eerie foreknowledge, that Cadbury had become a good place for feeding.

Chapter XIV

THE WORM HOLE IN THE APPLE

Paradise may have existed once. Christian and Hebrew teachings speak glowingly of Eden and its perfection, but human beings can neither recognize nor appreciate such a golden state. If asked, a man such as Targo would have called Eden rather boring, and perhaps that failing is why all the good in the world is constantly undermined for the sake of any pursuit that is exciting and hints at forbidden fruit.

Artor had created a small slice of paradise on Cadbury Tor, fortunately freed of tedium by the existence of implacable enemies. If he missed the pleasures of Roman baths, Artor still found that the streams, with their clean waters, were perfectly acceptable substitutes, even when he was forced to break the ice during winter. The fields were fertile and well tended, the tor was a miracle of defense, and both the burgeoning town below and the palace above were planned and organized so that disease rarely troubled its citizenry. Roman habits of cleanliness still colored most aspects of Artor's thinking, to the benefit of Cadbury's population.

But the sweetest and most juicy apples can hold perils that are unseen. From within the sweet pulp, the worm twists and turns, and devours the good flesh, causing the whole fruit to blacken and rot.

Like the worm in the apple, Artor's troubles were soon to come from within.

The wedding banquet was a reflection of the deterioration that was to follow. From the morning of her bridal day, Wenhaver had invaded Artor's quarters with her servant women, gowns, piles of discarded clothing, unguents, and fripperies. Sensing ructions ahead, Artor had ordered that his clothing be removed to a smaller set of apartments where he had the luxury of quiet thought and some solitude.

Wenhaver was not amused by the new arrangements, but she had enjoyed her wedding. Hers were the finest jewels, including those given to her by Artor, and these she couldn't resist wearing immediately. Her hair was the purest gold, and compared favorably with the red-haired daughters of the northern kings and the brunette coloring of their equals in the south; and her gown eclipsed all others in luxury and worth.

Or so she had thought until she saw Myrddion's apprentice leave the church and glide across the courtyard.

How dare she be here on this day? Why should the bitch look so attractive in grey, for everyone knew it was the color of grand dames and women of advanced age. Why did the young warriors cluster around her? And as for that hair! The little cow was a barbarian to the core.

Wenhaver continued to fume and to think. Artor's passion for surrounding himself with thoroughly disreputable persons was about to end, if she had any say in the matter. Only aristocrats should surround the king and the queen, not foreigners and strumpets with no breeding worth mentioning. As for Myrddion, he had shown insultingly patronizing reverence to his queen. He did not bow deeply enough to her, and then he had had the temerity to lecture her about Nimue's qualities, while no mention was made of *her* patience and forbearance.

Several servant girls felt the full force of her tongue before Wenhaver managed to regain her self-control, and only thoughts of the magnificence of her wedding finery could placate the sense of insult to her person. She had chosen cloth of gold for her wedding feast, knowing it would suit her blond beauty, and she was busy putting on the last of her jewels when Artor knocked tentatively at her door.

"Enter," she called coquettishly, which immediately warned Artor to be wary.

When he saw her magnificence, Artor found himself unable to say a word.

"What does your silence mean, husband?" Wenhaver asked dangerously. "Does my dress offend you?"

"You look magnificent, but I was raised in the Roman way." Artor tried desperately to extricate himself. "I didn't mean to cause offense."

"The Roman way? How do I offend the *Roman way*, husband?"

Wenhaver smiled sweetly, but Artor wasn't deceived. He'd learned over many years just how dangerous women could be when their appearance was called into question. Unwisely, he chose to explain.

"My foster mother, Livinia, would never wear all her jewels at once, for she believed that the quality of a few superb gems far outshone the grossness of many. But Livinia has been dead for many years and I've no idea what current fashions dictate."

Every word Artor uttered merely made Wenhaver angrier.

"If you will kindly wait outside, I will finish my toilette and will join you presently," the queen replied before closing the door firmly in Artor's face.

Artor winced as he heard a piece of expensive Mediterranean furniture overturned. Then he heard a yelp from one of the servant girls and found his fists tightening with anger.

"How do you plan to get through your wedding night, you idiot?" he mumbled softly, but was quick to plaster a smile on his face when Wenhaver opened the door and swept into the corridor.

He was pleased to note that she had shed half her jewels and looked the better for it.

"Our guests await us, wife."

"Of course, husband. You have but to lead the way," Wenhaver replied with dangerous sweetness.

Not sodding likely! Artor thought with a soldier's vulgarity. This bitch wants to put a ring through my nose and lead me around like a pet bull. I didn't survive the dangers of Uther Pendragon to be her plaything.

At the banquet, Wenhaver found herself the object of Artor's considerable charm. In the great hall, she sat at the head table like a true queen, while Artor fed her titbits on the point of his knife and filled her golden cup himself. Occasionally, he would whisper in her ear and she would blush and smile exultantly.

From a lower table, Myrddion winced, and Llanwith did not miss Myrddion's expression of distaste. He glanced at the king and queen, and then back at Myrddion who was intently dismembering a chicken breast with his dagger.

"You have me intrigued, Myrddion. What's wrong?"

"Look at Artor," Myrddion hissed in Llanwith's ear. "Does that attentive lover resemble the man you know? She's done something to upset him." He stabbed a piece of chicken with the point of his dagger and devoured it savagely.

Llanwith watched the loving couple, and his expression gradually changed to alarm. "When he's angry, the boy has the same look as his father."

Myrddion winced again. "Doesn't he just! If Wenhaver were slightly less vain and silly, I would warn her that it isn't wise to trifle with a man such as Artor. But she's convinced that she can maneuver the High King into doing things her way."

"There's little chance of that."

"No, but the poor little cow will suffer for upsetting him. He has been thinking about Gallia and Licia all day, so he's on edge."

Llanwith blanched. "I wouldn't even mention those names, Myrddion," he whispered. "We must be discreet."

"I'm worried, Llanwith. Seriously worried."

In a far corner, where persons of lesser nobility were seated, Nimue was enjoying herself enormously. Targo, with Perce, Odin,

Gruffydd, and several young warriors who looked suspiciously like the High King, were paying court to her. She was enjoying the whole game.

Nimue had not bothered to change her dress, mainly because she owned only three, and the other two were far from suitable. Besides, the queen would eclipse every woman in the banquet hall, and who would bother to notice an apprentice?

When she had returned from her visit to Targo, Myrddion had tossed her a cloth-wrapped bundle. She caught it by reflex, noting that it was very heavy.

She unwrapped the rough cloth and a mesh of some silvery material was revealed. It was a necklace of forged links of silver that were secured at the front by a large disc of the same metal, inscribed with a fish. It lay in her hands like a chain of glittering scales. Nimue's small, sweet mouth hung open in surprise.

"What is this?" she asked.

"Are you lost for speech, my ever-garrulous Nimue? And, yes, I'll explain the meaning of the word tomorrow. The necklace is very old, and I cannot tell you its history, but I am told it's made of electrum and that it's more ancient than the Celts themselves. It belonged to my mother."

"Master, you cannot allow me to wear these beautiful jewels." Nimue devoured the necklace with her eyes, but resolutely attempted to hand it back to her master.

"Take it, Nimue. You need decoration if you are to attend this feast, and no apprentice of mine shall be considered dowdy. Consider that you do me honor by wearing it."

"Very well then, Master Myrddion, but how do I wear it? It has no clasp."

"Come here, my child. And lift up your hair."

Obediently, Nimue lowered her head so that her hair fell over her face, baring her white neck. Myrddion simply dropped the chain over her head.

Nimue threw back her hair and they both untangled a few stray curls that had caught in the chain. As they did so, their fingers touched, and Myrddion pulled away as if he had been scorched by fire.

"That looks lovely, Nimue. This necklace has been in my possession all of my life, but I have never known a woman whom I considered a suitable person to wear it. Your coloring is a perfect match for its beauty." Myrddion was babbling, and he knew it.

Now, at the feast, in her grey dress and with her extraordinary neck chain in plain view, more than a few powerful men gazed at her and wondered what the grey cloth hid beneath it. When Nimue threw back her head and laughed at a jest, she bared her white throat, and many wondered how it would feel to bite on that slim, white column of flesh.

One pair of eyes in particular lusted to watch her eyes widen in agony.

But Nimue was oblivious to any danger, and Myrddion was seated too far away to protect her from harm. Fortunately, Odin seemed to scent the reek of brutality in the room, and he felt the hairs stir on the back of his neck in prescience. As Artor's laws demanded, no man came to the great hall armed, but Odin had to resist an urge to reach for a sword that wasn't there. Unarmed or not, Odin vowed to protect the little wise woman until she was returned to her master.

In time, the wilder young men called for dancing, and, from his high throne, Artor smiled down on them and gave permission. Nimue had never danced a step in her life, but a succession of young warriors were soon spinning her and gripping her fingers tightly while they executed rather untidy patterns in the palace hall and forecourt. Her hair flew like a flag of silver, her skirts swirled out around her delicate ankles, and the whole world, or all who cared to see, recognized the dragon motif on her ankle and calf.

Artor and Wenhaver had risen to watch the dancing. By that time, Wenhaver had drunk a little too much wine, and she spotted the electrum necklace first and seethed inwardly.

"Myrddion's apprentice is enjoying herself," she cooed. "A little too much, perhaps, for good manners, so I will suggest to her that such boisterous behavior is not quite the done thing."

Artor looked at his wife. What was she about now?

"She's very young, wife, and has been raised far from the court. Allow her a night of pleasure, for tomorrow Myrddion will have her grinding herbs, collecting toads for their sweat, or learning the Latin names for any number of remedies. My loyal chief councillor is a hard taskmaster."

"I can't imagine any decently raised woman wanting to collect . . . sweat . . . off toads. How vile!"

Artor laughed as Nimue spun in a graceful circle so that her grey skirt turned into a bell and the torches caused hair and necklace to shimmer like water.

"She is so natural, it would be almost impossible to chide the child."

As soon as Artor spoke, he knew his words had been carelessly chosen, for Wenhaver's eyes glittered with fury. The necklace that Nimue wore was superb in its simple elegance, its rareness, and its beauty. As a young woman who worshipped adornment above all things, Wenhaver lusted after it, and her irritation rose proportionately.

And then she spied Nimue's tattoo.

"What is that thing on her leg, Artor?" she asked in a slightly shrill voice.

"Where?" he replied blankly. He had quite forgotten Nimue's tattoo.

Wenhaver rarely explained herself, and Artor was beginning to find her obtuse demands irritating. Like the grain of sand that causes a pearl to grow in an oyster shell, her selfishness and ego were rubbing away at Artor's nerves, but refulgent gems weren't likely to be the fruit of his annoyance.

"That tattoo thing on the leg of Myrddion's apprentice," Wenhaver snapped.

Artor disapproved of the queen's tone and was unimpressed by the suddenly ugly lines that pursed her mouth.

"That is a mark of ownership, my dear, and it tells the world that she is under my protection," he replied with a cold, flat glance in his wife's direction. "It is the Dragon of Britain."

Let the silly bitch think what she wants, he thought flatly.

Artor knew better than to taunt his new wife, but he was already sick of her behavior. The boy, Artorex, would have acted with tact and consideration, but Artor remembered the meaty sound of Wenhaver's open hand when she had struck her servant's face. He pursed his lips and refused to provide a simple explanation that would deflect Wenhaver's outrage.

Wenhaver leapt to a rather foolish conclusion.

"Then she's your woman! How dare you parade her before me?"

The babble of happy voices around them slowly stilled as the queen's voice rose shrilly over the sound of the music. The musicians' instruments trailed off into awkward silence, and the dancers came to a confused halt.

"How dare you question your king, woman?" Artor's voice could freeze blood. "Your judgment and mind are indescribably poor if you choose to shout insults at your husband on his wedding day in the presence of his guests. You will soon begin to learn some manners."

Had Wenhaver known that particular flat, grey stare, she too would have stepped backwards, as did every other person in the great hall. But Wenhaver was silly, spoiled, and fast becoming vicious.

She rounded on her husband.

"What do you mean when you say that she bears your mark? I am your wife, and I will not tolerate such a thing." Wenhaver stamped her small feet in frustration.

"In that case, my dear, you may enjoy your wedding night alone."

Artor simply walked out of the great hall and left her standing, impotent and humiliated. She was forced to acknowledge the hurried good wishes of all the departing guests, the greatest men and women in the land, who could not meet her stormy eyes. A wall of silence surrounded her as if she were invisible.

"Oh, for pity's sake!" Myrddion groaned. "What's she done now?

You had best take Artor's place," he said to Llanwith. "Perhaps you can speed the departing guests on their way, and say whatever you can to smooth matters over. We could explain to them that the queen is a little nervous about her wedding night. Yes! I know it's crude, but they might believe the lie. Wenhaver is only just sixteen, she's half Artor's age." He turned to Luka.

"Luka?"

"Yes, I know. You want me to take the young lady to her rooms and soothe her hurt feelings," Luka said with resignation. "Why do I always get the dangerous tasks?"

"Would you prefer convincing Artor to do his duty as a husband?" Myrddion answered his friend seriously. "Perhaps he might listen to you."

Luka paled a little. "No, no, my friend. You can depend on me to soothe and console the queen." He had a healthy respect for Artor's rage.

Myrddion found his way to Artor's new quarters. "That stupid little girl," he muttered to himself.

When Luka reached Wenhaver, Leodegran was already venting his anger at his daughter. His hair was a wild nimbus around his head, and his finger was prodding her firmly on her slim, golden-clad shoulders.

"A queen never acts like a spoiled child, and where will you be if Artor casts you off? He can do it quite easily, you know, as easily as that." Leodegran snapped his fingers. "You're a silly young girl, Wenhaver. You've made yourself look foolish before the assembled notables of the realm. Who do you think you are dealing with? I'll be extremely lucky if he's not on my doorstep tomorrow with his army for what you have done and the insults you have thrown at him tonight."

"He won't do anything!" Wenhaver hissed. "I won't let him!"

Leodegran laughed sardonically and then, in his fury, began to cough.

Luka insinuated himself between Leodegran, who was quite purple in the face, and his suddenly contrite daughter.

"My queen, you must allow me to conduct you to your chambers," he said smoothly. "Your father is upset, and we mustn't say things we don't really mean."

"No, I'm not going anywhere with you. Where is my husband?"

"Artor could be forgiven for removing all trace of you from his fortress!" Leodegran shouted. "You try to talk sense to her, Luka! No one else seems able to do it!" Luka later swore the man was in real danger of bursting a blood vessel in his brain.

"Come along, Your Majesty," Luka said brusquely. "It isn't fitting that you and your father should be shouting at each other in public."

King Leodegran appeared to realize the scene he was making in front of gape-mouthed servants and a few aristocratic stragglers. He bowed sketchily to Luka and his daughter, and flounced away.

"How can he say such things to me?" Wenhaver wailed, betraying her youth and her ignorance. "I am his daughter! And I am the queen!"

Luka smiled, and then took one of her hands and patted it before drawing it through his arm to escort her to her rooms. He had learned decades earlier to take charge of teary women by speaking to them soothingly as if they were small children or horses. He knew that both responded well to his ministrations. The debris of the banquet behind them, the guttering lamps, the spilled wine, and the great Saxon dogs scavenging on the table were mute testament to a feast that had gone terribly wrong.

Wenhaver still seemed unable to understand the seriousness of her position.

"Where is Artor? I want to speak to my husband," she demanded, although her eyes were swollen with tears.

"Majesty, if I might be so bold, you are so irritatingly young. Have you any idea what just happened? Do you not understand that your marriage can be annulled? With all respects, my lady, the High King is not a man to be commanded, or embarrassed, by any living person, even a close friend. I could never humiliate Artor in public, and I have known him since he was twelve years of age."

Wenhaver tried, and failed, to appear unconcerned.

"He started our argument. I was perfectly correct to object to the presence of my husband's whore at this feast." Wenhaver's mouth twisted, and Luka thought irrelevantly how very unattractive she could appear when she was racked by jealousy.

"Of whom do you speak, my queen?" Luka asked instead.

Two spots of color flared on Wenhaver's ivory cheeks. She halted, for they had reached her apartments.

"I refer to the apprentice of Merlinus," she said haughtily. "That bitch, Nimue!"

"Is your brain completely at sea?" Luka asked belligerently, trapping the queen between his two arms against the wall. "You have caused the most ill-bred scene in Cadbury's history, and you have risked losing your pretty head and the life of your father—all because you think Artor has taken Nimue as a mistress?"

"Yes . . ." Wenhaver wavered, then fought back. "I know he has. He said that ugly tattoo on her leg made her his property."

"My lady, you may hate me forever for speaking these words, but you have been extremely foolish."

Efficiently, and without sparing the queen the gory details of Nimue's birth or of Artor's revenge on the killer of Nimue's mother, Luka told her the reason for the Dracos tattoo.

"He should have told me what it was all about, then this argument would never have occurred," Wenhaver wailed like a sulking child.

"No, madam! Artor shouldn't have to tell you anything, for he is the king. He's killed more men personally than currently serve in your father's entire palace, and he's the only protection we have from Saxon invasion. He is tired from twelve years of hard warfare, and he has had to be persuaded to marry a silly little girl who immediately antagonizes him."

Luka knew that Wenhaver still didn't understand the scope of her offenses. Once more, he tried to use the truth to bring her to her senses.

"Forget the songs of love that you imagine exist within a marriage. Forget, too, the pretty lies you have been told over the years. Artor is a mature man, and he will never sit at your feet like a dog and adore

331

you for your beauty. Never! He doesn't love you, and I doubt that he'll ever love you. I've no idea what liberties your father permitted you, but Artor is not Leodegran, or your father would be High King in Artor's place. Artor will not be told what to do by anyone, except, perhaps, by Targo or Myrddion."

"That smelly old man and that . . . that . . . ?"

"Yes?" Luka said dangerously.

"I was going to call Myrddion a bastard," Wenhaver retorted proudly.

Luka rolled his eyes and tried again.

"Artor's father, Uther Pendragon, was a natural leader who was inhumanly strong, cruel to the bone, and ruthless. It was Myrddion who managed to keep Uther focused on ruling well for the benefit of the British peoples. And it was Myrddion who found the young Artor, groomed him to become High King after the death of Uther, and has guided him ever since. Myrddion has served four High Kings, starting with Vortigern, and he has served the Roman emperors before the City of the Seven Hills fell to the barbarians. He is one of the greatest healers in the world, and he is so far above you that you scarcely stir his imagination. Do you understand, you foolish woman? He has no equal in wisdom and cleverness. And right at this minute, this same man, the man you profess to despise and wish to call a bastard, is trying to convince Artor that you're too foolish to be put to death. If he does not succeed, you may be executed before the night is over."

Wenhaver was finally silenced. It was slowly dawning on her that her person was not sacrosanct.

"What set you against Nimue this time? Don't pretend, Wenhaver. I've watched you. You're so jealous of her beauty that you foam at the mouth. So what did she do to upset you tonight?"

"She . . . she didn't." Wenhaver began to cry, but Luka was relentless.

"So why? Let us see what silliness prompted this whole mess."

"I liked her necklace. Why should she own such a pretty thing?" Wenhaver rubbed her tears away with her fist and contrived to look about five years old. Even the hard-hearted Luka felt sorry for a girl too self-centered to understand the consequences of her jealousy.

"You have risked the kingdom over a necklace?" Luka repeated. "One that you couldn't wear anyhow, because it wouldn't suit your coloring?"

"But it's so pretty. Artor should have given it to me."

"Child, I have a notion that I would save everyone a great deal of time and trouble if I were to strangle you right now for the nonsense you continue to babble. The necklace is not Artor's to give. It's an ancient heirloom from Myrddion's house, and he gave it to Nimue, not to Artor!"

"But I wanted it," Wenhaver replied simply, like a woebegone child.

"You cannot have it, my dear. Artor loves Myrddion, and he cares for him far more than he will ever care for you. Myrddion is fond of Nimue, so he gave her the necklace, not you. You have treated him like a leper, so why should he give you anything? If Artor wants a woman, he takes her. His liaisons mean nothing, for Artor's heart was won and lost long ago, and you aren't clever enough to change the way things are in Artor's world."

He gripped her chin with his hand.

"I am only going to say this once, Wenhaver. I suggest that you take the advice of an old man and stop riding roughshod over everybody on Cadbury Tor. The people of his kingdom love Artor, and if you anger him, they will soon come to hate you. But if you are clever, and manage to give Artor a legitimate son, then you could become the most powerful woman in the west. If you fail, you'll become a distant and abandoned nobody. And you must leave Nimue alone, for Artor really did kill nine innocent men, and one guilty man, to find the warrior who murdered her mother."

Luka stared into Wenhaver's eyes to see if she had absorbed any of the advice he had thrust upon her. "Has anyone ever killed ten men for you?"

Luka was normally the most sensitive of men, but on this occasion he said the one thing to Wenhaver that she could never forgive or forget: he questioned her worth. Luka really liked Nimue, and he loved Myrddion; his desire to puncture the bladder of Wenhaver's self-importance made him careless.

Wenhaver's mouth snapped closed, and her eyes cleared. A feeling she had never experienced coursed through her consciousness, a fear that she really wasn't the most beautiful or the most valuable woman in the entire land. Like acid, the fear ate into her mind until it found a corner to hide and grow. Wenhaver was, in her own fashion, as brave as her husband, and as ruthless when she saw the need, but now her rock-solid faith in her own self-worth began to crack.

Wenhaver had never really hated anyone, or anything, for that matter. Why waste time on hate when no one else can attain the exalted pedestal on which you stand? But if Artor had the power to send her home to her father or have her killed with a negligent wave of his hand, then what was her real worth? Further, if a lowly apprentice could generate genuine admiration in the eyes of hard-bitten kings and courtiers, and if the High King had killed ten men for Nimue when she was still an infant, then Wenhaver could claim neither moral nor physical superiority over her.

"I suggest you go to your bed," said Luka, "and pray that Artor joins you there. I would also pray that Myrddion ignores your insults to him, and to his apprentice, and that he convinces Artor to give you one last chance."

Wenhaver followed Luka's advice, but a single thought pulsed through her mind. What am I worth?

BEGGED, CAJOLED, AND, in the end, ordered by Myrddion to face the situation that had arisen, Artor found himself standing outside Wenhaver's apartments. Odin, who knew everything and said nothing, smiled in his curiously barbaric fashion, while Artor leaned against the wooden wall and tried vainly to work up some enthusiasm for the seduction to come.

"Well, do I knock on the door of my own room?" Artor asked Odin testily. "You seem to be expert in most matters, my Odin. What would you suggest?"

"She is a woman," Odin said economically. "And she is upsetting you, so why bother?"

"Why, indeed?" Artor whispered to himself, and kicked the door open forcefully.

He strode through into utter chaos.

Myrnia, the maidservant, was attempting to tidy the results of Wenhaver's temper, while trying hard not to cry through her pain. She had been struck on the face, and the force had left cuts on her cheekbone.

The queen was sulking in her great bed, dressed in a froth of clothing that seemed excessively complex for sleeping in, but no doubt pleased female notions of what a seductress might wear on her wedding night. Artor summed up the situation at a glance, while Wenhaver tossed her golden head and smiled, suddenly reassured by his presence.

Artor decided it was time to put the little bitch off balance.

"Odin? I want you," Artor ordered.

Wenhaver was startled when Odin bent to enter through the doorway. For one terrible moment, she expected to be strangled by the hulking brute.

"You will assist this poor girl to clean this unseemly mess and then take her to have her face treated. Myrddion will make sure she is not permanently scarred."

Without saying a further word, Artor raised Myrnia's face and ran his fingers gently over the bruises and nail marks that could be clearly seen on one side of her face.

He winced a little.

"Please, Your Majesty, I'm really quite well," Myrnia babbled, tears spilling out of her soft brown eyes because of his gentle sympathy. "There's no need to disturb Lord Myrddion."

"Do as I say, Odin," the king instructed his servant. "Then ensure

that this pretty lass goes to her rest early. She has suffered a difficult day."

Wenhaver's mouth fell open and her brows drew together thun-
derously, but a glacial look from Artor kept her silent. Myrnia would
keep. After all, where could the servant go?

Odin proceeded to fold fabrics and place them in the chest opened
by Myrnia, who snuffled wetly and tried not to sob too loudly. The
two servants worked together, and the room was soon tidy.

"Take Myrnia away and do all that is needful," Artor ordered
crisply. "I believe I can manage one silly girl."

"I will care for the little one," Odin responded gently, his eyes
smiling at the thought of what was to come.

"I am sure you will," Artor stated urbanely.

When Odin and Myrnia had bowed their way out of the bedcham-
ber, Wenhaver seated herself at the very end of the bed.

"Undress, woman," Artor commanded without preamble. "Although I am very angry with you, Myrddion has explained that I was
remiss when I didn't explain what I require of a wife before the wedding took place. I shall remedy that situation at once."

Wenhaver would have argued, but Artor raised a single forefinger
in front of his mouth to silence her, and she gulped and resisted the
urge to defend herself.

"My wife will be a generous, courteous hostess at all times, and she
will never, ever, contradict me or argue with me in public. I am the
true son of Uther Pendragon and I am the High King of the Britons.
Whether you like it or not, you are a mere woman. Do I make myself
clear?"

"Yes. But—"

"There will be no *buts* in my household." He smiled lasciviously.
"And you are still in that ridiculous clothing."

Wenhaver tried to be seductive as she edged the frothing frills off
her shoulders, but Artor took no notice.

"I considered sending you home to your father, but Myrddion has prevailed upon me to give you a second, and last, chance. He believes that you may, perhaps, be worth all the trouble you have caused. If you don't prove yourself suitable to be my queen, the marriage will be annulled. You are not the only presentable princess in these lands."

Artor removed his shirt and the woolen undergarment that protected his body. His flesh was sculpted, golden, and heavily muscled. Wenhaver gaped at his extraordinary skin.

"Now, comb my hair. Your task is to see to my pleasure, and not the reverse. Don't expect fine words from me until you learn to school your manners and your temper."

Afraid for the first time of the raw masculinity of her husband, Wenhaver scurried to find her bone inlaid comb and a brush of stiff boar hair. Artor seated himself and unbound his plaits, allowing Wenhaver to ease the tangles and snarls from her husband's hair. The curls slid through her fingers pleasurably, and she could see the knotted muscles in his shoulders begin to loosen a little.

Wenhaver was used to the adoration of youths and young men, but Artor was the first truly mature man that she had encountered, for, in Wenhaver's lexicon, her doting father and uncles scarcely counted.

When his hair was tamed, Artor stripped off his soft breeches and his leather boots and stood naked before her. Wenhaver gasped, for she had never seen a man unclothed, nor had she any benchmark upon which to assess Artor's male beauty. She had heard that the king took women as he chose, and the maids taken had never complained of either his courtesy or his lovemaking.

But Wenhaver had no experience, and was unsure what was expected of her, or what to say, if anything.

"Stand, woman!"

Wenhaver obeyed. She was quaking inwardly, although she tried to summon up a knowing smile. Artor was not deceived. He knew that Wenhaver was a child woman who must be mastered. Then, perhaps, she would mature and give up her insufferable arrogance.

He reached out one firmly muscled hand, followed by the other, and Wenhaver made a slight movement of surprise when the sword callouses on his palms came into contact with her soft skin. Then, abruptly, he tore her sleeping confection from neck to waist.

The fragile fabric fell away from her shoulders and exposed her heavy, lush breasts.

She opened her mouth to speak, but Artor again raised his finger to his lips.

She shivered.

"Take off that thing," Artor growled.

For all her feigned sophistication, Wenhaver had never seen a man aroused before, and she was afraid. Artor stroked her golden curls and let his fingers linger around her ears and her throat. With a quick twist, he pulled her round so that he could no longer see her face, and then pressed his body against her warm buttocks and smooth back. His hands cupped her breasts, and his fingers gently teased her nipples.

Surprised, Wenhaver felt her breasts harden, and she pushed them deeper into his hands. Smiling with amusement, Artor set about arousing and seducing his wife. She was not Gallia, but if he did not look at her, he could imagine she was. His lips teased the tender back of her neck and his hands explored the gentle swell of her buttocks. As she shivered, his flat grey eyes were alert and rather cruel, but Wenhaver could not see his expression.

As his hands and the sensitive pads of his fingers moved lower and lower, Wenhaver was suddenly aware that there were advantages to marriage that she could not have imagined.

"Your body is mine, woman, to do with as I please. This possession you vowed was mine in front of the assembled nobles of the Britons this day, so do not flinch away from me. Besides, Wenhaver, you are beautiful and you're a warm, sweet peach that I plan to devour."

The tone of his voice remained unchanged, almost as if he was discussing a battle plan or a ride in the country; Wenhaver had no idea what to do, or if she should respond.

In the past, no one had ever dared to trespass on the privacy of Wenhaver's body, so she was surprised that Artor could do such magic in a manner so knowing and so distant. After a time of stroking and featherlight kisses, Wenhaver no longer cared if he ever used her name or professed his undying love for her. She had never thought she would find pleasure in the marriage bed, so she was surprised when Artor eventually mounted her. Amazingly, she found that her body, after a short moment of pain, responded to his mastery with joy and abandon.

Artor smiled, his face indifferent to his body's pleasure. But Wenhaver responded as eagerly as Gallia had, even more so, for she savored her new sensations and demanded them again and again as Artor began to school her in the arts of love.

She was an avid, greedy pupil.

"You're an insatiable little bitch, aren't you, my queen?" he murmured as he pressed her deep into the down coverlet. "You may be a novice, but you'll learn quickly."

Her body was sleek with sweat, and she had wrapped both legs about his waist, moving instinctively in ways that gave him pleasure. For one brief, betraying moment, it was Gallia's face he saw under him and it was Gallia's breasts and thighs he was teasing when he climaxed. He shouted his first wife's name in his extremity, and, even in the pleasure of bodily sensation, his heart felt bruised and yet alive, as it had not done for many years.

For a moment, Artor was grateful to his wife for forcing him to feel more than fleeting desire. In that brief period, the possibility of a long and happy marriage existed, but the young woman didn't recognize the gratitude in his eyes; she was focused on her own feelings of self-worth.

She realized instinctively that, in matters of sex, she was a potential master. Exultation vied with pleasure in the synapses of her brain, and, even as she panted with the satiation and exhaustion of successful sex and the languor that had turned her limbs into sweet honey, Wenhaver's single-minded egotism returned with a vengeance.

"Who is Gallia?" she demanded, drawing deep breaths into her lungs.

Artor turned away from her in the soft bed. His mood had now shattered, and he couldn't bear her to see his wounded, lonely face.

"She was the first girl I ever loved. She was only eighteen when she died, and I was little older. You need not be jealous of a ghost, and if you become half the woman that Gallia was, I will be well pleased with you."

Wenhaver must have heard some thickening in his voice. Regardless of her body's enjoyment of the sexual act and her husband's obvious skills, she still burned in that distant pocket where fear cowered, fueled in part by her abject terror of what Artor could do to her.

"Was she fairer than I am?" she asked guilelessly, although she guessed that the agony of his memories was one of Artor's greatest weaknesses.

Wenhaver may have been foolish, but she was intuitive, especially when self-preservation was her spur. She determined to lie smugly in the warm darkness and twist the knife.

"She wasn't half so beautiful in face and form as you are, Wenhaver," Artor sighed. "But people loved her because she laughed so often. And she hated cruelty above all things. Even ants and wasps were safe from her, but she could fight like a tiger and kill in defense of those folk who needed assistance. If you can learn qualities that match hers, then you will truly become a queen."

"If she was such a paragon, why didn't she become the High Queen of the Britons?" Wenhaver asked sharply. Scorn came, unbidden, to her lips, and jealousy of what she knew were qualities she lacked.

"She was Roman," Artor replied with finality. "Now, let me sleep, woman."

"Roman?" Wenhaver crowed in delight, although she had the presence of mind to whisper her triumph into her pillow. "I should think the Celtic kings would never accept a Roman queen over them." She had to stifle a giggle, with her face half buried in the pillow.

But Artor heard.

He rose, his anger like gall in his throat. All feelings of gratitude and forbearance fled. No one, and nothing that breathed, laughed at his memory of Gallia.

Wenhaver flinched as he began to speak.

"Beware, wife! Enjoyment of the marriage bed is not a coupling of minds and hearts. You have far to go to prove to me that you are anything but a foolish, spoiled brat who is no better than a kitchen maid, and much less willing and experienced. My brother is Roman, my foster mother was Roman, and the glass in that window that gives you so much pleasure is Roman. But unlike the Romans, you aren't sufficiently clean for my tastes."

Wenhaver gasped aloud.

Like all well-raised Celtic girls, she washed her body in bowls of warm water when needed, and her face and hands were laved every day. No one had ever dared to tell her that she was unclean.

Artor picked up his clothing carelessly, for if a king chose to be naked in his own home, then naked he would be.

"If I call for you at night, you will bathe all over and wash your hair with cleansing oils. I will not share a bed with any Celt who makes fun of Roman ways when she is less than perfect. Do you understand me?"

Wenhaver felt an anger that was so deep and so visceral that her heart almost stopped with fury and chagrin. All thought deserted her, but for her need to strike back at him and hurt him as badly as he had wounded her.

"We have consummated our marriage, husband, and I can no longer be cast off. If you don't like me as I am, then perhaps we should not meet."

Artor knelt, dropped his head, and spread his arms wide.

"I am sorry, sweet wife, for I would so miss your fair flesh."

Then he raised his face and she saw that he was laughing at her with eyes as cold as the rock of Cadbury Tor. Her hurt and rage gave her no words to respond.

Artor rose to his feet, every movement an insult.

"Lady, I will survive your absence."

• • •

THERE IS NO worse feeling of impotence than being unable to strike back at the person who completely rejects you. Human beings may populate the forgiving earth until the end of the universe, but they will forever remain the frail, malicious, and violent creatures they have always been, although they might have developed some endearing qualities along the path to wisdom.

However, no virtues were visible in Wenhaver's face when she rose early on the morning that followed the disastrous wedding banquet.

Myrnia took a single, frightened glance at the frozen face of her mistress and prayed that she would be elsewhere when the inevitable storm broke over some hapless head, probably hers.

"Myrnia, I require a large tub, big enough for me to immerse my whole body. And it must be watertight, unless you wish to lose the skin off your back before you clean up the mess." Wenhaver flashed her maid a brief, cruel smile. "And I would like my personal bath by noon today. You will ensure that your choice is attractive, for I intend to wash daily."

Myrnia blanched. She had no idea where to start on her quest. Nodding, and curtsying, she fled from the room, trying desperately not to sob with frustration and fear. As she bolted down the corridor, she heard her mistress screaming for her other maids.

"What shall I do?" Myrnia muttered, and wrung her work-roughened hands like an old woman. "What shall I do?"

Blinded by a sting of tears, she ran full tilt into Myrddion and Nimue, who were arguing amicably with each other. She groaned, bowed low, and would have reeled away had Myrddion not gripped her forearm.

"Slow down, girl! What causes your haste that you are a danger to all around you?"

Myrnia swallowed and darted quick, agonized looks at Myrddion and his servant. Then, to Nimue's horror, the girl burst into a flood of hot tears.

"My apologies, Lord Myrddion, but the queen has told me that I must obtain a bath for her. She wants one in her apartment by noon, and I don't know where to look. You've been very good to me, and my face hardly hurts at all, but I cannot stay and explain to you . . . even if I knew what I was explaining. I don't even know what a bath is!"

The last words of this explanation became a wail of distress.

"She'll have me whipped again if I fail, my lord," she cried piteously, the bruises on her cheek now a livid mixture of purple and green.

Myrddion and Nimue shared exasperated glances.

"How fortunate for you that we crossed your path, pretty lady." Myrddion smiled. "I am sure that my apprentice will know exactly where to look."

Nimue shot Myrddion a glare over the top of Myrnia's bowed head.

"Of course," Nimue soothed the flustered maid. "But why a bath? What is wrong with using the stream?"

"I suppose a stream or a pond would be cold and lacking in privacy," Myrddion replied urbanely. "I am far more interested in why the queen has suddenly decided to develop a Roman attitude to cleanliness."

Myrnia simply looked blank, as if Myrddion spoke gibberish.

"Perhaps we could make one of wood," Nimue thought aloud. "No. That would leak, unless it was lined with pitch—and that would be unsuitable for bathing."

She continued to muse over the problem.

"A bathing container cannot be bought at any marketplace."

"Ah." Myrddion had seemed lost in thought. "I wonder."

"Wonder what, master?"

"Come with me."

The two women pattered along behind him, sharing puzzled glances.

The trio made their way out of the palace, across the paved forecourt, and down the long, winding road that led to the town below.

Myrddion presented a sunny grin to the warriors lazing against the walls, while Nimue thought seriously about boxing his smug and self-satisfied ears. Plainly, Myrnia was terrified, but Nimue was bursting with curiosity.

"Where are we going master?" she asked, a little puffed from the haste of their journey.

"To see Glaucus, the sarcophagus maker."

"The what?" Nimue stopped abruptly, as did Myrnia, who was nearly in tears with ignorance and fear.

"A sarcophagus is just a fancy name for a stone coffin," Myrddion explained, as if he was delivering a lecture. "Some Romans prefer to lie above the earth inside a coffin after they pass into the Shades, while others choose to have their remains buried underground. Still other Romans, and many Celts, prefer to be burned—or cremated."

"How could anyone wish to lie in the earth?"

"Glaucus doesn't have much business, so he also builds kitchen implements and furnishings. Like all good Roman men of business, he always has an eye to the main chance."

Through the town they twisted and turned, past the marketplace where farmers had spread their produce on the grass. Apples, pears, nuts in wicker baskets, eggs wrapped in straw, live chickens, rabbits, and ducks in willow-wand hutches, as well as every conceivable type of bread and cake filled the square with noise, smells, and the excitement of commerce. One gnarled old man sold live pigeons, squabs, and quails while an old woman had been out of bed long before dawn collecting mushrooms, lichen, fungus, and a range of dried herbs that hung upside down from a wooden pole. Nimue's curiosity was such that she would have paused, but Myrddion ushered the girls on like two chicks. The women's skirts soon became fouled and bedraggled at the hems from the mud that lay along the walkways, although they managed to avoid manure from penned piglets, young calves, and even a couple of foals.

Then, before a gaily painted hut of wood and plaster, Myrddion stopped and gazed with admiration at a number of coffins displayed outside the building. In pride of place was an agate, body-shaped container with a lid carved in the likeness of a fair woman with ample, rounded hips. It bore a striking similarity to the goddess Andromeda.

With the lid removed, the size and the shape were perfect for their needs.

"I thought I'd remembered seeing this," Myrddion said to himself.

He banged his staff of office on the entrance wall that led into the hut. "Where are you, Glaucus, you old reprobate? You have customers! Come forth and stop lazing about."

The sound of hammering came from several open-sided huts behind the main building. Obviously, Glaucus had several servants hard at work.

The merchant proved to be a large, portly Romano-Celt with an oily smile and greasy palms. A leather apron covered his considerable girth, and he smelled strongly of sweat, sawdust, and fish.

"Lord Myrddion, my humble abode is open for all your needs. How may I assist a man of such obvious good taste?"

Myrddion sat in the sun on the lid of the stone coffin and accepted a cup of hastily produced wine. Nimue nibbled a proffered fig, while Myrnia seemed like a stone effigy of herself. She was almost catatonic with anxiety.

"I'm interested in Andromeda's sarcophagus. I hear that she is an order that the patron refused to accept. Why did she refuse it?"

The merchant flushed, and Nimue could see his agile brain trying to decide if he was in some kind of trouble.

"The lady in question desired the hardest and most durable of resting places. That would normally be agate, my lord, because any fool knows how hard that stone is. But she had an objection to the color. She took offense to the fact that it is black. What is an honest man to do? She refused to pay the bulk of the commission and insisted on marble, so I made very little profit by the time I found some of that stone, I assure you. Then the stupid woman decided that she disliked the green in the marble, so I told her it was that or nothing, and that I'd take my complaint to the High King himself if she didn't pay the money she owed."

"And that left you with the sarcophagus of Andromeda."

"Correct, my lord."

"Is it watertight, Glaucus?"

"Absolutely, my lord. We cannot have a corpse leaking fluids all over the place."

Myrddion gave a little grunt of agreement, while Nimue managed to avoid bringing up her fig. Myrnia simply gaped with an open mouth.

"How much?" Myrddion demanded.

Glaucus named a figure that caused Myrddion to laugh dryly.

"I'm sure that King Artor will forgive your little joke and your efforts to cheat him."

In an instant, Glaucus recalculated his costs and arrived at a figure that still seemed enormous, but was acceptable to Myrddion. The old man spat on his hand to seal the bargain.

"Your final part of this arrangement is to move Andromeda to the queen's apartments before noon. If you are late, the deal is off. Do you understand my terms, my friend?"

The merchant nodded frenetically. "Yes, my lord, for your wish is my command. But who will pay me?"

"Send the bill to me and I will give it personally to the High King. Fail me not."

Glaucus looked hurt.

"One more thing, Glaucus. I don't require the lid. I want you to smash it to rubble and then dispose of it. Personally. Is that understood?"

"Yes, my lord. I am to dispose of the lid."

"Not dispose of it, my friend. I want you to destroy it. Should the lid be seen again, your suffering will be considerable."

As the trio made the long climb back to the citadel, Nimue asked the obvious question.

"Will the queen wish to bathe in a coffin?" she asked. "I'd be happy to use it myself, but I can't see Queen Wenhaver enjoying her bath in such a receptacle."

"I certainly won't be telling her it's a coffin," Myrddion replied happily. "And I'm sure Myrnia won't explain to Wenhaver what Andromeda is either, will you, my dear?"

The servant girl shook her head so vigorously that Nimue had the unsettling thought that she might shake it off.

"So, as none of us intends to tell Wenhaver anything about her new bath and, as Glaucus will destroy the lid, I'm sure the queen will be content."

"My lips are sealed, my lord," Myrnia promised. "Besides, I can't even remember what the thing's called."

"Then we shall all keep it that way," Myrddion answered glibly.

The adventure of the sarcophagus, as Nimue thought of it, proved a splendid solution all round. No one at Cadbury Tor possessed such an object of practical beauty, so Wenhaver was mightily pleased at her good fortune.

Not so the kitchen staff, who muttered dark threats at the prospect of heating all the water needed to fill that bath, nor the warriors and maids who were tasked to fill and empty the receptacle in Wenhaver's apartments each time she felt the urge to use it. Rose petals, oils, and perfumes were placed within Andromeda's form to soften and sweeten the queen's skin as she luxuriated in the pleasures that were only hers, making Andromeda doubly precious to the queen.

After her second bath, Wenhaver instructed Myrnia to attend the High King's apartments with a message for Artor.

"You are to tell him that I am exquisitely clean," she told the terrified maid, who did not understand the meaning of the instructions she had been given.

When Artor arrived at Wenhaver's chambers in response to her cryptic message, he almost choked with suppressed laughter. He managed to control his expression and congratulated his bride on her purchase and the speed of her response to his demands.

Later, when Artor was talking to Myrddion, he raised the subject of the Andromeda bath.

"Myrddion, what possessed my wife to purchase a coffin to use as a bath?"

"It's a sarcophagus, sire," his chief counselor replied, with a bland, expressionless face.

"I know what it is, Myrddion, but where did she find it?"

"I found it, sire. I discovered the queen's bath at the establishment of Glaucus. But what I cannot understand is why she wanted it."

Eventually, Myrddion extracted the story of the disastrous wedding night from Artor, and his face grew grave to hear of the words that had been spoken in anger.

"No wonder the silly child threw a tantrum. She lacks any real subtlety, my lord, and she will always irritate you, but I fear you must do your duty and you should try not to hurt her feelings too deeply."

"Beware of censure, Myrddion. You are the closest thing I have to a friend after Targo, but do not presume to instruct me on my duty." Artor spat the last word out.

"I swear I'm not criticizing you, my lord. I am simply suggesting that embarking upon a civil war against Leodegran is not a clever strategy. You must face him in battle if you shame his daughter before all the tribes, no matter how much you are angered by her foolishness." Myrddion knew he had angered Artor and thought furiously how to put matters right, but a peremptory knock at the door interrupted his thoughts. The visitor was Wenhaver's maid with an invitation from the queen for Artor to attend her rooms that evening.

"Damn all women," Myrddion muttered.

"I heard that," Artor replied, in his natural, easygoing tone. But Myrddion was not deceived. Artor must be mollified.

Myrddion spread his arms wide, bowed his head, and fell to his knees on the stone flagging. Artor gaped. He had expected his strategist to rage at him, or to cajole him, or to try to bribe him; he did not expect abject groveling.

"What now, Myrddion? Is this behavior a bad joke?"

"My king, the fault for this whole embarrassing mess is ultimately mine. Yes, my lord, I am to blame. Wenhaver loves jewels more than anything else, and I was unwise enough to give Nimue my Etruscan necklace. I meant no harm, for electrum can hardly suit a woman of Wenhaver's complexion. But Wenhaver is so accustomed to eclipsing all other women in beauty, style, and manner that she was aroused to jealousy."

For one short moment, Artor looked so cross and impatient that Myrddion considered he had overplayed his hand, but then Artor's brow cleared. He understood female jealousy, although he had no patience with it.

"Do you wish me to send little Nimue away, lord?" Myrddion asked the High King. "Perhaps it would be for the best."

Artor stared hard at Myrddion's old-young face, which was down-cast and oddly bereft. Artor became suspicious.

"Do you want her to go, Myrddion?"

Myrddion shook his head. "No, my lord. She is so full of laughter and eagerness to learn that she makes me feel quite young. I would miss her."

Artor considered the problem.

Outside the shutters, the spring air was sweet with the scent of new-grown flowers and crops, and the king remembered all that he had wrought, and how much Myrddion had contributed towards making these dreams real.

Suddenly, and painfully, the High King felt excoriating guilt.

"I am the one who is ultimately to blame, my friend, for I have kept you as my confidant to further my own ends. I have demanded all that you had to give during your many years of loyal service. The final responsibility has always been mine."

"No. That's simply not so. What I have given, I offered willingly. And I'm even prepared to relinquish Nimue if the kingdom should demand it. After all, I was the person who pressed you to marry Wenhaver in the first place."

Artor raised Myrddion to his feet and warmly embraced his friend.

"Hades, Myrddion! If you are prepared to cast away your valuable apprentice, then I can at least try to beget a child on that silly cow. But Nimue stays at Cadbury. I like her, and I admire her intellect and her happy courage. Wenhaver must learn to act like a queen, and Nimue may even have some part in the process, if my wife is prepared to learn from the child."

Myrddion shuddered slightly. "I don't think that's likely, lord."

He knew that if Artor suggested that Wenhaver should emulate Nimue's gay courtesy and ease of manner, his apprentice would not live a week.

"Will you go to Wenhaver's bridal bed once more?" he asked.

"I'll go. But I can't promise to perform, especially if she starts to speak. I can't stand women who whine."

Thinking hard, and mentally preparing himself, Artor set forth for the queen's apartments. While his steps were neither jaunty nor urgent, he no longer felt intimidated by the task ahead.

In a tavern on the outskirts of Cadbury, the three travelers of old sat at their ease over glasses of cheap Spanish wine while servants cleared up the mess around them. Luka had his feet on the table, while Myrddion had loosened the collar of his black robe. Llanwith just looked sleepy, and continued to drink.

"A toast, gentlemen," Luka suggested, and all three men raised their glasses. "I offer a toast to us, for we have managed to avert disaster over two entire nights. Firstly, my felicitations go to me for my golden tongue. Then my congratulations go to Llanwith for his tact. And, finally, my enduring gratitude goes to Myrddion for his tale of his search for a bath."

The three men touched goblets.

Llanwith pushed one of the innkeeper's hounds away. The dog had developed a sudden affection for his leg.

"Let's hope that Artor shocks Wenhaver into silence for a day or two," Luka said. "And not the way he did on his wedding night."

"And let us pray that she becomes pregnant quickly so she has something else to occupy that empty head," Myrddion added.

"Artor has proved his virility any number of times, so I don't expect any difficulty with that aspect of our plans for the succession." Llanwith absentmindedly scratched the head of the persistent hound.

"Hmmn." Myrddion sounded glum and depressed. "The one thing I have learned about Wenhaver is that if circumstances can go disastrously wrong around her, they do."

"At least Nimue is safe." Luka tried to cheer up his morose friend. "Damn me, but I like that girl."

"Never mind me," Myrddion muttered. "I can still feel a storm blowing up, and Wenhaver is at the center of it."

"You and your sensitive feelings," Llanwith joked. "Are you sure your father wasn't a demon?"

"I'm quite sure. Otherwise I'd have turned you into a toad by now, my large friend."

Chapter XV

A MATTER OF TRUST

The mysteries of what took place behind the sealed doors of the royal apartments were of endless interest to the common people of Artor's realm. The wedding feast had given all of Cadbury, its surrounds and the whole of the Celtic west a source of excited gossip, and the tale of events in the great hall grew in the telling. Far to the north, Morgan found herself almost happy, as discord had begun to tear away the veneer of paradise within the kingdom.

But in complex matters of the heart, Morgan misunderstood Artor entirely, for he was nothing like Uther Pendragon, a man who was cruel and calculating until his death. Although Artor had been changed by the untrammeled power of his position, he had spent his childhood as the butt of jokes and knew, too well, the unrelenting misery of one who has strayed from his destined path in the world. Unfortunately, he had also experienced the simplicity of true love, and Wenhaver was no Gallia. Unfortunately, Leodegran's daughter wasn't a queen either, although she'd been raised for that role.

But Artor was an accomplished seducer, and he was perfectly capable of ensuring that his wife would come eagerly to his bed. If he could curb his impatience, distaste, and an unmanly desire to puncture Wenhaver's smug self-satisfaction, the silly girl would learn her royal role. Her delight in sex was an added bonus that Artor could use to gain her loyalty and what affection she was capable of feeling.

On the second, true night of their marriage, Wenhaver was very clean, and Artor complimented her on her skin, which now smelled of roses. She purred with gratification.

As he smoothly explored her healthy, golden body and kissed her willful mouth, Wenhaver was quickly aroused. He was so handsome that the queen found it easy to forget his advanced age. Everyone told her that their blond good looks complemented each other, and, according to the peasants, they were like rulers of the Otherworld, fair and beautiful beyond human understanding. Of course, Wenhaver devoured such praise.

No, Wenhaver had no legitimate complaint to make of her husband and his bedding of her. In fact, the scars and marks of violence on the High King's body brought home to her, for the first time, that Artor was a great warrior first and a High King second. At times, she secretly hugged herself with glee that such a mighty man had taken her for his wife.

But if the worm is scooped from the apple, the sweet white flesh will still continue to rot. The corruption has taken root and cannot be winkled out by sexual conquest or the promise of greater glory. No matter what the heart possesses, it desires more than it should have, and so the contagion in Wenhaver's soul spread.

Cadbury Tor was filled with beautiful young men eager to praise her hair, the ruby redness of her lips, the narrowness of her waist, which stayed obstinately slender. And when Artor left to ride to the border cities, Wenhaver was left alone, except for a small group of girls, the daughters of kings, with whom she surrounded herself.

They flattered her endlessly.

"You are so fortunate, my queen," Ludmilla of the Iceni murmured as she brushed the queen's knee-length hair. "Most women with fair hair have brassy tones in their curls, but yours are like spun gold."

Wenhaver preened and was gracious to Ludmilla, going so far as to give the girl a small thumb ring from her childhood hoard, for Ludmilla was tiny and dark.

"You are married to the greatest man in Britain, perhaps in the world," Ludmilla enthused. "He is handsome and strong, and so very, very attentive."

"Yes, he is, isn't he? Still, at times I feel like a brood mare, and I swear all of Cadbury looks for signs of quickening. I would prefer to enjoy our marriage for a while, alone."

"It's all so romantic," Ludmilla sighed. She put down the silver brush and returned to her embroidery.

"Mostly," Wenhaver agreed, although she was no one's fool when it came to matters of pride and consequence.

And that one factor ate away at her self-esteem like a slow-acting poison. She knew that her need for Artor's body was far more urgent than his desire for her flesh. She didn't love her husband. She didn't love anyone, but she wanted him, and he knew it. Fear stirred in the dark corners of her brain, and then surged to conscious life. What was she worth to him? Very little, she decided with bitter resentment.

Artor came to her chambers when he felt like it, regardless of her wishes. Then, when she was prepared to do anything to keep him by her side, to lie in the crook of his arm and feel loved, he would yawn, smile carelessly, and wander away, naked and oblivious to her feelings.

So easily are earthly kingdoms jeopardized.

Meanwhile, life in the apartments of Myrddion Merlinus was quiet and, for the first time in his long life, filled with laughter. The sight of Nimue transfixed him, as she practiced new words with the tip of her pink tongue peeping out of the corner of her mouth in concentration. He told himself that he was turning into a doddering old fool to be so taken with a girl who was young enough to be his granddaughter, yet every day he rose with a spring in his step and joy in his heart. Myrddion tried to persuade himself that she was just another curious child, a little brighter than most young people, and a trifle unusual compared with other striplings of either sex. Yes, the king's most sage counselor tried to rationalize his feelings, but he was aware that he was only contriving to fool himself.

Myrddion's sojourn in contentment couldn't last.

Artor was absent, called to Venonae by Pelles to reorganize its defenses, so Cadbury was quieter than usual, and Wenhaver was listless and bored. Autumn had come knocking at the tor with heavy rain, grey days, and damp walls that set the nerves of the courtiers on edge. Many of Wenhaver's ladies nursed colds, and the corridors echoed with sniffles, coughing, and dismal conversations in corners. The queen spent most of her days in the tedium of sporadic bouts of sewing, spinning, weaving, and gossip. Needless to say, her mood was irritable and dissatisfied.

Perhaps Wenhaver never meant to cause such a disagreeable and vulgar display, but as Myrddion would later say, if wishes were horses then beggars would ride.

Targo put his interpretation of her behavior more bluntly.

"You can't turn a whore into a queen. She'll always love the muck."

Wenhaver happened to see Myrddion leaving the fortress to walk to the township below, so she decided to amuse herself. She sent Myrnia to summon Nimue to her apartments.

Nimue was busy grinding herbs with a mortar and pestle when Myrnia disturbed her, and, surprised by the invitation, she brushed her hands clean, tidied her hair, and sallied forth.

"Be careful, mistress," Myrnia whispered, her eyes darting around the hallway for any listening ears. "The queen is in an odd mood today, and she's no friend of yours."

Nimue grinned widely and pressed Myrnia's cold little hand comfortingly.

"Don't worry on my account, Myrnia. Your mistress has no power over me. After all, she can't order me to do anything I would dislike."

Nimue was sadly mistaken.

In her overwarm morning room, Wenhaver reclined on a couch, surrounded by her ladies, who were busy with various tasks of embroidery, mending, and spinning. By comparison, Wenhaver's hennaed hands were idle, although she toyed with a late, rather sad rose whose petals had grown unevenly in the unseasonable wind.

"Please be seated, Mistress Nimue. I'm pleased that you answered my request so readily, for I fear I've been tardy in becoming acquainted with you."

Wenhaver toyed with her heavy red gown. Because the color was scarlet, rather than crimson, its folds clashed with the queen's pink blondness. By comparison, Nimue's plain grey garb was elegant and understated.

"Would you enjoy some warmed honey wine? A sweetmeat? Water?" Wenhaver asked with disarming courtesy. Her pretty hands stripped a leaf off the stalk of the rose.

"I'll have nothing, thank you, Your Majesty. But I appreciate your offer," Nimue added as an afterthought. She was puzzled, for the queen's manner was confusing and out of character.

"What shall we talk about, ladies? How might we come to know Mistress Nimue better? I know!" Wenhaver raised one finger dramatically.

The maidens smiled nervously and went on with their various tasks, avoiding Nimue's eyes.

"We all know that Mistress Nimue is the trusted apprentice of Myrddion Merlinus, whom the king swears is the wisest man alive. Only an extraordinary person could hope to study with such a mentor, so what special instruction did you receive in your youth to make you eligible to enjoy such an honor? Don't be shy, Nimue. We're agog to discover your secrets."

The queen continued to smile, rather like a cat playing with some small, terrified prey, so Nimue felt uneasy. Instinctively, she knew she was out of her depth in the spiteful games played by aristocratic young women at Artor's court.

"None that I can recall, Your Majesty. My childhood was very ordinary."

Wenhaver cooed in mock surprise, and shredded another leaf from the stalk of her rose.

"You're far too modest, mistress. I heard that you were very close to the intrigues of Venonae. Servants know everything, don't they?"

"Not so, my queen. Someone has been prattling nonsense."

"Did you not have Gruffydd, the sword-bearer, as your foster father?"

"Aye, my queen, that's true." Nimue's brows drew together with suspicion.

"Did he not visit you regularly? Now, where did you sleep? I was told . . . yes, I remember. In the kitchens, with the servants." Wenhaver laughed with a tinkling peal of genuine amusement, laced with rancour.

"Yes, Your Majesty."

Nimue now understood the tenor of her audience with the queen. It was intended to be a torture of ridicule posing as conversation, and it was meant to end with an inevitable argument, one that a mere apprentice couldn't win with any honor. Nimue's hands clenched inside the rough wool of her skirts until her knuckles were white.

The aristocratic young maidens tittered, and Wenhaver tore another leaf from the rose.

"How odd, my dear, that you learned so much among the roasts, the pots and pans, and the ovens. It would seem to be a marvelous place to learn philosophy, science, and healing. I can tell that your master chose you for your wonderful experience and dedication to your studies, so you must have found a way to achieve an education. Somehow."

Sarcasm dripped from Wenhaver's lips like honeyed poison, but Nimue merely pressed her lips together so she wouldn't shame Myrddion with the rage that bubbled up into her throat.

Wenhaver saw the little fires in Nimue's blue eyes and continued to strip the rose.

"Who was your foster mother?" the queen continued her attack. "I heard she was the cook, but I can't believe that such a superior education came from such a person. Or does porridge, gravy, and cake making now rank as good education? My father was very remiss, for I'm afraid that I can't cook a thing."

"I'm sure Your Majesty was fortunate indeed in her learning," Nimue answered, attempting to divert the queen's attack on Gallwyn.

A rose petal fell to the flagging, and Wenhaver raised herself into a sitting position so that one elegantly shod foot could grind its softness under her heel. Nimue watched this small carnage with blank, detached interest.

"A sword-bearer and a cook. Remarkable, isn't it, ladies? Yet I suppose even such humble beginnings were preferable to being raised in a Saxon dung heap by barbarian savages. Yes, you'd have had dirty hair and fingernails, a foul tongue, and a fouler smell if your real parents had raised you, so I suppose we should be grateful to the cook who taught you to be clean."

The maidens tittered on cue, but their eyes were nervous and didn't stray from their sewing.

"Even a slatternly peasant is better than a Saxon, I suppose. But tell me, Nimue, what attracted Lord Myrddion to you? Does he actually like common muck? Does he see something special in you other than your mind, or your tattoo? Gracious, surely he couldn't . . . no, I'll not believe an aristocrat, even a bastard lord such as Myrddion, would want to . . . well . . . you know, my dear." Pretending delicacy, Wenhaver bent to smell the remnants of her rose, pulled a face as if she had discovered something rancid and then tore off two more petals.

"No, Your Majesty. I don't know." Nimue's voice could have cut glass.

Wenhaver laughed and her eyes were cruel and cold.

"Of course you do, Nimue, growing up in the kitchens as you did. Your education must have been quite . . . broad . . . by childhood's end. No wonder Myrddion Merlinus couldn't deny your charms."

Slowly and carefully, Nimue rose to her feet. Her cold eyes raked the queen from head to heels with a slow, insolent carefulness. Her face was very pale by the light of the sconces, and she stood up spear straight and proud. Wenhaver was forced to stare up at her as Nimue took several steps forward until she was within Wenhaver's reach.

"You may say what you will about my birth, my childhood, my

education, and my morals, Your Majesty. I'll not respond, for you do far worse harm to yourself than you do to me. You may be as vulgar as the worst of the camp followers that I heard around the fire pits of Venonae, but I'll not answer nor insult you." Nimue drew in a deep, shuddering breath.

"Dear Gruffydd was a peasant and he rose to become one of the greatest men in the land through his own ability, rather than through an accident of birth. Yes, my sweet foster mother, Gallwyn, was an ignorant peasant as well, but the king entrusted me to her care, and I remain under his protection. Nor will I fall into your trap by reacting to crude insults to fine persons who have won the respect of our entire world. I am no foolish girl interested only in superficial pleasures, so your insults cannot harm me."

The maidens quailed before Nimue's blazing northern eyes, but Wenhaver thrust out her chin in a clear challenge. Blue eyes met and clashed, ice to ice, and Wenhaver rose to her feet.

"But when you impugn the honor of my master," Nimue continued implacably, "a man of unimpeachable dignity, decency, and goodness, then you have gone a step too far, and the king should hear of your perfidy. I must ask myself how any well-raised maiden could possibly know what indecencies take place in the servants' quarters unless she listens at doorways. How could any woman of breeding discuss such matters of sexual license so freely, unless she was well versed in such matters? Before words are said here that cannot be forgotten, I beg leave to remove myself from your presence."

As Wenhaver untangled the insults that were buried in Nimue's graceful attack, two red spots appeared high on her cheekbones. Then she struck Nimue across the face with the leafless stalk of the rose.

"How dare you! Are you suggesting that my conversation is vulgar and inappropriate? Anything the queen chooses to discuss with an ignorant savage like you cannot be inappropriate. I am the High Queen of the Britons, and I decide when you may leave my presence." She raised the rose stem to slash at Nimue's face once again, but this time Nimue held up her arm to take the blow instead of her face. Blood was already trickling from the thorn cuts across Nimue's cheekbones and nose.

"Your Majesty has forgotten her manners once again, so I must remind you that I am not a servant who will accept a cowardly whipping without complaint. Good day to you!"

And, while Wenhaver fumed with impotent rage, Nimue turned on her heel and left the queen's chamber with her dignity intact. It was only when she was cleaning the wounds on her face and arm caused by the slashing rose thorns that she began to tremble like an aspen in the winter wind.

And so Myrddion found her, crying with frustration and reaction.

Over a warm bowl of chamomile that had been sweetened with honey, Myrddion winkled the whole tale out of his apprentice. Experienced in political intrigue as he was, Myrddion still found it difficult to believe that Wenhaver could play such filthy games.

"I am sorry, master. She insulted Gallwyn, and I let that pass . . . but when she suggested that you chose to take me as your apprentice so you could seduce me . . . I told her such a suggestion was vulgar and inappropriate. I became angry, and I lost my temper."

No man can listen to a beautiful woman apologize for defending his honor without some small stirrings of pride, and Myrddion was no exception. But he was restless and uneasy, for Wenhaver had ventured out into the open, and both master and apprentice should now be aware of her intentions.

"You must promise me, Nimue, that you will never enter the queen's presence without a friendly supporter behind you. Wenhaver's viciousness has no boundaries, and she's a harridan in the making. Avoid her at all cost, for both our sakes. I know you weren't to blame, but you're my responsibility and I must keep you safe." He frowned down at his young charge. "Listen carefully, Nimue. You must tell no one of your disagreement with the queen. Not even Targo. Artor would not tolerate such behavior from his wife, and, after the High King had punished her, she would search for a way to destroy you."

361

But Targo and Odin were soon made aware of the confrontation, for too many had witnessed it and rumor recognized no barriers.

But the incident of the rose, as Nimue thought of it, was never mentioned in public. The queen raised her chin in challenge to Myrddion when next they met, but when the scholar said nothing, either to her or to the High King, she allowed matters to rest. In truth, Wenhaver lost some of her dignity through her display of bad manners, and several young princesses returned to their tribes earlier than would normally have been expected because of what they had witnessed. Servants gossiped as well, and the queen suffered in their recitation of the disagreeable incident. Nimue continued with her accustomed duties in the fortress, but now Myrddion, Odin, and Targo watched her surreptitiously, in the full knowledge that she had made a dangerous and ruthless enemy.

DAY AFTER DAY, Myrddion honed Nimue's young intellect, far beyond what he had originally intended. Over many hours of talk, they analyzed numerous problems, and Nimue devoured the memoirs of Caesar, and then went on to dissect Myrddion's own written recollections of the reign of Uther Pendragon. Inevitably, his apprentice wanted to discuss what she found within the dusty scrolls.

"I find the differences between Lord Artor and his father far less interesting than the similarities," Nimue informed Myrddion, causing her master to lift his head from his reading.

Although Myrddion felt a little peculiar as he discussed matters of state with a young girl, something about Nimue's frank curiosity robbed the topic of its more inappropriate qualities.

"Uther was withered at the core," she stated unequivocally. "From your memoirs, I believe he came into this world with an emotional lack, and the emptiness in his soul was ultimately filled with fury and vindictiveness."

"If nothing else, Nimue, your vocabulary is improving," Myrddion muttered softly. "I'm surprised that you've managed to find echoes of the old king in Artor's nature. I can't see any similarities myself."

"You're not trying, master. Artor came into the world totally whole and strong, and without any emptiness. I can feel it. But he lacked birth parents who loved him."

"I'm pleased that you recognize his motherless state." Myrddion felt a strange shiver of pride run from the crown of his head to his long, narrow toes. Nimue's mind was quick, logical, and transparent.

At Myrddion's bidding, Nimue carefully considered the concept of aloneness.

"Neither Artor nor I fitted into the worlds of our childhood," Nimue continued aloud. "We were oddities and outcasts, I suppose, and Artor, like me, was without noble birth to smooth his way in the world."

Nimue thought deeply, one foot tapping as her mind raced.

"But Uther must have understood the qualities he lacked, even when he was young. The boy in him must have been very lonely. Artor certainly was, and so was I."

"I am an old man, but I can hardly be expected to remember the experiences of Uther Pendragon when he was a lad," Myrddion countered astringently.

"You're not that old, master," Nimue replied automatically, her mind still focused on her argument. "No. It was Gallwyn who made the difference in my development—dear, sweet, ordinary Gallwyn. Really, all she could do was organize the kitchens well, and care enough to bribe the steward so I had some learning. A piece of good simnel cake goes a long way," Nimue joked.

"And Artor had Frith, a slave woman, to help him adjust to his world," Myrddion said. "Frith adored him, and she gave him all the good advice and balance that a young boy needs. Livinia Major also saw to his training, especially when it became necessary for him to learn the peccadilloes of females. Both of those women loved him."

"Livinia was a Roman matron, a paragon of virtue, but she wasn't given to displays of affection. You described her well, master, and you also explained why Artor protects the loathsome Caius for the sake of his mother—because the king would never break his word to a woman like Livinia."

"True, Nimue. Artor loved Livinia, but more in the way you would admire a great teacher. It was a slave, one who was below Gallwyn in the eyes of the world, who was Artor's mother in all but birth, the mother of his heart."

Nimue leapt impulsively to her feet, her homespun gown rustling as she paced impatiently around the room.

"I've learned from my talks with Targo that Frith, the slave, was far from ordinary. She seems to have been a strong woman."

"That's also true, although I don't understand your point. She trained Artor in ways that Targo couldn't, for she taught him the value of absolute trust." Myrddion sighed deeply. "And here your argument about their similarities collapses completely, for Uther trusted nobody."

"At some time during his youth, I'm sure that Artor learned the dangers of trust. Today, the High King's every action and every word seems to be measured and calculated. He uses Livinia's justice and Frith's loyalty as his yardsticks, but sadness has taught the king that the world has a black and uncaring heart. Uther always believed in the vindictiveness of fate, and our king has learned to be like his father in this regard. In their desire to retain control, they are alike." Nimue turned to face Myrddion, and her face was very grave. "Should the High King lose those friends whom he loves, especially those men and women who humanize him, then the legacy of Uther will rise in him like a waiting pike, all teeth and viciousness. He is as many men have made him, but Uther Pendragon remains his father. I have seen something cruel in him. I hope it springs from necessity, and not from a need to inflict pain."

Nimue's words sent cold chills through Myrddion's body. Waking and sleeping, in the hours that followed, her assessment tortured him with its warnings of the inexorable march of time. When Targo hobbled into his room on the arm of his servant, Perce, Myrddion was jaundiced and upset.

"A fair afternoon to you, Lord Myrddion! What's wrong with you? You look as sick as an old grey cat! I'm not good for much these days, but I can listen, so out with it, old friend."

"I'm perfectly well, Targo," Myrddion retorted. "Your wits are wandering."

"Now I'm certain that you have a problem!" Targo settled himself into a deep, cushioned chair. "You're never discourteous, and you've just been rude to me. So tell Targo everything."

As he looked into Targo's face, Myrddion registered that the old man's features formed a lively nest of wrinkles, rather like those of an ancient monkey that he had once seen in his youth while at the court of Ambrosius.

"You do me an injustice if you suspect I'll tittle-tattle," Targo stated. "I won't blab, not even to Artor, if you don't want me to. I can't speak plainer than that." To show his good faith, he turned round to his young servant and ordered him to depart. "The boy's gone, so we're alone now. Whatever you've done can be kept private, between us."

"I've made a mistake, Targo," Myrddion began, in little more than a whisper.

"What? Speak up, Myrddion, for Mithras's sake. I'm old, and so are my ears."

"I've made a sodding mistake, Targo!" Myrddion's voice was sharp and almost desperate. "A huge error of judgment."

Targo's eyes disappeared into the folds of his eyelids like an old tortoise's.

"I've spoken too freely about our master, and heard advice that has upset me."

Now Targo's lips pursed as well. "Then you deserve to be upset, Myrddion. Go on. Spit it all out."

Myrddion recounted his lesson with Nimue, feeling rather shame-faced as he watched the old soldier frown in disapproval.

"Nimue didn't mean any harm to our king, old friend," he assured

Targo, though his voice was uncertain. "I have never really considered her opinions of Artor's character problematic before. In fact, I've been more worried about my reactions to her as a young and desirable woman, if you understand me."

"I'd rather you didn't bore me with your sudden rushes of blood to the head—or elsewhere—over a woman. Your whole conversation with Nimue yesterday was wrong! Nimue's a sweet girl, and I don't begrudge her an education, but you shouldn't treat the king like one of your specimens in a jar."

The king's counselor nodded. Targo's point was valid.

The old soldier gazed around Myrddion's comfortable room and observed the many shelves supporting glass jars of powders, liquids, and other sundry objects that the old mercenary would prefer not to imagine. His face was disapproving and his voice had the bite of suppressed anger.

"You were wrong, Myrddion, to let the girl talk about her king in such a fashion, and doubly foolish to permit her to state the sodding obvious."

Myrddion looked up sharply. "You think that I consider Artor to be a monster? No, Targo. No. Artorex was a fine youth, and Artor, as a man, has avoided all the pitfalls of power that have been thrown at him."

"He allowed Gaheris to be an emissary, didn't he? You may fool Nimue. You may fool the world if you want, Myrddion, but you won't fool me. Artor does what he must do, without scruple. I love him more than myself, but I can see the truth in him that you find so hard to admit. That's why you've been looking so upset today. Nimue rubbed your nose in the unblemished truth about our king, and you didn't like it.

"We should consider his deficiencies from Artor's perspective," Targo went on relentlessly. "Artor never acts on impulse, or to no purpose, even when those closest to him are at risk. Those people he loves maintain his humanity, but I sometimes believe he would sacrifice us all if it was necessary to keep the west safe for the Celtic peoples. Yes, he would. That's why he's a king worth worshipping, a man who has been forged for these terrible times. Our king knows what he is, and he often hates himself. Doesn't he? How far can self-loathing be stretched before the man breaks into a thousand little pieces?"

Myrddion's face was white with strain, but he couldn't deny Targo's assessments, which were as cruel as Nimue's, and uttered with sad certainty.

"God help us all if Artor loses those friends who offer him some measure of happiness," Targo concluded. "If that dark day ever dawns, he'll be adrift in emptiness and the silence of loneliness."

Both Myrddion and Targo sat silently, in their own separate miseries. Typically, Targo stirred first.

"So was that all you discussed? Ye gods, but you've been indiscreet—and you've allowed the girl to know far too much. You can be such a fool at times, Myrddion, such a sodding fool!"

Myrddion was affronted and showed it.

"You committed treason by discussing the High King's motives so recklessly," Targo said bluntly. "But, worse than this, you've half convinced yourself that Artor has some type of choice as to whether he acts like a saint or a sinner. His choice is the choice of a soldier, which means kill or be killed. Will this action harm the kingdom or help it? Will this man, or this family, be a danger to the security of the realm or not? And, if so, what should I do to protect the land? Should I kill the offending person? Should I kill the whole family, or the whole tribe? At the end of the day, Artor is responsible for what happens to the west. Whether he's like his father or not doesn't matter a fuck in the passage of time. He's trying to stop the wind from blowing or the rain from falling, and, because he's brilliant, brave, and so bloody determined, he's mostly successful in all that he does. Yes, he has beloved friends, but he'd survive without us."

Oddly enough, Myrddion felt a little better, and said so. Then, as he heated wine over a small iron stove, Perce returned to the room, looking a little better for having washed himself in the stream.

Odin also arrived, dwarfing the document cabinets and scrolls that were stored in Myrddion's study. Artor was enclosed with the queen, so his shadowy bodyguards were free for an hour or two.

"How goes the weapons training, Perce?" Myrddion asked, mentally shaking his thoughts back to more mundane and bearable channels.

Perce shrugged, but Odin was uncharacteristically garrulous.

"Perce moves like the warrior he is soon to become. He is very strong and determined, and he almost had my axe today."

"Well done, Perce." Nimue clapped her hands in pleasure.

The men turned in surprise as Myrddion's apprentice, the subject of so much discord, tripped into the room.

"What's the matter?" she asked as Myrddion and Targo stared at her. "Is my hair coming undone?"

"No, Nimue. We old men aren't used to having beautiful young ladies among us," Targo murmured gracefully.

"How nice." Nimue smiled. "But Perce is the hero here."

Perce flushed with embarrassment and joy. Myrddion knew that the young man was the son of a thatcher, and that current wisdom gave him little hope of winning a warrior's sword. But Artor was a fair man to his bones, and he would not forget his oath to Targo if it provided the old servant with some pleasure. Myrddion was certain that Perce would soon become one of Artor's warriors, regardless of convention and the absolutes of birth.

"What name will you take for yourself when you enter Artor's guard?" Myrddion asked in all seriousness.

Perce looked uncomfortable.

"Out with it," Nimue demanded.

"She's a bossy little piece, isn't she?" Targo commented to no one in particular. "Look at Odin. He was given his title because we couldn't pronounce his name, least of all understand it."

"My given name was Sven," Odin revealed, without a hint of resentment. "But Odin will do, may the gods forgive me."

"Your given name, at least, has a noble ring about it," Myrddion said. "But your birth name sounds like a basket full of snakes."

Nimue was impossible to deflect once her curiosity was aroused.

"Don't tell me you haven't decided on a name yet, Perce. Knowing you as I do, you've been planning a suitable name for years."

"I want to be known as Percivale," the young man muttered. He was acutely embarrassed.

"I beg your pardon?" Myrddion asked. "These old ears are hard of hearing."

"I want to be known as Percivale Maladroit."

"Maladroit?" Nimue looked at Myrddion for clarification.

"The ill-made man," Myrddion explained. "It seems rather apt if you consider your past life." Then he smiled at the young man to show his approval of the name. "Artor wears his pearl ring to remind him of some truths that, mostly, he would prefer to forget. In particular, his kinship with Uther Pendragon. At least you will always have a tangible memory of what you once were."

"Pearls are for tears," Nimue said softly, her eyes far away.

"Yes, and tears are the substance and the history of that ring," Myrddion said. "It decorated the lid of a pearwood box in which Uther kept jewels he took from Artor's mother. The pearl serves as a salutary reminder of the corruption of power."

"The king does his best," Targo added, his voice as rusty as a very old gate. "I never met a great man who was not assailed by the power he held in his hands." Targo met and trapped Myrddion's eyes as he spoke, reminding him that there was a fine line between academic study and betrayal.

"Heart always mattered to our king . . . and motives, regardless of the outcomes."

"But the berserker still lives on in his heart," Odin said simply.

Nimue was ignorant of the northern term, and insisted upon a full explanation from Odin and Myrddion. Her mouth made a little moue of wonder as Odin haltingly explained how blood and battle rage could make a warrior impervious to terrible wounds, and how the warrior's response was fueled only by the lust to kill.

"I have felt just like that. When that kitchen maid stole Gallwyn's bed and her treasures before her flesh was even cold, a red haze filled my eyes and I wanted to kill her." Nimue was so solemn that the men had difficulty keeping straight faces.

"The berserker never goes away," Odin warned.

"But you can bury your anger under grand words and sensible thoughts, little one," Myrddion said encouragingly.

"Julius Caesar didn't bother trying to civilize the northern lands," Targo added as an aside. "And by all accounts he was one excellent soldier. But he wasn't foolish enough to waste his legions on an enemy like the berserker hordes who'd fight until nothing and no one remained."

"So this berserker thing is bad?" Nimue asked.

"When it's set free, it is very, very bad," Myrddion said seriously.

"Poor Artor." Nimue sighed deeply.

FOR ALMOST TWO years, life was tranquil at Cadbury Tor and in the thriving town below. Artor was regularly abroad, seeing to the demands of his kingdom by settling petty tribal squabbles, and crushing the Saxons if they attempted to extend their holdings. Myrddion enjoyed the pleasure of a woman's company, and learned that a rare few, like Artor's Gallia, had the power to be a companion rather than an object of sexual gratification. But with increasing insistence, Myrddion's heart and body craved more than his mind cared to demand of Nimue. If she recognized his burgeoning love, she remained silent, for Myrddion would have been shamed by his attraction to her youth.

But two years is a long time in a dangerous land. One day, a Brigante warrior arrived at Cadbury Tor with a dirty bandage round his head and another, more dangerous wound in his thigh. Both wounds were suppurating with infection, and Myrddion was forced to use fire, hot cauterization, and a sharp knife to remove dying and dead flesh.

The warrior was impatient, eager to demand an audience with the High King, but fever laid him low, so Artor visited the Brigante in

Myrddion's makeshift infirmary. The news he brought turned Artor's face to ice and sent the fortress into organized chaos.

Luka had become separated from his attendants while on a hunt, and had been set upon and killed by brigands. His body was found hacked to pieces, but his weapons were gore-spattered: he had marked his murderers before they nailed the bloody pieces of his body to an ancient oak.

Artor's rage poured forth like a volcano of hot lava, scorching the very air in its passage.

By first light, the High King was abroad with a troop of one hundred men. For love of Luka, Myrddion braved the long and brutal ride to Verterae, deep in the heart of mountainous Brigante country. The warriors rode like madmen, driven on by Artor, whose eyes were ghostly orbs in the deep, exhausted hollows of his face.

At Verterae, one of the warriors beat on the locked gates of the fortress with the pommel of his sword. Pale and shaking servants admitted the High King to the hall where Luka's remains had been taken, and Artor saw for himself the butchered, quartered, and beheaded body of his friend. Artor's rage knew no bounds, his grey eyes burned, and Myrddion remembered Nimue's warnings that Artor's reaction to the death of a loved one could be excoriating rage followed by a cold, blood-freezing hunger for revenge.

Verterae woke to fear, hushed citizenry, whetstones sharpening weapons, and a miasma of dread.

"The Saxons or the Jutes didn't kill my friend, for this isn't their way. They are barbarians, it is true, but this murder was subtle as well as brutal. Luka's murder bears all the marks of an assassination by his own people, who have always treated him like a pig. By debasing his body, they've left their signature on the flesh of my poor friend. They will rue the day they took Luka from me."

The captain of Verterae was shaking with apprehension and his bones turned to jelly under Artor's basilisk glare. The man wished he were a Christian so that he could swear by the Virgin that he had no part in the assassination, but, as a distant relative of King Luka, he was

371

suspect, and he knew it. With rolling eyes and trembling fingers, he cast about desperately for some means of saving himself and his fortress, which Artor had threatened to raze to the ground.

Rhys ap Cernach, for such was his name, admitted that he had heard whispers of dissatisfaction among the ranks of the Brigante aristocrats. King Luka had been the first tribal lord to send cavalrymen to Artor when he was appointed Dux Bellorum by Uther Pendragon, and if gold was needed to pay and feed the High King's forces, Luka would levy his own vassals to pay the Brigante share. Nor did he spare himself, giving gold, sons, and time to the Celtic cause, and the rumblings against his rule had grown louder during his many enforced absences.

While Artor was still at Verterae, he sent Odin, Bedwyr, and a small group of warriors to the tree where Luka had been executed, and, from there, they were ordered to track the killers and hunt them down. Odin was charged with the task of bringing the murderers to Artor—alive.

Beset by more bad news, Rhys came to the High King and his adviser, Myrddion, late on the second day after Odin's departure. His face was ashen with dismay.

"Why the miserable face, Lord Rhys?" Artor grated, for Rhys remained suspect of complicity in Luka's murder until such time as he had positive proof of his innocence. "I'd swear someone had murdered your own mother."

"Better they had!" Rhys muttered under his breath. Artor heard his words and his knuckles whitened.

"What's happened now?" Artor demanded.

"Word has come from Lavatrae of more treasonous murders in the Brigante towns. I'm loath to make you angry, but, in this instance, I'm fortunate that I've been in Verterae with you for the past week."

Artor's brows rose. "Tell me and be done with it! I'll not punish you if you have no part in treachery."

"The king's three sons are dead, my lord. Murdered in their beds. Lord Luka's grandson, who has just become a warrior, has fled to parts unknown, trusting that you will see justice done and punish the murderers. No one knows who is behind these crimes, as common men wielded the knives, but King's Luka's cousin, Simnel, has declared himself to be the new king, and rides to Melandra fortress to take up the reins of governance."

"Does he now?" Artor whispered, and Rhys thanked the Tuatha de Danann that he wasn't in Simnel's shoes.

The room was cold, grey, and damp after days of rain. Artor pushed both hands deep into the folds of his tunic and sat with his wolf cloak around his shoulders to warm his body. In the weak afternoon light beside the shutters, Gruffydd was sharpening Caliburn. His countenance was bland as he feigned concentration on his task.

"Are you loyal to King Luka's legitimate heir, Rhys, or will you support the usurper? I don't really expect an answer, for how can I trust you to speak the truth? Instead, I ask you to place your warriors under my command and ride with me to Melandra to see that justice is done." Artor's voice was clipped, but not unkind. And, like any sensible man, Rhys thought hard as he considered his options.

Finally, he answered his liege lord.

"I will hand over the entire resources of Verterae Fortress to you, my lord, for the Brigante tribe needs security. We cannot survive a war with all the tribes that will gather under your banner, Your Majesty. But most important, this cousin of mine, Simnel, has always been a sly and dangerous man, and no Brigante will be safe under his rule, including me. Better a civil war than obedience to a despot who leads the whole tribe to disaster."

The next day, before a pallid dawn, Artor rode out and a force of 250 armed men rode behind him. A day later, at Melandra, the cavalry camped, conspicuously, on a hill beside the fortress. The Roman structures of Melandra had never been subject to serious threat from enemies, so Luka had retained the buildings as an administrative center. The Brigante lands had many other, easily defended fortresses, and Luka's father had cherished Melandra for its deep forests and its fair views of the lowlands. Luka had also loved its vistas, so Artor felt a grim satisfaction in waiting for Odin's return in the dim, green trees and the wide sun-drenched glades of Luka's favorite town.

Odin and Bedwyr arrived five days after Artor had set his battle tent before the Melandra fortress. Two prisoners, their wrists and ankles chained together, were securely tied over their horses and their eyes were blackened and terrified from the ordeal they had undergone. One of the men sported a nasty sword cut across his ribs.

"String them up to the nearest oak so all the assassins will know my intentions," Artor ordered, his eyes aglitter with something that was colder than frozen iron. "I'll speak to the murderers shortly."

Artor drank clean water and ate some nuts, fruit, and stale bread with slow deliberation. Because he was expected to wait on Artor's pleasure, Rhys served the spartan meal with his own hands in Artor's leather tent. Behind the Brigante, Gruffydd cradled Caliburn and watched Rhys with unblinking attention. Rhys's fingers trembled when he filled Artor's cup with water, but he was past embarrassment in the presence of such dangerous men.

"It's time to question Luka's murderers now," Artor decided softly, and rose to his feet.

The oak tree selected by Artor to enforce his punishment grew on the very edge of the forest in a place where the prisoners could be clearly seen with the naked eye from the hall in Melandra. The tree was huge; a forest giant from the old days, and Artor marveled that it remained standing, for the pragmatic Romans regularly destroyed the sacred trees used by the Britons in their religious ceremonies. Always practical and knowledgeable, Myrddion explained that the Roman legate of the garrison had used this same oak to execute those Celts who resisted their new masters, or to torture any unfortunate Druids who were captured alive.

Artor would have shuddered, but he was steeling himself to be stern, implacable, and just. The High King was under no misapprehensions: he would order cruel torture and execution in order to extract details of the plot that killed his friend, and he would ensure that even the most obdurate Brigante warrior could not ignore his resolve.

A flag of truce was planted before the oak and its grim, weeping fruit. Myrddion himself approached Melandra and invited all citizens, servants, warriors, and aristocrats who loved justice to come forth and witness the High King's justice.

They came, strong warriors, old men, women, lordlings in their gold and finery, squabbling children, and even house slaves, just as Artor had predicted.

"Kill us!" the two ragged mercenaries begged the crowd from the tree. "We are Brigante; we are loyal servants of the people while the bastard Artor is an ill-begotten, bloody despot who keeps the people poor. He will torture us for our patriotism. For love of the goddess of war, kill us now and be merciful!"

Some of the crowd rumbled in agreement, but most of the warriors present had either ridden with Llanwith's cavalry or had stood at the shield wall at Mori Saxonicus. They knew, beyond any doubt, that every piece of gold given by the tribes had paid for weapons, food for the bellies of the warriors, and as reparation to the widows of the dead. Brows furrowed and many men would have walked away if Artor had not ordered them to stay.

"Your king, Luka, was my mentor and my friend. The Brigante are honored by the legends of the three travelers, of whom even the smallest children have heard. For forty years, as prince and king, Luka slew Saxons in bloody campaigns across our lands, and kept you safe in your fine homes. How did he warrant what was done to him? Look on your king that was, and bear witness to the type of death he was given after forty years of service to the Brigante tribe and the Celtic peoples."

Myrddion had labored to reassemble the rotting corpse of his old friend and had laid him under a length of fine cloth. The smell of death was a sickly prelude to the obscenity that Artor revealed to the gaze of the crowd, nail holes and all.

"People of Melandra, I ask you to walk past your erstwhile king, and remember his father, remember his sons; remember your pride in Brigante courage, in the salvation of the realm, and then look at what King Luka's sacrifices have earned him. Look!"

Under his stare, most of the citizens that were present filed past the bier, some out of curiosity but most out of fear. Several warriors laid an earring, a cloak pin, a ring, or some other treasured possession on the livid skin of the mutilated body, and women laid flowers, but many citizens looked at the body and seemed utterly unmoved. Simnel was conspicuous by his absence and remained inside Melandra, under the protective cloak of fifty loyal warriors.

Once the citizens had viewed Luka's corpse, Artor began his interrogation of the assassins.

"Who paid you? How much were you given, and what were your orders?" Artor demanded of the two men as they hung by their wrists with their feet barely touching the ground. Unsupported as they were, the stress on their chest muscles was agonizing.

But twisted faces, panted breathing, and labored curses were the only replies that the two Brigante warriors gave to Artor's questions.

"Odin! Prepare to crucify them! And, while you do so, you will put out their eyes, for they have no right to look upon the sun and this fair land that they have betrayed. Remember King Luka and the laughter he gave us so generously."

Odin began his preparations, but the assassins still refused to speak. Throughout that long and blood-soaked day, ever-increasing measures of pain were inflicted upon the bodies of the miscreants, and, although many citizens were sickened and turned away, still more watched the atrocities committed with ghoulish appreciation.

The felons were hung on different sides of the great trunk where they were unable to see each other or to take comfort from shared pain. Nails were driven through their wrists and anklebones. Their fingers were removed, as were their toes, their ears, and their noses. Only when hot spearheads were applied to the bleeding bodies did the men finally break, and confess those details of the plot of which they were aware.

Afterwards, Artor showed the population that he could also be a merciful king.

"Honor should go to these warriors, dogs as they are! They've proved their courage and their loyalty to their cowardly master, Simnel, who has not lifted one finger to save them, or even fire off an arrow shot that would kill them and release them from their pain. They earned the right to die as warriors, for all that I've been forced to lose a friend I loved. Release them, Odin!"

The Jutlander beheaded them at once.

The crowd sighed.

"People of Melandra, do I leave you to the rule of Simnel and his fellow conspirators, rather than Luka's grandson, who has been spared with the help of his loyal servants? Tell me what you want. I'd be loath to cut Brigante lands from the union of kings and leave you to fight alone next summer when the Jutes and Angles pour out of Eburacum, Cataractonium, and Petuaria, but you may be sure that I will leave you to your fate if you wish to follow the usurper. I'll sign no treaties with a man who murdered my friend."

The crowd stirred as if a sudden gust of wind had caught them unawares. Faces paled, for no sensible man could be ignorant of what breaking the union would mean. Those warriors who had fought at Eburacum remembered the threat of Katigern Oakheart and decided Simnel's fate, as Artor had known they would.

That night, Brigante hands delivered the usurper and his coconspirators to Artor. Those men who confessed to their part in the plot were granted a speedy, painless execution, and their wives and children were permitted to keep their land and property so that the children did not suffer for the sins of the fathers.

But Simnel received justice in full measure.

Artor had to fight against his own rage day and night. Of the murderers involved in the assassination, Luka's cousin was the least fortunate in his fate. Simnel was hung on the door of the great hall of Melandra with the same nails that had impaled Luka thrust through his quivering and still-living flesh. He was then left on the door to die.

The ordinary folk were completely overawed by Artor, who came each morning to speak to the dying man. The mouth of Luka's cousin was parched with thirst, and his wounds were festering and black with flies. As he suffered, the High King took his ease and recounted to the traitor his memories of Luka. Although Simnel screamed, gibbered, and begged, he was forced to live until his body could no longer endure.

For subtle cruelty, Artor could almost be Uther Pendragon's superior.

When the unfortunate man died, his body was cut down and left for the dogs on the hall's midden heap. Then, with Luka's grandson firmly installed upon his father's throne, Artor and his warriors disappeared like the cold wind of winter that had brought them to Luka's lands.

But they left few friends in their wake.

In the months that followed, the use of Luka's name was forbidden within Artor's hearing, but Myrddion and Targo would laugh as they recalled Luka's irrepressible spirit, his bright irony, and his gift with a blade. They were comforted by their memories, even as they remembered his sardonic, irreverent joy. But Artor was bereft. Targo and Myrddion exchanged worried glances, but neither man was prepared to voice the sudden reality of what had been vague fears for the king's well-being only a few months previously.

To the entire Celtic population, the message from Artor was unmistakable. To harm any person under the protection of the High King would bring inevitable retribution and merciless justice would prevail.

"Our people are fortunate that Artor's loyalty extends across the whole of our nation, for the tribes would have disintegrated years ago without the enforcement of his commands," Myrddion said to Targo with great earnestness.

Targo's eyes were hooded, and his old man's mouth was pinched with regret.

"When you make a weapon, friend Myrddion, it should serve your will," he said softly. "When you make a man, he should serve his own will. We were arrogant, my brother, for Artorex wasn't meant to be any man's weapon."

Myrddion winced. "He was all we had. And I would use him again if the circumstances were the same."

"Would you?" Targo asked earnestly. "Truly?"

"Probably. Just as I believe you would batter Artor into unconsciousness a thousand times to prevent him from sharing Gallia's fate at the Villa Poppinidii. Even now, you'd do the same to save him if you had the muscle for it."

"Aye," Targo whispered. "Nothing really changes where the heart is concerned."

Or the mind, Myrddion thought dismally.

But changes in the fortunes of a nation, coupled with extremes in human ambitions, can bring years of bad luck that seem to have no ending, or so it appears to those suffering mortals who experience these travails.

Artor's trials were just beginning.

Chapter XVI

CONTAGION

Later, no one could, or would, say who brought the contagion to the population of Cadbury. Traders were considered the most likely source of transmission of the disease, for their travels took them to a variety of locations, both clean and unclean, throughout the land. These men came to Artor's western fortress because it had become a center for the exchange of luxury goods, grain, mead, honey, and the many varieties of pasture meats that were smoked and dried against the long sea voyages to the continent, and even to glittering Constantinople.

The disease found its way through every nook and cranny in stone, wood, and thatch. It struck indiscriminately and without pity. When most of Gallia's family had died of plague in Aquae Sulis so many years before, money and power were no protection against the steady and inexorable march of an illness that led to death or infirmity.

A fever was the first symptom suffered. In the early stages, it did not seem severe, but it proved to be debilitating. Then, within a few days, the patients found that their flesh was covered with sores, particularly under the arms and in the folds of the body. Then came delirium, and contagions of the lung, followed by death.

Even Myrddion, with all his learning, was powerless to halt this strange, alien disease that sapped the strength, and then the will, to survive.

Remembering Ector's quarantine of the Villa Poppinidii, Artor sealed off the tor completely from the outside world.

Soldiers manned a series of barricades that prevented travelers, petitioners, and pilgrims from climbing the hill leading to the palace on Cadbury Tor. The inhabitants of the tor were told that, if they journeyed outside of the quarantined area, they would not be readmitted.

In Cadbury town, the houses of those afflicted were locked up or, on some dire occasions, burned to the ground. The High King knew that new houses could be built, but the terminally ill had no magical route to return to the land of the living.

Insensitive as always, Wenhaver complained pointedly and publicly about the stink of funeral pyres and burning homes. She bewailed the boredom of her isolated life until Artor fled from her as if she was the source of the contagion. Then she began to regale anyone who cared to listen with tales of her husband's abandonment.

Perhaps if Wenhaver had become pregnant, her selfish, childish ways would have passed as an aberration of her youth. But fate had rendered her sterile, a state in which she was secretly pleased, for she feared to lose her trim waist and soft round breasts in the birthing of new life. She remained obstinately uninterested when Artor spoke of the need for progeny, never considering for one moment that the High King could still dispose of her if she failed to provide an heir to the throne of the Britons. Her belief in her father's influence over the High King remained irrationally strong. Inevitably, the situation created an argument of epic proportions between husband and wife in the first weeks of Cadbury's baptism of fire with disease.

Wenhaver spoiled a relatively pleasant evening by complaining of her boredom after Artor had rolled away from her willing flesh and was considering whether or not to sleep in her oversoft bed.

"There is absolutely nothing to do, Artor. I can't go riding, and one can only sew a certain number of samplers before tedium sets in.

You won't permit strangers to visit us, and I can't even call for my robe maker."

Artor considered her flowerlike face with hooded, untrusting eyes.

"Would you prefer to catch a disease where you'd swell with festering sores, vomit up green slime, and then choke to death?" He lifted one of her hands and examined its pink perfection. "If not, I'd suggest you continue to weave or spin. Of course, you may well develop callouses on your beautiful hands with unaccustomed work."

"Don't be horrid, Artor," Wenhaver snapped. "I just don't like sitting here doing nothing day after dreary day, and I don't want to slave like a peasant."

"Since you haven't borne sons for me, then perhaps you could serve some usefulness by collecting worn or unused cloth or rags for those townsfolk who are dying. If you can't become a mother, then perhaps you could become a queen."

Artor's comments took Wenhaver's breath away, as well they might. Secretly, although she wanted no children to thicken her narrow waist or cover her clean flanks with stretch marks, the inability to bear a child was a wrench. She was used to being feted for her appearance, her style, and her feminine perfection, and she was mortified that she had remained childless.

"Don't blame me, Artor," she snapped and bit hard on her thumbnail until it tore.

"There are young men at Cadbury who have been sired by me, and several of my daughters are approaching marriageable age. I would seem to be potent. But before you accuse me of shaming you, I have refrained from bedding any willing women since I made my wedding vows."

Artor's bastards were the last straw for Wenhaver. She knew of Artor's sexual prowess, of course, as did every person on Cadbury Tor, but to boast of his infidelity? She threw her silver brush at him, conveniently forgetting that an unmarried king may sow his seed wherever he chooses.

"I hate you," she hissed, and Artor shrugged as he climbed out of her bed.

"I take it you are choosing celibacy rather than further physical congress with me. After all, my efforts seem to bear little fruit in your eager body."

Naturally, Wenhaver had meant no such thing. The pleasures of the bed were a great solace that bound two otherwise incompatible people together. And now her husband was offering an even greater insult than sneers at her childlessness. He was suggesting that he had only bedded her to get her with child in the first place.

How could she answer him, even if she had been able to control her rage? Wenhaver could never beg him to share her bed without admitting that she desired him. Worse still, how could she confess her mortification that she was unable to carry the son that Artor craved? She felt like a royal joke.

Wenhaver could have wept with misery.

Artor was ashamed of his cruel response to her childless condition. The queen was still under twenty, and he understood her days had been wearisome in recent times. After chiding himself for the whole morning, he approached Wenhaver's rooms to apologize.

What he found in her apartment made his blood boil.

Wenhaver had joined her ladies elsewhere in the king's house, but, as Artor turned to leave the disordered apartment, a rustle of clothing halted him in his tracks. In the belief that a thief had somehow penetrated the security of the tor, Artor drew his knife. Then Myrnia, who was curled into as small a ball as possible on the floor, screamed aloud when she saw his shadow.

"What are you doing on the floor, Myrnia? Heavens, child! I could have stabbed you by accident." Then Artor's eyes flared with shock. "Who has done this thing, Myrnia? I order you to tell me!"

Myrnia tried to cry, but one eye was damaged, torn and bleeding sluggishly. The lid was almost ripped away, while her nose was raggedly sliced on the same side, and her nostril was torn in the outer corner. Her mouth had received a similar wound.

Even with the ministrations of a skilled healer, Artor knew that the girl was scarred for life.

"Who did this, Myrnia? I swear that they will be punished."

Her head turned carefully, for Myrnia was in obvious pain.

"No, my lord, even you cannot save me." Her one good eye was full of tears, and her wounds were slowly oozing blood.

"The queen did this terrible thing to you, didn't she? Answer!"

Artor's mouth twisted with shame, for he knew that he must share some of Wenhaver's guilt, for he had provoked his wife to anger.

"What did she use to cause these wounds?"

Myrnia opened her hand and a simple, elegant object lay on her palm, marked obscenely with a smear of the servant girl's blood at the tip. A small, beautifully carved bone handle held a very thin but sturdy length of silver as long as Myrnia's palm. At its very tip was a simple, blunt hook. Myrnia had been attacked with a tool used for hooking and twisting strands of wool.

Artor winced, took the nasty little object from Myrnia's unresisting hand, and lifted her into his arms. She was absurdly light and trembling with shock. Protectively, the king carried her through the palace to Myrddion's apartments.

Nimue fussed over the terrified, suffering girl, who flinched away from her sympathetic hands. Myrddion took charge, his face unreadable.

"Fetch the poppy juice, Nimue, in honey for sweetness, and then find my finest needles and narrowest thread." As Nimue ran to obey him, he laid Myrnia on a simple pallet, held her hands with both of his warm palms, and looked earnestly into her eyes.

"I will make you feel so much better very, very soon, Myrnia. I'll not promise that you won't be scarred, because you will be, but I'll try to keep that beautiful face as fair as I can. Unfortunately, you will probably lose the sight in your left eye."

Nimue arrived with the poppy juice mixed into a golden paste with honey just as Myrnia screamed, shook her head, and began to shake with pain and terror. Gently, master and apprentice coaxed her to swallow the potion, which began to work almost immediately. Her eyelids became heavy, but she struggled to hold up her head, fighting against the drug, and then mercifully slipped into unconsciousness.

"Quickly, Nimue, the softest cloths you can find, clean water, and the juice of lemons."

"Did you have to tell her the whole truth?" Artor asked tetchily, although his heart wasn't in any display of ill temper.

"She deserves my honesty. If infection sets in, she could be blinded in both eyes. This sometimes happens when one eye is damaged. I can't repair an eye where the pupil has been torn. No one could do it, not even the sons of Isaac or Ishmael, and they are the best in the world. I don't even understand how the eye truly works, so I shall simply do the best I can. I'll wash the wounds with clean water, again and again, until I'm sure that they are clean. Afterwards, I'll apply the lemon juice to all but the eye itself. I've noticed that lime and lemon juice can clean metal, and I find that they clean wounds as well, where the use of apricot brandy would have a harsh effect on the flesh. Then I'll try to stitch up any tears in the flesh as best I can. Perhaps I'll ask Nimue to sew the most difficult parts—her eyes are better than mine. Then, we wait. And we wait." Myrddion looked at his king. "What created this hellish mess?"

Mutely, Artor showed Myrddion the innocent little tool.

"A simple object to cause such devastation. What did poor Myrnia do to upset Wenhaver?"

Artor winced. "Is the guilty party so obvious then?"

"Who would deliberately strike Wenhaver's personal maidservant other than the mistress herself? Who else would dare? More to the point, Artor, what are you going to do about this atrocity?"

With Nimue close by his side, Myrddion began to clean the wounds with water, forcing the ragged edges of the skin open so that the torn flesh could be thoroughly cleansed. Once the healer was satisfied that the deep scores were free of dried blood, rust, or any other pollutants, he took from Nimue a fine needle attached to a thin strand of flaxen thread. Carefully, and with such intense concentration that Artor scarcely dared to breathe, Myrddion drew the edges of the wounds together.

When he reached the thin, delicate skin of the eyelid, master and apprentice exchanged places, for Nimue's eyes were young and acute. With stitches so tiny that the High King marveled that Nimue could see what she was doing, she stitched the inside and the outside of the lid, right into the inner edge so that Myrnia would be able to blink and weep easily in the long years of life that still lay in front of her.

When he was sure that Myrnia was as safe as her wounds allowed, Artor returned to Wenhaver's apartments, where he found his wife raging and sulking by turn as she tried to find her favorite peplum.

"Where is that lazy bitch, Myrnia? This is what comes of treating her so well—she avoids her duties," Wenhaver grumbled.

Artor looked at her, dumbstruck, for the queen really had no idea what she had done.

"Why are you looking at me like that? Where's Myrnia? I suppose she's been telling you tales about me."

Artor felt his lips curl.

He held out the small tool in his right hand, and Wenhaver took it carefully, her eyes never leaving her husband's rigid face.

"I should use this pretty little thing on you, woman, as you used it on Myrnia. I should blind you in one eye, tear off your eyelid, rip open your cheek, and slash your lips—but you wouldn't understand, would you?"

"There's nothing wrong with Myrnia," Wenhaver mumbled defensively, although her eyes were fearful. "She's just pretending. Anyway, it's not my fault. You put me in a temper, and she tore my best shawl, and . . . and . . ."

"The world will look at you, and then at poor, scarred Myrnia, and what will they think of you?"

"It's your fault! You're always cruel to me . . ." Wenhaver wept, great wrenching sobs, because in truth she was rather frightened by what she had done to her maidservant.

"I'll fix this matter, woman, but you will stay out of my sight for a while until such time as I forget the wounds I saw on Myrnia's ruined face. I'll send her home with a bride price of red gold, so a husband will overlook her physical deformities. Perhaps, one day, she'll become a happy woman and mother. In which case, her lot in life will be far better than yours."

Wenhaver gave a brittle, ugly little laugh.

"In that case, she should be grateful that I lost my temper. She'd never win a respectable husband otherwise."

Artor's self-control broke down completely.

"You're such a cruel, stupid woman, Wenhaver, that I rue the day I wed you, and, if I could, I'd undo the pact tomorrow. You are sickening, to suggest that poor Myrnia should be grateful that you've blinded her. I should parade the two of you through Cadbury Town so the world can see what manner of woman you are, but such justice would humiliate Myrnia, and hold her up to public pity and, possibly, ridicule. I'll not shame or upset her any further, especially when plague knocks at our doors."

Wenhaver backed away from her husband, for she could see his fingers curling as if they were firmly gripped on her throat. He looked at her with a loathing so palpable that she felt physically sick.

Then, kicking over furniture as he went, Artor stormed out of the queen's apartments.

For many months, she saw Artor only briefly, and then only when their roles demanded it. On one occasion, she saw him kissing a serving woman, and, in response to her gasp of shock, his eyes snapped open and he simply stared uncaringly at her.

Myrnia's wounds didn't fester, for she was young, strong, and used to obedience, so Myrddion was able to keep a close watch on her treatment and medication. Mindful of his promise, the High King commissioned an eye patch of thin, embossed gold, padded with soft wool for comfort, that tied around her head with a golden cord. On the patch, Artor's dragon symbol spat fire, so all who saw Myrnia and thought to laugh at her scars would see his mark upon her face and be warned of the king's anger.

Eventually, after the plague had passed and her wounds were completely healed, the High King sent her back to her village as a woman of substance. She was accompanied by a manservant and her own maid, and possessed a pair of fine grey horses, a leather purse filled with gold, and a wagon containing furniture, clothing, and woven lengths of cloth. In time, the young woman became the wife of a tribal chieftain's young son, who treated her with great respect for the dowry that she brought to the marriage and the protection of the High King that came with her.

Wenhaver resented every coin that was spent on her maidservant, but she was fearful of making any complaint lest Artor carry out his threat to expose her cruelties. She was aware that most of the citizens of Cadbury would believe him.

By the time the epidemic reached its height, Wenhaver was bored and had become eager for new stimulation. She longed to hurt her husband to his arrogant core.

Although Myrnia was still recovering from her wounds in the fortress, Wenhaver's shame over the ugly injuries had become just an inconvenient twinge in her memory. She blamed Artor for the whole tragedy, for Wenhaver was used to apportioning blame on to anyone but herself. To add to Wenhaver's woes, she spent a great deal of time embroidering and sewing like any good wife, but her workmanship was abysmal.

Her view of her own worth rested largely on her ability to attract the admiration of men. Artor had rejected her over the Myrnia affair, but Cadbury Tor was full of virile young men.

Filled with vanity and devilry, the queen began to actively search for a diversion.

She deliberately began to wander from the clear rules of behavior required by her noble position in life. She wantonly lowered her lashes and blushed prettily whenever men were near her, regardless of their station in society or their birth. Myrddion and Nimue watched in amazement as her flirtations and indiscretions increased, and Myrddion became deathly afraid. Nimue, little barbarian that she still was, watched the queen's vulgarities with amusement.

"She's been a figure of fun for years, master, for she's always puffed up in those ridiculously tight gowns that she wears. Wenhaver truly believes she's the only woman alive who has breasts."

"But can you imagine what Artor will do if he becomes aware of her involvement with another man?" Myrddion murmured.

"He'll be forced to kill her, I hope. And then life at Cadbury will be delightful once again."

"Will it really?" Myrddion asked. "Unfortunately, I don't believe Leodegran and his son would take kindly to violent recrimination against a member of their family. And, although they are supposed to be our allies, King Lot and his faction would immediately tell the world that the soul of Uther Pendragon had returned to the west. I'm afraid that this problem requires a great deal of thought."

"All I ever seem to hear is the name of Uther Pendragon! The man has been dead for longer than I've been alive, but every person I know still whispers his name in terrified undertones as if he were still alive and breathing. Just how bad could he have been if he continues to instill such terror?" Nimue was unused to major disagreements with Myrddion, but she had the confidence and certainty of opinion that is the province of the young.

"Uther was so terrible that his son still bears the taint of his name," Myrddion replied. "So don't wish that disaster upon us."

But the indiscretions of the queen were a serious matter for the crown, the court, and the realm. Cautiously, and unwillingly, Myrddion drew Artor off to one side in an attempt to have a private discussion on the matter.

"I have a matter of some sensitivity to discuss with you, my lord," he whispered. "I am concerned that the queen has been so unwise as to—"

"Be silent on the subject, old friend, for I'm afraid I cannot hear you." Artor's lips were pressed firmly together, and his eyes were very cold.

"But my lord, I am obliged to tell you that—"

"There are some things that a king must know," Artor interrupted, "and others that are far too dangerous to be spoken aloud."

"Even by me?" Myrddion asked sadly.

Artor roughly embraced his friend, and then whispered in his ear. "Even by you, old friend. But have no fears, for the queen will soon become more circumspect. I will see to it."

What else could Myrddion do or say? Like most souls on Cadbury Tor, he was forced to wait and to watch.

And then, two tragedies struck simultaneously.

Gawayne had come to visit Cadbury at the beginning of summer, and Queen Wenhaver was immediately entranced by his red-haired beauty and supple strength. Unlike his brothers, Gawayne had resisted early marriage, having a passion for hunting, battle, and available women, preferably married, to circumvent any encumbrances. Once the tor was sealed off from the outside world, time lay heavily on Gawayne's hands, for he could only groom his horse so often and drink with his friends on so many nights.

Cadbury town was quiet during the day and completely silent at night, when few lights burned and the streets were deserted. Artor had ordered that markets and all places where groups of citizens congregated must be closed to slow the spread of the disease. The citizens shut themselves within their homes and relied on warrior volunteers to deliver food. Tedium prompted Gawayne to join their number. Provisioning the townsfolk, guarding all exits and entrances to and from Cadbury town, and burning houses where whole families had perished provided distraction for a time, but it soon palled through the daily grind of predictability.

The town was a place of ghosts, both living and dead. The trees in the orchards still bore fruit, the animals still dotted the fields and raised their heads when a stranger passed, and grain still grew in the fields, although, mostly, it was untended. Soft breezes stirred the verdant vegetable patches, but no smoke rose from the conical roofs of the farms. The only sound to break the preternatural silence was the pained lowing of cattle with full udders whose owners had died, leaving them unmilked. Eventually, the crows came as if they smelled the path of death, and they, too, called hollowly over the still villages.

Thick black smoke obscured both the sun and the moonlight on wasteland on the edges of the township. Here, the dead were incinerated by warriors—their hands protected by gauntlets; their mouths and noses and all exposed areas of flesh covered by cloth. No matter how hot the day became, the fires continued to burn, and the smell of incinerating human flesh turned the air fetid and vile.

One afternoon, Gawayne joined a troop of soldiers who had volunteered for duties outside the fortress. He thought to show his courage once more by facing this invisible enemy that struck its victims at random. But he quickly found that he did not have the stomach for the foul labor of burning swollen, corrupted bodies in the hot sun. He returned to Cadbury Tor at midnight, by simply climbing over the ramparts.

When Artor discovered that Gawayne had broken his strict rules, the High King was incensed, especially when the prince strolled into the hall, frightening several servants and setting the hounds to baying.

"But I'm perfectly healthy," Gawayne pleaded his case. "I've never felt better, my lord. I thought you would be eager for word of how the town goes, and I'd never have risked the fortress if I considered for one moment that I might be ill."

In exasperation, Artor looked at Gawayne's freckled and handsome face and knew that he could berate Gawayne for hours, but the prince would never really understand what he had risked. Only one of the sons of Lot had inherited their father's intelligent cunning, and Gaheris was long dead. The others were very much like their idle, pleasure-loving mother, Morgause. But then, none of them had inherited Morgan's capacity for hatred either. Gawayne was the hero of a hundred forays against the Saxons, and was known to be a useful man in difficult straits, as long as someone told him what to do.

"At least stay away from the very young and the very old; this contagion sometimes clings to the healthy so it can creep into corners to trap the weak. I'd appreciate your showing some consideration for other dwellers in this fortress."

"Of course, my lord. I will have all my clothing burned and will cleanse myself thoroughly. The Jew physician in the town has told me that the number of new illnesses has declined in Cadbury. He believes that the contagion is passing." Gawayne grinned at his king irrepressibly. Artor tried to quell his irritation; Gawayne, at forty, was still an impressionable, irresponsible youngster, and would never be other than what stood before him, a smiling warrior with a genuinely equable nature.

"If I punished you for disobeying my orders, it would be like expecting a rabbit not to breed, or a hawk not to hunt birds. But shite, Gawayne, we don't need the sickness inside this fortress. What if the queen becomes ill? Or Myrddion? Or me?"

"I hadn't thought of that," Gawayne looked blankly at his king. "But now I can see what you mean."

Artor could picture the slow, patient machinery in Gawayne's head as it worked on the answers to the problem.

"So, you will do as you're told in future?" Artor asked, but his mouth began to quiver in the beginnings of a smile. Gawayne had that rare capacity that could bring humor to any situation, even when he had no intention of complying with instructions from any authority.

Ironically, when Targo suddenly became ill, he didn't catch the contagion from Gawayne, who never visited the old warrior. It was Artor himself who eventually brought death to the man he loved most of all those souls who dwelt upon the earth. Perhaps the illness had nestled in Artor's plaited hair, or had curled, serpentlike, into the folds of his cloak. Or perhaps the sickness had begun as a chill from sitting up too late with the High King.

One day, Targo was his usual sharp-witted self. The next, after a late-night visit from his king, he began to sicken.

Perce sealed the doors of Targo's rooms immediately, for the ill-

393

ness must not be allowed to spread further. Word had no sooner been sent to Artor than Nimue was pounding at the door, a leather satchel over one shoulder and a mulish look in her eyes.

"Who is it?" Perce called through the door.

"It's Nimue! Let me in right now, Perce, or I can promise you that there will be trouble."

"You cannot enter, Nimue. Targo has told me what to do for him, so I think we'll both survive this illness."

Nimue kicked and pounded even harder on the door.

"Listen, you great oaf! Only by the greatest persuasion have I prevented Lord Myrddion from insisting on caring for Targo himself. I will not have my master threatened, so I've come instead. You will open the door this minute, or I swear by Jesus, or Odin, or any other god that ever was, that it will be broken off its hinges."

These last words were shouted, and Artor, who rounded the corridor at a run, saw a red-faced Nimue perfectly prepared to batter at the door with a stool.

The young woman's blazing face turned at the sound of Artor's footsteps. She registered his anguished mouth, his desperate eyes, and hunched shoulders, and she felt a stir of fear for her king. Nothing could have calmed her temper faster.

Gracefully, she bowed low to him.

"My lord, I am trying to convince Perce to open the door a crack so that I can enter. I have preparations made by my master's own hands that might save Targo's life, but"—Nimue kicked the door again—"Perce won't let me in. They are both being incredibly noble."

Artor sighed, and his torment was so clear on his usually controlled face that Nimue felt her hand begin to rise in a gesture of comfort.

"Perce, this is Artor, your king, at the door. Will you please allow Nimue to enter."

The sound of a muffled discussion could be partially heard within the apartment.

"Targo forbids me to risk her, my lord," Perce replied, his voice not quite steady. "He says he will not be responsible for her death."

"I am the one who is responsible," Artor replied. "As his only visitor, I am the one who brought this evil illness to Targo. But what has been done is done, and cannot be changed. So open the door, Perce, and give Targo a chance at life."

"Targo says that you are not to enter, my lord," Perce insisted. "He says he'd rather die alone than risk your life."

Nimue could see Artor's face contort, and she believed he was about to help her to batter the door down, but with a great effort of will he controlled his face and his shaking hands.

"Tell Targo that I will bargain with him. I'll not enter the room, regardless of what might prevail, as long as Nimue is permitted to care for him during his illness. I will send whatever food and drink you need and have it placed outside the door. I will respect his wishes in all things, provided he allows Nimue to enter."

Artor could hear Targo's reply without straining his ears.

"Ah, shite! The boy has always had ways of getting what he wants. Let her in, Perce. I don't think even Hades is ready for a difficult Nimue."

The door opened a crack, and Nimue slithered in lithely before Perce could change his mind. Artor heard the long wooden bar rammed home, and knew the oak door would not reopen until the contagion was gone, or all those souls within the room were dead.

Through eyes filming with tears, Artor saw Myrddion running towards him. The scholar's hair was wild, and his robe was only partly fastened, revealing a smooth, white torso.

"Nimue? Nimue?" he yelled at the door. "That lying little bitch!"

"She lied?" Artor asked simply.

"Of course she lied! I asked her to pack my satchel with the herbs and salves I needed while I dressed. When I came out of my room, she was gone. And my satchel left with her."

Artor could hardly tell if Myrddion was violently angry, distressed, or terrified. In fact, all three emotions chased themselves across the healer's face.

"I'll kill her for this! She is the most disobedient, fractious, troublesome . . ." Myrddion ran out of appropriate adjectives.

"How about courageous?" Artor added. "Let her remain, my friend, while you go to Gawayne and order him to stay in the stables in quarantine. If I see him, I may kill him out of hand. I, too, will remain alone until we know if the fortress has been breached by this illness."

"You're not at fault, Artor. Targo's an old man, and his health has hung in the balance for years. Don't crucify yourself with guilt, because it's still possible that Targo may not even have the contagion."

"I should have quarantined Gawayne immediately." His voice began to break in his grief for his friend. "I visited Targo, so the contagion must have come from me. If Targo has the fever, then I am at fault."

Myrddion gripped his master's arm. Artor was surprised at the sinuous strength in his fingers.

"Don't do anything stupid, Artor. Gawayne is a fool, but the west should not fail over an idiot who knows no better. Seal off all that you can of the tor, and call me if anyone else sickens."

In the capricious ways of destiny, Targo was the only person in the fortress to become ill. While Artor waited for news of his sword master, his face was ashen with anger and fear, so the court kept out of his way, as if he carried the taint of death in his wake.

Wisely, Gawayne settled into the stables of the fortress with his horse. He remained there, snug in the straw, until the king's mercurial temper had improved. Even Gawayne understood that if Targo died of the contagion, there would be no safe refuge for him anywhere in Artor's kingdom.

Chapter XVII

A SUMMER OF MADNESS

Nimue took careful stock of Targo's room with its open fireplace, shuttered windows, and a narrow, pallet bed. The room was small but well appointed, and the fire provided a source of hot water that would be essential if Targo was to have any chance of survival. In a pool of diffused light, a pile of furs and homespun wool covered the simple pallet and the shrunken form that lay beneath it. Nimue squared her shoulders and prepared to do battle with old age, infirmity, and a killing disease.

Kneeling by the pile of furs, Nimue drew back the cocoon that Targo had formed about his face. His bright, raisin-brown eyes were as alive as ever, but his face was sunken, and she could see the skull beneath the paper-thin skin. The sheen of sweat beaded the old man's forehead.

"Come, Targo, tell Nimue where your pains lie?" she ordered the old man with the brisk tones of a mother.

Targo ignored her, focused as he was on Artor's conversation with Myrddion on the other side of the heavy door.

"They mustn't come in," he wheezed, and Nimue could hear the thick phlegm that filled his lungs as it gurgled under the effort of his labored speech. The old man called out his instructions once again, and the effort seemed to further weaken him.

Purposely, Nimue left Targo and strode to the locked door.

"Please go away, master. My lord Targo is tiring himself by worrying about your safety. He is my patient now, so you must trust me to do everything that can be done."

"How old is she, this apprentice of yours, Myrddion? Sixteen?" Artor asked.

"She's seventeen, lord," Myrddion muttered ruefully. "And she really is hoping for some form of a miracle. It's a futile hope, but she is uncontrollable."

"Then perhaps you should get rid of her," Artor snapped.

"I can't, so please don't demand it of me. I know that I should, my lord, but whenever I try to find her a suitable husband, I find myself procrastinating."

Myrddion sounded so miserable that Artor eyed his old adviser with sudden interest. Myrddion had colored across his cheekbones.

"Well, well. The great Myrddion has been hooked at last."

Myrddion's face twisted with so powerful a mixture of embarrassment and shame that Artor felt his heart go out to the man.

"I'm over sixty years of age, and I've managed to defy time up to the present, but I can't live forever. And Nimue is little more than a babe. My love is obscene and unworthy, and it will never be reciprocated by so fair a girl. It's useless to deny that I love her, if for no other reason than I admire her agile mind and her indomitable manner. I would be able to show my feelings if she were older, but my Nimue is a child in all things, and so I attempt to remain her master."

Myrddion paced across the wooden corridor, and his mind was filled with the smells and images of the women he had loved. They came to him now, as if his hated fits had returned to him and conjured them up from death, so he could almost hear the sweet susurration of their skirts on the adzed floors. First came Olwen, his grandmother and more than a mother, followed by a girl with scarlet hair and freckles whose name he had forgotten. Myrddion shook his head with shame, for this sweet and giving woman had taught him the mysteries of sex with generous grace and deserved to possess a name in the shadows of the Otherworld. Then his companions of the road appeared before him—Brangaine, Bridie, and Rhedyn—women who had loved him with pure, sexless devotion, sufficient to cause them to leave their homes and follow him across the world. They had slaved for him, protected him, and cosseted him to the detriment of their own bodies and souls.

Flavia tripped through a wall and into the corridor to stare around her with imperious, sneering eyes. Myrddion was sure that his first great love had been dead for years, perishing before her time from her own excesses, but his memory conjured her up without effort as she had been in her glorious youth, especially her extraordinary, mismatched eyes. How he had loved her! He had defied his father for her sake and dared the wrath of the Magister Militum of Constantinople, Flavius Ardabur Aspar.

Finally, Andrewina Ruadh joined him with eyes that understood everything and forgave him anyway. She had died somewhere close to the Villa Poppinidii, and she was both unburied and unmourned, except within the secret places of his heart. But Andrewina Ruadh had saved the Britons at a crucial moment when Fortuna's Wheel had shivered as the goddess decided who should be cast down into the muck of history. Why did she gamble everything, including her life, on a small, newly born child? Because she had loved Myrddion Merlinus!

And now, Fortuna had decided that the healer should pay for his long period in the goddess's sunshine. Late in life, he had tumbled into love with a younger woman who was out of reach. Now Nimue risked death, and he must watch and twist on the fires of indecision while she gambled with a life that had become more precious than Myrddion's own. As the healer paced back to the stubborn, scarred door of Targo's room, Artor's concerned face stared at his oldest mentor, trying to find words of comfort that could never be taken seriously.

Myrddion had finally begun to pay for years of existence with a frozen heart.

"Wenhaver is only a little older than your Nimue," Artor replied casually. "My father, like King David in the Jew book, took girls into his bed to ease his bodily pains by transferring his diseases to younger, stronger flesh. Your foolish maunderings are misplaced, old man; age always mates with youth. I'm not saying such a pairing is ideal, just that it's not unusual. I can't understand why you should be so . . . scrupulous in your feelings for her."

Myrddion gazed sadly at Artor, as if he could force this older, sometimes inexplicable Artor to understand his reservations. The young Artorex would have immediately understood how his sense of duty and decency tortured him. Artorex had known how youth calls to youth.

Myrddion squared his shoulders in sudden resolution. He would enjoy the life that remained to him with Nimue, rather than waste precious time in frustration and doubt. If she remained untouched by the contagion, he might have time to untangle his unfamiliar feelings. But for now, she needed him to be decisive and impartial. The sun seemed to rise over the dark waters of his thoughts and flooded his doubts with light for, as always, tomorrow would take care of itself.

One by one, his memory women disappeared from the forefront of his mind, all but Andrewina Ruadh. "Only wait, master, and all will be well," she murmured while she laughed throatily in her old, familiar fashion, with an ironic recognition that life is a gamble and a jest. Then she, too, was gone, as if she had never existed, leaving behind a tangible trace of the perfume that she had carried in her curling bronze hair.

"We must help Nimue, my lord. She will need a large basin for water, some ewers, fine cloth, clean rags, several covered pans, a goodly supply of easily heated food, and water. A servant must be posted here to do her bidding immediately she wants it done, but only one servant, and always the same one. All that comes out of that room must be burned."

"All what? I don't understand."

"The body still has its needs and its functions, my lord." Myrddion coughed respectfully until the king reddened.

"Of course," Artor said crisply. "I never thought of the practicalities. You can organize everything needful in my name, but I expect you to keep me informed."

Myrddion nodded and the two men parted.

Within the room, Nimue heard the departing footsteps and was glad. If the most important task in her short life was simply to ease Targo's pain, then she had a noble cause. Gallwyn had often told her that to survive her terrible birth, the gods must have had a purpose for her; her future was laid out like a golden ribbon that only Nimue could untangle.

"Well, Targo, it's just you and me and Perce now. You haven't told me exactly how you feel, so out with it or I will be cross. Believe me, old man, you'd be wise to keep me happy."

"Bloody women!" the old legionnaire wheezed. "They're more trouble than they're worth, especially the pushy ones."

"I heard that," Nimue replied sweetly.

After carefully sponging Targo's seamed and decrepit body, Nimue was certain that Targo had caught a fever, but she was equally certain that it wasn't the fatal contagion. Either way, the treatment was the same for both illnesses, and it served no purpose anyway to dwell on what she couldn't change. She convinced the old man to ignore any embarrassment when his bodily functions demanded to be eased, and then had to endure Perce's fierce protectiveness over the same matters. She checked a small cubicle where Perce slept and decreed that this little compartment would be their temporary latrine.

Perce was persuaded to move his pallet, and then was given the task of collecting the articles and medical supplies that had been left outside the locked apartment door and storing them inside his erstwhile sleeping cubicle.

"Myrddion hasn't failed me," Nimue noted with satisfaction. "He has provided everything I could possibly need."

"I can see he's taking care of our delicate sensitivities," Targo responded dryly.

"Of course he is. Perce and I need a latrine as well, so don't be difficult, old man." She smiled sweetly. "And now, Targo, it's time for some herb tea to reduce your fever."

"I won't like it, will I?" Targo grimaced in anticipation.

"You'll hate it," Nimue replied cheerfully. "But get used to the idea."

Targo's body had been worn away by time. Nimue held out little hope that he could fight off the infection that was spreading through his lungs.

Targo took some days to die, for Nimue used every trick in her repertoire to keep the old man alive and breathing. Three times a day, she would lay the old man's head over the end of his pallet, push several pillows under his shrunken buttocks, and then pound his back and rub strange concoctions into his chest and sides. Targo would cough out the vile green mucus that seemed to be gradually drowning him. After each session, the old man would talk about his long, adventurous life, and he asked Nimue to write down exactly what he said. It was the deathbed story of a life filled with the devastation and excitement of war, the only thing Targo loved other than Artorex.

In the strange and terrible business of killing, Targo was a master. In another world, with parents other than the peasants who had briefly guided his life, he might have risen to great heights, for he was intelligent and was a natural survivor. But the Roman legions had become both mother and father to him when he was little more than a boy, and his comrades-in-arms were his only family. All that was required of him was unquestioning obedience and a talent for carnage.

In the late evening, Nimue pondered the horrors of Targo's tales and the map of old injuries on his frail body. The old man's cheerful recitation was at odds with the violence he described. He seemed quite untouched by what he had seen and done.

Nimue gazed at the moon as she leaned against a narrow window slit. The sky was clear of cloud. Far above, distant and freezing, stars glimmered. The sound of drunken laughter rose on the wave of a light breeze that feathered her pale hair and cooled the close little room.

Targo is like a child who plays with toy soldiers, and he's always been careless of the slaughter in a game that is much loved by kings and masters of men, Nimue mused. I suppose that he's a realist; the world is a cruel, ruthless place, and he has dealt with all manner of ugliness by treating battle as a business.

"I miss you, Master Myrddion," Nimue told the wind as it rose to stroke her forehead. "I miss our talks."

But the dark is not always friendly. Small children will tell you how horrors conceal themselves in dark corners that the light cannot pierce. Nor is darkness comforting, for its black folds are secretive and can hide all manner of sins that would wither in the brightness of day.

In the king's stables, rosy with forbidden thoughts and a deep itch that demanded to be soothed, the queen so forgot her honor and her duty as to kiss the flushed face of Gawayne. The supper she had brought for him was forgotten as the queen and the prince settled into the welcoming straw and surrendered to temporary hungers and casual treasons. And if Gawayne was a more eager and attentive lover than her husband, it was only because he was obeying Wenhaver's royal commands, or so he reasoned. As was his habit, Gawayne acted without thought of the consequences. Certainly, the queen's rounded arms, her long, curling hair, and the sweet, pert breasts that somehow found their way into his hot mouth didn't allow for prudence or conversation. Any consideration of familial betrayal never entered his feverish mind.

So are kingdoms lost and men brought to ruin.

As for Wenhaver, her excuse was that she sought to punish her husband. He had rejected her after Myrnia had left Cadbury. While neither Artor nor Myrddion had uttered a word of blame towards the queen for her brutality, whispers crept through the busy corridors of Cadbury like tendrils of smoke, so that warriors, servants, and even citizens of the town viewed Wenhaver with a blend of disapproval and gruesome curiosity.

Wenhaver could not face her detractors without proclaiming her guilt. In her lavish bed, waited upon by careful maids who kept their distance, she fumed and hated her husband even more for a predicament that in her heart she knew to be her own fault. But her response, as ever, was to shift the blame. It was Myrnia's fault. Artor was responsible. She would have described every insult, real or imagined, that had occurred since she had arrived at Cadbury to justify her actions.

Her seduction of the king's nephew permitted the queen to feel much, much better.

THE NIGHT WAS always a time for killing. A thousand tiny murders were committed in the fortress under the cover of darkness, as owls, rats, and creeping insects followed their instincts and ambushed whatever prey crossed their paths.

In one secluded corner of the citadel, a pair of cold, dispassionate eyes watched the glint of moonlight on Nimue's hair. The dark flat irises masked a desire to crush, to rape, to sink sharp teeth into her small, perfect breasts. Distantly and instinctively, Nimue felt his presence and her flesh shivered with a sudden chill. She left the slit in the window and covered her patient where his fevered tossing had bared his side.

Morning came after a restless night when the wind rattled the shutters as if strong fingers sought entry. Targo was failing, his old lungs struggled for air and his heart was swollen in his thin chest. Nimue had seen this illness before in Gallwyn, and she knew that her efforts were fruitless. His dwindling frame gave no sign of the presence of the contagion, so Nimue took a great chance. She opened the door a crack and whispered to the waiting servant.

"Inform the High King that Targo is near death. Tell the king that old age is his friend's undoing and not the contagion. Targo's soul readies itself to make the dark crossing from this world to the next, and he wishes to bid farewell to his master."

Targo was fretful and his face had an unhealthy, feverish tinge.

"It's a bugger to be old and dying, little one," he whispered, his eyes proclaiming that wit and intelligence had not deserted him.

"It comes to us all, dear Targo. How well you have lived, though, for you have seen many strange places and known men who are now the stuff of legend. You will go to your rest knowing your life was full."

"You're sweet, my dear, to try to comfort me. But the mind still wants more of life, regardless of the body's ache. A lovely face like yours is far better medicine than those nasty syrups you make me drink. I'd really like a glass of good red wine now, my lovely. It can't hurt, can it?" Targo grinned with his old wickedness. "I'm dying anyway, lovey. Please?"

"You're a devil, Targo." Nimue laughed sincerely. "Perce will chase up a mug of a good Spanish wine. Or, better yet, he'll find a flagon and several cups so we can join you. Hades can wait until we have our toast."

"Good girl!" Targo whispered. "Let the bugger wait for me! He's hunted me for longer than I care to remember and he has to sneak up on me to catch me, so he'll cool his heels till I'm good and ready. Besides, I don't feel too bad . . . considering." The old warrior patted Nimue's hand. "I sometimes think that it would have been better to have died in battle at Artor's back, but then I remember I'd never have met you. Yes, old age is a bugger—but there are compensations."

"I heard my name mentioned," the High King interrupted as he entered the room. He knelt beside Targo's pallet and gripped the old man's hand tightly. "Nimue says you're thinking very seriously about leaving me. How can you trust me not to fuck up without you to guide me?"

Nimue's face flushed at the soldierly language, but Targo grinned, baring his few remaining yellowed fangs.

"That's my boy! Yes, you'll probably fuck up, but so would a Caesar in this country of boneheads and sodding rain. Can't be helped, boy. It can't be helped."

The old man lifted Artor's hand and kissed it. Nimue felt tears prickle behind her eyes and was forced to dash one hand across her cheeks to wipe away their traitorous tracks. The death of a great warrior was no time for weeping.

"I've loved you like a son, my boy. I loved little Gallia too. My heart hurts even worse to think of little Licia all grown up, and a wife, and us not there to see her on her big day. Old Frith was always right, wasn't she? Fate gives some men greater burdens than others."

Artor was dangerously close to tears; Nimue could sense them hovering in his shark's eyes, which were now simply wintry and sad.

"If the priests are right, Targo, then Frith and Gallia are both waiting to greet you. Lady Livinia, Ector, Luka, the Scum . . . so many friends will be there awaiting your arrival."

Nimue had no idea what the two men were talking about, but the shared love and life experiences that bound them so tightly were revealing the High King of the Britons to her in a totally new light. Before her eyes, Artor was becoming a true man, capable of love in full measure as well as the ruthless capacity for power that she had previously seen in him.

Perce hurried into the room, balancing a dusty flagon and some rough pottery cups on a simple wooden tray. He bowed to the king and commenced to fill the crude pottery with a rich, ruby-red wine.

Artor raised one eyebrow at Nimue, who explained Targo's last desire was for a fine glass of wine, and of her decision that they should join him in his tipple. As she spoke, Myrddion entered the room and was also handed a full cup.

Perce lifted the old man tenderly and supported him on cushions. With Nimue's help, Targo drank deeply and a little color came back into his pale face.

"To Artor, King of the Britons, my lord and my last master," Targo said gravely in his failing, thin voice. "My best master, who has given me my greatest triumphs."

Just as solemnly, Nimue, Perce, and Myrddion drank with him to Artor's good health.

"In recompense for my loyalty, I ask that you remember your promise, my lord," Targo added craftily, his eyes alight. "I ask that you do right by young Perce. He's nearly ready, and he'll be a loyal warrior who will guard your back for the love of me. I'll sleep better if I know that he has taken my place."

Artor raised his cup, drank, and saluted Targo.

"By the hours you once spent teaching me to stay alive, by the tears we shed together and by the losses we bore as one, I swear I will keep my word to you, my friend."

"That's fair enough," Targo wheezed. "Now, what's a man got to do to get a drink around here?"

Perce glanced an unspoken question at Nimue, who nodded almost imperceptibly. The young man filled Targo's cup.

"How fast are you, boy?" Targo asked slowly.

"I'm fast enough." Artor's voice broke. His eyes streamed with tears, although his mouth was held firmly by the force of his will.

Targo drank a little, and then waved the cup away with ebbing strength.

"I'm very tired," the old man whispered, and closed his eyes.

Odin came to the door, summed up the situation at a glance, and then stood guard at the entrance like a stone effigy.

Targo dozed for five minutes or so. His breathing sounded very loud within the confines of the quiet room. Nimue held his liver-spotted hand and stared into the cup of half-drunk wine on the stone floor beside her. It seemed to swirl like a pool of pumping blood.

The old man's eyes flickered, and then opened tiredly.

"How strong are you, boy?" The words whistled through his shriveled lips.

"Strong enough," Artor replied evenly, although his face was wet.

"So think before you act . . . Targo's law! Remember?"

Once again, the old man's eyes drooped shut as if he now lacked the strength to keep them open. His breathing was slower and more labored, until Nimue thought that the heaving chest wouldn't rise again. But Targo's will to live was still strong, and he opened his eyes once more.

"Nimue? Lovey? My short sword is yours."

"Never mind, you old darling. Just sleep, and we'll watch over you while you rest. Artor is here. And Myrddion, Odin, and Perce will stay close to you."

She caressed the old man's forehead with the long, gentle strokes of a mother, as if Targo was a small child. The old man obediently closed his eyes once more. Targo was a husk, a shell that was cracked and broken beyond repair. His heart still labored on, but Nimue knew that his soul would soon be free of his useless body.

His eyes snapped open.

"Odin!" he called, his expression suddenly desperate. The Jutlander stepped forward into the light of the lamp so that Targo's fading sight could see the outline of the familiar, shaggy body.

"Promise to guard his back! Whatever it takes, you . . . heathen . . . lump. Guard my boy's back."

"To ruin! To the death!" the Jutlander swore, and Nimue began to sob. She could no longer watch in silence, but she couldn't turn away either.

As she watched the final minutes of Targo's life, it was almost as if his god smoothed the wrinkled old face with a great invisible cloth, until the years that burdened his body began to fall away. Now Nimue could see the narrow, clever face that Targo once wore when he was young and vigorous, and her sobs increased in frustration and despair.

"He's gone," she whispered with a blend of joy and anguish. "His heart is still beating slowly . . . but his soul has fled."

Gradually, so quietly that the watchers could barely discern the small differences, Targo's breathing slowed and weakened . . . and then stopped.

A single heartbeat stirred the frail chest one last time, and then Targo's body was dead.

Artor kissed the dead lips and rose to his feet, ignoring the tears that darkened his short beard. His face was twisted, with regret, loss, and something darker that reminded Myrddion that the king had borne more than his share of losses during the past year.

"I will wash Targo myself, my lord, and sew him into his shroud," Nimue promised.

She gazed up into the ashen face of the High King and stroked his hand hesitantly. Artor seemed oblivious to her small, comforting gesture.

"Do you wish him buried?" she asked, proud to give this final, woman's grace to the old warrior. "Or burned?"

"Targo will be burned as a true Celtic warrior. And his ashes will rest at the Villa Poppinidii where he spent so many happy years."

Artor's sharp gaze turned on Nimue, and he seemed to see her truly for the first time. For one brief instant, she thought his eyes would pierce her heart, and she shivered under his fierce regard.

"I will send a shroud to you, the very best that my kingdom possesses. I thank you, Nimue, apprentice of Myrddion, and I am forever in your debt."

"I live to serve you, my lord. You only have to ask."

Artor bowed, turned abruptly on his heel, and strode out of the room. Myrddion stared fixedly at the iron-straight back with a kind of fear and, reluctantly, followed his master, the High King of the Britons.

ARTOR ENTERED HIS wife's apartments like a tidal surge. His raw emotions caused the perfumed air to crackle around him.

"Wenhaver? Where are you, woman?" he bellowed.

The queen's ladies fled from him like gaily painted birds disturbed by a hawk.

Wenhaver entered from her sleeping room, her long hair unbound, and looked at Artor with something very like disdain.

"I am here, husband. There is no need to shout."

"Where is the cloth of gold that came as a part of your dowry? I want it!"

Artor's voice was crisp and curt, and the maids observed him cautiously from under lowered eyes.

"I plan to make that length of cloth into a gown, my husband, so I must decline to give it to you."

"Your desires are of no interest to me. The cloth is mine, and was paid for when I married you. I have a use for it."

Artor's right fist clenched and unclenched unconsciously. The maids clustered in the corner of the sumptuous room to avoid the coming confrontation.

"Don't force me to search for that cloth, Wenhaver. It's mine, not yours, so it will be used to shroud old Targo, my most trusted servant, who is newly dead."

A wiser and less grasping woman would have acquiesced in the face of her husband's obvious distress. But, as usual, Wenhaver saw his demands through the filter of her own desires. She had found a replacement for her husband in her bed, and she had set her heart on an ostentatious gown, one designed to eclipse every woman in the west.

"That smelly old man! No, he cannot have it! My father owned it, so it's mine and I mean to keep it."

Her voice had risen until she was quite shrill. Artor, by comparison, became dangerously quiet.

"You'll obey, woman, and you'll comply with my wishes this very minute. Now!" He pointed at the prettiest of Wenhaver's handmaidens. "You! Find the cloth! This instant!"

"I am warning you, Linnet. Don't you dare do his bidding," Wenhaver shrieked.

Linnet's loyalty swiveled between Wenhaver's spiteful face and the king's implacable eyes.

"Linnet, you will obey! I am the king!"

Her decision had been made for her. She ran to a large chest, opened the heavy lid, and began to search through precious lengths of fabric until she struggled to lift out a bolt of shining gold.

Wenhaver stamped her small foot. "I will have you whipped, Linnet, and I don't care who your father is. You are not the king's servant, but mine. I order you to give that cloth to me."

"If you touch that child, Wenhaver, I will visit the exact same injuries on your body as you inflict on her, after I publicly tell all on Cadbury Tor of the reason for your punishment. Beware what you say, madam, for I am the High King, and you have never paid for Myrnia's scars. She may have been a servant, but she was in my service, so you

410

will have a care. You are merely my excessively tiresome and stupid wife, who can be removed from your position at my whim."

Any clever young aristocrat in Wenhaver's service soon learned to cover their ears so they could swear on either the Tuatha de Danann or the Christus that they'd heard nothing during the course of their duties in her chambers.

Without another word, Artor eased the glittering cloth from Linnet's unresisting hands and strode out of the room. Behind him, he heard the crash of precious glass pots of unguents and perfumes strike the wall, and Wenhaver's voice shrieked until he swore she sounded like the coarsest prostitute.

"Let her rave," he whispered softly, as he strode back through the rabbit warren of corridors. "The selfish bitch will live my way, or not at all."

Nimue raised her tear-stained face as he entered. Targo lay naked on his pallet, except for a strip of cloth that concealed the old man's genitals. Perce and Nimue, between them, were washing the old man's body.

"Here!" Artor said softly, as he draped the wonderful, expensive cloth over a stool. "Targo deserves the shroud of a king, and so he shall have the best that I own. In three days, his funeral pyre will be lit in the forecourt of Cadbury Tor."

As quickly as he had come, Artor was gone again.

Odin chanted in his own tongue while Nimue was sewing Targo's remains into his shroud. Then, as she was about to finish the last of the stitches, the Jutlander slipped a small carving of a wooden ship onto Targo's breast.

"Once the maidens take his soul to Valhalla, Targo will have a boat that he can row through the heavens," Odin explained quietly.

"Targo believed that he must pay the Ferryman his fee to cross the River Styx. The High King has left the fee with me," Nimue said sadly, and laid two golden coins on Targo's closed eyes.

She sewed the last stitches, and the remains of the old Roman were hidden from the light.

"By sea, by fire, by boat, or by the horses of the air," Odin intoned, "our friend will go to the gods as all great warriors must." He turned to face Nimue. "You did the best you could, little dragonlet."

Nimue flashed a quick, surprised glance at Odin's broad face. "You speak excellent Celt when you think no one will notice," she said. "It's something about you that I have never noticed before."

Odin bowed his head and smiled slyly. "Targo always knew. He taught me to speak your language, so I listened and learned. Targo said I could serve my master better if everyone thinks I'm stupid."

Nimue laughed for the first time in many sad hours. It was an appreciative gurgle of amusement at Targo's foresight—and Odin's duplicity.

"I certainly won't tell anyone," Nimue promised. "And I'll swear that Perce won't reveal your secret either. After all, you're Perce's mentor now."

"Nimue! As if I would!" Perce protested with mock affront.

The three friends gripped hands across Targo's withered corpse, and laughed and wept by turns. The old warrior would have appreciated their laughter.

Nimue, Perce, and Odin remained with the shell of the old man, and kept a long watch through the night. Nimue prayed, and every breath she took was a hymn to speed Targo on his way to the afterlife. She had seen his soul depart his body, and she had no doubt that Targo lived on in another world that was beyond her knowledge or understanding.

There were no more deaths from the contagion. It vanished from Cadbury as it had come, speedily and without fanfare. It was as if Targo's death marked a return to normality. Always sensitive to the power of symbols, Artor set his considerable energy to the task of galvanizing the population for one purpose, building a massive funeral pyre for his friend. Carts were sent out of Cadbury into the forests, and they returned, groaning under the weight of long, straight trees that had been stripped and prepared on site for the ritual conflagration.

The population did not begrudge Targo the efforts they expended

412

for his funeral. As arms master to the High King and the last Roman warrior in Britain, he had the romantic gloss of legend. He had stood at Artor's shoulder for many years and, in his great old age, had assumed a giant's stature in the eyes of the common people. He stood tall for all of them, for he was a common man who had touched the gods and, like the ordinary citizens of Cadbury, he had died as they, too, would eventually perish.

The funeral pyre took many days to build, so Artor sent word of the coming event to Targo's old friends. Only Wenhaver had nothing praiseworthy to say of the old soldier, so she sulked and nagged by turns. Artor simply ignored her childish behavior. The queen could bear insults, but indifference drove her half mad with rage. When a number of the loyal kings arrived for Targo's last ceremony, she was an unwilling hostess, completely lacking in charm. The fact that those who had known Targo cared nothing for her rudeness simply added to her feelings of injustice.

A week after Targo's death, his body was placed atop an impressive pyre of massed logs. The air was sweetened by the heady odors of precious attars set in wax combs among the wood to mask the smell of corruption beneath Targo's golden shroud. Artor ordered that the old man should go to the afterlife without armor or weapons for, as he told Llanwith, Targo had proved his status as a warrior and had no need of swords to proclaim his courage as a man.

The morning of the burning dawned sweet and clear. The fortress walls had been opened, and it seemed to Nimue's eyes that the whole of Cadbury town filled the square and every raised structure that gave them a vantage point. Excited boys swung their legs over the edges of the roofs while they waited to see the great Artor honor his sword master. A festive air filled the square with a hum of excitement, and many women had collected flowers that they threw onto the pyre, where their brilliant colors softened the harsh majesty of the rough-hewn logs.

Nimue had dressed in her finest, cradling Targo's old sword in her slender arms. She followed directly behind her master, clad in his customary black, as he stood to one side of the tribal kings. As always, Myrddion's tall, slim figure was both graceful and manly, and was now adorned by a serpentine gold chain across his chest.

The crowd sighed as Artor came forth from the great hall, accompanied by his queen. Wenhaver had dressed ostentatiously in a gown of many brilliant colors. As always, she was heavily adorned with gems and wore her hair long and loose like a maiden. Several women in the crowd pursed their lips with disapproval at such a festive display, but the younger girls were awed by Wenhaver's undoubted beauty, even if it was marred by a surly, proud expression.

The king was a somber figure, dressed in deepest sable without adornment. Only his amber hair and gold dragon crown provided any color.

Artor's face looked stern and strong, but Nimue knew that the king had wept for hours the previous night, for she had heard him when she strayed near his apartment. Gruffydd had told her that Artor was inconsolable, and had kept to his room as much as possible. She alone among the crowds saw the pallor under the king's tanned skin, and the swollen eyelids hooding his grey eyes.

When the assembled guests had settled, Myrddion Merlinus stepped forth and raised the symbol of his office, a tall black staff that was carved in the likeness of a sea monster.

"Hear, people of Britain! We have come here today to honor a man who arrived in our lands as a stranger, in a time of strife and danger. He dwelt among us for many years and served us with great courage and skill. All who wish to honor him should speak now, and remember Targo, sword master and bodyguard of the High King of the Britons."

Artor stepped forward and the crowd was suddenly still. With his back to the pyre, Artor surveyed the crowd with his head lifted in pride at the honor he was about to bestow on his friend.

"Targo, my friend, had only one name. There was no family nomen by which we might know his ancestors. All that we know of him was that he was of common stock, and was born under the hot sun of the Roman hills.

"He was already well past his youth when I first met him. It was an unwilling meeting, for I was a feckless boy and he was a hard taskmaster. I can still remember how he would sit beneath a linden tree and set me tasks that made no earthly sense to the boy I was. If I made an error in judgment during my weapons training, he would say, 'You're dead, boy!' He guided me towards making sound decisions based on thought and logic. He helped to turn an unwilling child into a man. That I can stand before you as High King of the Britons today, undefeated by the Saxons, can only be attributed to the lessons taught to me by Targo. These lessons were Targo's laws.

"Targo followed me through weariness and pain. He gave me laughter, hope, and courage, and the strength to face the task that still lies ahead of us. And he never ceased to challenge me to think, and to rule, and to be a warrior, even as he lay dying.

"I honor Targo, my oldest friend and my staunchest servant. He was a stranger who came to a new land, and spent the rest of his life keeping the west free for all Britons.

"Ave, Targo! Sword master and man! Honor him, free men of the west!"

Artor stepped back, to be replaced by other men of renown, Myrddion among them, who spoke of Targo's courage and his manliness. Gruffydd, too, bearing Artor's great sword, spoke of his drinking friend while he wept unashamedly.

Then the swell of speakers was done.

Nimue bit her lip. These men had touched on those aspects of Targo's character that warriors prize, but so much was left unsaid, so much that she had seen since she had first come to Cadbury.

Gathering her courage, she smashed custom and stepped forward, her heart in her mouth in fear and trepidation.

The crowd howled in protest, joined exultantly by Wenhaver, for all women were precluded from speaking praises of the dead, least of all a maid who was largely unknown and of peasant heritage.

Nimue stood before the angry mob, a tall, slender woman of silver and grey, and waited until Artor raised his hand.

The crowd stilled.

"I know that I speak against custom," Nimue spoke in a loud, clear voice, "but I break with tradition because Targo was my friend, and he would have known that I loved and respected him for the true man that he was. I wish to speak for Targo and I will *not* be silent!"

The crowd exploded with shouted insults once again, but Artor strode to Nimue's side and silence slowly fell.

"Have you gone witless, girl?" he asked in a whisper. "You could easily be killed if you affront this assembly. I might not be able to dissuade them from violence if they feel insulted."

Nimue stared directly into Artor's stormy eyes. "My lord, all men obey you. I was there with Targo at his deathbed, and I know what manner of man Targo really was, deep in his hidden heart, where neither weapons nor killing ever owned him. Someone must speak for the Targo who lived beyond his trade in death. I am an alien, as he was, but we understood each other, my lord, and I know his history from his own lips, and wrote it down as he requested in the nights and days before his death. I claim the right to speak for Targo himself."

Slowly and deliberately, Artor faced the crowd. His eyes were shadowed with the recognition that there were facets of Targo's life that he had never cared to discover.

"When Targo was struck with illness, this woman physicked him at great risk to herself. She was prepared to remain with Targo to face the whim of the contagion. Nimue nursed our friend through his last illness, and obtained a history of his life from the man as he lay dying. She knows and understands Targo's mind and spirit.

"It's unseemly to shout and threaten while Targo waits above us in his golden shroud that has been sewn by the hands of this extraordinary woman. I propose that we break with tradition and permit her to speak, although she is a woman and our customs do not generally permit such license to a female.

"The famed Boedicca, a great Briton, who almost drove the Romans out of our lands, was also a woman, and she suffered a man's fate from the justice of Rome. Our enemies made no distinction. How can we?"

The affronted muttering of the crowd indicated that many men were still enraged by Nimue's request, but others agreed that the disturbance made by protest was more unseemly than the trivial words of a mere woman.

Silently, Nimue waited, a silver light in her grey dress, until the crowd lapsed into attentive regard, or an insulted silence.

"As you can see, I am a woman. And my hair, my eyes, and my tattoo mark me as a barbarian woman at that. No doubt I was born to ignorant, savage parents who worshipped pagan gods from the frozen north. Therefore, I wish to speak for Targo, a man who came from the pagan south, where the winds stir softly through the green olive groves, and the grape vines shiver in the summer breezes; where the air is heavy with the smells of aromatic wood smoke and the racks of drying fish. So he told me in the days before his death, for I've never seen such a land and can only imagine it."

The crowd remained silent but stone-faced.

"Targo was robbed of children of his own, a loss that he regretted throughout his long life. What stole this basic right from him? Women know these things and we understand. When the land was threatened, the young men and boys were taken from their simple homes and forced into the Roman legions. How well we also know of the need that robs us of our husbands, our fathers, our sons, and our brothers. But Targo never lost his love of the quiet land with its fertile fields, its village life, and the deep springs of water from the earth that is the first love of all, the memory of home."

Now the crowd stirred.

Nimue felt their sudden change of mood, but she still waited, a girl of moonlight under a brazen summer sun.

"Here, in this land that is so different from his birthplace, he forged a new life and a new home. Yes, he missed the sun when his old bones ached in the winter, but he made his place among us and learned to love the quiet patterns of the earth once more as he became attuned to the rhythms of all green and growing things. He was happy at Aquae Sulis, far more content than he had ever been. He took a widow to his bed and raised her young sons, but fate did not choose to give Targo the peaceful old age he had earned.

"A boy called out to him, a man child unsuited to the burdens of his birth, and so Targo put away his contentment and took up the sword once again. Many were the men he killed, too many to remember their faces, but in dreams they came back to him as shadows, and they reminded him that life is precious and hard won.

"For love, he put aside his contentment. For love, he bore the constant weight of his dead. For love, he grew old in service after he was, so briefly, a free man. For love, he put aside the comfort of a woman's constancy. And for love, he permitted himself to forsake the greening fields for the red earth of the battle lines.

"Is there a greater love than that which is given freely and without regret, but which plunges the giver into the world that he rejected years before? No, my friends! We should honor him as the warrior who served his master beyond his arm's strength or his heart's desire.

"So, I speak for this selfless man. He was a soldier and had great courage, but he was also a soul of gentleness who was trapped in a body that had been fitted for war. He harbored no regrets at his choice. Simply, and with sadness, he regretted that his new home called him forth from the peace and obscurity that he craved. A king, a great scholar, a serving man, a barbarian, and a mere girl attended his dying, and, as always, his thoughts were for those others who would live after him, and not for the travesty of his own life."

And then Nimue stood even taller, and raised one clenched fist in an unconscious mimicry of the salute used by soldiers and gladiators for hundreds of years before she took her first breath.

"Ave, Targo! You gave us your old age and doomed yourself to loneliness for a dream of glory in which you wanted no part. Today, we stand and honor you, for what you fought for were the gentle fires of home, ours and yours!"

As she finished her oration, the crowd roared their approval, and even Artor was amazed that such a delicate creature could touch that deepest part in every man and woman which dumbly accepts suffering and loss of life so that the hearth remains alive and full of warmth. He bowed to Nimue, who blushed deeply as she stepped back behind the shadow of her master.

Only Wenhaver narrowed her eyes, and her hatred was a tangible thing.

Artor stood forth once more.

"And so, let us consign this ordinary man to the flames," he roared over the noise from the assembled crowd. "And we shall pray that when we have Targo's choice to make, we will give as he gave, with fortitude, grace, and laughter, so that the west will live forever."

Artor took up the torch held by a waiting warrior and plunged it deeply into a corner of the pyre, and then another, and another, until logs, flowers, perfume, and oils began to burn fiercely. As the flames rose into the sky, the white smoke plumed about Targo's gold-shrouded corpse and it seemed that his body stirred as if to rise again.

Few eyes were dry as the pyre consumed itself and the body wait-ing at its zenith. Priests muttered prayers, echoed by the ordinary citi-zens, who felt themselves committed to some greater cause embodied in the death of the old man. Many of the warriors examined their own souls, and each wondered if he would be found wanting if he faced the choices made by Targo, so far from all he had once loved.

And so Targo entered legend, and ultimately myth, as the human symbol of a great leader who pursued the beast of war to slay it, but never defeated his quarry, although he expended his life in the quest. What humans know in their hearts, they will ever glorify in the sym-bolism of any single person who embodies what they wish to become.

As for Nimue, now renowned as the Maid of Wind and Water for her silver hair and dress, and for the way the vortex of the flames lifted her shining tresses into a flag of light, she was feared, for great beauty is always oddly inhuman, and the common folk called her a queen come out of the Otherworld to be the conscience of Cadbury. Even

419

Targo's dented, ancient short sword, mounted on her wall with all its age and hard use freely open to scrutiny, became a symbol of protection, conferred by its grey blade and her slim white hands. She could hide no longer.

At last, she would achieve the position that Gallwyn had dreamed her foster daughter would assume, within a mantle of superstitious love. Whenever she walked in the fields that surrounded Cadbury, collecting herbs and roots for Myrddion's potions, men swore she left a track of silver water, as if a lake had been her mother and her father was the moon. The truth, that she walked early when the grass was thick with dew, meant nothing, for she was the Maid of Wind and Water and beyond the ken of mortal men.

How Wenhaver raged as the stories grew. How she bit her scented pillows late at night when Artor avoided her, and swore that Nimue would suffer for every reverential bow the upstart received as she passed through the corridors, the streets, and the fields of Cadbury. Deep in the stygian darkness of her spirit, Wenhaver yearned to tear down all that her husband had built about Nimue's ears so that the mob would know her for the witch she was.

So Wenhaver cast away the bearing of a queen, and chose the whore's way as her revenge, trusting that her husband would be ignorant or, worse, compliant for the sake of peace, and that Gawayne would cleave to her alone, putting her body before the safety of the kingdom. In her golden net of hair, hell beckoned, as seductive as the sweetest wine, and her milkless breasts were poisoned with avarice. Yet, in the streets of Cadbury, she smiled as she spread coin and bread to ease the cares of the people, and gloried as they slowly came to love her.

"I will be a true queen, and I will watch the white witch perish," Wenhaver swore silently as she lay in the arms of her lover, careful that no prying eyes should winkle out her secret. "And Artor shall lose everything he now has, and will know at the death that it was I who destroyed him."

Chapter XVIII

THE NAKED EYE

Perhaps Wenhaver's spite and malice would have become nothing but a whore's dirty little secret. The realms of the High King were peaceful in the main, for the Saxons rarely left their footholds in the east, and Artor's warriors patrolled the mountain chains, reacting with speed and deadly force against any rash incursions into the territory of the Britons.

Perhaps.

But the soul is a curious arbiter. The best of men deceive themselves if they believe that base desires are more than a fingernail's breadth below the surface of personal will. The worst of men, those who know their weaknesses better, soon learn to hide, and to deceive.

So discord, and worse, came to Cadbury.

The first sign of the terror that was to come occurred when a crucified sheep was discovered. It had been nailed to an old oak in a copse of trees beyond the rich fields. Human hands had slit the ewe from belly to breast and torn the pink entrails from its body while its heart was still beating. A shepherd discovered it, just before morning light, and vomited away his early meal of porridge as he cut the carcass down and retrieved the skin and the meat.

Shortly afterwards, one of Artor's great hounds was found with its paws cut off and its teeth torn out so that the bloodied muzzle was an affront to the decency of the men who discovered the atrocity. Out of mercy, Artor was forced to cut the dog's throat himself to put the poor creature out of its suffering. Warrior looked at warrior, and women kept their children close indoors at a time of year when the long dusks beckoned the young boys to play at soldier's games in the woods, and encouraged the young girls to collect garlands of flowers. The scent of dried blood seemed to hover in the air, and Artor watched his foster brother with eyes that had never learned to wholly trust the man.

Anticipating the High King's concerns, Caius sought Artor out.

The king's lands had profited from the careful stewardship of Artor's foster brother. Caius had also grown wealthy, probably from the manipulation of his position at court, but few men cared, for all servants took their profits from well-managed estates.

Caius, now Sir Caius in the people's regard, knew all too well that only three people still lived who remembered a blood-soaked night, an underground temple where children had died cruelly before being dumped, unshriven, in unsanctified graves, and how Artor had saved his young foster brother from his own foolishness.

Artor was studying field reports when Caius entered his private rooms unannounced. The steward saw the flash of irritation in Artor's eyes at his unwelcome intrusion, and the speculative look the king gave him before it was quickly quashed. A surge of resentment filled Caius.

"I regret my interruption, my brother, but such doubts as I see in your eyes deserve plain speaking."

Artor pushed the scrolls to one side of his rough table, and turned to face Caius. Courteous as always, he offered his foster brother a stool and some good wine, and waited to hear what urgent matters had prompted this meeting.

Over time, Caius had grown older and heavier in the jowls and in the upper body, but his legs, incongruously, were as slender as in his boyhood. Indulgence had blurred his delicate features, and the passing decades had marooned his once dark, carefully groomed hair in a mere fringe of grey around his ears. His mother, Livinia, would have believed that the years had lent him gravitas, that old Roman word for dignity, but Artor saw a soft man who had been spoiled by luxury and the sweetness of life at court.

"What are you talking about, Caius? Why should I doubt you? Few men have served me as well, or as honorably, as you've done," Artor replied, succeeding in pushing away his impatience.

"I am concerned about these atrocities. I cannot help but remember those days of long ago when the Severinii ran amok, and I wonder if you still believe me capable of such vile behavior. I sometimes think of Severinus and how charming he could be, and how filthy his soul became." Caius kept his open, guileless eyes fixed on those of his king.

"The Severinii are long dead, and the earth where their villa once stood was sown with salt over twenty years ago," Artor said softly. "There may be some form of man beast who walks among us, but I could never believe that you would have cast aside your oaths or the memory of your blessed mother so easily. Why would you risk all that you have won for the blood of a sheep or a dog? No, Caius. In truth, you have done nothing that causes me to doubt you."

Artor spoke levelly, with eyes that were grave and unswerving, and Caius was relieved. But Artor was now the High King of the Britons, and not the honest Artorex of their youth. He, too, had learned to dissemble.

"Thank you, brother," Caius said, his hands playing unconsciously with the curled fringes of his hair. "This matter has caused me concern for some time. I thought that my involvement with Severinus all those years ago could mean that I might be suspected of involvement in these abominations that have taken place. I thank you for your trust."

"Of course, Caius. Now, may I help you further?" Artor's civility did not waver, nor did the kindly interest in his stern face.

"No . . . no . . . my apologies for the interruption, my lord. You are busy with your duties towards the realm, and heaven knows I need to inventory the grain reserves before the harvest begins . . ." The nervous voice of Caius trailed off, and he bowed deeply to his brother and left the apartments.

Artor stared at the wall of his room, more like a priest's cell in its lack of comfort and its practical simplicity than the apartments of a supreme ruler.

"Why did you bring up the name of the Severinii, brother?" Artor murmured aloud. "And why should some random acts of cruelty to animals bring those perverted bastards to your mind? Guilt never quite goes away, does it?"

The lime-washed wall gave no answers. But, in his far memory, Artor remembered old Frith seated before the kitchen fires in the Villa Poppinidii, stitching up a torn tunic and dispensing natural wisdom as she worked.

"Them as looks you in the eye and swears to their gods that they speak the truth most surely lie," old Frith had informed the boy, Artorex, with grave certainty. "Never trust a man whose eyes never shift when he speaks. He's playing a game of some kind, and you may be sure, sweetheart, that it's not one you would be liking."

The face of the old slave, with its dried-apple wrinkles and faded blue eyes, was so clear in Artor's memory that he knew he, too, was growing old. Of late, the Villa Poppinidii and its verdant fields had seemed more real than anything he had built at Cadbury, or Venta Belgarum, or any of the fortifications in the west.

The young Artorex shivered, but the older Artor thrust his fears aside and returned to his duties.

Gawayne had ridden north a few days earlier, for he had finally consented to marry. Queen Morgause had chosen the girl, a gentle, brown-haired woman child who was the daughter of a nearby clan chieftain, and Gawayne had hoped, dimly, that this untainted girl would remove Wenhaver from his waking thoughts. Even Gawayne's rather slow thought processes had decided that he was acting in a fashion that his peers would deem traitorous if his liaison became public knowledge. Never before had he cleaved to any woman for more than a month, but Wenhaver's body appeared to hold some magical property that blinded his mind whenever she turned her knowing eyes upon him, with their promise of secret pleasures that he could not resist. Like any sensible warrior, he realized that there were times when it was best to vacate the field of battle.

At first, Wenhaver was enraged when Gawayne excitedly shared his plans with her, but as she contemplated the presence of a wife in their relationship, she realized that his marriage could be a perfect foil against discovery. Gawayne felt a moment's revulsion at her words, a reaction that must have been visible to Wenhaver's keen eyes, because she wept, sulked, and begged before she finally elected to deny him her body. Inside, Wenhaver was being devoured alive by jealousy.

Autumn in the citadel of Cadbury was, therefore, an uncomfortable few months for everybody. Artor was increasingly distant, while Myrddion was abstracted and clumsy in the presence of Nimue, and seemed always on the point of bursting into some rash, self-effacing speech. Nimue found the people's awe of her amusing and irritating by turns, while Wenhaver gave petulance a whole new meaning.

As Gruffydd confided to Percivale, the fortress had the feel and intensity of a place over which a great cataclysmic thunderhead was building. He, for one, didn't care to be present when the storm clouds finally burst.

Percivale nodded and kept his own counsel. But his sharp young eyes missed nothing, especially the queen's sneers when Artor was not present. True to his oath, Percivale awaited the day of reckoning.

The harvest was almost done when a gleaner disappeared. As in all nations, at all times, and in all customs, the indigent were permitted to seek out the fallen grain heads after the fields were reaped and the grain was collected and threshed. From dawn to dark, the elderly, the poor, children, and widows bent their backs to find a little measure of grain to guard against starvation during the winter. As the crop was particularly plentiful that year, Nimue often saw women holding aprons heavy with grain as they made their way home to their children in the autumn evenings. Wood smoke perfumed the air as the thrifty citizens smoked fish taken from the streams, or cured venison and ham. The world of Cadbury seemed pregnant with life, ripe and ready to be plucked and enjoyed.

A single woman, especially one who lived on the fringes of the wild woods with her infant son, was scarcely likely to be missed.

After spending a night in the woods, a hunter carrying a brace of coney heard the plaintive cry of a child as he was returning home to his cottage. Usually indifferent to others, on this occasion the man halted to investigate the sound and found a six-month-old boy child in a deserted cottage. The infant was soiled, hungry, and alone. The fireplace in his mother's hut was cold, and the child's condition, while not critical, was sufficiently worrying for the good man to take the infant home to his wife.

The next morning, the concerned hunter, Alric, informed the fortress guard of his find.

Artor had ordered that widows within his realm should receive special care, for many men had lost their lives during the war years when he had been consolidating his kingdom. But his warriors were not always so diligent. Several of their number checked the one-roomed cottage at random, but the gleaner seemed to have been swallowed whole by the earth. Even her name was forgotten, for she was simply the widow of the wood to those few persons who knew of her existence.

After a week, with no sign of the woman, the warriors decided she must have found a new man and that she had departed, forsaking an unwanted child. Life was often cruel, and no one, not even the hunter, wondered at her continued absence.

Coincidence rarely happens, and the gleaner's disappearance would have been forgotten, but for Alric, the same hunter who had found the babe. He had set his trapline along the banks of a small rivulet. A man of habit, he checked his lines before first light each day. One morning, nearly two weeks after finding the abandoned child, as he was expertly breaking the neck of a trapped buck rabbit, the night breeze suddenly changed and an odor of corruption came with it. The stench was one that Alric could not help but recognize.

Suddenly, the comforting darkness seemed to be filled with watchful eyes. Every noise in the forest, every creature that stirred in the underbrush, now seemed to be menacing.

Nervous and cautious, in spite of many solitary years spent living in the forest, Alric took to his heels, slinging the rabbit into his hide bag as he ran. He deftly avoided holes and the darkest coppices until he arrived, out of breath and shaking, at his cottage.

Inside, the widow's son was howling lustily. He was a fine boy, and Alric had been secretly pleased that he could raise another son. Now, with the memory of the vile stink that had been carried to him on the night wind, and with his imagination conjuring up images of its source, Alric vomited against the outer wall of his cottage until his revolted stomach began to heave up bile.

Shortly afterwards, he reported his suspicions to the senior officer at the tor.

Warriors were dispatched to the scene, and, on this occasion, Myrddion Merlinus accompanied them. Artor's interest was stirring with suspicion, and he required his most trusted eyes present.

Alric had been instructed to accompany the armed warriors, at least until the source of the corruption had been found. He was unwilling but could think of no way to deny the High King.

The peasant crossed himself in superstitious dread. "I won't be wandering through the Wildewood so carelessly in future," he told Myrddion. "There's something wicked walking along my traplines. I can feel it. It's fair been giving me the shivers, because I've been thinking that someone has been watching me. I hope that smell isn't the widow, but, if it is, I have her boy in my cottage and we'll see him raised right."

And then the seasoned hunter crossed himself again and soundlessly guided the search party towards their destination. The shadows of the trees swallowed them, and Myrddion wondered at the loneliness and solitude that a hunter embraced so willingly.

The warrior escort studied the traplines, and wound strips of fabric over their lower faces to weaken the stench of rotting flesh. Myrddion scented the breeze like a hunting dog. He had inhaled this sweet evil practically from birth, so one more dead body held no fears for him. Having determined the direction from which the odor was coming, he walked the length of the trapline, his eyes fixed firmly on the ground. Other than a scuffing of leaves under a young birch and faint scars in the tender bark of several trees, he saw nothing worthy of note.

Then he spied the first signs of violence.

A hand had gripped this sapling tightly in the darkness, with sufficient strength to break the narrow stem. Scrambling feet had churned the ground, leaving faded scars that led in the direction from where the vile stink was permeating the air.

Myrddion instructed the warriors to fan out into an extended line, and to avoid disturbing any traces of previous movement left behind on the forest floor.

A mere thirty steps into the blue-black shadows of the mature trees, one of the warriors made a grisly discovery.

"Lord Myrddion?" he called, his voice a little shaky for one so used to carnage.

The searcher had found the body of the missing woman where she had been tossed like a rag doll into a crack in the earth, worn by the spring thaws of countless years. She lay, half naked, with her flesh swollen, split, and greenish in the filtered light. She was tightly curled into the fetal position, and Myrddion realized that she had probably lived for a short time after the attack that killed her. She had died forsaken and in an extremity of pain. Even worse than the marks of decay on her body were the unmistakable signs of scavengers who had further desecrated her damaged flesh. The creatures of the wild, both great and small, had feasted on her.

At the back of his mind, Myrddion heard Targo's pragmatic voice. "All things must eat," Targo had often explained, and Myrddion could clearly see how much damage had been wrought on dead human flesh in the past three weeks, even though the nights were cold as the days sped towards winter.

Myrddion sighed, and commenced to sketch the body quickly with chalks and charcoal onto a piece of vellum. He knew that Artor would require a detailed record, no matter how unpleasant. Then he picked his way into the shallow gully, calling for the most capable of the warriors to accompany him.

"Her poor face," Myrddion exclaimed as he eased the tangle of hair away from her profile. The flesh had sunk so that the skull was almost visible and the skin was black from exposure. Myrddion was unsurprised to note that the eyes, lips, and the fleshy part of the nose were gone, lost to scavengers, but even so, the abused and rotted flesh had a ghastly tale to tell. She had been beaten just before death, and the livid remnants of burst blood vessels and cuts to her skin marred features that had already begun to show signs of tiredness and aging. Her mouth gaped, and Myrddion could see her tongue had been torn out. Maggots fed in her throat, and he felt his stomach spasm with revulsion. Other scavengers had attacked her remains postmortem, and her exposed flesh was torn and partly devoured.

"Turn her onto her back," he told the greying warrior in a voice that was harsher than he intended.

Her ash-green flesh gaped from breastbone to pubic hair. Within the cavity, scavengers had feasted and did so still, so that her dead flesh was invested with a strange, writhing life.

"I've seen my share of blood and guts," the warrior growled through his makeshift mask. "But nothing like this. Look at her legs!"

The woman had bled copiously, but not only from her terrible wounds, for a large quantity of blackened blood had trickled down her thighs from her distorted genitals.

"She must have been alive when she was raped, for blood doesn't flow after the heart stops beating," Myrddion stated.

He was revolted, despite his long experience as a healer and a physician.

"And the ground is thick with dried blood," the warrior added. "It's almost as if she bled to death right here."

"Lord Myrddion?" The voice of a younger soldier interrupted from the edge of the fissure. "Someone sat on his heels over here and watched her die. His heel prints are deep, and they're very clear to see."

Rain had fallen softly on most nights that the corpse had been in the eroded open grave, but the misty falls of autumn had been gentle and had only blunted the clear marks of boot heels and footprints where a man had hunkered down and rocked on his heels.

For Myrddion, that information was the worst part of this ghastly tableau. Plainly, a man had raped this poor, friendless woman, gutted her as he rutted inside her body, and then he had sat calmly and watched her bleed to death.

"Did she beg? I wonder. I suppose she did—for the sake of her baby, if not for herself," Myrddion speculated. "Well, it seems that we hunt a beast in human form."

He looked reflectively at the blurred imprints of the boots worn by the killer. The soles indicated they were made of good, strong leather, and the depressions in the muddy ground showed deep but indistinct crescents.

"From what we can see here, I believe that watching her die probably gave him his greatest enjoyment, because she took some time to bleed to death. Perhaps the rape was a mere foretaste of the pleasure he was seeking."

"May the gods preserve us," one young man exclaimed, sickened by what his imagination visualized.

"Aye," Myrddion replied with a sigh. "We shall bury her here alongside this stream. Her body has told us all it can, and I lack the heart to heap further indignities upon her. I shall send a priest to say prayers over her remains."

The warriors obeyed, breaking the eroded banks of the gully with their shields to form a shallow depression in which they laid the woman's form. They used their axes and fallen pieces of timber to heap earth on top of her until her body was covered.

When Artor received the report from Myrddion, his face turned grey with consternation.

"Peace seems to elude us, doesn't it, old friend?" he muttered darkly, while he stared ponderously at his sandaled feet. "Sometimes I think I've seen too much to remain human, so I hope you'll forgive me if I'm grateful that you discovered this victim and not I."

Artor began to pace, his long legs covering the spartan room in just a few strides.

"We must warn all the women in the fortress and the township to avoid the lonely places," he said thoughtfully. "But I've no doubt that rumors are circulating through the whole of Cadbury already."

"Then I hope we find the perpetrator quickly," Myrddion responded. "The animal who carried out this violence is a madman, and his hunger will not be slaked with just one killing."

After Myrddion had bowed and departed, Artor was left alone with his dark thoughts.

A vicious and disturbed man who liked to kill lived close at hand in the Cadbury environs. From the quality of his boots, he was obviously a person of means, and he was driven by impulses that Artor couldn't understand. He was a man who hunted for unwary women—to hurt, to kill, and to feed on the fear that came with imminent death.

Reluctantly, on the evidence of Myrddion's eyes, Artor acquitted Caius of the murder. This crime was quite different in method and motive from the Severinii atrocities. Artor had thought of Caius as an unpunished monster for so long, deep in his secret heart, that he had almost hoped his foster brother was guilty. Caius made a convenient scapegoat, but now Artor must face facts. A monster other than the one he had always held close to his breast had chosen Cadbury as his playground.

The High King thrust his bleak thoughts aside and spat the sour taste from his mouth.

Midautumn was marked by another missing person, this time a child, a girl, who had been gathering fallen branches for the winter store of firewood behind the cottage where she lived. She had not ventured into the forest, but the earth showed drag marks, as if her hair had been used to pull her bodily into the shadows of the trees.

431

Her butchered corpse was found swiftly, for Artor's warriors had learned from Myrddion what signs to seek during their searches. The injuries inflicted on this girl were identical to those found on the rotted flesh of the widow, but this victim was discovered within twenty-four hours of her disappearance. She lay curled in a pathetic little ball, the marks of her beating still livid on her cooled flesh. Although the rigidity of death had passed, the warriors were superstitious about even touching her until Myrddion ordered them to roll her body onto a rough stretcher of tree branches covered with an old cloak. The child was buried while a priest intoned prayers for her soul, and, suddenly, all of Cadbury reeked of fear.

Perhaps the murderer would never have been caught if sheer chance had not trapped him in the end. Sheer chance, and the folly of a sudden urge by Nimue, the Maid of Wind and Water, to collect ingredients for her medicines.

During late summer and early autumn, Nimue had had vague sensations of being observed by an unseen presence within the fortress. But she had simply shaken her head, and put the prickling of her scalp down to an overactive imagination prompted by the troubled times in which she lived.

Still, no matter how her conscious reason told her that she was being foolish, Nimue took pains to latch her door at night and lean a large clothes chest against it for good measure. On one occasion, when she was walking past the stables with her basket of herbs over one arm, she had seen the flicker of a moving cloak in her peripheral vision. When she turned to stare into the afternoon shadows, no one was there.

Shame-faced, she took her half-serious fears to Myrddion.

"I think someone has been following me and watching my movements, master."

Myrddion looked up from his calculations and stared blankly at his apprentice.

"What?" Myrddion's eyes were distant, and Nimue could tell that he was still absorbed in the task of calculating the number of troops necessary for the spring levee.

"I feel sometimes that someone is watching me, and it frightens me a little," Nimue repeated, feeling obliged to trivialize her fears.

Myrddion's eyes sharpened, and one elegant white hand nervously pulled his long silver hair behind his ears.

"You're not excessively cautious, Nimue. When did you first notice this . . . feeling?"

Nimue lowered herself onto her accustomed stool, and Myrddion's heart lurched as her beautiful face frowned deeply in concentration.

"Since the time of Targo's death . . . at least I think that's when I first felt a prickling sensation on my neck. Do you know what I mean, master? It's as if someone is staring hard at me behind my back. But when I turn to look, there's no one there. Sometimes, in the great hall, no one seems to be paying the slightest attention to me, but I know that someone has just turned away."

"Perhaps Wenhaver is amusing herself by making you feel uncomfortable?"

Myrddion was worried, and, unaccountably, his concern steadied Nimue's nerves.

"She stares at me like an angry, fat, and fluffy cat, but she stares directly at my face." Nimue gurgled with amusement at the thought of Wenhaver being her stalker. "There's no subtlety in Wenhaver. I could be dressed in a covering of rags, but I swear she'd begrudge me the right to wear them. No, master, it's not Wenhaver. I know her particular feel, if you understand what I mean. I know I'm not making myself clear, but it seems to me that a strange man stares at me. He wants me, but not as a man should, and I have been stared at with lust often enough to recognize that look. This man hates me, and I don't know why."

The last few words were whispered, for Nimue knew how formless and foolish her words sounded, even in her own ears. She wished then that she hadn't troubled Myrddion, for, spoken aloud, her suspicions seemed self-indulgent and vain.

"As of this day you must carry Targo's sword with you whenever you go out into the fields. I'll ask Percivale to hone a sharp edge on both sides of the blade. The weapon is short enough to be easily carried in your basket."

Nimue opened her mouth to speak, but Myrddion ignored her protests.

"The man we seek is capable of insane obsession and will be motivated by some twisted logic of his own. You say you feel his eyes within the fortress? This narrows the field of potential culprits considerably. If you aren't being fanciful, then I must accept that our murderer is one of Artor's personal guard, or a provisioner from the town, or a trusted servant, or a member of Artor's court. It's a wide group of potential murderers, but it's narrower than the entire population of Cadbury."

Myrddion's concern was contagious, and Nimue shivered in the overwarm room.

Every warrior, every smith, the servant who drew water, and the aristocrats who bowed in the hall all had the potential to be a threat to her. The possibilities for danger opened like a yawning chasm before her unwilling feet.

"Unfortunately, we are forced to wait until we can reduce the field of suspects further. Each murder will tell us something new about the killer. But you must be cautious in the extreme, Nimue, for I don't know what I would do without you."

Myrddion offered this admission reluctantly, but Nimue's whole face was transfigured, and she glowed with pleasure.

"I'll speak to Odin and ask him to show you a few nasty tricks you could use with Targo's sword," Myrddion added thoughtfully. "Don't worry yourself to flinders, for we might trap the creature. He takes risks and he exposes himself more and more with each kill he makes."

Myrddion's face was drawn with fine lines, and, with a pang, Nimue saw that her master was finally beginning to show his age.

"You shouldn't have to worry overly about me, dear master." Nimue impulsively kissed Myrddion's hand. "I will do whatever Odin asks of me."

Hours, days, weeks followed, and the nerves of women from both within the forest and without were sorely stretched. Then, as winter sent out its first tendrils of heavy mist and the cold weather chained men and women to their hearths, a young boy went missing from within the citadel itself.

Artor was enraged.

The child was a minor son of a northern king, sent as a hostage against his tribe's disaffection. Afflicted by a bad case of hero worship, the twelve-year-old boy had dogged Artor's steps and he had become fond of the lad. The boy's constant chatter of questions and his bright-eyed interest in the business of government had charmed the High King, despite his determination to remain aloof. The lad, Grigor ap Gilleasbulg, been a great favorite with the guards, and had whiled away his days poking his nose into the stables, the kitchens, and the servants' quarters.

He never ventured outside of the fortress, so his sudden disappearance sent a frisson of fear running through every inhabitant of the tor. No one could now deny that the murderer had access to everyone within its walls. Wenhaver had treated the previous deaths as inconveniences that caused a pall to settle over her amusements, but now she importuned Artor to *do something* whenever their paths crossed.

"His victims have all been fair-haired," Wenhaver nagged. "And who possesses more golden hair than I do? You cannot know how frightened I am, and, as usual, you are more concerned with your silly work than with the safety of the queen."

"Madam, you are not the only fair-haired woman in the fortress. In fact, Myrddion reported to me only an hour ago that Nimue suspects she's been watched by a hidden man for several months."

Irrationally, Wenhaver was incensed. She couldn't bear to think that, even in unimaginable danger, Nimue eclipsed her. How dare a monster wish to kill Nimue before her?

"That creature has an unseemly habit of seeking attention whenever she can," Wenhaver exclaimed in her temper.

"Have you any idea how ridiculous you sound?" Artor sighed wearily. "Why must you always be at the center of everything, even disasters? Believe it or not, Wenhaver, you could die tomorrow and the world would go on without you. Your egotism is unseemly, madam, not Nimue's fears."

Artor was tired, dispirited, and gravely worried, so he spoke with unaccustomed violence.

"When will you think of anything other than your own selfish hide, woman? When will you not demand full attention at all times? When will the Saxons cut your throat to shut you up?"

Wenhaver fled, and then wept real tears before her ladies-in-waiting, stirring up even more fear among them than had existed before.

When Artor wearily recounted this latest squabble, Myrddion became agitated.

"I have been an idiot," he exclaimed. "Wenhaver has stumbled on what I, for all my learning, have missed."

Artor raised his mobile brows.

"All the victims have been fair-haired. The murderer must be obsessed with a certain appearance rather than a certain age or sex. The widow was in her thirties, the girl no more than nine, and the lad twelve, so it's beyond doubt that age is no indication of his preferences."

"I follow your reasoning, Myrddion, but how does this help us?"

"Apart from being of fair complexion, all the victims were vulnerable. The widow had no close family support. The girl was an only child with no known father, and your ward was five days' ride from his friends and family comfort."

Myrddion was certain that Nimue must be extremely careful.

TO BE FAIR to Nimue, she tried to obey her master, but circumstances were against her.

Winter passed without a single violent incident. The citizens and villagers of Cadbury and its environs were of the opinion that a madman had dwelt among them for a short time but had since moved on to find fresher, sweeter kills. But Nimue still sometimes felt those hot eyes of her watcher, and as the spring thaw filled the rills with clean, icy water and new shoots leapt up from the earth, she continued to keep Targo's sword within easy reach. After an evening's earnest advice from Percivale, she always strapped a knife to her thigh when she left the fortress, just in case her sword should be wrested from her. In addition, Odin taught Nimue how to use a blade most effectively, and showed her that even with her stiffened fingers she could hurt an attacker. Odin's instincts told him that the monster hadn't disappeared but was simply watching and waiting, using anticipation to sharpen his desires.

"You must practice with the knife, little wise woman. A man who has such lusts as this man possesses will desire what is cool and unapproachable, a woman such as yourself who shows so few weaknesses. Even while he watches you, he has killed other, weaker victims in your stead. He awaits an opportunity to catch you unawares, and, if you should fall into his power, he will want to feast on your fear of pain. Don't give him what he wants. You must never show him that he terrifies you."

"Ugh!" Nimue shuddered. "Such creatures should not be permitted to live. Why can't we see the wickedness written on his face, friend Odin?"

"He knows what he is, so he is used to hiding his true self behind a friendly smile. You can trust nobody."

Nimue grinned. "But I trust you, and Perce, and my dear master . . . and the High King, of course."

Then she sobered, for Odin tapped her right hand with his calloused fingers.

"You know what I am saying, little wise woman. Targo would bid you to be very, very careful and to obey your instincts. I will keep you under observation when my duties permit, but if this creature wants you, he will wait patiently until you come within his reach." He smiled suddenly. "Be careful, or—"

"I'm dead. I know." She grinned up at the Jutlander. His clear, northern eyes were open windows to the concerns that he felt, and his anxiety stiffened Nimue's resolve. "I will carry Targo's sword with me whenever I leave the fortress, and I will ponder what you have said," she assured the Jutlander. "I will practice dutifully, for, in truth, I refuse to be murdered without striking back at my assailant."

For all her precautions, Nimue still didn't feel safe.

The remains of the laughing, curious boy who had disappeared in the autumn were found during the spring thaw. The body had been reduced to gnawed bones and scattered fragments of fabric. Now, Artor's eyes watched the denizens of his fortress with a new, icy suspicion, and Myrddion's dreams were often disturbed by the horrors of a bleeding willow tree that his waking mind understood all too well. The past had come to torment the present.

Gawayne returned to Cadbury in the early spring, accompanied by a pale, brown-haired bride with kind, green eyes and a sweet, Otherworld smile. Enid, for such was her name, was soon a favorite with the citizens of the citadel, for she was good-natured and shy. Gawayne took great pride in his young wife; she placed so few demands upon his time and his emotions, and she made his days comfortable and easy.

Like the termagant she would become, Wenhaver alternated between cloying civility and spiteful rudeness in her dealings with Enid. The mere sight of Gawayne's wife devotedly kissing her husband's hand before he embarked upon a day of hunting was quite sufficient to cause Wenhaver to find fault with her maids until they were bruised and battered. She directed the acid of her tongue at the well-born ladies of the fortress with almost equal venom. One of her so-called companions tearfully returned to her father's household rather than face Wenhaver's wrath.

Eventually, Artor was forced to intervene.

He entered Wenhaver's luxurious apartments where she reclined, sulking and pretending to stitch a hem. His nose itched with the mingled aromas of scent: dying flowers, female flesh, and rosewater that roiled together into an unpleasant sweetness. With a dismissive wave of his hand, the High King sent maids and ladies running for the door until he was alone with the woman whom he had come to actively dislike.

"You've gone too far this time, madam." Artor snapped at his queen. "Myrddion has had to treat the injuries of another maid after one of your temper tantrums, and this poor creature had done nothing but try to serve you. Don't bother to speak of laziness or greed. You find it difficult to remember that you are a queen, and, as such, you are supposed to be representative of the best of Celtic womanhood, not the worst!"

Wenhaver put aside her sewing, and daintily selected an almond encased in a sweet paste. She popped it between her red lips, sucked on the morsel noisily before crunching the nut between her perfect teeth, and then raised her limpid eyes to her husband's irate face.

"I will do precisely as I please, husband. I don't see what you can do about it."

Then she picked up another morsel and smiled.

Artor crossed the room to her bed with two quick strides. His eyes were unreadable, but his muscles clenched like coiled springs along his still-firm jawline.

"You risk much when you wager your pretty skin on that belief, wife! You are barren, and are of less use to me than your lowliest servant. You are queen only because I value the alliance with your father and, unfortunately, my wedding vows."

Feeling safe within her scented, rose-damask room, Wenhaver made the mistake of laughing, and Artor's large hand reached out with reptilian swiftness and gripped her chin and cheeks so tightly that her tender flesh was bruised.

"You're hurting me," she whispered, her eyes wild and frightened.

"I'll do worse if you cross me, or shame me, or continue to flout my authority," Artor hissed.

He flung her away from him with such force that she was thrown off her stool and slid across the flagstoned floor. Her mouth sagged open in amazement, and tears started to leak from her eyes.

"You can save your tricks for one who does not know them for what they are. Gawayne's wife is worth ten of you, and yet you take joy in her tears. You are idle, useless, stupid, boring, and sterile. You are my hair shirt, as the monks would say."

Artor's expression was flat, cold, and merciless. Suddenly, her blood ran like ice through her veins. Did he suspect that she spent her nights in the stables with Gawayne? Had that sorcerer devil, Myrddion, discovered her amusements? What would Artor really do if he found out?

"You have never loved me, Artor, so why should you care what I do?"

"You are my queen, woman. I warn you now that I will burn you at the stake for impugning my honor if you stray from your vows and I am forced to wear the horns of a cuckold. Don't test my resolve. Your father would himself light the fire that burns the soul of a whore."

Artor turned on his heels and marched out of the apartments, leaving his wife bruised, shaken, and yet, regardless of her terrors, still burning for revenge. I will let Gawayne keep his plain little wife, she thought resentfully. I can wait. He will tire of her quickly enough, and Artor will be off soon on his summer campaign. I can wait for years if I must.

And then, because nothing could ever really be her fault, she blamed her husband's age for her barren state, and swore that she would foist a bastard upon him at the first opportunity.

"Then we'll see who is stupid," she shouted aloud, and hugged herself with secret glee.

Most of the citizens who made up the population of the citadel saw the fingerprint bruises on Wenhaver's painted face, and smirked behind their hands. Wenhaver was despised and feared within the fortress, so any discomfort that came her way was viewed as being her just deserts.

"She must have really asked for it this time," Gruffydd said conversationally to his fellows once he was free to eat his evening meal and drink a jug of cider with Artor's bodyguard. "That slut is a fair trial. I'd put nothing past her!"

"Gawayne doesn't let any parts of her pass him by either," one wag retorted, to a roar of ribald laughter.

Gruffydd paled and rose to his feet, his cup spilling on the rough table top.

"You're foolish to make jokes about infidelity and the queen in the same breath. If he ever considered the queen to be dishonorable, Lord Artor would be forced to execute her. Our whole world would fragment, and the Saxons would quickly come calling. Neither Leodegran nor Lot would accept the execution of their children for adultery or treason, and that would be the result if Artor believed that Gawayne was bedding the queen."

"Aye, you're correct in what you say, Gruff," the joker replied, his face suddenly somber. "Why couldn't our murderer have killed the queen before he left Cadbury far behind? We'd all be better off."

Odin shook his huge head. "The beast has not gone from Cadbury, and nor will the queen change her wicked ways," Odin said softly to Percivale and Gareth when they were alone. "Artor's kingdom unravels already as his luck deserts him and runs away like water. But I will always be Artor's man, and, when the time comes, I will die for him."

"As will we all," whispered Percivale.

And Gareth spoke like an echo. "As will we all."

Chapter XIX

ENDINGS AND BEGINNINGS

No thoughts of death or infidelity troubled Enid's mind as spring brought forth its full promise of flowers, newly greening fields, and a child that was quickening within her womb. Like everybody in the fortress, she consulted Lord Myrddion whenever she felt unwell, and she went to see him because she couldn't bear to eat a morsel of food in the mornings. She was becoming paler and more wan by the day.

"I rejoice for you, Lady Enid," Myrddion congratulated the young woman once she had described her symptoms with many blushes and much embarrassment. "Your husband will be a king one day, and your child will follow in his footsteps, should Fortuna grant you the boon of a son."

Enid stroked the tiny swelling of her belly, and Nimue felt a visceral stab of envy as she ground the preparation of dried herbs to cure the morning sickness. How she yearned to be gravid with child to a man such as Myrddion.

"I hope my lord Gawayne will share my joy. He is distracted at times, but he is really a very good husband. And King Lot will be pleased at our news, for he has desired a grandson since we were first wed."

Enid was looking remarkably pretty. Her long, plaited hair was bound with a yellow ribbon that gave its soft color a richer glow. Small spirals of curls had escaped her braids, and they framed her face. She was slender and fine-boned, and her countenance reflected her contentment and completion.

"You can see, Lady Enid, how my excellent apprentice is likely to put me out to pasture soon, just like an old horse," Myrddion said. "She has prepared a mixture of dried herbs for you that you must drink with very hot water in the mornings, and whenever you feel the nausea coming on. You must eat well and get some color back into your pretty cheeks."

Nimue felt a stab of envy as Myrddion fussed over Enid. He never treated her like fragile glass, nor did he stroke her cheek in that gentle fashion that was peculiarly his own.

Then, because Nimue was a fair-minded young woman, and because it was impossible to dislike Enid with her sweet ways and pliant nature, she smiled at the young mother-to-be, offered her congratulations, and put the ground herbs into a cloth bag.

"You need have no fears, Lady Enid," Nimue reassured their patient. "These herbs will not harm your child, and you will soon be blooming. I will act as your midwife when your time approaches, for my master has trained me well, and I predict you will bear a beautiful son for your husband."

"I am in your debt, Lady Nimue, and I thank you for your kindness." Enid smiled her appreciation. "I am glad now that I never believed any of the horrible things that the queen always said about you. My mother warned me to beware of gossip before I came to Cadbury, and I've discovered that she was right." She sighed. "Queen Wenhaver dislikes me. I have tried and tried to please her, but nothing I do or say seems to have any effect on the way she treats me."

Nimue pressed Enid's narrow hands in commiseration. "I suspect that the queen feels chagrin at her childless state. It's probably best that you feel pity for her if she says anything to hurt you. I find this helps me not to lose my temper with her."

Enid smiled her appreciation of Nimue's words, and her rather ordinary features were transformed into a soft but earthy beauty. Impulsively, she embraced the startled apprentice.

"The people here call you the Maid of Wind and Water, but I don't find you strange or frightening at all."

Myrddion smiled indulgently at both young women, although he knew that Nimue was distinctly uncomfortable under Enid's praise.

"I'm glad you feel comfortable with me, because I don't think I'm frightening at all," Nimue responded. "Unfortunately, I'm a common person, and a barbarian at that. I'm simply Nimue, and any worth I have derives from the status of Master Myrddion."

Enid squeezed Nimue's hand to acknowledge her words, before bowing low to Myrddion and tripping out through the doorway.

Myrddion began to laugh. "You say that you're simply Nimue? I doubt your sincerity, for you are far from simple."

"Rubbish," Nimue snapped. "Now I'll worry about Enid all the time, and I'll be driven demented trying to live up to her expectations." Then she smiled at Myrddion, and the sun seemed to shine more brightly. "And I could kill that Wenhaver bitch, if there wasn't such a long line of volunteers ahead of me," Nimue continued, her face pink with indignation and rueful humor. "How can she be so cruel to such a gentle creature as Enid?"

Myrddion kept his thoughts to himself.

Gawayne received the news of his wife's condition with the excess of pride and bravado that is customary with men who believe that they have fathered the perfect child. He celebrated his good fortune by purchasing a plain, golden band for Enid's wrist, before becoming royally and expansively drunk with the warriors from his troop.

In her bower, Wenhaver became white with envy at the joyous news. Alone in her rose-scented bed, she prayed that the whey-faced Enid would die unpleasantly in childbirth, and that her cloth-witted lover would choke on his own vomit.

As spring lazed slowly towards summer, Gawayne became a model husband and doted on Enid, whose glow of happiness lent Cadbury a festive mood. Gawayne was so attentive that Enid's heart was wholly lost to him. For the first time in his thoughtless, fickle life, Gawayne was forced to consider the burdens, responsibilities, and joys of adult-hood. Secretly, he found that he was enjoying the experience, especially the hero worship that his wife gave him so unstintingly. Nimue's herbs managed to keep the morning sickness at bay, and, as the babe grew within her, Enid became even more beautiful. She also became less trusting, for now she had the full measure of the queen. One small exchange had brought out the tigress in the placid Enid.

Wenhaver had been fanning herself in a small arbor that had been built for the queen and her ladies. Artor had insisted on the installation of a fountain, a concept that was alien to Wenhaver but one that she came to prize as the days grew hot and humid. The water splashed from the mouth of a bronze dolphin into a large bowl, whence it overflowed and formed a shallow, pebbled pool where fish darted like silver shadows between the flowering water plants. A dragonfly darted over the water, leaving tiny circlets where it had touched the smooth surface.

"How hot it is," Wenhaver complained to no one in particular. "These summer days are so like those hot months before the contagion came. You should be careful, Enid, for Gawayne has no common sense. He's always off hunting or carousing with the common people, and heaven alone knows what illness he might bring back to you in the fortress. He's irresponsible!"

Enid laid aside the tiny garment she had been sewing and placed one hand instinctively over the now-pronounced swell of her belly.

"My Gawayne does all that a good man should, Your Majesty. He is a fine husband, and will make an excellent and doting father. As for any contagion, my master would never wish me harm, though we all risk illness every day. I trust in the love of our god."

"Your god won't save you, or any of us, for that matter," Wenhaver replied. She was completely unconcerned at the gasp of shock that came from her ladies at her blasphemy.

"The men of Cadbury are like broken reeds, interested only in war, lovemaking, and pleasure. And Gawayne is the same as any other man in this fortress. You shouldn't rely on him overmuch, Enid, for I know he has left a string of satisfied women from Cadbury to Venta Belgarum and onwards to King Lot's domain. He was neither born, nor inclined, to cleave to one woman."

Enid was badly hurt by the queen's comments, but instead of bowing a docile head, as was her usual custom, she caught the queen's amused glance and was suddenly very angry.

"My mother always told me that men are fools in the hands of unscrupulous women," Enid responded as demurely as she could. "They are so easily manipulated, especially by those vulgar creatures who cannot be content with holding one man of their own. Such whores always seek to steal another woman's husband away from her to feed their own vanity—or so I have been told by those who should know."

Wenhaver's cheeks paled, and her blue eyes narrowed and darkened at the implications of Enid's insulting words. Did the little mouse suspect her liaison with Gawayne? Or was she simply attacking her because of rumor and innuendo?

"Those are harsh words, Enid," Wenhaver said with cloying sweetness, her mouth pursing dangerously. "Are you saying that your husband is a mere toy in the hands of unprincipled women?"

"Perhaps that would have been the case at one time," Enid replied guilelessly. "My Gawayne is a dear, sweet boy, even though he is so much older than I am. I believe that all men are boys when they are truly happy, no matter what their age is or how powerful they are. I sincerely hope that you have experienced such felicity with King Artor."

This barb, delivered so quietly, drove deeply into Wenhaver's tender ego. She had to force a smile of agreement, for she could not admit that her husband avoided her.

"Well, don't say you weren't warned," she replied lightly, while swearing to herself that she would drag Gawayne into her bed as soon as Enid's condition rendered sex difficult.

Wenhaver was left wondering what Enid had guessed, and the

queen's ladies enjoyed gossiping about her obvious discomfort for several days. Every woman of any wit in the fortress was aware of the queen's precarious position with her royal husband.

But such exchanges were rare, for Enid spent her days quietly communing with her unborn child as she prepared for the birth, so the summer flew by into another autumn.

One morning, Nimue rose early, long before first light, for she needed to replenish her stocks of lavender, rosemary, rue, and mandrake root. Lavender and rosemary grew in the fortress's herb garden, and Nimue was almost certain she had spied rue growing there as well. But mandrake, if it were to be found at all, would be discovered only within the Wildewood. Since she must enter that grim, dark place, Nimue decided to hunt for some of Myrddion's precious lichens, mushrooms, and mosses, for these rare fungi could be turned into medications to cure wounds that stubbornly refused to heal.

Although fears of murder and bloodshed in the community had been largely forgotten, and it was many months since Nimue had given any thought to her demon watcher, she had not forgotten the warnings given by Odin, Gareth, Percivale, and Myrddion. The sword of the legions, accompanied by an even smaller hand knife, fitted into her long, shallow basket where they were covered by a small hand trowel. For once, as the day was threatening to be unseasonably warm, Nimue left her dagger behind, and she sallied forth into the early dawn with a broad-brimmed straw hat crammed over her long plaits.

Her feet left a slight track in the rime of frost that covered both flagging and the brittle grass. Within the simple herb garden, she cut a good store of lavender, rosemary, and rue that completely covered Targo's blade. Waving to soldiers and early visitors, Nimue tripped down the long curved path to the base of the hill, passing through the fortifications without really noticing the wondrous practicality of their design.

But then, Nimue was accustomed to her master's inventive works, be they medicinal, alchemical, or mechanical.

She wandered through the market of Cadbury town, buying a scarlet ribbon and examining a length of fine woven wool that had been dyed to the color of deep water. But her purse was well nigh empty, and she had no desire to browse if she couldn't afford to buy.

As she passed through the bustling laneways, the townsfolk smiled in her direction. The Maid of Wind and Water was a singular creature, as all the townsfolk knew, but she was also a fetching lass and was always ready to talk and give cheer as she passed among them. She was not above agreeing to see a sick child or an elderly grandparent and, on many occasions, had sent herbs or poultices from the fortress to soothe the ills of her patients. Nimue would have been surprised to discover that she was more highly respected than the noble Wenhaver, queen to King Artor.

Nimue loved her herbal rambles. Her passion for walking in the early morning had started in her childhood, when she had risen in the dark and played hide and seek with her shadow under the dappled trees. Ever mindful of the dangers of the wild places, Gallwyn had remonstrated with Nimue when she was caught outside the gates of Venonae. Nimue had tearfully obeyed Gallwyn's demands because her foster mother had seemed so frightened. Gallwyn had tried in vain to cure Nimue of her tendency to wander, for the young girl loved the trees, the shadows, and the still water within the deep forests.

Now, as she ambled through the places where the laneways turned into rutted tracks between the fields, Nimue began to whistle in a very unladylike fashion. She smiled as she remembered how often Gallwyn had boxed her ears when she caught her trying to warble like a bird, or creating songs of her own devising. With no one to care what she did, Nimue caught the hem of her trailing skirt in her girdle so that her long legs were bare below the knees, and she swung her basket with its precious clippings in sheer exuberance at the joy of being alive.

The wood gradually ate into the fallow fields, and the sun, as it rose through the sky, sent long, green-stained bands of light through to the forest floor. Nimue overturned a rotten log, and found a rich source of lichens growing in serried, orange flanges like some strange flower. She deftly cut away the spongy flesh and scraped a handful of common moss from the wettest sides of the log.

The morning passed quickly as she hunted for her lichens and the elusive mandrake plant. She swam through the shadows from tree to tree, harvesting useful specimens from the roots and adding to the supplies that were filling her basket. Then, just as the sun had finally started to angle down in the sky, Nimue's sharp eyes spied the foliage she sought, the familiar leaves of the mandrake plant, growing in a cluster of smaller specimens.

She was on her knees in a trice, digging for the special root that had derived its name from its resemblance to a child's rough manikin. She was happily humming under her breath and singing softly as she imagined Myrddion's joy when she brought him her booty.

Nimue felt no inkling of fear, and completely missed the sounds of quiet feet that were slowly creeping up behind her.

Then, as she placed the mandrake root in the basket and stowed away her small trowel, she saw the movement of her stalker's shadow. A hood was thrust over her head and jerked tightly round her throat in one swift, practiced movement.

Blind panic overtook her as darkness and pain, but at the exact moment when the cord of the hood bit into her neck, Nimue managed to slide two fingers under the cord. It allowed her a tiny space in which she could maintain an airway, albeit in great, wrenching sobs.

"You bitch! I'll make you scream before you die. You'll beg to be dead . . . you'll howl for it," a male voice whispered in her ear so softly, so insidiously, and with such a hiss of hot breath that she shrieked with panic.

The man snickered.

All Nimue's instincts, coupled with Odin's instructions, told her that she must keep those two bruised fingers under the cord and keep hold of her basket, for her life depended on her presence of mind.

"Morturi!" the voice gloated. "Let the games begin."

The hands that jerked her off her feet were very strong, and she found herself forced backwards over rocks and fallen branches like so much flotsam in a swollen river She heard her trowel fall, then her pruning knife, and she knew that all her carefully collected specimens were tumbling out of her basket as she was forced towards a place where the man intended to rape her, then take her life.

And she lacked a free hand to snatch up Targo's sword.

What if the blade falls from the basket? Nimue thought desperately. If I cannot get to it, I'm dead! Don't panic. Don't fight yet. Just think, she told herself.

In the blinking of an eye, she realized she had one frail chance, almost impossible, but better than no hope at all.

She dragged a lungful of air in through the constricting hood, and then pulled her fingers out from under the cord. Immediately, she started to choke, to die, but she knew this animal had no intention of letting her strangle to death before he had had his fill of her body.

"Don't waste time thinking, Nimue," she almost heard Targo's spirit whisper in her head as she plunged her free hand into the basket, and through a stray frond of rosemary that had become wedged in the wicker. "Just do it!"

Her questing fingers found Targo's cold blade. Her hands desperately searched along the sharp edges until she found the hilt, although her fingers were cut badly in the quest.

"Die!" she keened with the last of her breath, even as her sight darkened from lack of oxygen. And she stabbed the short sword backwards and upwards from her waist.

A cry escaped from all too human lips, although it was quickly muffled, but the iron hands restraining her head released the cords of the hood, allowing Nimue to draw in lungfuls of rather musty air. The cloth of the hood stank, and Nimue wondered briefly what other terrified women had smelled its rankness. She spun on her heels and fell to her knees, still blinded by the hood, and slashed out in front of her with Targo's sword.

The ancient blade had drunk blood for more than one hundred years. It had been used long before Nimue or Targo were born, for

451

the legions never wasted good weapons. Now it drank again, eagerly, as if its will and lust were as strong as the man whose blood it tasted.

The man screamed again, shrill and high like a woman, and she heard something metallic fall to the ground with a thud. Then she was thrust down with great force, still clutching her sword as she fell on her back.

Heavy footsteps blundered off through the fallen leaves, and Nimue heard the smashing of twigs and branches under a hasty tread. She held the sword before her, and then silence fell, as terrifying and as horror-filled as her few moments of battle had been. Only rasping breathing disturbed the silence of Wildewood, and with a childlike wonder Nimue realized it was herself who was panting.

Disregarding a lance of pain in her elbow, Nimue raised her left arm and tore off the black woolen hood.

In the steadily darkening forest, she was utterly alone.

Breathing raggedly, and with blood oozing over her hands, Nimue took stock of the pains in her body. Her knees and heels had been scraped almost raw, her right hand was throbbing from long cuts, and her throat was bruised so she could barely croak a sound. Her left elbow had struck some hard tree root with such force that she had heard the sharp little crack of breaking bone.

In a strange, dreamlike state, Nimue gathered up the hood and the discarded dagger, and then paused, listening and looking. She spied traces of blood on the bracken and ferns, but was unsure who had bled there, herself or her attacker. Where she had fallen, the message was more clearly written. Dark blood spatters showed that Targo's blade had bitten deeply. She began to retrace her steps. She forced herself to recover every piece of lichen, moss, and herb, including her trowel and pruning knife, a task that took some time as the mandrake root was difficult to find. The sunlight was almost completely extinguished, and every rustle in the underbrush sent a shiver through her body. Clever in the ways of illness, Nimue realized she was in shock, that strange, suspended period after a battle that could kill a man as quickly as a knife wound. But for now, she blessed the unnatural calm that forced her to think slowly and with clarity.

Then suddenly she was too tired to walk a single step, and she sank to the ground.

The shock is beginning to wear off, she thought aimlessly, and every wound was burning like fire or aching so fiercely that movement was agony. The left arm that had dragged off the hood was now immobile, and its swelling joints and steady, thudding ache indicated at least one broken bone.

I must go, she admonished herself. Rise, Nimue, for your master will be worried. Besides, the beast might return. Get up, you stupid cow, for you cannot die here.

She struggled to her feet, gripped her basket with painful fingers, and began to trudge out of the forest. Weariness settled over her like a shroud. On several occasions, she leaned against forest trees, and left her own blood spoor behind her. But at last, the green aquarium of the Wildewood was at her back, and the fields stretched away to the serried towers of Cadbury Tor in the late afternoon light.

"One foot in front of the other, girl," Targo told her in his kindest voice.

Nimue swore she saw him stand at her right hand, his old face serious.

"I'm doing the best I can, Targo," she replied irritably.

"Not good enough, darling. It'll soon be full dark, and he'll be waiting for you. Head towards the lights."

Nimue carefully turned her pounding head towards her left side, and Gallwyn hovered beside her.

"You're both dead. Am I dead too?" she asked the shades querulously.

"Not hardly, lass, you're just a little bent around the edges." Targo smiled. "You got him, girl," the ancient warrior continued proudly. "I never thought that dull old sword of mine would prove useful again."

Nimue noticed irrelevantly that Targo no longer needed his canes.

"I'm that proud of you, lovey, I could burst," Gallwyn whispered on the other side. "Look what you've made of yourself. Look how far you've traveled."

"The girl's got a big heart, hasn't she?" Targo added. "And she has warriors as ancestors, for all that we called them barbarians." The shade smiled again. "Keep walking, lass. You're doing well."

"You always were a bossy old bastard, Targo, even if you are a figment of my imagination," Nimue panted.

Then her foot slipped over a clod of earth on the rutted track, invisible in the half-light. Nimue fell on her injured arm, and, for a moment, her vision went black. When her breathing returned, she began to cry aloud from the pain.

I think I'll just lie here, she decided, and in her imagination the mud was a deep, soft, featherbed.

"Get up, Nimue. Right now!" Gallwyn ordered in the voice she used when she was very angry with the kitchen girls.

"I'm ashamed of you, girl," Targo snapped. "Everybody hurts some time. Think of Myrddion. Who will look after him if you die in the roadway?"

"Why are you both so angry at me?" Nimue moaned, but she used her good arm and her strong thighs to force herself to her feet.

"Because we love you, girl," Targo replied, the moonlight shining through his eyes.

"And we want you to live," Gallwyn finished for the old warrior. "We watch over you, you know. And I'm now quite fond of this little pipsqueak here who helps me care for you."

"Pipsqueak? I trained a king, woman, and you only fed him," Targo snarled, in mock fury. "Keep moving, lass, you're doing very nicely, my girl."

"And I trained Nimue," Gallwyn retorted.

"There's a light ahead, Nimue, so make for that," Targo ordered, and Nimue responded, while her two shades argued and bickered and encouraged her to keep moving. She forced one foot in front of the other, still clutching her precious basket.

454

Lamplight poured out of the slit windows in a beehive-shaped hut as Nimue approached. She leaned against the door and tried to knock.

"Bye, lovey," Gallwyn whispered softly.

"See you soon, lass," Targo added.

"Not too soon, I hope." Nimue giggled, knowing that she hovered on the edge of hysteria.

The night wind sighed around her as she tried to summon the strength to knock more loudly.

"Yes?" a frightened female voice stuttered from behind the latched barrier.

"Let me in," Nimue called softly. "I've been attacked."

Behind the door, the silence was absolute.

"I am Nimue, the Maid of Wind and Water," she added. "I am apprentice to Lord Myrddion Merlinus. He will pay you well if you let me in and take care of me." She moaned softly, despite her intention to maintain her strength.

The door opened the slightest crack. Nimue lost her balance, and slowly began to fall down . . . deeper and deeper . . . to a place where she was without her comforting shades, and nightmares waited in the darkness.

"Run to the fortress, boy," Nimue heard a coarse female voice shout as she was falling. "Run to speak to Master Merlinus. He will know what to do with her, for it's certain that she is the Maid of Wind and Water. Run, lad, there's gold for us this night."

At least someone will be happy, Nimue thought vaguely, as she continued to fall into that soft, endless darkness where there are no dreams or nightmares, and where absolute silence reigns.

AFTER A TIME, fragments of thought and confusion intruded; hugely exaggerated faces; disembodied voices; her hand being kissed again and again; tears and laughter.

And a voice that hissed in her ear, "I'll get you yet, bitch."

Nimue woke slowly as a stray ray of light found her eyelid in the stygian darkness of her room. A black-robed form was lying across a chair, snoring gently. Long white hair fell over a face that was etched with worry. A naked sword lay across his knees.

"Master," she croaked.

Myrddion's body snapped into instant life. The sword fell to the ground with a metallic clatter and his dark, anxious eyes fixed themselves on her face. In the darkness, half blind and even half dead, she would have known her protector anywhere.

Myrddion, her master, was watching over her.

Even though her head was pounding with an unbearable headache, and her left elbow was splinted and immobilized, she opened her arms as best she could and Myrddion eased his body into her embrace.

Kneeling beside her bed, with his face close to hers on the pillow, and with her right arm holding him close against her breast, Myrddion was neither able nor inclined to move.

"You're real. And I'm alive. Oh, my lord, I have searched and searched to find my way back to you and to the fortress."

"I've been here ever since you were found, Nimue," Myrddion whispered soothingly. "I haven't left your side."

"Then I must have been having a nightmare."

She kept her grip round Myrddion's neck.

"Move over, woman. If you intend to strangle me, at least have pity on my old back."

Nimue released him and moved to one side of her pallet, and Myrddion stretched his long legs beside her. She held him again, cradling his head on her good arm and, in perfect peace, apprentice and master fell asleep.

Artor found them together in the early evening. Myrddion was lying with his face against Nimue's breast and their hair intermingled so that man and woman seemed woven together. Nimue's lips smiled in her sleep, in stark contrast to the livid bruises on her throat, and Artor felt a pang of bitter jealousy, for no one loved him in the way that Nimue loved Myrddion. Then, as he recalled the decades of selfless service to the crown and the old man's unswerving devotion, he shook off the uncharitable emotion and was pleased at the good fortune of his most loyal servant.

"Myrddion?" he whispered, and two pairs of eyes snapped open. One pair was ebony dark and the other pair northern blue. Myrddion eased himself out of Nimue's embrace.

"What do you need of me, my lord?"

Myrddion's normally pale complexion slowly suffused with blood as he realized the king had found him asleep in the embrace of Nimue. All his past guilt concerning the disparity in their ages surfaced as he struggled to rise on numbed feet.

Artor held out a hand to his friend and helped Myrddion up.

"You're blushing, friend. Why?"

"I shouldn't be here, my lord. I shouldn't compromise her, for so I have done by my stupid behavior. A man is never too old to be a fool."

Artor grinned wryly. "Perhaps you're finally being clever, my dearest and oldest living friend. Nimue might yet be your salvation."

Artor glanced down at Nimue, who was also struggling into a sitting position. Bandages covered her palms, cut by Targo's blade. Myrddion himself had stitched those wounds closed lest her hands be permanently useless. He had also eased her elbow into a bent position, while forcing the broken bone and its dislocated fellows back into position, and then binding the whole arm into place with carefully shaped wooden splints. The worst injury seemed to be a superficial cut on the back of Nimue's head, for the area immediately around the wound was very swollen. Myrddion feared that her skull had been breached, and both men knew that those poor creatures who survived such wounds often became drooling idiots or were changed beyond recognition.

The blue eyes that now met Artor's open gaze were those of the true Nimue, and the mobile brows that rose under his careful scrutiny were Nimue's brows. Obviously, her brain had suffered no damage.

"We must discover who's responsible for this attack, girl. And why. I regret my haste, but the blood trail led us in the direction of Cadbury Tor. I can't be seen to be harboring a savage murderer within these walls."

457

"I understand, my lord," Nimue responded gravely. "Now that my thoughts are clear, I can recall much of what happened during the attack."

"Are you hurting, Nimue?" Myrddion asked. "We can investigate this matter at a later time if you don't feel well."

Myrddion held her free hand, careful not to press upon the stitches that crossed her palm.

"Did you find the lichens and mosses I collected, lord?" Nimue asked. "I found some excellent samples, and I was careful to collect them again after the monster went away."

"Yes, I found them. And they were unharmed from their ordeal—unlike yourself. We can examine their medicinal properties together when you are well."

Artor was beginning to grow impatient. "I must know the details of the attack on you, Nimue, and I need to hear them immediately. Every moment is precious, with an animal guilty of rape and murder on the loose somewhere. He must be found before he takes another victim. We might not be so lucky next time."

"Oh!" Nimue said, her eyes glazing with shock as a memory returned. "He's definitely in the fortress. I remember that he came into this room and threatened me, but I thought it was only a dream."

"What do you mean, Nimue?" Myrddion demanded. He glanced fearfully around the room as if a crazed murderer could leap out from behind a clothes chest.

"Tell me," Artor ordered.

"I was half conscious but I remember the whisper in my ear," Nimue said softly, and she shivered at the memory. "How could I not remember what he said? He called me a bitch, and he promised to come for me soon to finish what he had started. What have I done that someone could hate me so?" A tear snaked down from one eye.

"We are upsetting her, my lord," Myrddion warned his king angrily, but Nimue placed her one good hand on his arm.

"I must tell the king all that I remember, Myrddion. I must, or I will never forget it, and I'll not give that coward the satisfaction of a lifetime of fear. Let me speak, please."

"Why do you call him a coward?" Artor asked.

"He attacked me from behind, and, because he knew I would be able to recognize him, he covered my face with that vile hood. Only a coward, or someone I knew well, would want to hide from his victim."

Both men nodded in agreement.

"He moves silently and knows the woods very well; I had no idea that he was there until the hood went over my face." She glanced across at Myrddion once more. "I was engrossed in freeing the mandrake root. Did you find it, master? I took some trouble to put it back in the basket."

"I have it, child. Just tell Artor your story."

Nimue did so, and fulfilled her task without any particular distress except for satisfaction when she spoke of how she struck the monster twice, once with the point of Targo's sword, and once with a blind slash. She was more circumspect about her description of the long journey out of the forest and her eventual arrival at the sanctuary of the weaver's cottage. Both men knew at once that she was holding something back.

"Can we reward the weaver's wife? She was alone, except for her children, and she must have been frightened, yet she opened the door to a stranger and sent her eldest son for assistance."

"She has been well paid for her efforts," Artor replied grimly. Myrddion had been blunt in his discussion with his king. Untreated, and exposed to the night air, Nimue would probably have died of exposure and shock on the roadway were it not for the insistence of the weaver's son that he speak to Myrddion.

"If I had money to pay for it, I would like to ask her husband to weave me a sea-green length of cloth to thank them for their help," Nimue whispered tearfully, thinking of the delicate wool she had seen in the marketplace on that dreadful day.

"I will pay for the work myself, Nimue, so don't worry your head about it," Myrddion answered. "Now, what do you remember about your attacker?"

"He was very strong. I'm tall for a woman, yet he pulled me off my feet as if I was thistledown."

She thought for a second, and Myrddion could tell by her expression that she was reliving her experiences. He felt a surge of pure rage, something so foreign to his nature that he was taken aback by his reaction.

"He was a little taller than me, but he was thick in the body. I could feel his chest and belly against my back before I fell. And his cheeks were smooth." Nimue muttered as she stared at the splints and bandages on her arm, "I managed to block the cord of the hood that was cutting off my airway, and I felt his cheek against my hand. His face was plucked smooth."

Both men looked at each other. Most Celts wore facial hair as a sign of manhood. Only men of Roman heritage, Gawayne, some sentimentalists who emulated a younger Artor, and eccentrics such as Myrddion were still inclined to pluck or blade away their beards.

"Are you quite certain, Nimue?" Myrddion asked her quietly.

"Yes master, I'm certain. Even now, I can feel his smooth cheeks. At first I wondered if he was a boy, but he was far too strong and heavily bodied to be a youth."

Myrddion stroked her downy cheek, his eyes unreadable in the half-light.

"It's time you went back to sleep now, my dear. I will give you one of my bitter drafts to help you on your way and you'll feel much better when you awaken."

Nimue nodded like an obedient child, then her blue eyes flared with a sudden thought.

"The stab wound must have struck him on the side, for he was dragging me at the time I used the sword. It can't be very deep. I may even have caught his left thigh, for I was not standing upright at the time. But the slash wound caught him either on the lower right arm or across the belly. I was kneeling, facing him, and no other wound is possible."

"Well done, Nimue," Artor praised her. "You would have made an excellent warrior."

"But then I'd have to be all hairy and rough, my lord." She gurgled with laughter. "I think I prefer being female."

Outside the sickroom, after Myrddion sent a servant to fetch a sleeping potion, the two men planned their next move.

"Every word that Nimue spoke points directly at an aristocratic Celt . . . or Caius," Myrddion stated baldly. "Her description fits him exactly because he still holds to the Roman way of dress. I'm sorry, my lord."

"Aye, and he is about the same height as Nimue," Artor sighed. "While his guilt, or otherwise, is yet to be proven, I can think of an immediate way to settle the matter. I had acquitted him of any guilt in these murders because the method was so different from the Severinii attacks. I'll be sorry to discover I've made a mistake."

"Caius should be questioned and his body checked for injuries." Behind the reasonable words, Myrddion's thoughts were black with a fury that he hadn't known since his checkered youth. Artor could feel the old man's rage, like loosened fire, as suspicion of his foster brother's guilt moved towards certainty. Targo had been right to warn the young Artorex that a quiet, restrained man could go berserk when he eventually reached the limit of his self-control. Artor recognized that Myrddion had reached his limit, and that he could pose a problem in the hours to come.

"We'll visit Caius immediately," the High King said, to placate Myrddion's obvious rage. "And we'll take a couple of stout fellows with us to hold him down so we can check his person for injuries."

Had Myrddion not been so angry, he would have wondered why Artor's proposal was so indiscreet.

"I agree, my lord. It should be done immediately. Injuries such as those described by Nimue will be absolute proof of his guilt. But we should take no guards, my lord, for you cannot afford any gossip over this matter."

Artor knew this, but he had wanted his friend to be the person to suggest a surreptitious investigation. Even in such a desperate crisis, Artor's cold inner self was still manipulating his loved ones.

"Conversely, the absence of wounds will clear him of all blame," he said.

Endeavoring to act naturally, the two men negotiated the warren of corridors that led to Caius's apartments. Servants and warriors bowed as they passed, but the High King ignored their courtesies. Gruffydd approached his master, but when he saw Artor's stiff face he decided abruptly that his presence was needed elsewhere. Odin marched resolutely behind his master, his face reflecting the urgency of his master's actions, and wise men stepped aside and whispered furtively in corners.

The High King and his counselor found Caius in Queen Wenhaver's garden, telling amusing stories and looking relaxed and healthy. Such was the courtier's charm that the queen was purring with pleasure, and she even invited the two interlopers to join the merry group. Caius raised one eyebrow at his brother, for he saw through Artor's smiling lips and Myrddion's lying eyes. He grinned insolently at the High King.

"Why do you bring Odin to protect yourself from women, my king?" Caius joked, but his words had a certain bite. A little shocked at the steward's presumption, Wenhaver nevertheless smiled in amusement, for she noticed a whitening around Artor's mouth and nostrils.

"Odin goes with him everywhere, in case we women attack him with our bodkins and our needles," she said.

"Wife, leave us for a few moments, you and your pretty ladies, so my brother and I can speak plainly to each other," Artor ordered without bothering to address Wenhaver directly. His eyes were locked on the limpid, open face of his steward.

"Your manners are execrable, as always," Wenhaver retorted. "Play your little-boy games if you must, such masculine conversations are too boring for my liking anyway. Come, ladies. The king has spoken, and we must all obey the king."

As the last of the ladies swept out of the garden in an indignant swirl of brilliant skirts, Caius uncrossed his legs with studied unconcern and leaned back against the sun-warmed wall.

"I don't think your dear wife likes you overmuch, brother," Caius offered, his tone flat.

"Strip off your tunic, Caius, and then we'll discuss my wife," Artor replied in an inflexible voice. In his assumed air of superiority, Caius was visibly reverting to the bully whom Artorex had both feared and hated during their youth.

"Why should I, Artor? What am I suspected of that warrants a person of my lineage having to bare his arse in public?"

"We're not here to dance around the truth, Caius," Myrddion said, his face showing his distaste for the situation. "Your future hangs on your response."

Caius's smile was predatory. "You really want to see my body, dear brother? You really desire the truth? Very well, I'll give you what you want. What are a few commoners more or less? The lovely Nimue was a commoner the last time I checked, but she certainly has an air about her, doesn't she? How could I overlook her when I imagine she's such a good fuck."

Artor was sickened. His foster brother was showing the true man behind the affable facade he had built, out of fear and self-interest, since the killing of his mother. Truly, Artor thought, men never change, they simply learn to hide their flaws effectively. He wondered how long Caius had been a sadistic murderer.

God help me, Artor thought. Now I must wound my oldest friend.

"You are impertinent and insulting, Caius," Myrddion snapped. "And you still haven't removed your tunic. Perhaps you're hoping to avoid retribution because you're kin to the High King. You won't escape this time."

"Send Odin away, Myrddion," Artor ordered abruptly. "The game has changed."

"What?"

"You heard me, Myrddion. I am about to change the game."

"No, my lord! I'm sorry, but I won't allow my suspicions of this man to stand untested."

"Then I will do it myself." He ordered Odin to move out of earshot of the travesty that was about to take place. "Now, Caius, show me your wounds. No one, other than Myrddion and myself, will see them."

Caius smirked, and pulled off his beautifully tailored tunic.

A narrow slash wound, well bandaged, cut across the right side of his belly. It was low and close to a deep fold in his soft flesh immediately above his pubic bone.

"It's a shame she didn't castrate you," Myrddion snarled with obvious satisfaction.

Caius continued to smile.

"What of the other wound?" Artor asked.

Caius lowered his loincloth. An inexpertly stitched wound, also covered, had narrowly missed the tendons in his thigh. He was grinning, as if these wounds were badges of honor, although they must have caused him considerable pain. He seemed to relish discovery.

The cruelty in Caius's nature must have longed to assert itself once its outlet in battle ended, Myrddion thought with disgust. The soldier that slaked his demons in battle was safe during troubled times. But in peace, he became a monster. Targo had recognized the brutality within Caius. He had never been fooled, as his constant warnings down the years testified. Myrddion wondered whether the killings provided Caius with the opportunity to somehow act out the murder of his hated foster brother, for his victims had all been fair like Artor. Perhaps when he exulted in killing, Caius was once again slaying the well-born mother who had loved him so well but had ruled him so completely throughout his younger life.

Myrddion felt ill with a natural man's loathing for madness, and knew that Caius's motives would always be unknown. He was certain that Caius had stepped over a line in his mind, and now there was no going back. To keep his oath to Livinia, Artor might try to find a soft solution, yet still punish his brother as he had sworn to do on a blood-soaked night when they had all been younger. But Caius would never stop killing, not as long as there was flesh to desecrate. A worm lay in his soul that could never be killed.

"Arrest him, Artor. I hunger to hear this man scream when he confesses his crimes." Myrddion turned to Caius and almost spat out his accusations. "You lied all those years ago, didn't you, Caius? You assisted the Severinii to kill those poor boys. Is that when you learned to enjoy watching life drain away? Or did Severinus let you kill them once he had tired of using their bodies? What really lives behind that false face of yours?"

Caius laughed at Myrddion without a hint of regret. "You still don't understand, Myrddion. Artorex will never expose me, because he can't tear apart the kingdom by murdering his brother. That was Uther's way, and Artor will do anything to avoid comparison with his father. We all have our ruling passions, but mine are more honest than his. Besides, he promised Mother he would protect me from harm."

Caius's expression was almost demonic, causing Myrddion, the reputed son of a demon himself, to step backward.

"And he needs me," Caius added with a sneer. "As his steward, I keep his campaigns against the Saxons successful. Artor is a realist. Regardless of your wishes, old man, Artor will neither expose me nor execute me. Not this time. Not ever, if Artorex holds to his vow to my mother. And the noble Artor always keeps his boyhood vows. Nimue will just have to wait until I decide to visit her again. What fun! Antici-pation is half the pleasure!"

Artor drew in a deep, shaky breath with an audible hiss of air. "There are many good men who will line up to be my steward. No, being steward won't save you, or the oath I swore so many years ago. Nor any threat to persons I cherish."

Caius snickered, but his eyes were less confident.

"You neither know nor understand me, brother," Artor continued. "I don't think you ever have, if you trot out such tired reasons why I should allow you to live. You butchered my dog and left the poor animal to suffer. And you killed the Selgovae princeling, that lovely boy from beyond the wall. You've struck out at me personally, brother . . . and you know how I respond to personal attacks."

For a moment, Caius looked unsure of himself. Myrddion could see his confidence wavering as he stared into Artor's eyes. But he had lived his whole life on the edge, and his arrogance quickly returned to him.

"You've had opportunity after opportunity in the past, and I'm still here to haunt you. Is it sentiment, Artor? Was it because you loved my parents? Or is it because you don't want my wife and daughters to suffer? As if I cared about daughters. I only ever wanted sons. No, it's not sentiment, Artor, is it? It's personal. You don't want me blabbing about Licia, do you? I wonder how Wenhaver would use that bit of information. It would be like giving her a knife to stick through your ribs."

Artor said nothing, but motioned Odin to approach.

"You can't kill me out of hand," the loathsome, honeyed voice continued, "because I'm your brother and a lord of the realm. You would have to put me on trial just to retain the facade of the noble Artor. How could you explain the lies that were told at Aquae Sulis and at the Villa Poppinidii? And the lies told to the realm concerning me? In the first place, you didn't want to hurt my father, but when did you realize that exposing me would damage your own reputation? When did you decide that you couldn't afford one more monster in the family when you already had so many?"

Myrddion couldn't help himself. He took three quick steps and struck Caius across the face with all the force of his repressed anger and dread behind the blow. His ring caught on Caius's cheekbone and ripped the tender skin under his eye.

This small violence finally wiped the sneer from Caius's jowly face.

"I hope that makes you feel better, my lord Myrddion. Brutality is tasty, isn't it? And nothing eases the heart like running blood." Caius smacked his lips, and his pink tongue caught the rivulet that trickled down his face. "Very tasty."

Myrddion had no words to refute Caius's sneering remarks. How could any man respond to such unrepentant perversion? Nimue would never be safe while this monster lived, for Caius had proved that he had the patience of a spider.

Artor was silent, his brows drawn together.

"I'll dress now, if you don't mind, as I see no point in advertising my pleasures."

Myrddion turned his tortured face towards his king and protégé.

"You cannot turn a blind eye to what Caius has done, my lord. Steward or not, Licia or not, he must be forced to stop any actions that are born out of his murderous desires. He feeds on blood and pain. He inhales the screams of his victims, yet he only preys on those poor souls who are weak and helpless. Only you can stop this monster, for he will go on and on with his atrocities until he is exterminated." So profound was his disgust that Myrddion spat on the tiled floor. In truth, he would have preferred to vomit, for Artor had become a stranger by his lack of action, and Myrddion's whole life and every sacrifice now seemed to have been given for nothing. Artor's brow was furrowed, and Myrddion knew there would be no trial, no public execution, and no dangerous gossip. Behind his bitter disappointment, something broke in him as he saw what he had made.

Caius sat at his ease, poured a cup of wine, and began to clean his nails with a small fruit knife.

Artor recognized the wound he had inflicted on Myrddion, and his heart ached at the hurt he saw in his old mentor's eyes. He drew his old counselor down the corridor while Odin kept guard over Caius, who was peeling an apple. Caius's lack of concern made both men feel ill.

"I must consider my options, Myrddion," Artor struggled to explain. "You understand my dilemma. Were it any person other than my foster brother, I could act as I choose, but he knows too much. He protects the secret of my daughter, and he can leave evidence of her existence where I will never find it."

Artor held up one hand to stop the hasty words that came boiling up to Myrddion's lips.

"I know, I know. You believe that my brother's threats are nothing but words, and a creature like this worthless worm will say anything to protect his neck. But even the possibility of his revenge forces me to stay my hand—for the moment. But Caius really doesn't know me at all if he believes that politics will keep him breathing. Trust me."

Artor stared back at Caius's sandaled feet where they rested on his table. Odin's eyes followed his master's gaze, and one booted heel struck hard at Caius's ankle so that he dropped his apple in surprise.

"I'm still considering his fate, Myrddion. I would kill every man in Cadbury to keep my daughter safe."

"Even me." Myrddion sighed bitterly.

The old man's head dropped wearily, and Artor couldn't help himself. He stepped forward and embraced his old friend. One sword-calloused hand rested lightly for a moment on Myrddion's hair, as light as the kiss of a lover, and for a moment the old scholar's hopes were restored.

"I will punish Caius, but I will do it in my own way," Artor said. "You must believe in my justice. I am a king, and you made me such. You, of all people, should understand."

"I will never understand this madness, my lord." Myrddion stared at his sandaled feet as if he could find some comfort in familiar things. "I look at Nimue and her wounds, I remember her courage in fighting this . . . thing, and I feel revolted that Caius breathes the same air that we do. I imagine the slow death of the widow while he watched over her body, and I could kill your brother myself. How can you let him live, Artor? How?"

Myrddion's whole body pleaded with the High King, but Artor was like stone. Sadly, Myrddion remembered the many lessons that Targo had taught the young Artor about expediency and how the goal justified the means to attain it. Self-knowledge and blame curdled in Myrddion's stomach.

"We were at fault, Artor. Luka, Llanwith, and I were at fault, but I will always believe that we had no choice. My heart bleeds that Caius causes us both such pain because he has been permitted to live past his time. I wonder if Lady Livinia would have still asked you to swear your oath if she had known what the future would bring."

"You must leave me some illusions, old man," Artor growled. "But now for Caius. I have pondered for long enough on this matter. I am a king, but, like Targo, I am also a soldier."

Artor's booted heels warned Caius that his foster brother was approaching. Against his will, his shoulders stiffened and his fists clenched, although his face remained bland.

"The widow was very satisfying," Caius drawled. "I have often wondered why she clung so tenaciously to life . . . perhaps her babe was the motivation. Ah, Myrddion, if you felt the rush as she begged for her life, then you might understand me better. Why should I care what happened to either of them after I had finished with her? She was an itch I needed to scratch."

Artor struck his brother across the jaw, and Caius's head hit the rock wall with a sickening thud. His stool shot out from under him, and he landed on his plump buttocks in an untidy sprawl.

At Artor's casual violence, Myrddion knew a shiver of pleasure that made him feel even more distressed.

"Have there been others?" Artor demanded.

"Oh, yes, from time to time. I've always enjoyed my pleasures away from Cadbury until recent times. But lately there seemed to be fewer reasons to deny myself, and less need to hide. After all, your father tortured and killed quite openly, and no one tried to stop him. I can exercise self-control, but the urge to taste little Nimue was too strong to ignore on this occasion."

He smiled at the repulsed expression on Artor's face.

"It's odd how my inhibitions have faded as I age. I don't suppose I'll ever cease to kill, if I'm truly honest. And why should I, for I'm a connoisseur of pain. You should try it, Artor. You've always been so workmanlike in your killing."

Artor's face flushed with anger. "Caius, you are banished to Tintagel fortress in Cornwall, where my kin continue to reign. It consists of cliffs, predatory birds, and the wild ocean and, if you try your tricks there, you'll be drowned in an unfortunate accident. The nephew of Gorlois is still the master of Tintagel, and, while he has little love for me, he has even less for you. Should you speak openly of the reasons for your banishment, I may change my mind. In which case, you would not live to see the dawn of another day. Five of my trusted warriors will make sure that my conditions are met, and that no children, women, or livestock go *missing* around you."

Artor looked bleakly at Myrddion's distant, sickened face.

"You have cost me the trust of my true friend, Myrddion Merlinus, because of my decision to allow you to live. You aren't worth a moment of his pain, but I must break his belief in my justice to keep you breathing. You will always have to watch your back, foster brother."

Caius seemed uneasy, but he still hadn't learned to keep his tongue.

"So I am right once again," he blustered. "Artorex is far too squeamish to kill a member of his own family." He smiled knowingly. "I will see Nimue again," he leered, and his voice hissed with malice. "And soon!"

Artor drew himself up to his full, impressive height. "My name is Artor, Caius. The Artorex you knew died years ago!"

Yes, Artorex is dead, Myrddion thought regretfully, and I liked Artorex. Nay, I loved him. But I am less sure of this Artor.

Artor moved towards Caius with an impassive face, so that his foster brother struggled to his feet with a wince of pain. Something in Artor's demeanor shook Caius's arrogance and caused him to back away.

"Odin will fetch two members of my personal guard to ensure that you remain safe until I can organize your journey to Tintagel. Don't think to move anywhere without them, for I'll not permit any further harm to come to citizens within these walls at your hands. I suggest you pray to your ancestors beyond the River in Hades. Perhaps your blessed mother will intercede, and you'll be permitted to cross when death takes you. Perhaps not! Whatever you decide, you will confine yourself in your quarters to ensure your continued good health. There are many men here who'd relish a chance to hasten your departure by more violent means than you'd like."

Caius attempted to bluster, but Artor turned his back on his foster brother. The arbor was quiet except for the tapping of creepers and the rustle of the wind through drying leaves. A flurry of fallen petals was blown into a corner, and the pale pink fragments swirled and danced as the freshening air swept fitfully over the flagging.

Artor refused to turn, even when two warriors escorted Caius away to his lavish apartments. Only when the sound of their footsteps had faded into silence did Artor turn back to his friend who seemed older, beaten, and lost.

Artor gazed at Myrddion. "Please trust me in this decision. I will allow no harm to touch the head of Nimue."

"I must think of my position on these matters," Myrddion said to his lord, but his mind was already seeking out the pretty fairy mushrooms that grew deep inside the Wildewood, in the quiet places where even the wind was strangled by the ancient trees. It was a solution that didn't require the compliance of his lord.

Chapter XX

THE HOLLOW TREE

Five days later, Caius rode away from Cadbury, nonchalant and smiling, with many graceful, lying farewells ringing in his ears from his fellow courtiers.

Myrddion had reported the whole incident to Nimue, who was now risen from her sickbed and was trying to dry her herbs one-handed. Myrddion was surprised to learn that his apprentice knew an impressive range of curses when she found that she was having difficulty coping with her tasks.

"Poor Artor," Nimue sighed.

"Poor Artor? The king has released a monster who would happily kill again and again for as long as he is free to do it. And I can assure you that he will torture and murder again if he isn't stopped."

"But the king has so much to lose in this matter. People have forgotten that Caius isn't blood kin and is only a foster brother. To the world, Caius is family, and an execution would harm the honor of the High King. You must be fair, Myrddion."

Myrddion gaped at Nimue. He had not expected her to defend Artor's actions.

"I'm not defending Artor," Nimue continued. "I'm simply trying to understand him. His life has been one long series of losses ever since the details of his birth became common knowledge. He has had to repress the worst, and the best, in his nature, and he has no choice in this concealment, because he is the king. I'm certain that the king's secrets must die with Caius who will, I believe, have an unfortunate accident quite soon—probably during the journey to Tintagel. The king did ask you to trust his justice, didn't he? And if Caius should be fortunate enough to survive the journey, I understand that Tintagel is a very lonely and dangerous place." Nimue looked keenly at Myrddion, and his eyes dropped under her scrutiny.

"I know you, my lord. You play word games, just as a warrior plays with his weapons. You say that Caius *would* kill in the future. Yet you know with certainty that Artor will take steps to resolve this matter in secret, and that Caius will never be allowed to kill again. Gruffydd travels with him, which is an odd choice of companion on a long journey . . . unless Artor has chosen the way of Uther Pendragon to solve his problem with Caius."

Myrddion smiled distantly.

"Why did you choose the word, *would*?" Nimue asked calmly, although her heart skipped a beat.

"You must be innocent of all knowledge of my sins, my child, in case I am exposed. But the king's orders to Gruffydd came too late, for the death of Caius had already been arranged. For the first time, I doubted the word of my lord and master."

Myrddion's eyes were bleak, and a little catch of pain caught in Nimue's throat. Her master was kind and human, and murder was both an unnatural and an unforgivable act for him. But worse than murder was his loss of trust.

"Sometimes, you are a little barbarian in your thoughts," Myrddion said quietly. "But you are right, it was determined that Caius would die in an accident arranged by Artor. I should have realized that the king's intentions were for the good of the west, but he didn't tell me of his plans until after Caius had departed."

"You are too good a person, Myrddion, to understand the true viciousness or the pragmatism of human beings."

"Whatever the outcome, Nimue, I no longer trust Artor with our lives. He loves us, but he would use us up if it became necessary to save the west from danger. I've learned that I'm no better than he is. In fact, I'm worse because he has never failed me and I broke my faith with him. I don't know how I can live with the shame. I can't imagine facing him, the son I always wanted, and doubting him, as I will from this point onwards."

Nimue cradled his craggy face in her hands.

"Nothing is forever, master, not even love."

"He is now the perfect king because he has mastered his nature, but I regret that he has lost some of his humanity in the process. If the cause of the west could be advanced by our deaths, Artor wouldn't hesitate to sacrifice both of us."

"Of course," Nimue answered. "That choice is his burden, and also his fate. "But he would sacrifice himself as well," she added as an afterthought. "He already has."

Myrddion wept silently, and Nimue longed to raise her hands to his twisted face and wipe away his hopeless tears.

"I desired to make the perfect king, Nimue. In my hubris, I believed I could mold a suitable young man into another Caesar—for the sake of the people, and for my inflated pride. I was successful, but I find I cannot bear to face what I have done."

Myrddion looked so sad that Nimue hugged him hard with her good arm. Myrddion tried to pull away, but she gripped his hair and he laid his head on her shoulder. He wished he was younger and wiser.

"We must leave Cadbury," Nimue said quietly. "And the sooner the better. But it must be after Enid is delivered of her child, for I have promised to assist her with the birth. We should go far away, Myrddion, to a place where the Celts, the Saxons, Artor, or any of the warrior kings cannot find us."

"You have never called me by my name before," Myrddion whispered.

"I have called you by name a thousand times, but you were never listening. You thought yourself old and celibate, and that I was far too

475

young for you. You ran from me as if I had the contagion, when you are all I could ever want, or ever will."

"But I will be dead before you reach middle age, Nimue. You have not thought of the practicalities of such a union." Myrddion tried to pull away from her, but his efforts were only halfhearted. "And I am needed here in Cadbury."

Nimue chuckled richly and seductively. "Gallwyn was dead at fifty, and young warriors can be mown down like grain during the harvest. Death comes, sooner or later, so we should snatch what happiness we may while we can. I do not count the cost. We are friends first, and yet we can still be lovers. I have so much to learn from you, Myrddion, and you, my love, can learn from me."

Myrddion would have spoken, but she laid two fingers on his mouth to silence him.

"Artor needs you, but he will survive your loss. A gulf lies between you now, and you will both bleed internally in the full knowledge that the gap cannot be breached. It's better that we go, my Myrddion, with love for Artor still alive in you, rather than risk its erosion with the passage of time. Better to be with me, my love, even if only for a little time. Artor has his Gallia. And you shall have me."

"I will think on it," Myrddion whispered. "Enid has a month before the birth of her child."

"I can wait, my love. I have waited for several years, so what is one more month? But time is narrowing here at Cadbury, for Wenhaver grows worse and worse, and her spite knows no bounds. She'll harm me if she can, and I fear her spite far more than I fear the revenge of Caius. Artor may have defeated the Saxons, but Wenhaver will be the death of him in the end. I'd prefer not to watch the decay of a dream."

Myrddion winced, for he had shared that dream for the whole of his adult life.

"There must be some remedy," he exclaimed.

"The remedy will only be found if Wenhaver can change, and only if Gawayne can be persuaded to return to the north with his wife and child. Yet my reason tells me that Wenhaver would only seek out another lover."

"Then we are in the hands of the gods."

"No, my love. Our future lies in our own hands, and in no others. You have proved this truth in your judgment of Caius."

ON THE ROAD to Tintagel, taken in easy stages to spare Caius's wounds, Gruffydd waited his chance. His orders had come from the mouth of Artor himself, so Gruffydd knew that the needs of his king must be sorely pressing if he was forced to send a trusted friend to assassinate his own foster brother.

Gruffydd felt soiled at the thought of a cowardly stab in the darkness, but he had followed Artor for most of his life and he couldn't throw away an allegiance that had become an essential part of his life. Gruffydd could not know that his king was near to breaking point, for he was repeating an ancient sin committed by his father, Uther Pendragon, by imperiling the soul of a man who loved him.

Shortly after midnight, when the darkness was absolute and the fires had banked and guttered, Gruffydd waited silently behind Caius's traveling tent, his dagger sheathed at his waist. Eel-like, he slid through the tent flap and stood over the supine body of the king's foster brother.

Caius's eyes snapped open, and Gruffydd recoiled in surprise.

"Help me," Caius whimpered, even as a spasm rippled through his whole body.

Gruffydd saw that Caius's pallet was dark with blood where his wounds had pulled apart and bled anew. He shook his head in confusion. What other assassin lurked in the darkness? What was happening here?

Even as he shouted for the guards, Gruffydd's eyes and ears were straining to discover whether another killer was hiding in the shadows. As he lit the wick of an oil lamp with shaking hands, he thanked his gods that the blood of Caius would not stain his soul and that his master would be freed from guilt.

When light revealed the interior of the tent and its writhing inhabitant, Gruffydd could see clearly how the healing cuts on Caius's belly and thigh were now oozing blood, but no fresh wounds marked the man's body. Gruffydd's lips curled with distaste, for now his unpleasant orders made sense. Sword wounds were distinctive, especially on flesh that stretched over layers of fat. Gruffydd had seen Nimue return to Cadbury Tor, wrapped in warm wool with dried blood in her fine hair. Like the rest of the inhabitants of the fortress, he had speculated on the identity of the Wildewood murderer and the audacity that led to his attack on the Maid of Wind and Water.

So this sick bastard is the monster of Wildewood, Gruffydd thought to himself with contemptuous horror. No wonder Artor wants him assassinated.

"What ails you, lord?" Gruffydd asked softly of the desperately ill man. He was careful to ensure that his face was wiped clean of all suspicion.

Caius continued to thrash about in his sweaty, bloody clothing.

"I'm ill! My stomach and bowels boil, and my head aches abominably. I can scarcely see you, Sword-bearer. I command you to fetch a healer to tend to my needs."

"Of course, lord, you have but to ask," Gruffydd replied evenly, his thoughts firmly fixed on the remembrance of a laughing boy, a battered widow, and a disemboweled girl.

"And, in pity's name, leave the light," Caius yelped, for in the corners of the tent he could see pallid faces peering at him. Caius's dead had come to wait for him. The sick man gibbered as yet more faces loomed out of the darkness and smiled at him.

"What is wrong, my lord? Why are you frightened? The tent is empty but for your guards. No one here will harm you."

Caius whimpered and turned his face into the pillow. "Can't you see them? The girls? Who let in the dog? Get it out! Get it out! I am the king's brother, so obey me! Get the whole hell brood out of my tent."

Caius almost screamed in his hysteria, while the miasma of horror and illness in the tent was so thick that the warriors clutched their amulets and rolled their eyes superstitiously.

"What dog, lord?" one warrior asked nervously.

"Go to the nearest village and find a healer," Gruffydd ordered the frightened man, cutting smoothly into the silence. "But you don't need to be overly fast about it. For all that our master looks ill, he is still remarkably strong and isn't at death's door."

Gruffydd had his own nightmare visitors, the men he had killed and the friends who had gone to the Shades before him. But his dead weren't hungry for his pain, his fear, or his suffering, thanks be to all the gods of the tribes.

The sick bastard! Gruffydd thought viciously. I hope he hurts! I hope he shits his insides out before the healer returns with a cure. But his face remained impassive, even sympathetic, as he organized lighting, clean water for washing, and a fresh robe for the sick man.

As it was obvious that Caius was unfit to travel, Gruffydd decided that the party would remain in their present encampment until the situation resolved itself. Already, he was composing the report he would make to Artor on his return to Cadbury.

Less than two hours later, Gruffydd's messenger returned with a white-haired old woman from a nearby village. Desiccated, ragged, and yet dignified in her faded shawl and head scarf, the healer turned a pair of light-blue eyes on Gruffydd, a gaze that proclaimed her barbarian blood. Her amulet was a simple stone, pierced through the center, and hung round her neck on a crude cord of flax. She was small, bent, and lean, and Gruffydd could see the raised veins on her swollen hands.

Caius hissed as she approached him, and cowered in abject fear at the thought of a Saxon woman touching his body. She ignored him, sat on her heels, and stared at his flaccid, naked body that was leaking blood and serum from every orifice.

"Do you like mushrooms?" she asked her patient politely.

"What have mushrooms got to do with anything?" Caius howled. "Do your job and heal me, witch!"

She rose, nodded to her patient, and walked out of the tent. The old woman would have walked back to her village had Gruffydd not waylaid her.

Self-possessed and impassive, she stared into Gruffydd's soul through his frowning eyes. What she found there seemed to allay her anxiety.

"What ails the brother of the High King, mother?" the sword master demanded bluntly.

"Besides his many sins? I am not sure, master," the old woman replied enigmatically. "But it is certain that I cannot help him."

"Will he die?" Gruffydd snapped, irritated by her riddles.

"The woman's comfort mushroom has caused him to bleed. He ate it three days ago, and he is now beyond all mortal aid. His dead have come for him, so permit me to return to my people. I must wash myself clean of the stink of him."

Gruffydd raised his brows.

"Woman's comfort is a pretty little mushroom that all women know. Some Christians also call it the angel cap. Only the most pressing need, or the most overriding, consuming hatred, could be summoned to justify the use of angel's cap on another living creature. The very breath of your man is envenomed. I cannot tell what comes from his person and what from the mushroom poison in his blood." She looked at Gruffydd with a woman's sharp sense of wickedness. "Do not ask me to minister to your patient, for my hands would become polluted."

"By the poison?"

She laughed, freely and openly. "No. By him." She pulled her ragged cloak about her narrow, old woman's shoulders. "Have a care, good man, and bury him deep when he breathes his last, for he carries the death of others with him."

In the two days and nights that followed, Caius raved at unseen shades that taunted him.

The warriors pointedly refused to tend to his needs. Strange things seemed to hover in the shadows in the corner of the tent, just out of view, and no sensible man chose to gaze on a wight.

Only Gruffydd remained to assist the dying man. He left copious amounts of water within Caius's reach, but the patient remained parched, no matter how much fluid he drank.

Gruffydd took care to avoid asking what Caius had eaten, and from whom his rations had come. He did not want to know.

The son of Livinia Major took a long time to die, and the High King had not broken his oath in the process. Myrddion had given his last gift to his well-loved master.

ENID WAS HEAVY-BODIED and dreamy in her final month of pregnancy, and Gawayne was a proud father-to-be. Even so, the Otadini prince continued to seek out willing girls in Cadbury town.

And Wenhaver smiled until her jaws ached with the strain.

When Gruffydd returned with the news of the death of Caius, Artor's heart seemed lighter, but his eyes examined Myrddion speculatively. This mood lasted a mere day, and to everyone at the court of Cadbury, the relationship between master and healer seemed unchanged. But the eyes of both men were filled with shadows.

Artor rode to Venta Belgarum at the end of autumn. As was his custom, he sought absolution from the bishop of that venerable city, for his heart was heavy with guilt. He had come, late in life, to understand Uther's belated piety.

Every night, Artor squirmed in his bed as he considered the dangers to which his Licia and his grandson, Bran ap Comac, had been exposed by his failure to execute Caius as soon as he became aware of the man's guilt. And he found himself reliving Myrddion's expressions of disbelief, and the old man's scorn and anger when he informed him of the total inadequacy of Caius's punishment. Worst of all, Artor knew that only Myrddion had the skill to destroy Caius so thoroughly. Gruffydd had mentioned mushrooms, and who but Myrddion had such knowledge of mushroom and fungal lore? Artor also understood that the blood on the hands of the healer was his own fault because he had mishandled the whole affair when a little honesty would have spared his old friend.

The High King was scarcely gone from Cadbury when Wenhaver began her campaign to reel in Gawayne. Myrddion and Nimue, who both knew her methods well, watched with amazement as the queen invited Lot's heir to afternoons in the garden, even though the flowers were dying because of the cold night frosts. Her retainers were often sent away on various errands, and only those closest to the queen knew how she was flouting her wedding vows.

Gawayne, for his part, was beginning to experience unfamiliar pangs of guilt. As the baby moved inside Enid's belly and prepared for its entry into the world, he found himself unable to meet the gentle eyes of his wife, for he knew he had betrayed her innocent trust. He had come to realize that he had betrayed Artor as well, and his admiration for the High King had always been pure and total. Gawayne's true loyalties did not belong to Wenhaver, but she played upon his sexual weaknesses, and the lure of her body, luscious and inviting, was a more potent force than any notions of loyalty. If he sometimes wondered whether she betrayed Artor, and himself, with other men, he thrust such thoughts aside as unworthy. Gawayne really was a bonehead within the convoluted plotting of the court.

Nimue was called to Enid's rooms when she took to the birthing stool. The child was huge, and Enid was tiny at the pelvis. The labor was protracted, and Nimue began to fear that Enid would die.

After a night and a day of hard labor, Enid was exhausted. Gawayne had fled from the room once his wife began her travail. The sound of her screams from the contractions, and her agonized pleas, echoed through the fortress until Wenhaver huddled in her room, demanding that her maids sing for her so that the sounds of childbirth were muffled.

During one seemingly endless contraction, Enid held Nimue's hand so hard that her nails drew blood.

"Don't let my son die," Enid begged once the contraction had passed and she could breathe once more.

Nimue tried to feed her a little broth, and hid her fears behind practical action.

"I must call for Myrddion, Enid. I know he is a man, and he has no place in the business of women's labor, but you are too small to bear so large a child. You will both die if we don't use his skill."

"Then send for him, but tell no one," Enid panted, as another contraction arched her swollen body with agony.

Nimue ran to Myrddion's apartments, leaving Enid with her old nurse. Her hands were still stippled with blood as she burst into the study of her master.

"Enid is dying. The child is too large to be born, and the birth canal is tearing. I need your help."

Myrddion did not argue.

Snatching up several glass vials and a small leather wallet, he ran after Nimue. The route to the birthing rooms was obvious, for he could hear Enid in her extremity, although her screams were growing weaker. He had no doubt that Gawayne's wife was near to death.

The nurse was afraid for the safety of her mistress, so she wasn't overly scandalized by the presence of a male at such an intensely female event. She hovered over her mistress, so Myrddion sent her for water, and measured out several drops from one of his vials into the glass.

"She must drink. This distillation of poppy juice will take away the pain and Enid will sleep."

The narcotic gradually worked, and Enid drowsed in a half-conscious world. She still moaned occasionally with the pain of her useless contractions, but the empty corridors of the fortress were virtually silent as the poppy juice took effect.

"Bless you, sir, for if my girl must die, it's better she does so without pain," the nurse told him tearfully. Then she gasped with shock as Myrddion lifted Enid's gown to expose her belly and thighs.

"I cannot help this woman if I don't know what is wrong," Myrddion snapped. "Has the head crowned yet, Nimue?"

"Yes. But Enid is too small and the child is wedged in the birth canal."

"Have you ever delivered a foal, Nimue?" Myrddion asked.

"No." Nimue sounded affronted. "And Enid is not a mare!"

"The basic principles are the same. Wash your hands now, and do it carefully, for the Jews believe that contagion is carried on the hands."

Nimue immediately plunged her hands into a bowl of clean water and commenced to scrub her fingers clean. Her elbow still pained her, but Enid's need was greater than her own small aches.

"You." Myrddion pointed at the nurse. "I want you to hold the blade of this knife over the flame of the lamp, and hold it there until the metal of the blade glows red from the heat. We must make sure that the fire cleanses it of all corruption."

Nimue returned to his side with her freshly cleansed hands. When the nurse had sterilized the narrow knife blade, Nimue took hold of the hilt.

"You will have to cut her now, Nimue," Myrddion said softly. "I will tell you exactly where to make your incisions."

"Cut her?"

"You can see where the head is crowning, so you will have to cut on both sides of that point. You are about to ease the way for the child to come out of the canal. We can always stitch Enid up after the birth has been completed. Otherwise she will die, Nimue, and you know I'm not permitted to touch her myself."

"Heaven help us all," Nimue prayed, and commenced to slit the straining, swollen flesh. The babe's head burst into view and part of one shoulder, but the child's flesh was a bluish color.

"The cord is trapped round the baby's throat. You must remove it, fast!"

Nimue obeyed, but although the child's flesh gradually became pinkish, he was firmly stuck in the body of his mother.

"You must listen to me carefully, Nimue, and carry out my instructions as I give them. Is that understood?"

Nimue nodded.

"You must grasp the child by its visible shoulder and try to free its arm. Then, perhaps, you will be able to pull him out by the shoulder." His gaze flickered from Enid's body back to the face of his apprentice. "You mustn't faint, Nimue, or Enid will surely die. Do you hear me? Enid will die." Myrddion turned to the nurse. "We need water, a needle and thread, and as many clean cloths as you can find. Then I need you to start warming the water."

Nimue gently explored the shoulder of the child. A strong contraction allowed her to ease her hand into Enid's body to find the small arm and Enid's wound split further, and blood flowed.

"Now wait for the next contraction, and then pull."

"I might break the child's arm," Nimue wailed.

"Breaks will heal without too much difficulty, especially in children," Myrddion answered brutally, his face firm and calm in the lamplight. "You know that."

As Nimue saw Enid's belly begin to move with the next contraction, she pulled, gradually exerting more and more pressure. Then, just when she believed that she had failed, the baby slid from Enid's body, and Nimue almost dropped him.

"Nurse, wrap the child up in that blanket. Nimue, tie the cord off about a finger length from its body, and then cut it off. Come on, woman, there's no time to lose. This fine boy must be forced to breathe alone, and his mother must be prevented from bleeding to death."

Nimue's sure fingers carried out Myrddion's instructions. She opened the tiny mouth and breathed into its lungs. The nurse then slapped the child hard on its tiny buttocks, and he coughed out a plug of mucus, screwed up his eyes, and commenced to cry lustily.

"Nurse, wash the child and see to its warming." He turned back to Nimue. "You and I must save the mother. Use cloths to soak up the blood and move fast. That's good. Now thread the needle. Ignore the cord, because the afterbirth comes free of the womb naturally, as long as there are no hemorrhages."

Myrddion watched closely as Nimue worked to stitch the two gaping wounds together. His concentration was so great that Enid seemed little more than a piece of living meat to the old man.

"Remember that you must take one stitch at a time, both inside and outside the wound. Keep the pressure on each stitch firm and even. Too tight with even one stitch, and you bring extra pressure to bear on the stitches alongside it. Too loose with the stitch, and you have a weak area where bleeding and seepage can take place. You can do this, Nimue, so don't fail Enid now. Women's bodies are very strong, and so much better made than the frail flesh of a man. Gawayne would not have survived the agony that Enid has borne. Pain and shock can kill just as easily as a knife."

"Yes, master," Nimue answered automatically, her eyes fixed on each stitch as she repaired the damaged flesh. Her task was relatively simple where the blade had cut, but the tearing caused by the many hours of labor was very difficult to mend.

At last, she was finished.

Within the hour, Enid's body expelled the afterbirth. The nurse was cradling the boy child in her arms, and staring at Myrddion as if she was in the presence of a god.

"But for your skill, the mistress would be dead by now, my lord. May the gods love you, and you also, my lady, for I swear I could not have done what you did, not if I live to be a thousand."

Nimue washed her hands in the hot water used to remove the birth sac from the infant. She felt sick and drained, but triumphant. As she packed clean cloth between Enid's legs and tied it in place, Myrddion professed himself satisfied that Enid hadn't hemorrhaged.

"Unfortunately, Enid is not yet out of danger. When the old Jew showed me what to do in such cases, he warned me against overconfidence. A woman can suddenly start to bleed and, once the hemorrhage begins, nothing can stop it."

"May the gods have mercy," the nurse cried.

"Has Enid organized a wet nurse?" Myrddion asked.

The old servant nodded.

"The child is hungry and wants feeding, so you must look after that little problem." He nodded to her. "I appreciate your assistance."

He turned to his apprentice and smiled down at her exhausted face.

"Should Enid wake, Nimue, you must give her three more drops of the poppy, for she must be kept still. It is essential she does not move." He smiled once more. "I must go now, or I will face censure from the women."

"But you saved her life," Nimue answered, her eyes shining with pride.

"We Celts are still barbarians at heart, I'm afraid, and there are some things that are totally unacceptable to our people. The Greeks knew more about medicine than we do, and the Jews know more again, for all that they are the most despised of all races. When I was in Rome, I was taught by a brilliant Jew called Isaac, who was an acknowledged master of medicine. I also had occasion in Constantinople to meet some of the greatest healers in the whole world. I have heard tell that the sons of Ishmael are the finest physickers on earth. But I will be punished if I am found in this place."

"Then go, Myrddion, and find Gawayne. You should be the one to tell him he has a fine son," Nimue replied, and began to wash the sheen of sweat and blood from Enid's supine body.

Myrddion searched the fortress for Gawayne, but the new father had vanished. The warriors guarding the fortress wall had not seen him descending to the town below, so Myrddion knew that Enid's husband was not drinking in some vulgar tavern outside the fortress.

In all of Cadbury, there was only one place left where he could seek out Gawayne. Reluctantly, he determined to see if the warrior was closeted with Wenhaver in her apartments.

He entered the queen's bower unannounced. If Gawayne wasn't with the queen, he would apologize abjectly, and search further. If Gawayne was present . . . well, that possibility did not bear thinking about until he must explain his presence.

Gawayne lay naked in the queen's embrace on her rose-colored bed. At first, neither lover noticed his presence, so Myrddion coughed loudly, causing Gawayne to swear profusely and attempt to cover himself. Wenhaver simply lazed on her pillows, making no effort to cover her body, and stared insolently at Artor's closest confidant.

"You! Out! Get yourself dressed and wait for me in the corridor," Myrddion ordered Gawayne, who sheepishly dressed and obeyed.

"And close the door behind you," Myrddion added.

"Look your fill, Myrddion Merlinus." Wenhaver smiled her harlot's smile, and wriggled her wide hips on the coverlet.

Myrddion threw a light woolen robe at her.

"Cover yourself, slut," he sneered. "Your used goods don't tempt me in the slightest. The punishment for harlotry and treason, for such is the crime in your liaison with Gawayne, is the stake. You and Gawayne may regret this day ever began." He bowed with an exaggerated flourish that was worse than a slap. "I leave you to your vulgar amusements."

Outside, Gawayne waited. He looked like a ten-year-old child expecting a punishment from a parent.

"Walk with me," Myrddion ordered. "Your wife has been delivered of a large, strong son, although he nearly killed Enid in the birthing. While Nimue struggled to save the lives of your wife and child, you forgot your nobility and honor so far as to rut with the wife of the High King, your uncle. Have you no shame, Gawayne? Have you no honor?"

Gawayne was silent.

"No. Neither of you have shame nor honor. Your wife was dying in agony and you were behaving like an animal. No love was involved, for I don't believe either of you care for each other at all. Ultimately, someone must pay for your sins, Gawayne, for the gods will not be mocked. You've betrayed your kinsman and, even now, commoners whisper and laugh behind their hands at Gawayne's playing the game of the two-backed beast with the queen. In the process, they laugh at Artor, who has never caused you harm. He went to war for your brother. He has never treated you with suspicion, even when your mother and your aunt tried to raise rebellion against him and gave succor to his enemies. Do you want your king to be sneered at, you fool, and made the butt of jokes?"

Gawayne looked miserable and guilty by turn. "You don't understand."

Myrddion laughed. "I wasn't always old, so don't think I am ignorant of the tricks that some women play. Do you wish to cause a war between Leodegran, Lot, and Artor? Do you want the Saxons to claim all of Britain? You must begin to be a man, Gawayne. You must take your family back to the north. You will leave the queen to her amusements and run for your life, for she'll destroy you. And if she doesn't do it, then I will!"

"I will go, I promise," Gawayne began, but Myrddion cut him short.

"It's time for you to welcome your son."

"You won't say anything of this to Enid?" Gawayne pleaded nervously.

"I am not so unkind," Myrddion replied sadly. "I will say nothing to Enid, for she is truly noble, unlike the queen. Why should she suffer because of your lust? But you will leave Cadbury as soon as your wife can travel and, in the interim, you must keep away from the queen."

Gawayne actually shuffled his feet like a youth caught out in an indiscretion. "Thank you, Lord Myrddion."

The contrition on his face was real enough, but Myrddion knew in his heart that Gawayne would always be a headstrong, easily led fool whose brain was ruled by his sexual urges.

THAT NIGHT, THE king's adviser wrote a long letter to Artor in Latin, certain that the messenger who would bear it to Venta Belgarum would be unable to spy upon his last message to the High King.

Finally, at first light, Myrddion called Nimue to his rooms. She entered, her silver hair in an aureole around her face. He took her hand and kissed the palm.

"Do you still believe that you love me, Nimue?" he asked softly.

"Neither a single night nor a lifetime of nights will weaken my love," she replied gravely.

"I will become old and frail, and you will be forced to care for me," Myrddion warned.

"Such care would be a pleasure to me, my lord. I have told you so."

"And I will die while you are still young. I will not know of the years of enforced loneliness in far-off, empty places that you will be destined to endure."

"As I have said, I do not care for tomorrow."

"Then, my love, we must leave Cadbury immediately. I've battled against my feelings for you for a long time, and now, weakly, I submit to them. If you wish to have me, we must go, or I will change my mind for the love of Artor. I adore you, Nimue, with an old man's final flush of passion, but I have loved my king for years beyond counting, so you should never be jealous of my devotion to him."

He smiled at the look of joy that transfigured her face.

"I could never resent any love you have for your king, Myrddion. How could I, when I owe Artor everything?"

"You must prepare what supplies we need in panniers for the pack-horses, for we won't be returning to this place. Choose well. You must find wagons and hire servants. We leave as soon as possible, and our destination is wild and barren."

"Myrddion," Nimue cried, and held him tightly as if she would never set him free. Tears began to flow down her cheeks.

"Why tears, my sweet? Do you love Cadbury Tor so well?"

"Never! I'm happy, and I'm so joyful that I could fly."

"We leave at noon tomorrow. Finally, I ask that you wear your silver dress and your neck chain. Let us give Cadbury a parting that they will remember for many years to come."

She nodded, and her face was radiant with hope. "May I say goodbye to Gruffydd, Odin, and Percivale in a letter?"

"Of course. But you must hurry. For Artor will try to stop us if he can, and I hope to be far to the north before he realizes that we have gone."

So, on a wintry day when the sun intermittently broke through great banks of grey cloud, Myrddion Merlinus, believed by many to be a sorcerer and the spawn of a demon, rode out of Cadbury Tor for the last time with the Maid of Wind and Water. They were clad in silver and black, and they were smiling as the light reflected off their hair and struck sparks from the maiden's silver dress. Three packhorses and two carts accompanied them, and the common people felt a chill come over them for no one could remember a time when Lord Merlinus hadn't been at the king's back.

"Perhaps they go to join Artor," some citizens speculated.

"Perhaps the maid has stolen away Lord Myrddion's soul," hazarded others, who were less kindly disposed towards the forward young woman.

When they passed, the sun disappeared behind the dark clouds, and the day became grey and grim.

By the time Myrddion's courier delivered his letter to Artor, the lovers were far away to the north, heading towards the mountains and the deserted fortress of Caer Gai. No man or woman saw them again in the west, or, if they did, no word was sent to Cadbury of their discovery.

Without a single thought for the health of his horses, Artor rode to Cadbury posthaste in the vain hope that Myrddion had changed his mind. He wept late at night on the icy road when he believed no warrior could see his tears, but his bodyguard understood that Artor had been dealt a mortal blow. He drove the horses hard, almost to the point of death, but when the High King reached his fortress, he found Myrddion's study empty and already covered in a light coating of dust.

On the desk, a simple scroll in the Roman style lay waiting, ready for Artor's hand. He opened it and read the title. Then the High King laughed until he wept.

The scroll was the last part of Caesar's memoirs.

Artor called for a goldsmith and ordered that a box should be made, to hang on a long neck chain. When the plain box was finished to the king's satisfaction, he reread Myrddion's letter, folded it into a small square, and placed it in the box. The chain hung from Artor's neck so that the letter lay above his heart.

My lord, my friend, my son,

I am leaving you at last, and I beg you not to try to find me. I have given too many years in the saving of the west, and now I crave only peace and a chance to love, as you once loved.

I do not desert you because of Caius or because I believe that the kingdom will fail. Lady Fortuna spins her wheel and we rise or fall as she prescribes. No, I leave because I must, if I am ever to find myself again and share what is left of me with Nimue. As you know so well, all men must ultimately submit to their fates.

I am proud of the man you have become, but prouder yet of the man you are not. I have watched as you struggled with the shade of Uther Pendragon in your soul, but I promise that he will never gain the ascendancy in your nature. You learned as a young man what love truly is, and that knowledge, my lord, makes all the difference.

The west will fall when you are dead. I have studied the Saxons and the Celts, and of this I am certain. Only one Artor was born to weld the tribes together, and no other king shall rise after you have gone. Besides, the Saxons have nowhere else but here to make their home. They must adopt the west as their own, or they will starve. I predict they will not starve.

You think now that all you have endured and sacrificed is for nothing, but you are wrong. The ordinary people remember, for they are the true earth of Britain. As long as the sun rises and sets, your name will endure. This, too, I promise you.

We will not meet again in this life. But I have hope that your Christian Jesus spoke the truth, and that the soul goes on forever. Then we will embrace in the old way, without fear, or the duties of power, or misunderstandings, but in perfect trust.

Remember who you are, dear Artorex, the boy beneath the king, and I will be satisfied that I did not labor in vain.

Written in haste and love,

Myrddion Merlinus

Cadbury Tor

"Well, that evil old witch was right," Gruffydd commented to his two friends. "When Nimue was barely seven days old, Morgan predicted that the child would steal away the mind of the kingdom. And she has done exactly that."

"Nimue always adored her master," Percivale protested. "And he loved her, so I see no reason for them to be denied happiness together."

"They have gone to the far, quiet places and the hollow oak now swallows them," Odin stated ponderously. "Artor's kingdom will now begin to die."

"You're a cheerful bastard, I must say, Odin," Gruffydd growled. "I can't see much change in the kingdom myself. The fortresses are stronger than ever they were before, and we are still holding the Saxons at bay."

"But the heart of the king is broken," Percivale murmured. "Still, I will hold fast, no matter what our fates may be."

"And I," Odin echoed.

"And me too, I suppose," Gruffydd said, "since I'm too old to be a spy again, and the spymaster has gone awandering with his fair lady." He would miss Nimue, his foster daughter, the child he had found discarded and left to die in reeds near the body of her mother.

He shook himself free of the somber mood that was settling over him and thumped the table, startling his two silent companions.

"Why in Hades are we sitting here like three old women? I feel like a drink, or two, or more."

COMMON MEN HAVE easy lives by comparison with the great ones. While Gruffydd raised a toast to absent friends, Artor was congratulating Gawayne, whose son, the newly named Galahad, was cradled in the arms of the High King.

"Your boy is large, lusty, and strong, and he will try your patience," Artor said evenly. "Just as his father tries mine! You should accompany your wife back to the Otadini lands to spend some time with your parents. From there, you will proceed to the fortress of Verterae, for I have little trust in Brigante common sense."

Gawayne was reminded of his unpleasant conversation with Myrddion on the night his son was born. Was Artor aware of his liaison with Wenhaver? The High King was looking at him very oddly.

"If I have offended you, I'm sorry, Uncle. I'd never hurt you deliberately, any more than I'd harm Galahad."

"All is well between us, have no fear. Just travel to Verterae and ensure that young Rhys is behaving himself."

Artor handed over the babe, who immediately started to wail. Gawayne held the babe awkwardly, and his son took revenge by vomiting curdled milk on his fresh tunic. Gawayne swore pungently.

"Such are the joys of fatherhood, Gawayne. But you can rest easy in the knowledge that you now have an heir."

Gawayne could see the sadness in Artor's eyes, and he felt a jolt under his breastbone that he recognized as guilt.

"We shall leave within the week, my lord. Enid is recovering slowly, but she is eager to show Galahad to her parents and mine. You may not believe me, but I look forward to spending time with my wife and my new son during the hours left to us at Cadbury."

Artor smiled, and wished him well. Am I forever to give careful warnings to Gawayne and disguise how I really feel? he wondered. And is this all that is left for me?

Seeking something, an argument perhaps, or even comfort in his loneliness, he visited the queen's apartments.

"What do you want, Artor?"

The queen had pinned up her hair in a coronet of plaits and was dressed in a serviceable sleeping robe that was comfortable rather than fashionable.

"A promise," he replied with as much conciliation in his voice as he could manage.

Mystified, Wenhaver eyed him suspiciously and sent her ladies out of earshot.

"What promise?"

"I want you to stay away from Gawayne. If you are prepared to obey me, the whole affair will be forgotten."

Wenhaver was suspicious. If Artor knew for certain that she had presented him with horns over her liaison with Gawayne, he'd be ready to tear her into very small pieces. That he was almost conciliatory seemed to suggest that he wasn't sure. She reacted accordingly.

Wenhaver plastered an expression of outrage on her face. "How dare you accuse me of being a whore! I know you hate me, but do you truly believe me to be so vile?" *Artor cannot know for certain,* she thought feverishly, *or he would never be so calm and conciliatory.*

Artor sighed. "Long before we were betrothed, Morgan le Fey warned that I should beware of a woman with yellow hair. She predicted that you would bring me, and all my works, to ruin. Do you want the west to fail and to find yourself forced to flee and hide?"

"You're just trying to frighten me. Besides, Myrddion Merlinus predicted I would die in a nunnery."

Despite himself, Artor laughed. "You're far too fond of your bodily delights to willingly enter a nunnery, wife. I think that Myrddion must have been drunk when he uttered those words."

Wenhaver pursed her lips.

Artor seated himself on a delicate stool that seemed too insubstantial to take his weight. "I await your promise, Wenhaver. Come. It's not a difficult vow to give."

Confused and unsettled, she looked at her husband's lined and haggard face, and felt afraid. If Artor should die, she would not be the High Queen.

"I will promise what you ask," she said, "although I don't know why I need to make such a vow. I don't want the kingdom to fall, and it won't happen anyway, because our warriors wouldn't let the Saxons win."

"I used to believe that I could drive the Saxons out of our lands. I hoped that, with unification of the tribes and with a single, determined will to guide us, we could force the Saxons and Jutes out of the east, back into their boats, and across the Litus Saxonicus to their erstwhile homes. I was wrong." Artor contemplated his large knuckles and scarred hands.

Wenhaver felt unaccustomed pity. Artor seemed so lifeless and so defeated. She almost stroked his head, but their long enmity stopped her fingers.

"I don't understand what's wrong, Artor," she stated honestly.

Artor gave a great sigh that seemed to come from some black pit within him. Wenhaver shrank back from the finality of that sigh.

"We cannot win," he said bleakly. "We can only maintain the borders as they are, with huge loss of life. Should our alliances fail, the Saxons will flood through the breach like the great tides that they brave to reach our lands. More and more of them come every day, across the Litus Saxonicus. In time, our whole world will be Saxon, and everything we have built and fought for will be forgotten."

Wenhaver rose and knelt at the feet of her husband. There was nothing sexual or even sympathetic in her gesture, but her action caused the High King to raise his head.

"Really, Artor. I don't know why you're trying to frighten us all, but what you are saying isn't true. All my life, doom mongers have been moaning about the Saxon barbarians, but it hasn't happened, has it? And you won't let it happen, will you?"

The High King laughed. She was so serious, yet so lacking in understanding. How he longed to stride down to Targo's room and discuss his bleak thoughts with the old Roman. Or seek out Myrddion, busy with his potions and his long, careful notes on all manner of subjects. Myrddion's calm logic always eased Artor's heart.

But Targo was dead and Myrddion had gone. Only Wenhaver, who had betrayed him and sickened him, was left to hear his self-doubts.

He bowed over her hand and kissed the plump little palm, causing Wenhaver to flush like a virgin at his simple mark of respect. He apologized for disturbing her rest and left her rooms.

He strode out onto the forecourt of Cadbury Tor and looked up at the cold, distant stars that he had known since he was a child. Why did they now seem to be so far away? The sound of men singing and laughing floated up to him from the stables, and he recognized Gruffydd's distinctive voice. With a pang of jealousy, he wished he knew how to be so carefree and comfortable in the company of friends.

"You're crying for the moon and things that cannot be," a familiar, beloved voice seemed to whisper in his ear. "Do the best you can with what you have—that's Targo's law."

Artor swore he heard a chuckle behind him, but he knew that his imagination was calling up the sound of his oldest friend.

"But the dead are dead, Targo. And tomorrow I will still be alive, the Saxons will still hover near our borders and Saxon summers will continue to come, as they have since Hengist and Horsa were invited to these shores by Vortigern," he whispered softly into the night. "There's no turning back and no point in whining about what is to be. I must go on, even if I can't win."

Then, because he was tired of his own fears, he shouted into the night at the Saxons and at Lady Fortuna herself, until the guards drew their weapons and searched for the approach of an enemy.

Silence settled once more, and the stars wheeled above Cadbury Tor, in immutable and ordained paths.

EPILOGUE

At Caer Gai, trees had invaded the Roman ruins and oak roots had broken the stones and heaved up the flagged floors. Yet there was shelter enough, and there were hill people who were prepared to exchange labor in payment for lanced boils or medications and cures for the fever.

Odin had the edges of the Sight, for around a great hollow oak, so old that it had first sprouted before the Druids saw the light of day, a series of rooms had been constructed out of salvaged Roman stone. Myrddion felt he needed the power of the ancient tree to fuel his faith in some reason for his long and difficult life. If the hill people thought his design was peculiar, they chose not to speak of it. They worshipped ancient trees and stones, and they held to the old ways within their hearts.

Myrddion's house was neither large nor elegant, but the reed-covered roofs kept out rain, sleet, and snow, and the tree formed a great protective shell.

Myrddion spent his days healing, reading, and writing down the chronicles of two kings, while Nimue broke the earth for a garden. In time, flowers grew in the old fortress, and herbs, and fresh fruit and vegetables flourished. As their needs were simple, they had all they desired.

A fresh spring was harnessed for irrigation, and Myrddion amused himself with the building of a fountain and a bathhouse, although he lacked the skills of the old Romans.

In time, Myrddion and Nimue were loved for their wisdom, and were protected from the outside world, for the sturdy hill people would not let such provident lovers be taken from them.

While they were strange outlanders, Myrddion and Nimue were also gentle, for all that they bore weapons of bright iron. Women in labor knew that they would assist at the worst birth, and the wounds of the hunt that had once killed were now treated safely and successfully.

The villagers told no one of the great ones who had come among them, for fear they would vanish on the wind.

And in the fullness of time, Nimue bore Myrddion his first son, a strong boy with hair the color of ebony, apart from a stripe of silver growing from the forehead. His eyes were midnight blue and were far older than any infant's eyes should be.

They called him Taliesin.

ACKNOWLEDGMENTS

A number of acquaintances, men and women, read *Dragon's Child*, Volume One of this trilogy, as a "taste test," and as a means for me to discover if I had the capacity to write historical fiction that was suitable for public consumption.

In particular, I would like to mention David Hall, Guy Ogden, and the family and friends of David and Jolene Hill. Their kind words of encouragement have been a great fillip to my confidence, and their positive comments were the spurs that kept me writing, especially during the boring times when the work was hard and creative thoughts got lost in the muddle. I have never thanked them. But I do so now.

Still other acquaintances, like my beautiful friend, Pauline Reckentin, never wavered in their unshaken belief that I would make the grade as a writer. At times, Pauline embarrassed me with her faith, but whenever my spirits flagged, there was Pauline (who herself leaps tall buildings with a single bound) telling me that I was unstoppable. Such friends are beyond price.

Finally, how can I find the words to thank those who are nearest to me—Michael, hard taskmaster and savage critic; Damian, my highly intelligent son, who is the prototype for several of the characters in my Arthurian legends; and Brendan, my prodigal son, whose work habits, courage in impossible situations, and absolute dedication to his children forced me to understand the difficult choices that confront Artor. I am blessed with extraordinary kin.

It was a special day for me when Johanna Castillo became my

mentor at Simon and Schuster US. There are too few superlatives to describe how the crew at S&S has changed my life and how greatly I admire their publishing skills. Johanna and her cohorts deserve my gratitude because, without their expertise, Artor would have vanished into the darkness. So live the dreams of authors.

Finally, I wish to thank my agent of agents, Dorie Simmonds, who is a friend, a lifesaver, and a genius in her chosen field. She is lovely in every way that matters.

Life is a cruel teacher, and we all learn, like Artor, that only by facing the great beauty and the suffering of life can we become that which makes us strong. Ultimately, facing ourselves is the lesson that we learn and carry with us until we go to whatever fate awaits us in the Great Unknown.

I hope Arthur will forgive me for the liberties I have taken with his life when eventually we meet.

DRAMATIS PERSONAE

Artorex/Artor   The legitimate son of Uther Pendragon,
High King of the Britons. He is sent to
the Villa Poppinidii as an infant by Bishop
Lucius of Glastonbury to protect him from
Uther's spite.

Ban   Named the Firebrand of the West, he is
Uther Pendragon's champion. He fights
Artorex in single combat and is defeated.
Ban accompanies Artorex in a suicidal raid
on the Saxon fortress at Anderida, where he
is killed.

Bedwyr   Son of the guardians of Arden Forest. He is
from the Cornovii tribe.

Botha   Captain of Uther Pendragon's guard, who
is ordered by Uther to kill Artorex's family
and destroy the Villa Poppinidii.

Bregan   A blacksmith in a village close to the Villa
Poppinidii. His son, Brego, is saved by
Artorex from the depravities of the Severinii
family, and in gratitude, Bregan makes
Artorex a gift of the iron dragon knife.

Caius   Son of Ector and Livinia and foster brother
to Artorex. He later becomes steward to
King Artor.

Cerdic ap Cerdyn The head of the party of envoys sent by Artor to parlay with Glamdring Ironfist while under a flag of truce. Cerdic is the first of the envoys to be killed.

Cessus of Aquae Sulis Breaks the rules of truce between Cerdic and Glamdring Ironfist by hiding a knife in his boot. When the Saxons begin to slaughter the envoys, Cessus responds by killing the Saxon nearest him by stabbing him in the eye. He is killed by Glamdring.

Cletus The elderly steward of the Villa Poppinidii.

Ector Celtic husband of Livinia, master of the Villa Poppinidii near Aquae Sulis, and the father of Caius and foster father of Artorex.

Enid Wife of Gawayne and mother of Galahad and Gawayne's other children. She will become one of the Three Queens of legend.

Frith Elderly female slave in the Poppinidii household. She mothers Artorex during his childhood and is his confidante. She becomes maid to Artorex's first wife, Gallia, and dies with her during an attack on the villa by renegade warriors sent by Uther Pendragon.

Fynn ap Finn Son of Finn Truthteller, the former apprentice healer who served Myrddion for many years.

Gaheris Gawayne's youngest brother and King Lot's youngest son.

Gallia The first wife of Artorex, daughter of a Roman trader from Aquae Sulis who died in an epidemic of the plague. She is murdered on the orders of Uther Pendragon.

Gallwyn	Mistress of the kitchens at Ratae. She is the foster mother of Nimue.
Gareth	The grandson of Frith; protector of Licia; and, for a time, steward of the Villa Poppinidii.
Gawayne	The eldest son of King Lot and Queen Morgause of the Otadini tribe, and the brother of Gaheris. Although a philanderer of note, he is one of King Artor's staunchest supporters.
Glamdring Ironfist	The Saxon thane who combines the remnants of the western Saxons under his rule out of the old Roman Fortress of Caer Fyrddin.
Glamdring's messengers	Ulf of Caerleon, Justus of Aquae Sulis, and Bryn ap Cydwyn are sent back to King Artor by Glamdring Ironfist after the Saxons ambushed Artor's envoys.
Glaucus	An erstwhile sarcophagus maker who has diversified to survive the end of Roman burial customs. He possesses a sarcophagus called Andromeda, which Myrddion purchases as a bathtub for Queen Wenhaver.
Grigor Gilleasbulg	A twelve-year-old boy who has been sent to Cadbury Tor as a hostage to guarantee the continued cooperation of his tribe who lives between the two walls in the north of Britain.
Gruffydd	One of Myrddion's most able spies. He saves the infant Nimue from freezing to death at Durobrivae after her Jute mother was raped and murdered. He becomes Artor's sword-bearer.

Julanna   Wife of Caius and mother of his daughter, Livinia Minor.

Licia   Daughter of Artorex and Gallia.

Livinia Major   Wife of Ector and the last of the Roman Poppinidii line. She is mother of Caius and foster mother of Artorex. She is accidentally slain by Caius during a domestic dispute.

Livinia Minor   Eldest daughter of Caius and Julanna.

Llanwith pen Brynn One of the three travelers, Llanwith is a friend of Myrddion from his childhood and helps the young Artorex to reach the throne.

Lot   King of the Otadini tribe and fierce enemy of King Artor. He has allied himself with the eastern Saxons.

Lucius   Bishop and leader of the Christian community of Glastonbury.

Morgan   Eldest daughter of Gorlois and Ygerne, sister of Morgause, and the half sister of Artorex. She is a witch woman.

Morgause   Second daughter of Gorlois and Ygerne, and the half sister of Artorex. She is married to King Lot of the Otadini tribe and is the mother of Gaheris.

Myrddion Merlinus (earlier called Myrddion Emrys)   The shadowy figure who serves Ambrosius and his brother, Uther Pendragon, during their reigns as High Kings. He is both a healer and a spymaster in the service of the High Kings of Britain, and presides over the birth of Artor.

Myrnia   Wenhaver's personal maid who accompanies her to Cadbury on the occasion of her marriage. Whenever she is upset, Wenhaver physically mistreats Myrnia.

Nimue   The infant girl saved by Gruffydd. She is made a ward of Artorex when he is Dux Bellorum.

Odin A Jutlander and member of the Scum, the mercenaries who assist Artorex to capture the Saxon fortress of Anderida. He becomes the bodyguard of Artorex.

Pelles (Pinhead) A member of the Scum and a talented bowman.

Perce (Percivale) A kitchen boy at Ratae who aspires to become a warrior.

The Scum A small group of some twenty mercenaries who are recruited by Artorex for the raid on the impregnable Saxon fortress at Anderida. Rufus, Pelles, and Odin are three notable members.

The Severinii A Roman family, domiciled in a villa in Aquae Sulis, consisting of Severinus (an epicure), Severina (his mother), and Antiochus (his catamite). The Severinii have been responsible for the rape and murder of at least eight children from the local villages. Severinus is a friend of Caius and is brought to justice by Artorex. The Severinii are executed and their villa is burned to the ground.

Simeon (Simon) A Jewish priest at Glastonbury. He is a master metalsmith who fashions Artor's crown and re-forges Caliburn, Artor's sword.

Targo A professional Roman soldier who is Ector's sword master at the Villa Poppinidii. He instructs Artorex in martial skills on the instructions of the three travelers.

The Three Travelers 1. Myrddion Merlinus: Chief counselor

to Uther Pendragon and, in turn, to King
Artor; a healer, philosopher, architect,
strategist, and spymaster. 2. Llanwith
pen Bryn: Prince (and later king) of the
Ordovice tribe of the northern Britons.
3. Luka: Prince (and later king) of the
Brigante tribe of Cymru.

Ulf of Caerleon   One of the mounted guards who are
handpicked by Artor to accompany the
envoys to the meeting with Glamdring
Ironfist. Ulf and two others are given the
task of returning the heads of the slain
envoys to King Artor at Cadbury. Ulf is
forced to memorize a message to King Artor
from the Saxon thane.

Uther Pendragon   The successor to Ambrosius as High King of
the Britons, and father of Artorex.

Vortigern   The King of Cymru several generations
before the time of Artor. He is remembered
because he welcomed the Saxons into Dyfed
to placate his Saxon queen, Rowena. He
attempted to sacrifice Myrddion in a bid to
build his fortress at Dinas Emrys.

Wenhaver   Wife of King Artor and a great beauty and
strumpet who sulks, hinders, and runs
roughshod over the court of the High King.

Ygerne   Originally the wife of Gorlois, the Boar
of Cornwall. After his death, she married
Uther Pendragon. She is the mother of
Artorex.

GLOSSARY OF PLACE NAMES

The following is a list of place names in post-Roman Britain with present-day equivalents.

Abone	Sea Mills, Avon
Abus Flood	River Humber
Anderida	Pevensey, East Sussex
Aquae	Buxton, Derbyshire
Aquae Sulis	Bath, Avon
Bravioniacum	Kirkby Thore, Cumbria
Bravonium	Leintwardine, Herefordshire
Bremenium	High Rochester, Northumbria
Bremetennacum	Ribchester, Lancashire
Burrium	Usk, Gwent
Cadbury	Cadbury, Somerset
Caer Fyrddin	Carmarthen, Wales
Caerleon	Newport, South Wales
Calleva Atrebatum	Silchester, Northamptonshire
Camulodunum	Colchester, Essex
Canovium	Caerhun, Gwynedd
Castell Collen	Llandrindod Wells, Powys, Wales
Causennae	Saltersford, Lincolnshire
Corinium	Cirencester, Gloucestershire
Cymru	Wales
Deva	Chester, Cheshire

Dinas Emrys	Beddgelert, Gwynedd, Wales
Durnovaria	Dorchester, Dorset
Durobrivae	Water Newton, Cambridgeshire
Durobrivae	Rochester, Kent
Durovernum	Canterbury, Kent
Dyfed	Dyfed County, Wales
Eburacum	York, North Yorkshire
Forden	Welshpool, Powys
The Giant's Dance	Stonehenge
Gelligaer	Gelligaer, Caerphilly, Wales
Glastonbury	Glastonbury, Somerset
Glevum	Gloucester, Gloucestershire
Isca Augusta	Caerlon, Gwent
Isca Dumnoniorum	Exeter, Devon
Lavatrae	Bowes, Durham
Letocetum	Wall, Staffordshire
Lindinus	Ilchester, Somerset
Lindum	Lincoln, Lincolnshire
Litus Saxonicus	English Channel
Llandovery	Llandovery, Wales
Llanio	Bremia Llanio, Cardiganshire
Londinium	London, Greater London
Magnis	Carvoran, Northumberland
Magnis	Kenchester, Herefordshire
Metaris Aest	The Wash
Moridunum	Carmarthen
Nidum	Neath, West Glamorgan
Noviomagus	Chichester, West Sussex
Onnum	Halton, Northumberland
Pennal	Machynlleth, Snowdonia, Gwynedd
Petuaria	Brough on Humber, Yorkshire
Portus Dubris	Dover, Kent
Ratae	Leicester, Leicestershire
Rutupaie	Richborough, Kent

Sabrina Aest	The Bristol Channel
Segontium	Caernarfon, Gwynedd, North Wales
Seteia Aest	The Mouth of the Dee River
Sorviodunum	Old Sarum, Wiltshire
Tamesis River	Thames River
Tintagel	Tintagel, Cornwall
Trimontium	Newstead, Borders
Vectis Island	The Isle of Wight
Venonae	High Cross, Leicestershire
Venta Belgarum	Winchester, Hampshire
Venta Silurum	Caerwent, Gwent
Verterae	Brough, Cumbria
Verulamium	Saint Albans, Hertfordshire
Viroconium	Wroxeter, Shropshire
Y Gaer	Brecon, Wales

AUTHOR'S NOTES

While writing *Dragon's Child*, I grew very fond of the young Artorex, and it was only with the greatest reluctance that I let go of his character as he developed into a mature man. I fall in love, a little, with all my characters and hate to kill them off, but it's an inevitable process in such a long chronicle. Targo, especially, captured my heart, and I have continued his tale into *Warrior of the West*. I was particularly sorry that Targo had to die and, if you found his death sentimental, then blame me, not him.

Poor Artor! As the novel progressed, and as the legend thickened and darkened, Artor was forced to become more pragmatic, accepting much of the violence and, it must be said, the wrongheadedness of his father. The difference between Artor and Uther Pendragon is that the son cared, profoundly and guiltily, that he sent Gaheris to die and that he knew that Caius (Kay) was likely to kill again. Uther would not have cared. Artor never succumbs to hubris, so he remains rather likable but also becomes more distant.

In several strands, I vary from the accepted, populist legends in this novel. For example, I was never comfortable with the wicked character of Nimue as portrayed in the medieval tales. Arthurian literature abounds with wicked women, a device that was fashionable when the various early accounts of the life of Arthur were written, and the straitlaced Victorians added to the old theme of woman as seducer. This is no longer a particular trend in the twenty-first century in which we live. Nor, to be fair, did Celts see women as inherently wicked creatures, as the position of Boedicca and females as low-caste Druids attest.

My Nimue is an outlander. To be truly alien in those times, it was necessary that she be a child of the great enemy, in this case a Jutlander. However, to become close to Myrddion, my Merlin, she had to be welcome at court, so she was raised in Celtic lands as a freeborn girl and was the foster daughter of Gruffydd, Artor's sword-bearer. In this woman of lowly birth I have attempted to devise someone of acute intelligence who is capable of great devotion and who possesses considerable practical leanings. This novel is largely hers, and she provides a counterpoint to the character of Wenhaver (Guenevere).

How appropriate then that Nimue fulfills my invented prophecy concerning her part in the tragedy of Artor. She steals away the mind of the kingdom by capturing the heart of Myrddion Merlinus. Essentially, when they leave Cadbury, they leave Artor to his fate.

I have never much liked the Guenevere of the legends, and I hated her relevance as a woman who could destroy Arthur's kingdom for the love of another man, while still remaining likable as a person. My Wenhaver has all the flaws of a spoiled beauty, and she is as different from the pliant and lovable Gallia as I could make her. At times, I am sorry for the queen, for I can understand her frustration at being a tool in great affairs of state, even though her sense of self-importance doesn't allow her to feel any guilt. Wenhaver depends on her beauty to disguise her character flaws and, other than that trait, she is depicted as a profoundly stupid woman.

Gawayne (Gawain) was the original hero of the legends, for Lancelot was an invention of the French romances. I have returned to the older versions, so my Gawayne is brave, boneheaded, charming, and feckless. I like Gawayne, as did Artor, but I wish the young man thought his actions through before he acted. He is perpetually prey to his libido, and is only rescued from venality by his willingness to accept his faults without argument.

When the time came to reconstruct the many battles that Arthur is reputed to have fought, I must admit to a great deal of skepticism in the locations championed by any number of sources throughout the British Isles. After many years of research, and access to countless documents, I have formed the opinion that the most accurate account of Arthur's reign comes from *The Keys to Avalon: The True Location of Arthur's Kingdom Revealed*, by Steve Blake and Scott Lloyd. It's inarguable that Arthur was forced to stabilize his throne by fighting a series of wars that take place all through his virile years. I deal in depth mainly with the final war, one that I have set in the border country between present-day Wales and England, where, I believe, most of the Arthurian battles probably occurred, although my own wars range across Britain. The details of this battle are my own personal inventions. However, Vortigern did create a Saxon enclave in this part of Britain that, even today, flies the flag of the Red Dragon, derived perhaps from the Dracos Legion that was quartered in Wales in Roman times. I like to think that Artor smashed this enclave and established political stability.

I have been silent concerning Myrddion (Merlin) and his capitulation to the lure of Nimue. I could not bear to make him the "dirty old man" found in Tennyson's *Idylls of the King*. My Myrddion would never have lost his life and his intelligence in pursuit of a pretty face.

Myrddion is reluctant to acknowledge his love for his apprentice. More important, he isn't vulnerable to seduction by a fair face and a lush body. It is Nimue's spirit and intelligence that undo him, as we should expect from a man who is so powerful, so knowledgeable, and yet so inexperienced in matters of the heart. He is prepared to kill treacherously to keep Nimue safe. Myrddion has no choice but to leave his beloved Artor when he finally accepts that Wenhaver will never permit Nimue to live safely at Cadbury.

As always, the common and faceless servants are my heroes, including the courageous, plain-speaking Gallwyn, who gives Nimue the love that is so necessary for her to grow to adulthood as a whole person; the faithful and cynical Gruffydd, who is gruff by nature but a sentimentalist at heart; and the gallant Percivale, Gareth, and Odin, who are a little careful about showing their real faces but who amply prove what loyalty really means.

I am also sorry if you find King Artor a little less likable than the youthful Artorex. He is Uther's son, after all, but he attempts to grapple with this aspect of his character as sternly as possible. It's certain that gentle, decent men make terrible rulers, killing more of their followers than those leaders whose motives are less pure. No saint could survive years of war, political struggle, and cultural division. Although he gives of his best, my Artor often creates the outcomes he attempts to avoid, but his flaws and his virtues are necessary to hold the kingdom together.

The Garden of Gallia is also my invention and is perishable, although the legends often refer to various places of great beauty within the Arthurian setting.

Cadbury is another matter entirely, and many scholars believe it to be the site of the legendary Camelot. I've made it as beautiful as I know how without creating a fantastical world. After all, it was a Celtic fortress, and it was softened by the lives of the common people into something that remained rare, fleeting, and fragile. When you stand on Cadbury Tor, you know that the man who ruled here and designed this fortress was no cuckold, no weakling, and certainly not a distant, faceless dream. Real blood, great heart, and a fierce intelligence made Cadbury strong. Go there, and taste the sense of history that time has bequeathed to us as you gaze out into the morning mists.

Ultimately, I chose to interpret the legends my way. You may agree with me or not, for you are the true arbiters of the tale. My story is very violent at times, and occasionally vicious, but so is the story of humanity, and I make no apology for my excursions into blood and sin.

At times you might find my lovers are overly romantic and noble, but others, such as Wenhaver and Artor, are foils for any rosy view of love. As for the pure love that exists between friends, I believe that such caritas is possible, and even desirable, in a world devoted to dog eat dog.

My hero does the best he can with what he has—and who can ask for more of anyone?

Ave, Artor!